Firethorn

A NOVEL

Sarah Micklem

HarperCollins*Publishers*

HarperCollins*Publishers*
77–85 Fulham Palace Road,
Hammersmith, London W6 8JB

www.harpercollins.co.uk

Published by HarperCollins*Publishers* 2006
1

A catalogue record for this book
is available from the British Library

ISBN-13 978 0 00 719306 6
ISBN-10 0 00 719306 8

Set in Sabon

Printed and bound in Great Britain by
Clays Limited, St Ives PLC

To Cornelius Eady

THE DIVINING COMPASS

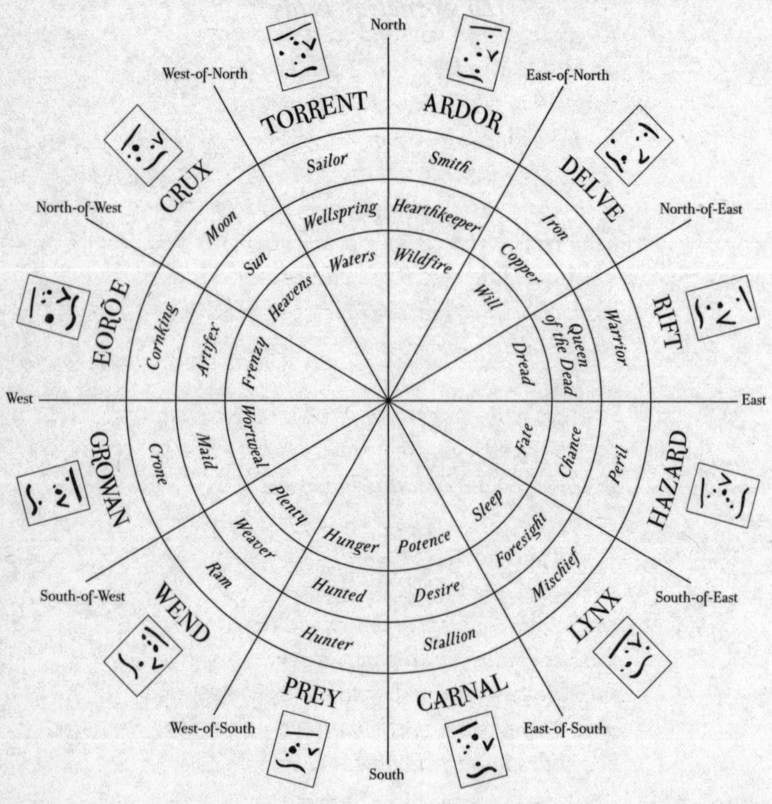

Particularity

In search of the desert witch, the shamaness
forget the archetypes, forget the dark
and lithic profile, do not scan the clouds
massed on the horizon, violet and green,
for her icon, do not pursue
the ready-made abstraction, do not peer for symbols.
So long as you want her faceless, without smell
or voice, so long as she does not squat
to urinate, or scratch herself, so long
as she does not snore beneath her blanket
or grimace as she grasps the stone-cold
grinding stone at dawn
so long as she does not have her own peculiar
face, slightly wall-eyed or with a streak
of topaz lightning in the blackness
of one eye, so long as she does not limp
so long as you try to simplify her meaning
so long as she merely symbolizes power
she is kept helpless and conventional
her true power routed backward
into the past, we cannot touch or name her
and, barred from participation by those who need her
she stifles in unspeakable loneliness.

—Adrienne Rich, "Turning the Wheel"

Firethorn

PROLOGUE

Kingswood

took to the Kingswood the midsummer after the Dame died. I did not swear a vow, but I kept myself just as strictly, living like a beast in the forest from one midsummer to the next, without fire or iron or the taste of meat. I lived as prey, and I learned from the dogs how to run, from the hare how to hide in the bracken, and from the deer how to go hungry.

I was then in my fifteenth year or thereabouts. I had been taken into the Dame's household as a foundling, and when I came to a useful age, she made me her handmaid. I was as close to her side as a pair of hands, and as quick to do her bidding without a word having to be said. I stood high in her regard; many a daughter of the Blood is not so well regarded, being counted more a debt than a gain to her house until she is safely married and gone. When the Dame died, and her nephew and his new wife inherited the manor, I became just another drudge. The world had its order and I my place in it, but I could not whittle myself small enough to fit.

In sorrow and pride I exiled myself to the Kingswood. I shunned fire for fear the kingsmen would hunt me down, and so by way of cold and hunger, I came near to refusing life itself. I never thought to anger or please a god by it. Sometimes I wonder if it was my stubbornness that caught the eye of Ardor, god of forge and hearth and wildfire. And sometimes I wonder—was it by my will alone that I fled to the Kingswood? Maybe Ardor had already taken me in hand, to test my mettle as armor is tested, under blows.

I was not such a fool that I could go hungry in high summer, when the wild plum waited for the touch of my hand before letting go of the tree. I could put a name to each useful plant, I knew its favored ground and the most auspicious season and hour to seek it. The Dame had taught me all this when we'd ridden to the Kingswood to gather dyestuffs for her tapestries and herbs for healing or the table. By root and stem, flower and leaf, seed and fruit, she'd shown me how every plant was marked by the god who made it, that we might know its nature, whether benign or malign or both at once. She'd taught me songs for many herbs, so I might keep in store what I'd learned: these songs were half riddles, half prayers. And the Dame's housekeeper, Na, and Cook had given me other names for these plants, in the Low tongue, and other uses as well. We mudfolk have a green lore of which the Blood know nothing.

When I fled to the forest, I gave up begging the gods for favors, for my prayers had been ignored; I threw myself on the mercy of the Kingswood. But turn away as I might, I couldn't turn my back on the gods, for they were everywhere before me. The Kingswood was their garden, everything named and known, fruitful and pleasing to the eye, ripe with signs.

What I couldn't gather freely I stole: grain from the fields, fruit from the orchards, beans and seeds from the burrows of field mice, bulbs hoarded by squirrels. At times I felt I had stolen the Kingswood itself, for there was a heady freedom in roaming where I was forbidden to go, in lazing when others were working. I walked for days and days, from the slate-bedded ravines to the mossy woods high on the mountains, where the trees are stunted and stooped, and never lost my way. I have the gift of knowing where the Sun is, even if the Sun is behind clouds and I am under a fir tree at the bottom of a narrow valley.

Though I've traveled farther now and know the world is vast, I still think the Kingswood, inside its compass, may be endless.

Our village was an island in a sea of trees, one of many such islands, each with crofts, fields, hedges, orchards, and pastures, scattered across the great round waves of the mountains. The Dame held that village and two more at her father's pleasure, and at King Thyrse's pleasure too, for her holdings lay within the Kingswood and under forest law. The king had given her dispensation to take dyestuffs from the woods, as he prized the tapestries she wove. So she had wandered at will, and I'd attended her, and thought I knew more of the Kingswood than the other drudges of manor and field.

The villagers had leave to travel the market road that threaded the wood from one village to the next, and certain grants to underwood, pasture and forage, clay pits and such. All for fees, of course, always something owing to the king's foresters and woodwards. It was said King Thyrse was so jealous of his belongings that he kept a tally of every deer and oak in his forest; and the pigherds swore he counted every acorn too, when they drove the pigs into the woods in autumn to fatten on the mast. The drudges could cut no wood save hazel and ash poles from the coppices, and every man had leave to fell an oak when he took a wife and built his house. Otherwise they were not allowed past the wards.

But I found signs of their trespass: a burned patch planted with a fistful of grain, a tree felled or stripped of fruit, a deer strung up in a snare. I never saw a poacher. They were too cunning, and for cause: the foresters would take a man's eyes and hands and leave him to the mercy of the wolves for such an offense. It was bad enough to steal the king's game, but snares were an abomination. The gods abhor weapons that leave the hand, cowards' weapons such as javelins, bows and arrows, slings. No man or beast save vermin should die by such means.

The village folk kept other secrets, and I found those too: great circles of ancient elm, ash, or oak, their limbs so entwined that no sapling could take root under them. I supposed the groves deserted, but still I felt the prickling on the nape of my neck when I saw the lofty spaces and blackened stones inside. I'd heard tales of such places from Na when I was small. Late at night she'd whisper to me of the old gods in the woods, the numina of trees and groves, stones and rivers, until I feared to sleep. The Dame had given these tales no credence, so I too had come to disbelieve them. When the Blood took these lands many generations ago, they said the gods of the mudfolk were not gods at all, but rather malicious wights. They banned even their names.

It's one thing to forbid the worship of a god, and another to command that it be forgotten. One day I found the oldest tree of all, a black oak bigger than twelve men could encircle with their arms, and I knew it for the one Na called Heart of the Wood. Dolls of twigs and shucks dangled from its branches: right side up to cure barrenness, upside down to bring on a miscarriage. Mudwomen had dared to put them there, knowing that if the kingsmen had caught them in the woods out of turn, they might also hang from those branches.

I was not the only inhabitant of the Kingswood. There were some few others there, with the king's leave or without. Besides the foresters, there were woodcutters, charcoalmakers, miners, armorers, drovers, all to supply the needs of king and kingdom. I stayed away from them, with their noise and stink of smoke. Feral men and uneasy shades also dwelled in the woods, or so Na had said, and sometimes at night, when the strangled scream of a vixen sounded like a haunt, I believed her. I should have been afraid, but I was merely wary. I thought I was safe enough, as if I were a shade myself, who could go unseen and tread without leaving footprints.

Late in summer I crossed the pass between Barren Woman Peak and Bald Pate, and walked south along the ridge and down and uphill and down, until I came to mountains I couldn't name and a forest groomed so that a man could ride through it at a gallop without bowing his head. It was a place of old trees, great shafts rising to a roof of leaves, lank grass underfoot. I saw a red stag cropping the grass, moving between the gray trunks in a green hush. He wore a crown of thirteen tines covered in tattered velvet.

He lifted his head and snuffed the air, and then I heard the hunters, a rumble of hooves and voices and the chink of bridles. The stag smelled nothing, so I clapped my hands and we ran, he in one direction and I in another. The bellhound had the stag's scent and chased after him, belling as he went. The other dogs were gazehounds, running silent beside the dogmaster while the huntsman signaled the chase with his horn.

I ran downwind until I could no longer hear the horn over the roar of my own breath. I waded in a stony stream and burrowed my way into a stand of horsetail rush on its bank. There I lay gasping and sweating and shaking in a black swarm of gnats. And there I lay even when I heard the horns and bellhound again, coming closer. I saw the stag lunge across the stream and up the other bank with water streaming from his flanks, his breath harsh as a cough. The hounds brought him to bay and tore him down, their lean bodies straining and wriggling at his chest and belly. A small dog, a lapwarmer, wormed his way in between the gazehounds like a puppy after a dug. The dogmaster whipped them off. The stag strove to gain his feet. The lead huntsman thrust a long knife into the stag's chest and leaned upon it. The stag sank again, and the huntsman drove one antler into the earth to bare the stag's throat to the knife.

I was frozen like a hare in a meadow that seems to think the boy with the cudgel won't see him hide in plain sight. And I learned that the hare is not deluded. It's just that he can't move when the fear is on him, limbs won't work, eyes won't blink, only the wheeze of breath and roar of blood distinguish him from a stone.

The hunters made a libation of stag's blood, and passed around the cup until their lips were red. It took a long time for me to pluck words from their roars, to realize they spoke the High tongue of the Blood. Even then I couldn't make sense of it, I was so deep in my silence.

The huntsman in his stained leathers took the antlers and held them to his head and pranced up and down, and the other men laughed. Yet it was not mockery. They were calling the Hunter, stag-headed avatar of the god Prey, and I could swear I felt his breath on my cheek as I lay hiding.

The stag was unmade: gutted, skinned, and quartered. The horses stood quiet, trained to bear the smell of blood, while the dogs fed on bread mixed with the entrails. When they were gone, leaving scraps on a bloody bank, I thought of a red haunch blackened on a fire, and I craved the taste of meat until my belly cramped.

The hunt taught me to be afraid, day and night. I moved to higher, wilder ground, to the domain of the beasts of prey: bear, lynx, wolf, and boar. I studied their habits and avoided their territories. I feared them, but not as much as I feared the king's men and the king's dogs.

I found myself a lair, a cleft rock cut into the crown of Bald Pate. Only eagles claimed such high, stony places, and they paid me no mind. I roofed the cleft with a flat slab of rock and filled it with a nest of leaves, and strewed twigs around to warn of any approach. From this aerie I could see down the valley to the village, a mud warren next to the stone manor walls. The river winding past the village changed with the weather, sometimes silver under the Sun, sometimes brown and full of silt.

I watched two drudges and a mule plowing a spiral field, tilling the strip that had lain fallow that year to ready it for sowing in the spring. Three bands of color coiled one inside the other: the brown ribbon of dirt, darker behind the plow than before; the golden stubble of the summer rye; the luminous green of the winter wheat. Hawks circled below me, looking for unwary mice gleaning the grain.

The world the gods made is too big for us, so we make ourselves a smaller one. We go round and round, every path we take a thread, the threads tangled. From outside I could see how tightly the villagers had knotted their world about them; hadn't I done the same, as if my little tracks could contain the Kingswood?

I knew by the signs that it would be a hard winter. The hollies bore a heavy crop of berries and birds stripped them bare. Crows quarreled in the reaped fields and owls cried in the mountains, mournful as widows. Fur and moss grew thicker than usual. Cold rains came, driven sideways through the trees by north winds, and snows followed.

I had brought two things with me to the Kingswood: the dress I wore and a sheepskin cloak Na had made for me, dyed with ward signs against ill winds. This cloak kept death away, but could not keep out winter, the old Crone, who crawled under it while I slept and wrapped her icy arms around me.

I thought I'd been diligent in the harvest months, drying fruit and burying nuts and seeds for the lean times ahead. It was not enough, not nearly enough. As I went hungry my belly grew, making a hollow space under my ribs for the chill to roost.

The deer scraped snow from the ground, looking for a hint of green. Though I was listless and shivering, hunger forced me from shelter. After my caches of food were gone, I began to eat unnamed plants from deep in the forest where the Dame had never gone. I sucked on frozen roots, gnawed twigs and tender inner bark, wood ears and lichens, and the powdery, worm-eaten wood from hollow logs.

Poisons come in many guises, not all bitter or foul smelling. All signs given us by the gods are true, no doubt, but our reading is often at fault; so I found I couldn't rely on the signs the Dame had shown me. I made a trial of each new plant by sniffing it and holding a morsel on my tongue. I'd always been able to guess what herbs Cook had used in the pot, and now my senses were honed by need and fear. The more I erred, the more I was tutored. I was often queasy, sometimes feverish. When I got too sick, I ate clay to purge the poisons.

My blood stopped its monthly tides, and I feared that if I lived, I would be barren, a dried-up old woman before my time. Scratches healed slowly and my teeth loosened in my gums. I'd seen this wasting before, when the Dame was dying.

It's a blessing that the pangs of hunger, like the travails of childbirth, are duller in recollection. What comes back to me now, sharp and clear, is the sight of four or five red deer bounding up a snow-covered hill in the pale yellow light of morning. The deer were not pursued; they ran, it may be, for the joy of it. The trees were black against the snow and the long stripes of their shadows were a color between blue and violet.

* * *

Short winter days made for endless nights. I envied the bears their long sleep in an earth den, feeding on dreams of fish and berries, and I envied sleepers such as I had once been, behind shutters and doors, safe in their beds; I envied anyone with a lamp, a candle, a hearth. I lay long awake, and sometimes the dark pressed in close and stifling, and sometimes—far worse—the dark grew immense around me, and I was alone in a night that covered the world.

When I slept, I sank into the ocean realm of Sleep, as we all do. Sometimes Sleep lapped me in balm and floated my woes away, but often I encountered nightmares as I went deeper, and had to flee into wakefulness. Sleep is an avatar of the god Lynx, and therefore capricious.

In time I learned to drift in Sleep's shallows. There, just below waking, I could catch soothing dreams the way a boy might tickle a fish into a net. I learned to hold them fast too, for dreams are shapeshifters, likely to turn baleful if they slip your grasp. The Dame visited these dreams and brought me a joint of lamb, bread, a withered apple, and she ate with me, as she never did alive. I'd dream it all so plain, the cream in a glazed bowl, a green fly buzzing in a shaft of light. She'd tell me to make sure the wine casks didn't leak or to gather willawick for yellow dye: many tasks and all left undone.

I fear I shouldn't have dreamed of the Dame so often. The dead are not beyond suffering and want and even curiosity, so we're forbidden to speak their names in the year after they've left us. The priests say that their shades might linger to eavesdrop, distracted from the journey they must make. Perhaps dreams have the same power as speech to hold a shade close, for when I bade the Dame stay awhile in my dream, I felt her near. But I awoke hungrier and more desolate than ever.

In the dark-of-the-Moon before Longest Night, I had a true dream. Some such dreams foretell the future, but this one foretold the past, and I knew it for true even while I slept in its grip, by the scent of it; in ordinary dreams I have no sense of smell. I couldn't recall that I'd ever before breathed this incense of herbs crushed underfoot, this dusty redolence rising from the rocks as if they were bread in an oven. Yet I knew it: the smell of mountains, but not the mountains of the Kingswood.

I followed my father up a trail to a high pass between higher peaks capped with snow. The mountains were rocky and steep, arid and open. I had a small pony because I was small. He was on a big roan gelding, leading a pack mule, singing a bit for me and for his own pleasure. The road was a cobbled track with a wall beside it, and as he reached the top of the pass, he turned in his saddle to watch me and grinned in his ruddy beard. I hunched over the pony's withers, feeling her labor to climb the last stretch. She was eager, knowing as I knew that home was down the other side of the pass. I saw clouds flying below us, and under them cloud shadows moving over the long, narrow lake in the valley, and our town among the other towns along the shore. The lake was a deeper blue than the sky. Where the Sun struck the water, it threw off white sparks. Then my father looked behind me and cried out without words, or in a language I understood only in dreams, and I knew he cried danger. He pointed over my shoulder at a line of men on horseback on the breast of another mountain. Their helmets glinted and their banners were black. Dust smoked around their horses' hooves, coming our way.

When I awoke I was so taken with the image of my father that I gave little thought to the soldiers. The Blood can trace their lineages back to the gods, but we mudfolk call a man lucky whose wife is so faithful he sees his own features sketched on his children's faces—as my father saw himself in me, in my dream.

It's no great shame among drudges to be fatherless. Still, I wanted to know mine. I didn't feel the lack of a mother so much. When I was very small, I was content to think Na was my real mother. Later I wondered if I were the by-blow of some gardener or groom she thought beneath her.

But she'd told me often enough that I was a foundling. I came to the Dame's household when I was old enough to run; by the number of my teeth they'd reckoned me to be about four years of age. I understood neither the High tongue nor the Low, and when I spoke, no one could understand me. They called me Luck for my hair, the color of new-forged copper, for redheads are favored by Chance, the female avatar of Hazard. No one in the village had seen such hair before. I don't recall the time before I came to the manor, and no wonder. We dream our infancy, and forget that dream when we awaken to our selves and our duties.

They gave me simple tasks: sweeping and scouring, combing the fringe on carpets, emptying slops. I was always running off and leaving things half done, always distracted. Na would make me fetch a willow wand for the beating I was due. Afterward she'd soothe me and call me her own little Luck. That was my childhood until the Dame took me in hand one day. I thought the manor and the village made up the world and all its inhabitants.

* * *

Memory can be a churlish and disobedient servant, out of sight when you bid it come, insolent when you have dismissed it. Perhaps that's why the memories that insisted upon coming, as I grew weaker, were the ones that harrowed me most: how the Dame looked after five weeks of fever had whittled away her ample flesh, leaving skin on a scaffold of bones, how she lay in the bed closet and threw off the covers. She couldn't bear the weight of the linen, though it was the finest weave we had. Her fingers kept plucking and twisting invisible threads, pulling the air about her face as if she already felt the shroud.

Once when I brought a basin to bathe her, the Dame pushed herself up on her elbows and said, "When my nephew takes the manor, he has promised you'll not be bound. He says he'll give you a place as his wife's handmaid if you suit her. And if she doesn't suit you—well then, you'll be free to go. I can make no better provision . . ." She lay back down and I dampened the cloth with cool water and wiped her arms and chest. Even such a short speech and she was short of breath. "It will serve you best to serve them well." She smiled faintly. "And try to keep a bridle on that tongue, for I've heard it run away with you from time to time." I smiled back, though it was no jest.

It didn't seem such a gift to be permitted to leave the manor; each stone in the walls was dear to me, and even the weeds that took root in the mortar. I was a weed too, clinging to what I knew. I gave little thought to what I might do when the Dame was gone.

She didn't die then, and she didn't die easily. She'd taught me many remedies, but all failed. She never moaned or cried out until the last days, when she forgot herself, already on her way down the long road. In the end I gave her fare-thee-well to dull the pain. It has no healing in it.

We had a scant tennight after the funeral rites to ready the manor for her nephew. The priest made the Dame's clay death mask to send to the clan's temple to join the Council of the Dead. We gathered the belongings that might call to her if they were left behind: shuttles and bobbins, comb and hairpins of shell, her plate and cup, her knife with the amber hilt, the small clippers she wore on a chain, undergarments, shoes, and hats. We laid them on her pyre and watched the smoke fly up. The priest ground the fragments of her bones and scattered her ashes in the stream and plowed the black stain under. It was all done as it should have been done, to free her spirit. Afterward we were careful not to utter her name. We called her the Dame, and so I call her still.

That winter in the Kingswood I grieved more for myself than for her, crying blame on her that she'd left me nothing but pride, and that a poor inheritance. Better if she hadn't noticed me, when I was just a child, making a palace for ants behind a shrub in the garden when I should have been weeding. Better if she hadn't knelt next to me and pointed to an ant dragging a leaf and said, "See, they esteem the feverfew for their nests, for its sweetness. We crush it into a paste when someone is sick, because it has a healing smell." Better if I hadn't been quick to learn and eager to ask another question.

Then I would not be so proud, as if the blood of gods ran in my veins, as if I wasn't formed from dirt and spit like other mudfolk. I could have endured our new master and mistress the way the other servants endured them: with sullenness and grumbling and spite, but nevertheless as something to be borne.

Na wouldn't take the keys after the Dame died, saying she was too old and her backbone would crack under such a burden. When the keys came to me, and the duties with them, I marveled at how the Dame had kept the threads of a hundred tasks in hand, weaving them all together. I was glad of this tangle of worries, too busy to mourn.

I made the inventory in preparation for our new master. I knew how to read and write godsigns and how to tally; the Dame never held with the saying that a drudge who reads is a greater oddity than a pig that flies, and less use. I found a plan for her next tapestry rolled up in the locked cabinet in her workshop. The warp was on the loom, but she had not begun to weave before she was taken ill. She'd drawn a maiden in a meadow amidst an impossible profusion of flowers. The frostwort of late winter bloomed beside the corona of high summer, and garden gillyflower mingled with dragon's hood from the deep woods. Switches of yarn were pinned to the sketch, and for the maiden's unbound hair she'd picked copper-colored wool dyed with a rare pigment made from crushed beetle wings. I burned the drawing but took the thread for remembrance. I kept it with me in the Kingswood, sewn into my coat.

The nephew and his new bride arrived in springtime with a crowd of brothers and cousins, friends and servants to see them to their new bed. The only person of Blood in the manor was the Dame's old priest, so he greeted them at the gate and led them into the outer courtyard. The guardian tree, a red-leafed plum, dropped pink blossoms on their velvets and furs and the shining hides of their horses. The groom wore a crown of supple twigs with leaves of the newest green; the bride was wreathed in flowers.

That evening I served at table. My new master and mistress shared a plate in the place of honor. Sire Pava dam Capella by Alcyon of Crux, to give him his full name, was so young his beard was still thin on his cheek. His bride, Dame Lyra by Ophirus of Crux, had a face as pale and plump as the well-kneaded dough of white bread. She was younger than I was, having no more than thirteen years.

After the faces of the guests grew red and their jokes coarse, after the bones were picked clean and drink spilled on the cloth, after the last song and libation, the couple were sent to bed in the Dame's own cabinet with her best tapestry hung in front. We drudges worked late in the dim light of the tallow lamps, while the new steward had us move everything in the storeroom from here to there. I wouldn't have been surprised to see him piss in the corners, like a dog making his mark. We gave up our pallets in the hall to the guests and slept in the outer courtyard. Not that I slept. When the Sun came up over the wall, I heard the doves sing, *What will you do? Oh, what will you do?*

That morning when I helped Dame Lyra wash and tightened the laces on her dress, I saw her wince, and asked if she felt pain, for I knew an ointment to soothe chafing. She had such a child's shape, slender hips and small breasts, and she was round where a child might be round, cheeks and wrists and knees and belly. But she had borne a man's weight, and I supposed it was too heavy for her.

She slapped my face and told me never to wag my tongue without permission. I learned to serve her in silence. I came to know her well, from her tricks to make her skin pale and her lips red, to her pisspot and the rags for her monthly tides, but she seemed not to see me.

I often wished I were as invisible to the steward. From the day I handed him the keys, he found fault with me and the way the manor and its holdings had been run. He was a lesser kinsman of the clan, sent by Sire Pava's father to keep a tight grip on the household. I got more than my share of his blows. I was uppish and my manners abominable, so he said. If I looked him in the eye, he'd give me a bruise, and the same if I mumbled his name, or failed to keep a smile stitched to my face when I served at table.

Pride in my work drizzled away. I was not the only one who found hands had turned clumsy and tasks that used to take an hour lasted a whole day.

The warp threads tangled on the loom of their own accord. When things went wrong, Na would say, "A rotten egg hatches no chick." In the Low, on the back stairs, we discussed the weather: the clouds on Steward's brow, Dame Lyra's storms, Sire Pava's droughts of silence. Hate was our bread. Daily I saw Na treated like a laggard and put to tasks too heavy for her years. I had the right to go, but what household would welcome a drudge who dared seek a new place?

I could hardly draw breath indoors, when I knew that pintle shoots were green by the river and maiden's kiss in bloom in the high meadow, and it was past time to collect the seeds of prickly comfort. So I learned to lie my way past the gates, telling Steward one thing and Dame Lyra another; I learned the barefaced lie, the lie of omission, and all the other ways a drudge can tie the truth in knots.

In those first tennights I prayed to any god I thought might hear me, but most of all to Wend. I offered twists of dyed lamb's wool to one of the god's avatars, the Weaver, whose little statue stood in a niche in the Dame's workshop—for though the Dame was descended from the god Crux, Wend had favored her. I prayed to know my place, to be woven in, smoothed down. The smell of burning wool brought the Dame to mind more than the god, and gave me no peace. My heart grew as hard and swollen as a gall around a worm.

Now I think that Wend Weaver did answer me, in her way, for her right hand carries the shuttle, but her left holds the shears.

The first time Sire Pava came to my pallet at night, I did not expect it. Besides his wife, just two months in his bed, he had brought from his father's house a mudwoman no better than the rest of us, except she already had a five-month belly and no duties to mention. He put her in a mud hut stuck to the outside of the manor wall like a swallow's nest, and he'd visit her when he pleased, no matter that Dame Lyra threw slippers and wailed.

I thought Sire Pava must be well occupied between these two. But what did I know of the appetites of men? Most of us in the Dame's house had been women, growing old with her; I was by far the youngest. The men who'd served her had been very old or very young, from the ancient priest to the boys who worked as scullions in the kitchen. Then Sire Pava came with his steward, jack, varlets, huntsman, forester, gardeners, and a toady of a horsemaster.

At night the hall was crowded with the pallets of those drudges who had a right to sleep there. If not for the sweetfern in the mattresses, the close air would have been too rank to breathe. I slept beside the master's bed closet, so Dame Lyra could wake me to fetch water or wine or empty her pisspot or kill a fly buzzing by her head.

I'm taking a roundabout road to this part of my tale, and what is it, anyway, but a tale so worn it hardly needs telling? Sire Pava came to my pallet one night. I put him off, told him my tides were flowing. A woman's blood—especially the unclean blood from her womb—can make a man fall sick. Unless it's blood from a broken maidenhead, which makes a man potent and is a cure for the canker besides. He went away, but I knew he'd be back.

I woke Na, who slept on the pallet next to me, to tell her what had happened. "What shall I do, Na, next time he comes?" I was so roiled that my voice rose above a whisper.

"Hush," Na said. "It would be well if Sire Pava took a liking to you. Get you out from under Steward's eye and Dame Lyra's heel."

This was not the advice I expected to hear. "I don't want him or anyone else," I said.

"Are you dead below the waist, then?" she asked me. "More's the pity. You're fifteen years old and still wear your hair down. You must be bred or wed; there's no hiding under the Dame's skirts anymore. If you don't please Sire Pava, you'll be sport for his men. So you'd best be thinking how to keep him, not send him away."

At these words I began to cry. Na came to my pallet and lay beside me, stroking my hair. I could see the waxy glimmer of her face near mine. "Now, now, hush now, Luck," she whispered, close to my ear. "I know a thing or two the Dame never taught you, to keep Sire Pava tied to your thumb. We'll find some kindlecandle and Cook will put it in his dish—but you must take it to him with your own hands. It will stiffen him up for an hour, and he'll think it's owing to your charms, for that's more than his wife can do. Haven't you heard them at night? Pava is quicker than a dog. No wonder Lyra is cross as two sticks."

I was angry with Na, not liking her counsel, and kept silent around her as if she were to blame for Sire Pava's wandering eye. Cook had better advice; she said dampwick would make his prick limp, and showed me where to find it, and she never said a word when I used it to season the dishes I served to Sire Pava. I also gathered the white berries of childbane, which the women in our mountains take against conception. If one didn't work, I would need the other. I knotted the hair between my legs to barricade the entrance to my womb. Many nights I lay awake, but he did not come to my pallet again.

When he ran me to ground, he was on horseback and I was on foot, gathering fiddleheads down the hill by the ravine. He said I'd led him a fine chase, as if the fox runs for the hounds' amusement. I'd planned to yield if I was cornered, but when the moment came, I scrambled down the bank toward the river stones. Before I could get a rock in my hand, he caught me by my skirt. I acquitted myself about as well as a stray cat, marking him with bites and scratches.

Shortly he was done. He got up and I pulled down my skirts. Everywhere I was seeping: tears, sweat, snot, bile.

He looked down at his prick as he tucked it into his leather prickguard. He straightened his hose and tightened the laces. "Where's the blood?" he said. "You had me fooled, going with your hair unbound as if you were a maiden. Did some horseboy have you first?"

I spat at him and jeered, "A horseboy rides better than you, Sire. It's just as your wife says: you can't stay in the saddle long." Dame Lyra had never confided so much in me, but I wanted to poison his mind as he'd poisoned mine.

I saw this taunt go home, but his smile didn't change. "I won't be in a hurry next time we meet," he said. "I'll clap on my spurs and teach you not to balk."

By then I was crying and couldn't speak. I've thought on it many times, what I should have done, what I failed to do, and I've dreamed about it too, bloody dreams; but unlike dreams, the past can't be altered.

When he got up on his horse, he tossed a scarf at me—a rag he'd tied to the pommel of his saddle—saying, "I brought you a headcloth. Put it on and stop wailing. Why all the fuss if you already gave it away? In all my life I never heard such an uproar."

I went down to the river and sat in the water to wash away the stains of mud and grass and white blood. And it was true; there was no red blood, though I'd never lain with a man before. The hairs I'd tied together over my quim had prevented easy entrance, like a hymen. Where they had pulled I was swollen and sore.

I wrapped the headcloth around my head with shaking fingers and went down the hill. It was a sign anyone could read.

Sire Pava didn't bother me again, despite his bluster. I think he preferred his women willing. And Na was right: it would have been better if I had pleased him. The spite of Dame Lyra, half-moon scars on my arm from her pinches, the japes and hands of Sire Pava's men, now that I was no longer his quarry, the steward's whispers in a dark corner, the coldness between me and Na, for we no longer understood each other—Wend Weaver cut the threads that held me, one by one.

In the village early spring is the leanest season; the grain is half dust from the granary floor, the hams have been scraped to the bone, and there's not much else but old coleworts and turnips. In the Kingswood deer stripped the buds from low branches. The weakest fell prey to wolves or lay down and suckled scavengers, even as linnflower trees flushed red at the bud and willows burned with a green flame by the riverside. Ferns uncoiled and the shoots of bulbs pushed their way through the dead leaves.

I felt sorrow uncoiling too, less tainted than the bitter thoughts that had kept me company so long. I missed the Dame, not just the place she'd made for me, but the woman herself. I recalled her face, how she would brown in the summer except under her starched blue coif, how I teased her about her pale forehead when I dressed her hair at night. On her right cheekbone she wore the small blue tattoo of her clan, Crux; her left was marked with the godsign of Lynx.

Lynx was her husband's clan. He'd been killed in one of the king's wars before I'd come to the manor, and Na said his kin had sent the Dame back to her father, claiming she was barren. Her father had settled her in his humblest manor for as long as she should live, or until she married again. But she never married again. "I'd not suffer it twice," she told me once, and that was all she said about it.

Two lines appeared between her brows when she was vexed. I was more afraid of that look than I'd ever been of Na's whippings. The Dame would turn it on me when I was careless in my work, or too haughty with the other drudges.

I feared her shade might be angry with me, for now I weighed up my ingratitude and it was heavy indeed. The pride was my own, nothing forced upon me. She owed me nothing, and yet she had bequeathed to me what she knew. She'd given me her eyesight, that I might see beauty in the patterns the world makes, and all the colors, named and unnamed, that dye the seasons. Was it any wonder I'd come to love what she had loved?

* * *

I had gotten out of the habit of eating every day. Comfort was another habit I had lost: I no longer expected to be warm when it was cold, or dry when it was wet. In submission to weather and need, I'd learned endurance—or indifference, it may be. But famine carried a goad, and drove me through the forest. Everywhere I found the promise of plenty, and too long to wait.

So I came to the firethorn, the only tree of its kind in the woods. It stood solitary in a glade where a great oak had fallen, and all underfoot were the blue stars of tread-me-down. The Sun lit translucent orange berries in a cage of gray thorns. Silvery buds on the twigs were just unfurling the first green flags. The tree is sacred to Ardor: wood as hard as iron and fruit like flame. The Dame had told me never to touch those berries. Even the birds avoided them. I had been there before and passed them by, but winter had not shriveled them, and they looked round and ripe. And I was hungry. Maybe I was dying.

I put a berry on my tongue and the juice burst from under the skin with a savor between tart and sweet: wine on its way to vinegar, fermented on the tree. Yet nothing that tasted of danger. I knew I should wait, but I ate another, and another. I stripped the berries from among the thorns until my hands were pierced and scratched: the blood redder than the berries, the berries tasting of blood. As if I consumed myself.

I lay where I dropped, and shuddered and shook and slept. I awoke in the deepest night to find I had been divided from myself. There lay my body sleeping and dreaming, and I was outside it, awakening. When we dream we may take shapes other than our own; a man may be his brother, a woman a king, and never question it. So, with the certainty born of a dream, I knew I'd become my own shadow. It was a moonless night, with clouds covering the stars, dark as it could be, but somehow the sky was bright enough to cast shadows, to make me out of a darkness deeper than night. I lay beside my body and under it, and I was tucked into the crook of my knees and elbows and the folds of my garments, and I hid under the hair at the nape of my neck.

Because it was a dream, I knew what to do. I seeped into my body through the soles of the feet, and as I flowed through the dreamer, I gathered my darkness to me, shrinking and thickening until I was a tiny homunculus. I followed the breath out of one nostril and stood on the upper lip.

The night had quickened with shadows, nothing but shadows, wantonly joining and parting, flickering, rising. I never knew that darkness had so many colors, all of them black. I strove to make the shadows into trees, but things had escaped their edges and lost their names. The harder I looked, the more baffled I was.

I saw something from the corner of my eye that vanished when I looked at it straight. I stayed just so, glancing sideways, and saw it again: a tree with berries like sparks. The tree caught fire, growing leaves of black flame, and one of the flames made a bird, and the bird began to sing. I turned toward it again and bird and tree disappeared. They could be seen only askance.

I saw all this on one in-drawn breath. When the dreamer exhaled the wind went through me and I faltered. I lost the certainty that gave me shape. From breath to breath I hung suspended. I was too tenuous to be called a thing. Without weight, how could I stand? I rose like smoke; another breath and I might smear into the wind, dissolve into the other shadows and become nothing.

But the bird began to sing again and this time I could see the song itself. It gave off a silver flicker, it was like a string on a dulcet, trembling under the player's touch, shaking sound into the air. Being thin as air I felt it shiver all through me, and I saw it shining through my darkness.

It was not so hard then, after all, to relinquish my fear, to drift upward; the song was a tether to my sleeping self, to the body below me, which seemed to be no more than glimmers and streaks. But I'd learned that shadows were mutable; I could make something of them by seeing. From the corner of my left eye, the dreamer became a fallen tree, splotched with lichens and moss. I turned my head and from the corner of my right eye, I saw a fist of cords and sticks clutching a sheepskin cloak, a mouth filled with shadow, hair stiff with mud and twigs and leaves. A puppet of wood, no more a part of me. A song bound me to it, a song spun so fine it could break, and there would be silence.

I drifted. I almost flew. But the dreamer twitched. Eyes shifted under her eyelids. I began to feel sorry for what I'd done, for I saw how I'd remade my flesh into something wooden and numb; I'd been altogether too willing to die. But there was still a single coal of the body's fire, an ember under soot and feathers of ash. I breathed on that coal and a flame crept out, and heat with it.

I don't know how many days and nights the fever burned in me. I was melted, cast, beaten on the anvil of the tree's root, and drawn to a point. Quenched at times, so the chills shook me, and then heated and pounded again. The pounding kept time with my heart. The heat purified instead of scorching, burning away the dross.

I awoke to a daylight world where shadows kept their places. The sheepskin was sodden under me, and the smell of sweat was strong. I'd bled from the nose and the blood had dried in a crust on my face and neck. I was weak as a newborn filly and just as thirsty.

I knew then that I'd been between Ardor's hammer and anvil. The god had come in the avatar of the Smith to temper me. I took a thorn and made a libation of blood to give thanks to Ardor for letting me live. And I took Firethorn as my name.

When one of the gods chooses you for a tool or a weapon, you may go on, heedless; nevertheless, you are marked. So I went on for a time, grateful that Ardor had saved me, and didn't ask why. I suppose I was unwilling to ask, for fear of an answer.

Yet I'd changed under the Smith's hammer. His blows had shaken part of me loose, and I felt weaker for it. What was my shadow, in the dream, if not my shade given form? Now I feared my shade might go wandering beforetimes, while I still lived, and leave the rest of me to rust. If that was a gift, I was ungrateful for it.

Ardor gave me other things: a song, a handful of berries, and the gift of seeing in the dark. It may be a kind of trickery, this way of seeing, but ever since, I've been able to make my way in darkness when others stumbled, so long as I looked askance.

Even in the day I saw more clearly, both the quick and the subtle: the hawfinch high among the branches, the lynx in the dappled shadows, the hare quivering in the long grass. Often, from the corners of my eyes, I glimpsed the shadows of presences, not quite seen, not quite unseen. The old gods had not fled the Kingswood after all. They were the trees of the forest, and they drew breath in winter and let it out in summer, year upon year, and all the animals of the woods flickered by while the trees stood still. The Blood accused them of malice, but they bore us no ill will unless we came with fire and axes.

And everywhere in the Kingswood I saw signs of Ardor's presence, signs that had gone unmarked before I ate the firethorn berries. The Smith, Hearthkeeper, and Wildfire were manifest in the distant pounding of the armorers' hammers and the smoke of the huntsman's cook fire in trees riven by lightning.

In such signs I have long since tried to read the god's wishes. But priests study all their lives to divine the will of the gods, and still dispute their omens. Each of the twelve gods has three avatars, by which they show themselves to us, but in truth the gods are so far beyond us they are unknowable. In their wars and alliances, they make and unmake the world. How can I be certain what Ardor made of me in the forge of the Kingswood, and for what purpose? Perhaps I have already done whatever I was meant to do.

CHAPTER 1

UpsideDown Days

watched for the Midsummer's eve bonfire from my lair on Bald Pate. I meant to return to the village a year to the day I'd left for the Kingswood. But why should the day matter? The seasons go round the year and never come back, for, as everyone knows, time moves in a spiral, not a circle. To persist in folly made me no less a fool. Once I'd counted myself brave for venturing into the Kingswood alone; now I wondered if it would not have been braver to stay among people. Solitude had withered around me like a husk. Yet I stayed until the bonfire released me.

On Midsummer morning I walked down through the ripening fields to the croft of Na's sister, Az. I carried my sheepskin cloak under one arm and shaded my eyes with my hand. A great humming and chaffering of insects rose around me as I walked, as if the fields had a voice under the Sun.

When I stepped through the gate into the mud-walled yard, the croft seemed deserted save for the hens scratching around the stone feet of the granary and a sow sleeping in the Sun. But I saw smoke coming from the summer kitchen, a lean-to built against the hut and roofed by the huge leaves of a golden hopvine that clambered up the poles. The yard smelled of dung and dust and meat cooking.

I stooped under the pitched roof of the lean-to and peered inside. Az was squatting by the fire pit in the scattered yellow light that came through the leaves. She was smaller than I remembered, and I wondered if she'd dwindled since I saw her last. I hadn't thought she was so old. Her head grew forward from the rounded hump of her shoulders, and she had to strain to look up at me. I couldn't bear for her not to recognize me, so I called out, "Az, it's me, Luck, that used to come by with Na. Are you in health? How is Na?" After a year in the woods without speaking, the words stuck to my tongue.

Az got to her feet, steadying herself on my arm, and came into the light. "Ah, Luck, did you think I wouldn't know you and your red hair? You look to be on fire with the Sun behind you like that. Come and sit." She led me to the croft's guardian tree, a rowan, and we sat on the ground in its shade. Az pulled her shawl close around her, though it was a warm day. The pattern was the loveknot; I'd made the shawl myself as a present for Na. I thought of the Dame, how she never could make a weaver of me. My mind would go wandering and leave my fingers to fumble, and mistakes unnoticed had to be picked out later. But Na had treasured the shawl. I wondered why Az wore it.

"How does Na fare these days? I don't want to go to the manor, so I hoped you might send one of the boys for her."

Az shook her head. "Na is gone. Carried off by the shiver-and-shake this winter. Others too: Min and two of his daughters, and some of those Herders who live off by themselves and never get along with anybody. Dame Lyra caught it too and miscarried. It was bad this year, with all the snows and the cold."

I was silent for a while, and wouldn't look at her. "I should have been here. With the Dame gone you were in need of a healer."

Az said, "Nothing to be done, it was that quick. I know Na missed you, though. She'd come to visit Peacedays, and we'd talk of you living on white bread and cream at the king's court."

A year ago, I'd stood beside Na watching the dancers around the bonfire, and told her I was going to the city of Ramus, where the king lived, to find work as a dyer. It was a likely lie, likelier than the truth. I lacked patience as a weaver, but I'd been drawn to the mysteries of dyestuffs and mordants, the transformations in the dyebaths. It was a kind of green lore, and all such lore came easily to me, as if I had only to recollect it rather than to learn it for the first time.

Now my lie came back to shame me. How could I admit I'd been in the Kingswood, so near at hand when Na was dying?

Az cocked her head and looked me over with her shiny black eyes. I'd taken care to wash before leaving the Kingswood, but my hair was a bramble thicket, my dress a rag, and my feet bare and hard as horn. She sighed. "But I see you were never at court. I wouldn't bother to kill a chicken as skinny as you. Wouldn't be worth the coals to cook it."

She fetched me a slab of unleavened barley bread and a bowl of greens stewed with bacon. I dipped the bread into the stew and crammed it into my mouth. Tears ran down and salted it. I was too full of sensation, I was drowning in it: the taste of meat after long fasting, the smell of burning wood, the flood of words coming up from underground, the sweet welcome and sad news.

Az let me eat and cry in peace until curiosity overmatched her courtesy. "So where did you go, then? You look wild as a bog wight come to scare the children into bed."

I said, "I've been on a hard road, truth be told, and I gained nothing from it but a new name. I'm called Firethorn now." I'd never spoken my new name aloud before, and I felt as though I overreached. But for certain Luck did not fit me well anymore, and sometimes one must grow into a name.

"Firethorn suits you," was all Az said.

She didn't ask again where I had been, and I was grateful for it. She spun a thread of gossip around the manor and the village, saying Sire Pava had sent away the old priest when he grew forgetful, and the new one was a Sun priest and not a priest of the Heavens, and what use was he? He had no notion of how to read the weather or the stars and birds, how to tell by signs which day to plow and which to sow, when to dig a hole or breed the ram to the ewes; he never looked up at all, as far as she could see. The crops and flocks had suffered for it—twenty lambs stillborn and another taken by an eagle, and a blight on the rye too.

And there was talk of war. It was said Sire Pava himself was going on campaign, and refused to wear hand-me-down armor from his father. He and the steward were squeezing the village hard to pay for his new harness and weapons. To be sure, a lot of coin stuck to Steward's fingers. "Rooster thinks he rules the henhouse, but Fox knows better," Az said.

Thinking of Na, I lost the thread. It was bitter to me that I'd turned my back on her before I left, had found so little to say to her in the way of farewell. Shouldn't I have known her time was short, or felt her need of me, even in the Kingswood? I put my head on my knees and Az fell silent. We sat like that for a time, under the rowan tree, while the chickens pecked for grain and a chiffchaff sang above our heads.

I'd fed on my pride a twelvemonth and it was near eaten up, but I didn't intend to go back to the manor and beg for a place as a scullion. Az let me know that I'd be welcome to stay, and gave me Na's second dress to wear and a rag to wrap around my head. The dress hung loose and left my calves bare. Still, it was more proper than what I wore out of the Kingswood. Soon her youngest son, Fleetfoot, came home to fetch the midday meal for the men in the fields, and I went to help him.

Az had borne ten children, and five boys had lived. The two married sons had built their crofts next to hers. Their huts shared the same wall and the gates were always open between the yards for the children to run in and out. Three sons still lived at home, but all five liked working their shares of the commons together.

It was a long walk to the field where they were haying, across the river ford and the valley to a high and stony meadow. One of the wives, Halm, came with Fleetfoot and me, with her baby slung in a shawl on one hip and a great basket on the other.

"I'm glad there's a rill up there," she said as we climbed the steep path. "I get so weary carrying the water bucket."

We called the men from the pool of shade cast by a great beech, and they came laughing and shouting. They'd stripped to loincloths, and the sweat shone on their brown shoulders and legs. Their bodies gave off heat, like horses. They ate and drank, tossing a few japes back and forth. One asked me where I'd been and I couldn't think how to answer. Another said, "Looks like her tongue swam away," and they laughed. I sat with my head averted, pretending not to watch. They drowsed until the shade moved away. The smell of sweat and cut hay and earth baking under the Sun went to my head like hard cider and made me dizzy.

And so I went to live among the villagers. Their houses were of mud mixed with dung and straw, daubed on a frame of poles and withies and thatched with reeds. They slept in one room and their animals in the next. Dirt was ground into their skin. Their clothes were as drab as peat and stone, fir and straw; the Blood reserved the most vivid dyes for their clan colors. Drudges spoke the Low among themselves, but they knew enough of the High to placate their masters. Now I saw that the villagers had another face than the one they turned to the manor. They never forgot that they were there first, before the Blood, born from the earth of those very mountains.

A cock belonging to the old alewife, Anile, was always the first to crow in the village, long before dawn. I rose at his summons to grind barley, oats, and rye for bread and porridge. Wheat went for taxes, so we never had the fine, leavened bread of the manor. The brothers complained until I learned to grind fine enough. We hid the mortar and pestle in a hole in the wall, because Sire Pava enforced his monopoly on milling. We'd take the miller a scant measure to make him think it was all we had, and he'd be sure to cheat us in turn.

Sometimes in the dark I heard the rhythmic scraping sound of other women grinding, and I wondered if in time I'd be worn smooth enough to fit in, smooth as an old mortar. A mudwoman's toil never ends and never lasts: clean clothes are dirtied, meals are swallowed, and there are always new weeds in the garden. I remembered the Kingswood, how I'd risen when I pleased—forgetting how restless my sleep had been, and how I'd longed for even the humblest porridge. The tedious chores wore away at me, but I was glad to spare Az the worst of them. She was not as frail as she looked, but there was so much that needed doing. She said we pulled well in the same yoke, and whatever had she done before I came?

I learned to tell her sons apart. The youngest was called Fleetfoot because he won all the village races. He was still a smooth-cheeked boy, with a deep chest and lean flanks like a gazehound. The second youngest was Ot; he was proud of his new blond beard, roaming out of the house at night to show it to the village girls. I started calling him Wheatbeard and the name was apt, so he kept it. Maken was the eldest still at home and in no hurry to be wed, for girls and widows (and wives, Halm said) were fond of his merry hazel eyes and his wide shoulders, and many had found him a sweet nut come cracking time. I found him unsettling, myself, and it made me shy of him.

On Peacedays, the one idle day in every tennight, I'd watch the green youth of the village go courting, with their banter and raillery, forthright stares and sly glances. No one looked my way. I'd been fair enough before the Kingswood, I suppose, fair enough for Sire Pava. Now my ribs showed plain as those on a stray dog; my hips had hollows instead of dimpled flesh. When I looked at my face in a basin of water, my cheekbones and chin were too sharp, my eyes too deep and too dark.

I found I couldn't sleep under a roof and within walls, next to Az and her boys when they unrolled the pallets at night. I slept under the rowan tree, and even there I rested uneasy. Carnal's female avatar, that fat voluptuary Desire, sent me dreams, and with them her itch and tickle. Better if she'd come when Sire Pava wanted me; now she was too late. I ate as much as I could, but Az's sons were hungry, and I never had my fill.

I saw old friends from the manor on market days and on Peacedays, before the village shrine. Cook was shocked that I was so gaunt, and brought me savories from the manor table. She said Dame Lyra could curdle milk with a look since her miscarriage, and no wonder: Sire Pava had brought his mudwoman right into the manor, and she'd started another bastard with a daughter just off the tit. I dreaded seeing Sire Pava about the village, but he heeded me no more than the dirt he trod underfoot. I didn't want his notice, but it angered me to know I didn't trouble his mind in the least, while he troubled mine.

When I lived in the manor, I thought the villagers dull witted, with their lazy way of talking. They lopped off the end of every word, as if they couldn't be bothered to pronounce it plainly, and yet they used so many: they dawdled all around a tale when a straight path would have been quicker. But when Az and I would go visiting, words went galloping past and I'd stumble after.

They said they were living like toads under a harrow since Sire Pava had claimed an extra day of labor every tennight, leaving them only five for their own fields. They said Steward was always watching, prying. Nothing was beneath his notice; he'd skin a flea for its hide and tallow.

And some went on to say that although the old Dame had been too meddlesome by far with her herbs and potions—being something of a canny-woman, after all—and too strict to wink at even a little hole in a grain sack, she'd never stolen the food from between their teeth. It rankled me, this backward praise. I thought of how the Dame and I had gone into their crofts, bringing remedies for their ills, how she'd tended women and children with her own hands, how they'd blinked and looked away in the darkness of those stinking huts, shuttering the whites of their eyes. I'd supposed them shy, perhaps bewildered by her kindness, surely grateful. Now I heard their ingratitude and distrust. But I said nothing.

They talked about me as well when my back was turned. Az was too kind to tell me what they said, but Halm and Betwyx, the wives of Az's sons, told me how the tittle-tattles clucked that Sire Pava had tried me and found me lacking—though a few said I'd run off to bear his child and bury it. I felt shame that such tales were bandied about. Perhaps they wanted my own account of it, good currency among the other wives, but I wouldn't oblige.

I gave the gossips another cud to chew, for I never said where I'd spent the year away. Neither the truth nor a lie would do, and that left only silence. Some took offense, saying I supposed I was too good for them. But all agreed that wherever I'd gone, I'd come back strange.

Word got about that I was god-bothered and the questions ceased. The Blood who are touched by a god are sent to the temples to serve as Auspices, or, if their wits are too addled, to be tended with care. Among the mudfolk, the god-bothered may become wandering Abstinents, pleasing their god by mortifying their flesh, or revelators who tell fortunes in the marketplace, or servants at a temple, drudging for the priests of the Blood. Most stay in their villages, sometimes shunned, sometimes sought after for their gifts of healing, hexing, or foretelling. Always pitied. It's said the gods most love those they most afflict. This I doubt.

As one of the god-bothered, I might have done anything—raved of voices and visions, fallen down in fits or gone naked—and no one would have been amazed, save Az and her sons. But I wished only to be unremarkable. If Ardor spoke to me now, it was no more than any woman might hear when she roused up the fire for the morning porridge: the fire song of Ardor Hearthkeeper.

A few women came to me for help, and then a few more. One pleaded for a blight to mar the smooth skin of her rival, and I sent her off with my rage at her heels; another asked for a charm to make her next child a boy, and I turned my back on her. But I did my best to soothe those who came to me with pains. I filled Az's hut with drying herbs, and her kitchen with tinctures and salves, and daily I brought home beneficial plants from hedgerows, fields, orchards, anywhere my duties took me.

I'd been mistaken to think the Dame was the only healer in the village. Every mudwoman knew simples and the charms that went with them to treat everyday complaints, but there was also a midwife and a woman who could cure a baby's colic with her spittle. The men had their own healer, of course; a woman could ease a man's aches, bruises, and fevers with a poultice or tisane, but if she touched his open wound, she'd sour his blood and cause the wound to fester. The men's carnifex, named Fex for short, came to his calling by way of gelding calves, colts, and hogs; his remedy for everything was leeches and more leeches.

They called me a greenwoman. I only did as the Dame had taught me, but they trusted me more now that they thought I was touched.

One morning Az saw three crows land in the yard while she was weeding the kitchen garden. The one on her left flew away over the wall; the middle one preened; the one on her right went into the byre and came out with a beakful of straw. I was next door with Halm and her baby and her daughter Lilt when Az called us to come and look. By the time we came, only one crow remained, strutting in the dust.

Az was shaken. "I must go to the Kingswood today. Will you come with me?"

Halm made the sign to turn bad luck away. "Why must you go there? Knock on Mischief's door, he's sure to bid you welcome." Like Na, like most of the village folk, she thought the forest was full of menace, and not just from the kingsmen. Those who thought otherwise were not inclined to speak of it.

I said I would go, and gladly. "We'll be back tomorrow," Az told Halm, and she gave me a basket to carry loaded with barley and a flask of goat's milk.

We followed the river toward its source in the mountains. The path climbed gently at first, then steeply, and I matched my pace to Az's. She panted as she climbed under the hot Sun, so I forbore to ask her questions until we stopped to rest in a field of blooming flax. Swallows darted over the field, the undersides of their wings catching the blue of the flowers.

"What did you see, Az? What does the omen say?"

To my surprise, Az began to cry. "The crows told me I'll have but one son left in my croft by wintertime, for one will fly and one will marry. We'll be begging the woodward for the king post to raise a new roof soon. Ah—change is hard for an old woman! Even good news comes like a thief."

"You think Maken will marry? Who will he marry?" It was a question I pondered often at the time.

Az shrugged her humped shoulders. "The crow flew right over the village with the straw, and there's no telling where he came down. Plenty of women in his path. I worry more for Fleetfoot. I fear he might not live to grow a beard." She rubbed tears from her face with both hands. "Come, we have a ways to go."

There is a path the fallow deer use when they come down from the woods to nibble on the heavy heads of ripening grain. We followed it through the wall of brambles, out of the Sun and into the shadows under the trees, and then Az left the path and led me deep into the forest to the great oak, Heart of the Wood.

I knew where she was leading me, of course; every step was familiar. Yet I wondered at how I could have forgotten—or put out of my mind—the sense of presence that fills the Kingswood. I had been a creature of the wood, one among many, so enfolded in that vast life that I'd lost myself there for a time; now I was touched by awe and dread, like any trespasser who strays too far within those precincts.

Az did not seem afraid. She had me put the basket with the barley and goat's milk in a crotch of the great oak high above her head. Then she began a low chant, standing between two roots as thick as a man's thigh, rocking back and forth. I sat on the ground nearby, and after a while I fell into a shadow dream with my eyes wide open. Before me a green veil stirred in the wind, woven in a shifting pattern of leaf and branch, light and shadows. I looked at it sideways and caught a glimpse of a black horse galloping, its rider cloaked in a green flame. But soon I became aware of other shadows crowding close, at the edge of vision. I felt we had a multitude around us, and it raised the hair on my nape.

Az was still murmuring, rocking. She wept again.

Late in the afternoon she came out of her trance. She cut a green branch with a fine spray of leaves from Heart of the Wood, giving thanks as she did so, and led me away, sure of her steps even without a path. We climbed a steep slope and then descended into a ravine between two long ridges, where one of the streams that feed our river had cut deep into the rock. The shale walls of the gorge were covered with ferns, sprigs of twinflower, and brilliant green mosses lush from seeping waters. The stream was shallow, swift, and cold. We scrambled on slippery rocks and clung to roots and saplings. Az's breathing was harsh and her limbs trembled. I begged her to stop and take some food, for I'd gathered mushrooms and starchroot and berries on the way. She shook her head and we went on, unspeaking.

Darkness comes early deep in the mountains. By the time we reached our destination, the bright blue ribbon of sky overhead had turned cobalt. Az had led me to the headwater of the stream. Where the two long ridges joined, the waters of a spring tumbled out of a fissure in the cliff face into a pool littered with great boulders. One side of the ravine was a wall of pure gray clay. It had been mined over the years, and the diggers had left a wide shelf of clay next to the pool. We piled up leaves in a hollow, and Az and I curled up to sleep.

I spoke in a dream, and woke myself, though both word and dream escaped me. I saw three lights moving near us and shook Az in a panic. "No fear," Az said. "They're here to keep us from harm," and she went back to sleep.

In the morning she was more forthcoming. "Our dead are all through these woods," she told me. "We buried them here to keep them close, so they'd look after us, each one under a sapling according to their nature. Many of these trees are our people. Then the Blood came along and made us burn the dead. We've lost six generations since they came from Oversea, six generations wandering who knows where. But those who are left here still come at need, if they are not forgotten. I think soon they may be forgotten."

She pointed at the ridges. "In the beginning our people were fashioned from this clay, right here between the Thighs. You'll not come into your strength till you know what clay made you. This isn't your place."

Tears started to my eyes as if she'd struck me.

She leaned over and took my hand. "Don't take it hard. I'm only saying I don't need an omen bird to tell me you'll fly away again."

I went to find food while Az worked all morning, digging and shaping clay. By the time I came back, she'd made a clay woman about knee high, forming it around the oak branch so that a topknot of leaves sprouted from the head. She smoothed the clay until it was like skin, and incised spirals over the round breasts and belly. Last of all she scratched eyes in the featureless oval of the face. I was amazed and afraid to see how the clay woman looked back at us from her new eyes, and I wondered if Eorõe Artifex had been surprised, when she shaped our forebears, the first people, to feel the clay come to life in her hands.

We left the woman behind rubble in a dry niche in the rock. Az said Maken would come to fetch her when he was ready to build his house, and hide her in the wall to bring blessings.

Az was in good spirits on the way home, for she'd heard under the great oak that Fleetfoot would not be dying just yet. She knew he'd be leaving, but not where he'd go or whether he would return. She'd made him a clay man the size of two fingers, with an acorn for a heart. She wanted him to keep a bit of the earth he came from, to keep Mischief from crossing his path. But some fates are beyond our power to avert; the more Az fussed over Fleetfoot, knowing she'd lose him, the more surely she sent him away.

When harvest came we reaped daylong in the fields and went to sleep with straw in our hair and grit under our lids. The work hardened me, until I could keep up with the fastest reapers. Everything smelled dusty. The stone granary within the manor walls filled up while Steward and the priest, Divine Narigon, stood at the door making the tallies, watching each other like two cats.

I pinched my arms and legs to feel the fat under the skin. Az made me a new dress from cloth Na had left her, dyed a dark blue with woad. My tongue got quicker, and keener too. Laughter came hard to me, but Fleetfoot liked to tease me and make me smile. Life with the Dame was like a tapestry locked in a chest; I stopped taking it out to look at the colors. Nor did I think of my year in the Kingswood, though sometimes I dreamed of it.

All this talk of war: rumors flew like chaff above the threshing floor, and it was hard to find a grain of truth in all the dust. King Thyrse had campaigned nearly every summer of his reign, and he'd reigned since before I was born. People said he loved war nearly as well as hunting, and better than women (for he hadn't found the time between campaigns to take another wife after his first died barren). His battles meant no more to me than a rumormonger's songs, so long as he kept war from our gates and took it to others.

The Dame had filled her levy with horses instead of men: she had an old battle-scarred stallion that bred true, and a fine horsemaster to train his get. A good warhorse was worth five times his weight in foot soldiers. And if, every year, a few younger sons among the mudfolk were hungry and restless enough to run off to war, well then—it made for peace in the village with the mischiefmakers gone.

This year was different. The king had summoned the troops to meet after the fall harvest, which meant a winter campaign. Nobody knew why but everybody made surmises. And it was true: Sire Pava was going to war. He'd called for four drudges from the village to serve as foot soldiers. Perhaps he wouldn't come home. Well rid if he didn't.

Messengers had gone back and forth between the master and his father, and Sire Pava had gone to Ramus to be fitted for his armor—and very fine it was: a helmet topped with a crest of gilt steel feathers and armor covered in silvery scales like a fish. They said his horse's barding alone cost enough to feed us all for a year. He was spending money in the village too, buying leather fittings, cloth coarse and fine, hams and preserved ducks, cheeses, dried fruit, grain, a thousand things. But what he paid the armorers he took from us, in new taxes and fines for every small offense. It made for quarrels, as some drudges had coins for the first time and others said the granaries would be empty by midwinter, and famine would come calling. But the boys liked to sneak off and watch Sire Pava train for war, his new armor flashing in the Sun.

Fleetfoot and I went to see him too, climbing a tree that overlooked the outer court. He'd cut down the manor's guardian tree. Until I saw it with my own eyes, I had not believed it. That tree had been beloved, fed yearly with libations of ale and pruned into a perfect dome. As a child I used to hide in its branches and eat plums and cast the pits at Na when she came looking for me. Its leaves were dark, but when the Sun came through, they'd shone red as wine. Now there was nothing left of it but a bare trunk and two limbs to make a quintain for jousting, standing in a muddy field where once there'd been a garden, with paved paths and lavender and roses and benches of turf.

It had rained after tennights of cloudless skies, and turned chilly. Sire Pava and Divine Narigon chased each other on foot, whacking away with wooden swords weighted with lead. They slid in the mud, grunting and cursing. I turned my head and spat on the ground, but I could tell Fleetfoot was taken with the sight.

A little before the UpsideDown Days that mark the autumn Equinox, a company of men came to the manor on the way to the king's new war. I was in Az's croft pulling turnips from the kitchen garden when I saw the banners over the wall and heard the boys yelling. I ran with the other drudges to see the warriors, and stood at the back of the crowd to watch them enter the manor gates.

We were dazzled by the sight, for the Sun, which had hidden behind massy clouds all week, chose that moment to send her rays to gild the metal of armor and weapons. Each rider bore, on a pole strapped to his back, pennants of cloth-of-gold for the king and grass green for the clan of Crux, that streamed and fluttered in the wind; the men held the reins tight to make a better show, and their horses pulled at the bits and stamped and neighed as they jostled before the gate. Far down the valley road we could see, still in the shadow of the clouds, a convoy of foot soldiers, a train of oxcarts and baggage mules and spare mounts, and a pack of war dogs with their handlers. Two boys, pushing between legs to get a better view, slipped into the ditch beside the road and had to be pulled from the muddy water and then roundly cursed for their folly.

I mistook this troop of the Crux clan for an entire army. I couldn't count them all, for they moved about, but I guessed there were near a hundred horsemen and about the same number of men afoot. But as the Blood count, there were only sixteen in the company—so I learned later—for that was the number of cataphracts, and Sire Pava was to be the seventeenth. Seventeen is a strong number, not easily divided. Each of the cataphracts had an armiger, also of the Blood, to carry arms and fight on his shield side. These men were warriors who'd fight for the glory of it—some of the glory being the plunder they'd bring home. Then there were the soldiers, mudmen who went to war at their masters' bidding: every cataphract had seven or eight armed varlets, several mounted, the rest on foot. But the Blood don't bother to number mudmen in a troop, neither alive nor among the dead on a battlefield.

The cataphracts were at the front, but we'd have known them anyway by their warhorses, which stood a good hand taller than the other mounts, and by their bright breastplates. Their helms were strapped to their servants' saddles. We could see their faces as they greeted Sire Pava and Dame Lyra at the outer gate. The eldest had a grizzled beard, though his hair was brown. His face was weathered, with a puckered scar running across his brow and down over the corner of his left eye. He dismounted first, moving as easily as a young man. He said, "Sire Pava, I bring you greetings from your father."

Sire Pava and Dame Lyra were kneeling right in the road before him—though they had a drudge lay a piece of cloth on the ground first. Sire Pava had donned his new armor for the occasion. "We are honored by your visit, Sire Adhara dam Pictor by Falco, First of Crux," he said. "My manor is but a hovel, not worthy to shelter you, but you're welcome inside. I wish we had a better feast to set before you, but the food we have here is more fit for swine than people." Dame Lyra said something I couldn't hear for the noise. She looked fatter than when I'd last seen her; her complexion was pasty.

We onlookers could read the meaning of this pageant, for it's the custom to mouth such humble-tasting words to our betters. But it wasn't all false courtesy. This man was titled the Crux, the First of his clan, and he was the living representative of the god Crux among the god's descendants. He led the clan's Council of Houses, and when the need was dire, he was the Intercessor who summoned the Council of the Dead. His prayers reached the god when others failed. Furthermore, as little as we knew of the court, we knew this, for Sire Pava boasted of it often: Sire Adhara dam Pictor by Falco, First of Crux, had the king's ear.

I stared at him, this man who stood so near a god and a king. We all stared and were not beaten for it. Sire Pava likewise descended from Crux, who long ago visited the mudfolk in the avatar of the Sun. She mated with mortal men and bore sons, the forefathers of the houses of the clan. God's Blood ran in Sire Pava's veins, sure enough, but I'd never seen a spark of radiance in him before. Yet that day the Sun parted the clouds and shone on the Crux with such brightness that I had to shield my eyes, and I was in awe of him and all his company, even Sire Pava. No matter that she shone on us onlookers too: we were dull and did not partake of her glory, as they did in their armor.

The First of Crux bade Sire Pava rise and gave him the kiss of peace. We lingered, after they went inside, to watch the rest of the company straggle in: foot soldiers and oxen and mules and horses and dogs. At last a manor drudge came out with a broom and barrow to collect the dung from the road. She was too proud to share a crumb of news with the likes of us. I could imagine the feast and the bustle in the manor in every detail, but I was outside now, looking in with the rest of the village folk. I went home in a bad temper.

I found an excuse to go to the back gate of the manor, though I'd stayed away before; I took tart striveberries and purse nuts to Cook and asked her what tidings had come with the newcomers.

"I can't stand here nattering," she said. "Come keep me company."

I stepped just inside the back gate and leaned against the wall by the kitchen garden. "Well, what news?" I said.

"Will you look!" she said. "The worms are at the coleworts again." She knelt and began plucking greenworms from the leaves and crushing them under stones. She said the king meant to cross the Inward Sea and make war on Incus, and it was his sister, Queenmother Caelum, who begged him to do it, and in winter too. Who ever heard of warring in winter?

In my lifetime King Thyrse had campaigned to the north against surly, sheep-stealing clansmen, and strewn the stones of their keeps over their stony lands. To the south he'd conquered a tribe of little men who rode small, quick horses; they used bows and arrows, and for this profanation of killing at a distance the king had slaughtered them without mercy when he could catch them, man, woman, and child. To the east he'd won and lost and won again a fertile river valley. Never had he gone west to war against Incus, and I said so.

"Ah, but he did," Cook said. "Maybe it was before you came along. It was a matter of the border, I think, or some island or other. Afterward he married his sister to the king of Incus to keep the peace. When the king died she ruled as queen regent until her son, Prince Corvus, came into his age. They say he married a serpent woman and she has him tight in her coils (and her forked tongue tickling his ear besides), and since she couldn't abide Queenmother Caelum, he turned against his mother and locked her up in a northern keep. I heard the Crux say at table that the queenmother led her garrison all the way around the north shore of the Inward Sea and south to Ramus, and she lay on the ground before King Thyrse and rubbed dust in her hair, and begged him to restore her due. How could he deny his sister?"

"I don't see the sense in it. She'd go to war with her own son?"

"She says he's bewitched, and unfit to rule. But I don't know. The Crux's cook told me she's more clabber than cream, however sweet she seems, and he wouldn't blame the prince for hoping she'd catch her death of cold and damp up there in the north country."

Cook moved to the next row of coleworts. I followed her a few steps farther into the courtyard and asked about the troop staying at the manor, for that interested me more than this talk of a far-off kingdom. She said the Crux had been granted the right to take five hinds and a stag from the Kingswood, and as many fallow deer as he could drive; it showed how high he stood in the king's favor. He'd promised them to Sire Pava for the UpsideDown Days and the Equinox feast, and Pava was wagging his tail fit to break his back for pride at the honor.

And one of the younger cataphracts was said to be a by-blow of the king, fathered on a Crux woman to strengthen the clan. He stood to gain a fief if he did well in battle. Iza had been coupling with his jack, and Dame Lyra caught her and gave her a beating, said she should at least have picked an armiger if she was going to make a fool of herself.

I laughed so hard at this—Iza was nearly thirty and too old to be chasing men—that my headcloth came undone. As I tucked my hair back under it, I saw Sire Pava come out of the stables with some of the visitors. I hugged Cook hastily and turned to go.

"Luck, bring me some spicewort and jenny-o'-the-fields, if you can find any," she called out. She could not get used to my new name. "And come to see me in the kitchen sometimes so I can fatten you up."

I shook my head. I had not yet set foot inside the manor. I was waiting for the UpsideDown Days.

In the hand of days each year called the UpsideDown Days, five days belonging to no month or tennight, anything can happen. Low is high and high is low, and people seize chances they've been waiting for all year, or are seized by chances unlooked for. Many children are born nine months later, and are counted fortunate, though perhaps they get more than their share of beatings from the father in the house.

On the third of the Days, Sire Pava was hooked to a plow and driven with a switch by the oldest drudge. He plowed half a furrow and swore he'd do no more. One mudman called out, "Your furrow is short. I hope you don't flag so quick when you plow your wife," and another said, "Oh, he likes to plow well enough. It's the sowing he shirks." Sire Pava made some light answer, but he was displeased. Everyone knew he'd scattered his seed all over and had but two bastards to show for it. Dame Lyra squatted down and watered the field, holding her dress up so it should not get dirty. There were other rude japes for her, and I was glad to see how they chafed.

The third night was given to the god Carnal. Women wore their hair uncovered, all maids again, no shame in it. Men roamed from village to village, and any woman who didn't want a pricking stayed home and barred her door. We danced our way to the center of the spiral fields along the plowed strips, to make them ready for the winter sowing, and back out again, round and round until we were dizzy. We called the god, and the god came among us in the avatar of Desire. The Sun went down; we lit the pitch-pine torches, and the torches drifted farther apart, dipping and swaying and going out, as the dancers chose partners for a different dance.

A man with a torch came running up behind me and threw my shadow flickering ahead over the furrows. He seized my shoulder, turned me around, and kissed me. Not having much time to think about it, I bit him and pushed him away.

He laughed. There was a drop of blood on his lip. "I was hoping I'd find you," he said in the High, a language I'd not used for more than a year. "Red hair is lucky."

"Might not be lucky for you," I answered back. My heart was pounding hard enough to shake me. I held myself still, thinking: if I run, he'll catch me anyway, and believe I am playing coy. And thinking: maybe I don't wish to run.

He was one of the Blood. He'd shaved his beard, the better to show off his clan tattoo. Such was the fashion in Ramus—or so we'd heard when Sire Pava had shaved too, and revealed his weak chin. This man had no such fault. He was breathing fast, and I saw the pulse jump in his neck. His long, curling hair was damp from dancing. He wore no surcoat, only a shirt and leggings, but those well made: his hose cut to the shape of his leg and gartered above the knee with jeweled ribands, and a shirt of linen so fine it was nearly transparent. A cataphract, then. An armiger was unlikely to dress so well.

He said, "Well, seen enough?" He held the torch high in one hand. With the other he caught my skirts and pulled me closer. He laughed to see me considering his question so seriously.

I liked his looks and his laugh that came so easily. I put my arms around his waist, stood on tiptoe, and kissed him. The taste was salty. "I'm not too skinny for you?"

He laughed again and replied with another kiss. He took my hand and we ran, far from the other lights. Behind a hawthorn hedge he drove the butt of the torch into the ground.

I asked, "Why don't you put it out?"

"Because I want to see you," he said.

We lay on earth turned and softened by the plow. He pushed up my dress, unlaced his hose, and I took the weight of a man willingly for the first time. There was not much pain, or pleasure either. I don't know why he wanted the torch. He kept his eyes shut most of the time.

When he was done he rolled off and lay on his side with his head propped on his hand, looking at me. The torch wavered and smoked as it burned low, casting shadows under his brow and cheekbones.

He asked my name.

"I'm called Firethorn."

He smiled and rubbed his lip where I'd bitten him. "I daresay you earned your name by being prickly," he said.

"It seems to me *you* have the prick," I retorted. He lay on his back and laughed. He had heavy eyelids, drooping at the outer edges. I began to like the shadow left by his shaven beard. I pushed my dress down around my legs and turned to look at him.

"What is your name, Sire?"

"Galan."

"And your mother's house?"

"Capella."

"Gods! Are you Sire Pava's kinsman, then?"

"Our mothers are sisters." He looked at me under his lids.

"Give me the rest, then—your father's house?"

"Falco." This time he laughed at me, because my jaw hung open. He took a lock of hair that had fallen over my face and tucked it behind my ear.

"The First's son?"

"No, his nephew. Aren't you pleased? They'll make much of you in the village."

"Why should they? You'll be gone soon enough. Besides, what's done on the UpsideDown Days must not be mentioned." Now this Sire Galan dam Capella by Falco of Crux put me too much in mind of Sire Pava. The Blood think we should be honored by their touch, as they were honored when the gods mated with their ancestors. They don't imagine we might disagree.

The torch guttered out. I could see the bright road across the sky and the twelve godsigns in the stars. In the sky each sign writes a god's name. But arranged one after another, in dots of ink on sized linen, with marks above, right, or below to indicate the avatars, the signs can be made to mean almost anything. So the Dame had taught me, when she'd taught me to read.

I didn't need to wonder what she'd say if she saw me lying with a man in a field. Perhaps she did see me.

"Look, there's Crux," I said, pointing. I was glad of the dark, for blood had risen to my face.

"I'm surprised you know the stars," he murmured.

I bit back a short reply.

He said, "I saw you at the gate the other day. When your red hair got loose it was hard to miss. And I thought to myself: that one's mine, come Carnal Night." He put his hand between my thighs and I felt a pulse start under his touch. "I see you're red here too." His voice was not as sleepy.

There was balm in this. I was glad to be sought after. Better that than to think I was all he could catch. I pulled my dress over my head and persuaded his shirt to come off, and then his hose. I wanted the heat of his skin on my whole body.

The second time, I touched him wherever I pleased, wherever he pleased, and I marveled that we each had ceded to the other the right to wander freely in so much new territory. I found him embellished with scars: a long, thin line under his jawbone; a weal on his shin; a crescent-shaped ridge on his back; nicks and scratches everywhere. They were pale against his skin in the dark, and they gave my fingers something rough over which to linger. I said, this one? and he said a horse had kicked him. And this? He didn't remember, or had other games in mind.

We lay in the field all night. In the morning I was sore and covered with goose bumps. Under the Sun my tongue was tied. He said he'd find me again, but I didn't believe him. We parted on the hill where one footpath leads to the manor's front gate and the other to the crofts in the village. He flashed a grin at me and said farewell.

UpsideDown Days are fickle days. I'd found a man who pleased me well for a night beside a hedge. It was Carnal Night, and no wonder Desire's lamp had burned for us. I hoped to remember the hollow of his throat and the taste of his sweat, the feel of muscles shifting under his skin, his fingers digging into my haunches, for such are gifts of the festival.

For the rest, I meant to put Sire Galan out of my mind easily, and most of all the way he looked before the torch burned out, when I was first under him. He'd raised himself above me with his weight on his palms, and reared back his head and closed his eyes and plowed me deeper into the furrow. I could have been anyone, or no one, the earth itself, like the clods that crumbled under my hands.

But I was a fool to think Ardor was done with me. Surely a spark of Ardor Wildfire had kindled Desire's lamp, and showed me the unexpected path at my feet.

That evening Sire Galan found his way to Az's door and asked for me. I was surprised to see him, and glad in a way that worried me. He lifted me up for a kiss. It was the UpsideDown Days, so Az shrugged and shut the door, leaving us out in the yard.

"Come back to the manor, where there's a bed," Sire Galan said.

"I can't. I'll be seen."

"What does it matter? We'll have a whole bed to ourselves. Sire Alcoba and I have been sharing one of the cabinets, but I offered to let him ride my black courser for the hunt tomorrow if he'd go elsewhere for two nights. He would do anything to ride Semental—and besides, he'll have no trouble finding a soft maid or two to pillow him."

I hadn't planned to go back to the manor that way. I was going to wait for the feast at the end of the UpsideDown Days, so I could see Sire Pava and Dame Lyra bend their proud necks to serve us mudfolk sitting at table. But this had a good savor to it: cabinet beds were for guests, not drudges. I'd never slept in one in my life. I ducked into the hut for my shawl. Az made a face and waved me out.

The hall of the manor was dim and smoky and smaller than I remembered it. There were men everywhere, some sleeping, some pricking women in the corners, and others dicing and drinking and gnawing bones. The place stank like a fox den. The Dame would not have allowed it, not even during the UpsideDown Days. She would not have used torches, either, for they cast sparks and blackened the tapestries. She never stinted on candles when the occasion called for it, thrifty as she was.

Sire Pava was sitting before the fire with Dame Lyra, the Crux, and two of the other cataphracts. They had a low screen about them to set them apart from the revels. Dame Lyra sat stiff and quiet with a wooden smile, and she kept her best gown tucked about her as if a flood of dirty water swirled around her slippers. Sire Pava was flushed, exalted by the honor or too much wine. He called out, "Look what Galan has dragged in. You worry me, Cousin, if that's the best you can find on a night when every woman in the village will flip her kirtle over her head."

Sire Galan answered back, "I have all the luck tonight. She fits me to the hilt." He put his hand on the small of my back and pushed me forward into the hall, through the crowd of men sitting on the floor. He wore an easy smile, but I noticed his other hand was on the dagger at his belt.

I'd have killed them both at that moment if I'd had the means—or less sense.

Sire Pava said, "She's a dry well, Cousin. I know because I've plumbed her. Don't waste your time. You ought to be doing your duty instead, begetting half-breeds to improve the drudges' blood."

Sire Galan took two steps toward him, saying his manners should be mended.

I grabbed his arm and found my tongue. "Everyone knows Sire Pava needs help siring bastards."

Such was the license of the Days that this earned me a laugh rather than a beating. I saw the Crux lean forward and touch Sire Pava's knee to turn his attention. Dame Lyra glared and I lifted my head high and went past her. There was nothing for it but to be as brazen as I was thought to be.

Though the feather bed was soft, I did not do much sleeping. When Sire Galan tired I goaded him on. Our bodies were greased with sweat, and the curtains held the smell of our musk close. When I cried out, sometimes I thought of Sire Pava and hoped I was keeping him awake. Rage can lend its own heat to desire, and that night I mastered Sire Galan more than he mastered me. I left before daybreak, stepping around the pallets on the hall floor.

That was the morning of the last UpsideDown Day, the day of the feast. I came back with the villagers in the evening. Plank tables were crowded into the hall, spread with white linens. They'd scrubbed and sanded the floor, and put out tallow lamps and candles. The master and mistress of the house and the rest of the Blood—even the Crux himself—brought our food, poured the wine, did our bidding. The centerpiece was a roasted stag, crowned with gilded antlers and stuffed with songbirds; they had hunted well. We were forbidden to kill the deer that fattened on our coleworts and stole our grain, and the venison tasted all the better for the salt of revenge.

I'd looked forward to the feast, but I'd never imagined Sire Galan, or how he'd steal my thoughts and make Dame Lyra's fetching and Sire Pava's carrying less important. Their humility was hollow anyway. When Sire Pava came around the table and bent his knee, offering a platter of pigeons baked in clay, he didn't keep his head down as was proper; his eyes promised that tomorrow we'd serve him again.

I watched Sire Galan. He had a walk like a stalking cat, and could carry a brimming cup so smoothly not a drop of wine would spill. Once he stood close behind my bench and pressed my back with his hip. I thought the feast would never end. Though I gorged until my belly was tight, I'd not had my fill of Sire Galan, and we had but one more night.

The next day was Equinox. The priest would start the count of tennights and months. At the feast tomorrow, we would take our proper places, and the villagers would kneel and swear fealty again. Balance would be restored. But when the world has been shaken and cast at odds, only the gods know what is balance and what is chaos.

That night I lay in the cabinet bed looking at the ceiling, tracing the carved and painted vine on the panel above in hearthlight that came through the curtains. The walls were too close, the air too still.

I could feel Sire Galan watching me, and my face stiffened. The Days were over, and he'd be going soon. I would not show I cared. I turned over in my mind what questions to ask, so I might hear his voice: if I asked whether he'd been to war before, and he had not, then I'd be more afraid; and if I asked how long the campaign would last, he might think I hoped to see him on his return, but I was not vain enough for that. There was mischief in every question.

He said my name twice, as if he liked it on his tongue, and turned my head toward him with his hand. "Come with me," he whispered.

I turned my face away, and tears came against my will, sliding down my cheek and into my ear. I'd heard what kind of woman followed a man to war: a sheath. A cataphract might share her with his armiger or lend her to a guest, and if he was not too particular, he might let his drudges have her now and then. If she didn't begin as a whore, she usually ended as one, wearing a striped skirt and opening her legs for any man with coin until she was clapped out.

He went on whispering. "You can ride the chestnut mare. She's steady. I'll get another mule for the baggage."

"I won't be shared," I said.

"Never. You shall be my own." He said this so fiercely I believed him.

"What of the Crux? He won't welcome me."

"Many a sword brings his sheath along; he won't blink an eye. Come with me, I'm intent on it. I'll care for you well, and you'll bring me luck."

I said nothing, only looked at him.

He laughed low in his throat and raised himself over me. "I can offer you better reasons, since you're not convinced," he said.

While we coupled, my thoughts went wandering. Sire Galan would tire of me someday and leave me standing by the roadside with a few coins and a new dress, and Sire Pava laughing to see it. And suppose he did? I'd lived a long year alone in the Kingswood. I needed no man's help.

But that was all bravado. Already—how had it come about so quickly?—desire had begotten need. A few whispered words (perhaps he didn't mean them) and I was ready to follow. It was worse to think of staying behind, to grind one day upon another. Nothing to hold me here. None to regret my leaving, save Az.

I wrapped my legs around him and gripped his shoulders and pushed back.

CHAPTER 2

Sheath

he First of Crux was not pleased, not at all, when Sire Galan took me to him and asked leave for me to travel with the troop. He said, "You know I don't hold with sheaths—useless baggage. A sheath is no better than a harlot, but more trouble." Sire Galan stood his ground, but I saw him flinch. He stood in front as if to shield me.

The Crux went on to call me a whore four or five different ways, and a sow and a vixen besides. I endured it. I was so set on leaving, it seemed impossible that I'd ever thought of staying.

But when the Crux said I was a bitch in heat and all the dogs in camp would fight over me, I stepped forward, eyes downcast. "Sire Adhara dam Pictor by Falco, First of Crux," I said, in the correct and formal speech I'd heard the Dame use when she was most irked with me, "I won't hold you back. I can ride, I can sleep on stones and keep a fire going in the rain. I know herbs for many uses." I showed him my palms, callused from the hoe, sickle, and pestle. "Does a whore have hands like these? I know how to work. And I promise you no one will quarrel over me—I keep to myself."

The Crux laughed, a short bark. He said, looking at Sire Galan, "You can tell your little braggart she'd never hold us back. Isn't that so? A bit of mud may cling to a boot for a time, but it's easily scraped off. Take her, if you're so ruled by your prick that you must have her, but keep her out of my way or I'll feed her to the manhounds. And tell her never to address me again, unless I give her leave."

I'd forgotten my place. If I'd been a man, I might not have survived my presumption. I should have let Sire Galan answer, for there was nothing I could say that the Crux was obliged to hear. My face burned. I dropped to my knees and touched my forehead to the ground.

The Crux turned on his heel and left us. Sire Galan pulled me up and kept hold of my hand. He'd seemed so assured before; now I saw how green he was, when he stood against a man. He saw me in a new light too, when I mislaid my country accent and my deference. I had dared to contradict the Crux. It frightened us both.

I'm not sure why the Crux changed his mind and let me come, unless it was to teach me my own inconsequence. Or because a god whispered in his ear.

While the troop was readying to go, I made my own preparations. I stitched myself a wide leather girdle, lined with hidden pockets for necessities: childbane, for it might not grow where I was going; simples to soothe pains, bring down a fever, poultice a wound; seasonings for the cook pot; chunks of rock salt. One pocket held a handful of berries from the firethorn tree, wrapped in oiled vellum; the berries were too dangerous to use for healing, but I kept them. They reminded me of the Kingswood and a god's gift.

From the belt I hung an iron knife with a bone handle and a copper fire flask lined with clay and firewort to keep a coal from the hearth alive. The flask was stamped with the sign of Ardor Hearthkeeper; I'd never willfully go without her blessing again. I also took my sheepskin cloak with faded ward signs and Na's threadbare old dress. A bit of cloth was too precious to waste.

Two days after Equinox I said farewell. This time I'd be farther away than the Kingswood. Az was the hardest to leave, so I left her last, and took care that I found her alone in her dim hut. I knew, like Na, she'd never live to see me again.

Az fetched a leather sack from a hiding place beside the clay house goddess, who kept watch on us through a tiny hole in the wall, safe from the prying eyes of the priest.

"I'm giving you these because you have no blood family," she said, spilling small painted bones from the sack onto the table. She held one against her index finger, so I could see it matched the last joint, and dropped it into my palm. The tip of the bone was painted red. "This is from the right hand of my sister, from Na. I'm giving her to you." She chose another bone, dyed a deep blue all over. "This is the Dame. Na wanted you to have her. They cared for you, and they'll counsel you well." She took up the other finger bones, one by one, and kissed them and put them back in the sack. Some were nothing but brown shards.

It chilled me to think of Na cutting off the top joint of the Dame's bloodless finger and tucking her hand back under the shroud. She'd dared the wrath of the priest and troubled the Dame's shade. She'd kept secrets, even from me. I wondered how many other secrets were hidden in the mud walls of the village huts, as these small bones had been hidden. A few months of grinding barley, and I'd been arrogant enough to think I knew the folk who lived here—and Az herself. I was daunted to find she had shades at her beck and call.

We squatted near the doorway where a patch of sunlight came into the hut. With a stick, Az drew a circle two handspans wide on the hard dirt floor and divided it into twelve equal parts by crossing it with lines for the twelve directions. Starting at the east and going around the circle, she named the god who governed each wedge-shaped domain. Then she scratched two concentric circles inside the greater one, so that the wedges were cut into three parts, one for every avatar of the governing god. She named these too, pointing with her stick as if she expected me to remember.

I do remember, as clearly as if the compass were before me now, carved in stone. I'd heard tell of the gods and their avatars all my life, though some had always seemed remote and indifferent to me, and others near at hand—too close, at times. Everyone knows the prayers of drudges don't wing their way to the gods as swiftly or as surely as those of the Blood, but they are still our gods and we belong to them.

The mudfolk used to live in ignorance, worshiping the numina of trees and boulders and waters instead of the gods, but even in those long-ago days, they knew of Eorõe Artifex, though they called her by another name. It's a tale everyone knows, how she formed our ancestors of clay—mud and Blood alike, we spring from those first people—and gave us her breath, the breath of life, and then she died. She is the only dead avatar. The god Eorõe lives on, still manifest to us as the Cornking and Frenzy, but the death of even one avatar warns us that the gods too may be mortal.

Az rubbed charcoal on her eyelids, the better to see, and she cast the bones for me. I was reminded of how I was cut off from the tree of generations, with nothing to bind me to my forebears but a fragment of a dream, for I had only two bones in the stead of a handful of ancestors. She had to throw the bones three times for every reading, to point to six signs all told.

The first reading is always for character. A drudge lives from one calamity to the next, and even a king can't guard himself against every hazard; so we are tried like a coin, and learn whether we are made of base or true metal. Az didn't ask the bones what was to come, but rather how I should meet my fortune. She pressed her fingers to her eyelids, smearing the charcoal, and swayed from side to side. Her voice altered. The Dame pointed to wandering, aimlessness, flood—or, it may be, discovery, resolve, wellspring, for every sign had two meanings. Na said beware of prisons, obstacles, shackles; their transformations were shelter, vessels, roots. Each warning was woven with its reverse, like a cloth with two faces. I could make little sense of it. Az said it was counsel to bear in mind on my journey, when I had to choose one path or another.

For the second reading the compass marked time: the inner circle the past, the outer the future, the present in between. Az tightened her lips as she threw, displeased with the pattern the bones were making. Three bones landed in the present: Crux Moon, Hazard Chance, and Ardor Wildfire. Only one finger pointed to my past, to Rift Dread. Two bones fell in the future: Ardor Smith and Rift Queen of the Dead.

I made light of it, saying I could see for myself that the present was ruled by a most mischievous assortment of avatars, and as for the rest, are we not all born in fear and living at hazard, and doesn't the Queen of the Dead lie in wait for everyone?

Az shook her head and said the bones were not so quick to give up their secrets. Avatars have many qualities, and the only way to tell which ones mattered here was to listen hard, for the bones spoke to one another.

Seeing she was vexed with me, I asked her more humbly: what did she see, what did she hear?

Az hesitated. "I see you've chosen a man who loves Chance. You'll find he takes his luck too much for granted. He'll wager, and the dice will tumble and the world will spin, and even when he wins, he'll be overset. I see you travel toward the past as well as the future: war ahead and war behind, and strife along the way."

"Nothing more?"

She said that I need make no provisions for old age.

Did she think I expected a long life? Such a reckless mood had overtaken me when I decided to go with Sire Galan that I believed I could greet whatever came my way, whether it be living or dying, with equal readiness; beneath that was a secret conviction—a folly of the young—that death was not for me.

The third and last reading was for the gods. Az said that of course I shouldn't shirk my duties to any god on its holy days, but the bones would tell me which gods I should honor with fealty, prayers, and sacrifices, and turn to daily for guidance and help.

On the first cast both bones landed in Ardor, one in the Smith, the other in Hearthkeeper. On the second cast in Ardor Smith and Ardor Wildfire. The third, both in Ardor Wildfire.

Az sat back on her heels, looking grim, saying nothing. She rubbed out the circle in the dirt and handed me the two finger bones with a little bag she'd made to keep them in, a circle of leather embroidered with the compass and tied with a drawstring. I kissed the bones and put them in the bag: red for Na, blue for the Dame. I didn't think I'd be able to hear them speak the way Az could, and surely it was selfish to keep them with me, tethering their shades to the world they'd left behind. Yet I felt that Na and the Dame would not begrudge me, and it was a comfort, that slight weight tied to my belt, the touch of the dead.

It turned out that Az wasn't sorry I was going; the future she'd seen in the flight of a crow had come apace, and Fleetfoot was leaving. She wanted me to look after him.

"Sire Pava wants him as a runner, and he means to go. Says I have enough sons to take care of me," she said.

There's a saying in the village: have three sons, one for dying young, one for a soldier, and one for your old age. Az was richer than most, with five healthy boys. But Fleetfoot was shy of twelve years old. She still nagged him to keep out of the rain and wear his hat in the Sun. I promised to take care of him, as much as he'd let me, and I rocked Az as she cried. She was not much bigger than a girl. I clenched my teeth against the tenderness welling up in me, this treacherous affection for Az, with her crooked back and brittle limbs, who cared enough to tie her sister's spirit to me. Treacherous, for I'd not be staying.

When I shut the gate behind me, I felt more relief than sorrow to leave that stifling hut. The world is wide, they say. No mortal has found the end of it.

Az and I were not the only ones reading omens. The Crux had his three Auspices out before dawn to make a sacrifice and consult their god. When these priests had arrived, we hadn't marked them because they'd been armored like the other warriors of the Blood. But for this occasion they wore green robes, peaked caps, and solemn faces. They whispered together, looking up and pointing, scratching signs in the dirt. A sliver of Moon sat near the horizon, and a wind from north-of-east pushed a freight of clouds over half the sky. Long before the Sun cleared Bald Pate, its light tinted the clouds lavender and rose and gold.

Sire Galan and I huddled under his fur-lined cloak, for the air had a bite to it, and he told me that these priests were the clan's best diviners, so renowned that the king himself called on them from time to time. One Auspex, Divine Hamus, had devoted years to studying the Sun, the female aspect of Crux. He was a rarity, for most female avatars are served by priestesses; Sire Galan whispered that this priest had been called to the Sun's service when he was a boy, and in his fervency he'd sacrificed his sacs for her, and would never grow to be a proper man. He knew the significance of her path in every hour and season, of the colors of her face from dawn to dusk, even of the shadows she cast. Divine Xyster was skilled in reading the ambiguous omens given by Crux Moon as he changed his disguise from sickle to orb. The third priest, Divine Tambac, could decipher the future in the realm of the Heavens, and anything that filled it: the shapes and colors of the clouds, the stars left covered and uncovered, lightning and storms, the flight of birds.

The horsemaster led out a brood mare, several years past her prime, and handed her halter to one of the priests. He kept his hand on her flank for a few moments, then gave her a pat and stepped back. As the rim of the Sun showed over the mountain, the priest cut the mare's throat. The jetting blood looked black in the dawn light and steamed when it met the air. The mare's forelegs buckled, and she lurched and fell with a thud.

The Auspices reported to the Crux in low voices. Whatever they learned from the Heavens, from the mare's ungainly death, they did not choose to share with the rest of us.

We stood about too long waiting for Sire Pava, and were late starting. Neither his men nor his supplies were in good order. The cataphracts' stallions began to quarrel, and a mule bolted into the crowd of onlookers and knocked down a little girl. The Crux masked his impatience behind courtesy when he spoke to Sire Pava, but he was not so courteous to the steward, who'd achieved such a muddle.

After the formal farewells at the manor, half the village followed us down the road, until the women with babes on their hips tired and waved us out of sight, and the men went back to the fields. At last the boys and dogs, dodging about the feet of the horses, gave up the chase.

But some of the village stayed with the company. On horseback there were Sire Pava; Divine Narigon, serving as his armiger and riding the second-best warhorse; Sire Pava's jack, Gaunt, armed with sword and stave; Harien, the horsemaster (that I trusted less than a weasel in a dovecote), with two spare mounts on a lead behind him; and Ev, the horseboy, riding an overburdened pony and leading an overburdened mare. Dogsbody, Sire Pava's bagboy, drove the oxcart, and three men—boys, rather—trudged beside him: Fleetfoot was one, along with Dag and Snare. Az had made Fleetfoot a padded leather vest, called a jack; I'd seen her stuffing it with horsehair and muttering blessings over it. He carried a billhook and the others bore scythes. They were younger sons all, big bones and meager flesh, who ate their fill once or twice a year at best. Their idea of plunder was roasted meat and white bread; they never stopped to think what kind of harvest they'd be asked to reap next with their blades.

Sire Pava heard that Sire Galan was bringing a sheath and he tried to add his mudwoman to the baggage. She refused, unwilling to give birth on the road; he left her to Dame Lyra's gentle care. So Iza and I were the last and least of those leaving the village that day. Iza, the drudge from the manor who'd made a mooncalf of herself over Sire Guasca's jack, followed him on a bony mule. I (no better than Iza, perhaps) came along on Sire Galan's chestnut mare. We had no place with Sire Pava's men, with the other villagers. In truth, we didn't know where we belonged, so we rode together. We passed the men afoot and lagged behind the men on horseback, in a gap that grew larger as the day went on.

When the Dame was alive, Iza had prepared wool and flax for weaving, which was dull, exacting work of many steps, each having to be done well or the next would be ill done. The Dame had preferred Iza's thread, for she spun very fine, but she couldn't abide her chatter. After I left the manor, Dame Lyra had taken Iza for her handmaid. No wonder the first jack to wink at her looked like a gift of the gods, if he could save her from Dame Lyra's pinches.

Iza would not stop talking. She boasted that her jack, Lich, had given her this new dress—and what had Sire Galan given me? And Lich was in Sire Guasca's good graces, and Sire Guasca (the king's bastard, you know) was a favorite of the king. And what of Sire Galan? She'd heard the Crux was vexed with him, over me. It rankled her that I was with a man of the

Blood and she was not, and she tried this way and that to get around it. I gave her curt answers, and after a time I took the lead without seeming to try, and I rode alone.

The troop had traveled north through the mountains from the capital of Ramus, stopping at fortified keeps and village manors to gather the warriors who had answered the king's summons on behalf of the clan. Sire Pava was the last to join the company. Now our road led west toward the Marchfield, to the place chosen by the king for his army to assemble. We'd started so late that the Sun was in our eyes. The Equinox had passed, and I could smell the change of season in the wind. Cold gusts from the heights stirred up the loamy scent of fallen leaves.

We followed the river road down the valley and around the shoulder of a mountain, and when I looked back the fields and pastures of the village had disappeared. But the Kingswood marched with us, ranks of trees on steep slopes, the evergreens in somber liveries, others bearing the gaudy banners of autumn. Sometimes the road went straight where the river bent, and sometimes it climbed a hill when the river plunged into a ravine. The way was ditched and banked for leagues, and the forest cleared around it to discourage ambushes, for that is part of the service owed by the master of each holding to the king, and therefore owed by drudge to master. Nevertheless, in some places the road was neglected, and saplings had crowded close, ditches had filled with marsh flowers and ruts with weeds.

The wind pushed the clouds of the morning beyond the horizon. Sunlight pressed on my skin through my clothes, like a weight, like a blessing. I watched the river running smooth and fast, muscular currents under the surface. Leaves shimmered on the poplars near the road, the undersides silver and the tops gold.

The Crux sent men back to make us keep the pace. Geese crossed our path, heading south, and I thought how we were like a flight of geese, with the Crux at the point and the Blood stringing along behind, and the rest of us jostling to find a place. I didn't want to catch the First's eye, so I urged my mare to catch up with the last of the horsemen. They were strangers to me, and I took care not to return their glances.

One said to another, "Is that a boy or a woman, do you think? By the sinews of the legs, I'd wager it's a boy."

A mudwoman can't spare the cloth to make a skirt lavish enough to drape over a horse's saddle down to the stirrups, such as women of the Blood wear to go on horseback. As usual when I went riding, I'd brought the front of my skirts between my legs and tucked it into my girdle at the back to make a sort of trousers, which covered me to my knees and left my calves and feet bare (I had no shoes, either). I'd never thought to be ashamed of it before.

"Maybe. For two copperheads I say it's a woman. Shall we see?" The second man made as if to ride toward me, and I stopped my mare in the middle of the road. He laughed and turned away. He'd never meant it.

When I dismounted that night, I wobbled and held on to the stirrup, unsure of my own legs. My skirts were stained from sweat and saddle leather. I hadn't ridden for over a year, and I was sore everywhere, from my legs to the back of my neck.

Sire Galan had a feather-stuffed quilt in his baggage. We lay down among his men and wrapped ourselves in it. He wouldn't wait until they slept to take his pleasure. Our breathing resounded in my ears, loud enough to be heard over the crackle and hiss of the fire. A man muttered a curse and turned away from us. When Sire Galan moaned I put my hand over his mouth.

Late in the night I woke up with Sire Galan's breath on the back of my neck. It was quiet, except for the wind, the river, and the whickering and rustling of horses. I nestled close to him, and he woke up fast. With his lips against my ear, he told me what to do, what he would do. He captured my hands in his, and I found it hard to care if anyone heard us.

In the morning I was ashamed. A man takes his wife on their pallet on the floor, among their sleeping children; drudges lie together in the hall. This was not the same. There were too many men without women here. The UpsideDown Days were over, and I was food for foul mouths now. I tied my headcloth tight and looked for something useful to do that would not be in the way.

The Sun was just peeking over the mountains through a fringe of trees. Sire Galan's jack had gotten up before me and built up the fire and started oat porridge while it was still dark. When I asked, he pulled a pot out of the baggage. His hair stood out on his head like a fodder stack, and his leather jerkin was stained down the front from wiping his hands on it. He had a smallsword and dagger hanging from his belt in worn scabbards.

I fetched water upstream from the camp, and found a handful of wake-me-up leaves to brew a tisane. Sire Galan's head had disappeared under the blanket. I squatted down, shook him, and handed him a wooden cup. He went under cover again; he was a stay-abed when the Sun came up.

The jack took a cup of wake-me-up and thanked me, after he tasted it. I began to hope he was sleepy, not surly. He unbent enough to say that his name was Spiller, and it was a pricking cold morning.

Spiller woke the bagboy, Noggin, with a hard nudge of his boot, but Noggin wouldn't get up. Spiller nudged him harder, then kicked him, and at last the bagboy scrambled up and pulled on a dirty tunic to cover his scrawny chest, and took the spoon to stir the porridge, casting sullen looks at Spiller.

"Mind it doesn't lump, now," Spiller said, "or I'll give you a lump or two."

Sire Galan's armiger emerged from his blanket. He took a bare few steps before he turned his back on us to piss; he didn't aim too carefully, for I noticed he sprinkled Sire Galan's foot soldiers before he was done. They were sleeping all jumbled together, without a cover between them, taking refuge from the cold in a twitching sleep.

When the armiger came back to the fire, he wore a lopsided smile. He sat down and wrapped himself in his blanket. He looked older than Sire Galan. He'd shaved his beard to show his clan tattoo, and his cheeks were dark with stubble. He'd lost most of the hair above his temples; what was left was brown and coarse as a horse's mane, and hung to his shoulders.

"Food, Spiller," he said. "And you," he added, pointing to me, "bring me some of that."

I poured him the last of the wake-me-up. He took a sip and spat it out. "This is foul!"

"Maybe you find it so, Sire," I answered, "but it will open your eyes in the morning."

"Fetch me something sweeter," he said. I didn't like his smile.

"I'm afraid I have nothing to your taste, Sire."

"Then mull me some wine, and stir some honey in it." He pointed toward the pile of baggage, where Sire Galan had his store of wine. The rest of us would drink ale, if we could get it.

So I was to be the armiger's servant? He'd bid me wash his dirty hose next. I turned and walked away, but not toward the wineskins. I let my stiff back answer for me. I didn't know if I could look to Sire Galan for help or not. Perhaps he had brought me for this: to drudge for all of them while I warmed his bed. I'd not wake him to find out.

"I know you've a honeypot hidden away; I'll stick my spoon in it yet," the armiger shouted after me.

I looked over my shoulder. "Mind the bees," I said. "They sting very fierce." I tried to turn it into a jest, but the armiger was glaring. I had not begun well, making an enemy so early in the morning.

I went around the fire to where Spiller was cooking bacon, and asked him in a low voice, "What is his name?"

"Sire Rodela dam Whoreson by Sowpricker of Crux, that's what I call him."

The bagboy snickered, said, "Sowpricker!" and jabbed the air with his spoon. Noggin's yellow teeth were crowded into his mouth, and now he showed too many of them. It was no mystery how he came by his name, for he looked as though he hadn't a thought of his own to slosh around in his wooden head.

"So what do you call the armiger to his face?" I said.

"Rodela dam Antlia by Musca. He's Sire Galan's cousin by bastardy—they have the same grandfather, but Sire Galan's father was bred on the wife, and *his* father on a Musca concubine. Although they do say Sire Rodela's mother is such a whore there's no telling who his father really is, and that makes him a bastard twice over, so say I. For sure, his blood is tainted with mud. I can always tell."

"Bacon, Spiller," Sire Rodela yelled.

Spiller tore off a piece of bread and put a slab of bacon on it. Then he turned his back on Sire Rodela and spat on it, winking at me. The spit looked like the foam of fat that sizzles from bacon, and the armiger was none the wiser. So we were at war long before we reached the battlefield.

Sire Galan rode his lesser courser that day, a dark bay a hand taller than my mare. He stayed ahead with his armiger and the other warriors of the Blood. Among so many men, I still could find him.

I rode with his horse soldiers, now that I'd made their acquaintance. Already Sire Galan's varlets had worn against each other enough to be at ease; even their gibes and scuffles, as they rode along, seemed a matter of habit. Each man knew his place and his duties, whereas I, a woman and a latecomer, could see no chink or cranny where I might fit among them.

Spiller was on my left, and Sire Galan's horsemaster, Flykiller, just ahead. Flykiller was short and wide, with thick muscles in his thighs and forearms and a torso that would have suited a much taller man. His face was half hidden behind a heavy black beard. Now and then he broke his long silences to scold Sire Galan's best warhorse, Semental, on a lead behind him, for snatching at grasses beside the road or dawdling to nip at my mare. The horseboy, Uly, had care of Sire Galan's lesser mounts; he led two geldings and rode a third. He was as slight as Flykiller was brawny, and too young to have grown more than a tickle of a mustache. Along the way, Spiller filled Uly's ears with such gossip—or lies, if I guessed right—as made his earlobes turn pink.

Noggin rode behind us in the baggage train, on a mule already laden with sacks. Since we had risen that morning, the bagboy had been clouted by Spiller, Sire Rodela, and Sire Galan, one after the other, for mislaying things. When he loaded the pack mules, I marked how he clouted the beasts in turn.

The three foot soldiers, Cinder, Nift, and Digger, trudged along with the baggage. All of Sire Galan's varlets would fight, of course, ahorse or afoot, but the footmen had no special duties; they did everyone's bidding, even Noggin's.

My mare's name was Thole and she endured me well. Noggin had ridden her before I came, and I daresay I treated her more gently. Her hide was the color and gloss of a polished chestnut. My legs ached from straddling the barrel of her back, and the saddle grew harder by the hour. No doubt the mare had the worst of it, for the Crux set a stiff pace that day to make up for time lost the day before, and soon Thole's belly and flanks were dark with sweat. When we stopped at midday, I watered her upstream from the other horses and rubbed her down with swatches of coarse grass. I fed her oats from my hand and scratched her under the chin as if she were a cat. Flykiller had not yet given me a word, but when he saw that I'd tended to her well he gave me a nod.

Sire Galan and the other cataphracts and the priests sat with the Crux, feasting on cold dishes conjured up by his provisioner. The First's men had conjured up a table too, and spread it with a white cloth. Stools appeared, clever contraptions of leather and wood, unfolded from neat bundles in the luggage. The cataphracts ate while their armigers served. Then the armigers were served by the Crux's varlets, and at last the varlets got the leavings—but the cook made sure there was plenty to go around.

I'm certain it was better than what Spiller gave to Sire Galan's men and me: cold pottage scraped from the pot with a bit of leathery brown bread, without even the grace of salt. I saw I'd have to look out for myself, if that was Spiller's idea of a meal. There was better food all around us in the woods and beside the road. I found some tiny wild pears and put them in a sack I made by tying knots in Na's old dress. There were walnuts too, and enough chestnuts for a feast (I dote on a roasted chestnut), and mouse ears for greens, gone to seed but good enough for stewing with a bit of bacon. Best of all, I found a rare patch of sweetrod, long white roots that cook up sweet as honey.

When I'd said good-bye to Cook, she'd told me I'd be wise to seek out the Crux's provisioner (who also went by the name of Cook); he'd be a good man to befriend, she said. So I took him some sweetrod in my gather sack. He was gruff at first, thinking I'd come to beg, but more amiable when he saw what I carried. He gave me a slice of mutton, and I made a fine meal after all.

I looked for Iza among Sire Guasca's varlets, thinking I'd given her scant courtesy the day before, and it would do my eyes good to see another woman, even if she was an empty-headed prattler. The men were taking their midday rest, sprawled in the shade under the poplars, waving away flies with an occasional flap of the hand or snoring like bellows. But Iza was nowhere to be found, not among Sire Guasca's men, nor among Sire Pava's.

Later I heard she'd turned back for home early in the morning. The story went up and down the line with laughter in its wake. Sire Rodela dallied behind to tell it to Spiller and Flykiller. He said, with a rapid, hammering laugh, "Her buttocks were so bony the mule complained. Lich took pity on the beast and sent the baggage home afoot." Some wag had said it first, and everyone after passed it off as his own.

Spiller said, "I heard she had meat enough, but she was stingy with it. Lich offered his friends a go at her—for a bit of coin, mind you—but she refused to take to the blanket. He says, 'You're no use to me then,' and she says, 'Oh, Lich, I beg you,' and he says, 'You will or else,' and she wouldn't, so she left. So I heard." Then Spiller, pleased with his own wit, repeated in a high squeak, "Oh, Lich, I beg you," while they laughed and whooped until tears ran down their faces and they leaned helpless over their horses' necks. As if they were the finest of friends.

Sire Rodela caught his breath and said, "That Lich is a greater fool than I thought him. A priggish woman is like a fish with feathers—can't fly, can't swim, no use to anyone. If it were up to me, I'd have plucked her. I'm sure that underneath she's as slippery as any woman." He turned in his saddle to look at me.

He was like a dog, grinning as he growled. I met his eyes for an instant and my hackles rose. I looked down. I thought I'd better find myself a dagger; my bone-handled knife was but a little stinger.

Then I thought of Iza, footsore and heartsore on the road home. All along, Lich had meant to make a whore of her, and be her pander. Under my breath I prayed for her to Ardor Hearthkeeper, that she might come home safe; to Wend Weaver, that she might find her place; to Crux, the Moon—that he might let her go. I prayed for myself as well, the only woman left in the troop now that Iza was gone. Yet I wondered if the gods mocked our prayers and us. I imagined them as giants, and we their toys, like straw dolls that come apart in the hands of a heedless child. Or maybe Iza was merely a fool, beneath the notice of any god, and I was a greater fool, still riding after my hotspur. A fool, a bitch in heat—hadn't the Crux called me that? Of course all the curs like Sire Rodela would come sniffing around. And Sire Pava.

It did not bear thinking on. I kept my eyes on the road, looking over the mare's ears as her head nodded and she picked her way among the ruts and stones.

By the next morning the story had changed again. Everyone liked this tale better, though it was untrue: they said Lich would take her only from behind, because she was so sour-faced she could pickle a man's prick just by looking at it. But he'd bruised himself on her bones, and so he'd sent her home, saying he preferred his hand or a boy's buttocks. By the afternoon there was a song about it.

When I went to mount Thole in the morning, the saddle was loose and I ended by sprawling on the road. Sire Rodela laughed and said to Flykiller, "You should take better care of Sire Galan's sheath." With a frown so fierce his black brows nearly met over his nose, Flykiller said, "The girth was tight when I put on the saddle."

In the afternoon Sire Rodela condescended to ride along and gossip with Spiller on the subject of Sire Galan's wife, with his voice pitched to carry back to me: how her skin was like cream, her eyes like a doe's, her lips two rose petals, her breasts round as apples and so on; how Sire Galan had married her last year, and with what ceremony; how the bride had worn a gold mask of the Sun and a robe of cloth-of-gold, and her unbound hair hung down to her knees.

Marriages of the Blood are consummated during the rites, before witnesses, so that the match will be beyond question. Shyness and constraint are to be expected, and the deed is quickly done. But sometimes a god blesses the bride and groom with holy abandon. Sire Rodela said there was no mistaking that Crux had seized Sire Galan, for he was tireless.

Spiller had been in the crowd outside the temple; he wanted to know all about it.

I turned Thole's head to the side of the road and slid off her back. I lifted her hoof as if I checked for a stone. But I was the one with the stone, a flint lodged behind my temple, sharp as a memory: Sire Galan leading his naked bride to the marriage couch, her skin golden in the light of a thousand candles, her body everywhere soft, everywhere round and ripe. Her nipples gilded.

That was a year ago; they had a son already three months old.

Of course he was married, and she was fertile. The Blood do not send their sons to war before they've sired an offspring or two. Sire Pava hadn't waited for his wife to bear, but then he was known to be overhasty.

My curiosity had failed me when I needed it most. There were so many questions I'd neglected to ask, so much willful unknowing. But why should it matter to me? It didn't change where I stood one whit; I was ever at the bottom.

I leaned against the mare's shoulder, blinking. An old beech hedge lined the road, the leaves already turning copper. They would cling all winter, color against the smooth gray branches. Someone had planted the hedge before I was born, and it would outlast me too.

Sire Galan was such a wastrel with his charm that he had lavished it even on me. He'd turned in his saddle once or twice every league to search me out with his eyes, and smiled when I saw him looking. How easily he could roil me! I cursed him for it, and yet I waited for him to bestow his look and smile, which both promised and remembered. That very morning he'd ridden back to cull me from among his men and take me into the woods, and by the time we were done, the baggage train had passed us. We'd galloped to the front again, and the cataphracts had howled and jibed. They understood his attentions well enough.

And I must have misunderstood, thinking there was something more—for I felt as if a rope tied me to Sire Galan by the keels of our ribs, it must tug under his breastbone as it did under mine. But I'd been a fool to believe it. Surely it was folly to believe it.

Flykiller rode back and asked, "Is she lame?" It was the first he'd spoken to me.

"I thought perhaps she favored one leg, a little hitch is all. But it's nothing." And I vowed nothing would show on my face.

He dismounted to see for himself, lifting each of the mare's feet in turn.

"She has a smooth gait," I said.

Flykiller checked the girth to see that it was tight. "She does. She has heart too," he said, and I could swear he nearly smiled at me. He bent his knee so that I could stand on it to mount and I put my hand on his shoulder. He was kinder now; still, I wished to ride anywhere but with Sire Galan's men.

A rumormonger overtook us one afternoon, riding at a smart trot on a dappled gray gelding, a very fine horse for a mudman. The horse soldiers called to him for a song when they saw his banner, the sign of his trade: a hollow red tongue that belled and flapped in the breeze. But he waved and rode on until he reached the warriors in front, where there was coin to be made. He had news of the court, of Ramus, of their keeps and kin; he brought messages for some and gossip for everyone.

That evening, after the cataphracts and armigers had supped and the Crux's fire had burned so low it barely crackled, the rumormonger brought out his fat-bellied dulcet and a drum he played by knocking his knees together. Spiller, Noggin, and I crept close and sat behind a bush to listen. The rumormonger plucked on the strings of the dulcet, and if I hadn't known better, I'd have thought two men were playing, for he played two tunes at once, braiding them together so well that they became one. He set such a sprightly pace that I couldn't see how his fingers could keep up. I'd not heard many rumormongers at the manor, and none to compare with him: a man of talents could do better than to travel the hard mountain roads from one poor village to the next.

Soon he began to sing, and his voice floated effortlessly above the melody, alighting on it only now and then. To please his hosts he sang a song of Crux, of the time the Moon had tricked the Sun into giving him some of her radiance, and the Sun had stolen it back, all but a tiny piece the Moon had hidden in his purse, which lights him still.

Next the rumormonger sang the ballad of Queenmother Caelum. It was a long tale, but he made it go by fast, for he sang it so well. I knew little about her, save that she was our king's sister, and it was her war on which we were embarked to fight against her son. I knew even less of Incus, her kingdom, which we call in the Low tongue Oversea. It was from Oversea the Blood came to settle in these lands, but that was long ago, so long ago it seems as if they've always been here.

The rumormonger played with a lilt at first, as he sang of Princess Caelum, slender and fair, and of how twenty years ago she'd crossed the Inward Sea to marry the warrior lord of Incus, King Voltur, bringing peace as her dowry. Within the year Queen Caelum was brought to bed and delivered up a prince, a boy with hair black as a raven's wing and eyes blue as twilight, and the king looked on him and was pleased, and named him Corvus. All Incus rejoiced, sang the rumormonger, and he turned the ballad into a jig that made my legs want to dance.

Then he struck his strings hard and made them jangle, and he added notes of discord. He sang that eight years of peace passed while the prince grew lithe and strong, but too much peace bred discontent in eager young men and greedy old ones. So King Voltur gathered his army to war on the kingdom to the south, to win a fertile valley with a lake of sapphire blue. He swore it should be his, for his mountains lay about it on three sides.

On the day of his victory, he was slain, not in battle but by treachery, for the Firsts of five clans had conspired against him, saying each to the other that the king had grown soft, and each to himself that he would rule in his stead, seeing he left a mere child behind.

The Firsts came back to the palace in the city of Malleus, and they laid the king's helm in Queenmother Caelum's lap, crying false tears and saying, "Woe to us all, for our good king is gone. We worthy men will take the burden of the kingdom from you until Prince Corvus comes of age, for it is too heavy for a woman to bear." And all Incus mourned.

But the queenmother sniffed out their treachery. She had the Firsts of the five clans torn limb from limb, each by four black horses, and she left their sundered bodies to feed the ravens.

Now the rumormonger sweetened his voice and played with a gentler touch, and he sang that eight years of peace passed under the rule of Queen Regent Caelum, while Prince Corvus grew tall and his shoulders broad, until he looked the very man his father had been. Then the southern kingdom sent the prince a portrait of a princess painted lifelike even to her size, as if she might step out of the frame. He stared at it long and longing, and the wide eyes of Princess Kalos stared back, and her lips were parted as if to speak. In his dreams, he heard her voice.

The prince said, "I will have her." Queen Regent Caelum said—being wiser—"Let me send for word of her nature, to see if she is fit to wed a perfect prince." She sent birds southward and when they returned, the birds sang, "Not a word is spoken against her."

The rumormonger plucked the twittering of birds from his dulcet, and he strummed faster and faster. He sang of one little brown thrush that carried back a different tale. The bird had spied on the princess late at night when she thought herself alone in her chamber, and saw her hold up a mirror, shinier than bronze, shinier than silver. In that mirror the princess showed her true self, gleaming all over with scales of the palest green. The thrush sang, "If you wed her, you will wed a lamia, a serpent woman, who means to catch you in her coils and squeeze the life from you. Your father stole the jewel of her father's kingdom, that sapphire lake set in an emerald valley, and she wants vengeance."

The prince drew his dagger and struck down the bird even as it flew, crying out that it was all a lie. But Queen Regent Caelum heeded the warning and would not consent. Prince Corvus said, "Mother, dear, in this you do not rule me. I will have her when I reach my majority." On his seventeenth birthday he wed his princess and all Incus rejoiced.

Bitterly Queenmother Caelum watched her son fall prey to the wiles of the lamia. She begged him to find the mirror Kalos hid in her wedding chest, to hold it over her as she slept so that he might see through her disguise. But Corvus raged, saying, "Mother, dear, the kingdom is mine, the woman is mine, and you shall not part me from one or the other. I banish you to the Keep of Northernmost, and there you shall molder for doubting me and my judgment."

The tune turned plaintive, and the rumormonger paused in his singing to let his fingers coax melancholy from the strings, and it was a wonder to me that he could turn the same simple melody to so many purposes. There was such a hush around his music it seemed even the trees stooped to listen.

When he lifted his voice again, he sang of the Keep of Northernmost, where for two long winters and a third Queenmother Caelum sat lonely in her tower, staring across the white wastelands, wondering how fared her son, her city, and her kingdom. Even her birds deserted her, flying south to roost in the orchards of Malleus and sing the winter out.

When the birds returned in spring, she asked, "What news of my kingdom?" For two years the birds sang of festivals that lasted winter long, of men clad in armor of beaten gold and women in gowns of gossamer. They sang, "The granaries grow empty, but the feasting goes on." And Caelum wept.

This spring when the birds returned, she asked, "What news of my son and his wife?" The birds sang, "Day by day Corvus grows thinner while Kalos swells. Soon she will bear a child, and all Incus is rejoicing." And Caelum wept, saying, "What serpent will she birth to sit on the throne of Incus?"

Then the queenmother said, "I have done with weeping." She whistled for the gray Wolves that guarded her keep, and they loped at her heels as she rode around the Inward Sea and south to Ramus, and the way was long and hard. She knelt before her brother, King Thyrse, and begged him to lend his strength to save her son and kingdom from the lamia's stranglehold. But he bade her go home to her northern keep, saying, "It more befits a woman to weep than to war." She rent her gown and showed under it a corselet of steel, saying, "Brother, by our sire and dame, remember the same blood runs in both our veins."

The king relented, and he summoned the Firsts of all his clans, saying, "Our forebears came from Incus long ago, and if you meet me by the Inward Sea before the Ingathering Moon has waned, the winter winds shall blow us to our homeland."

Now the rumormonger played the last verse, and he sang it as wistfully as he'd sung of Queenmother Caelum banished to the icy north, and there was such yearning in his voice that I felt the ache of exile; he made me pine for a place I'd never been. He sang of the yielding plains of Incus, of cedar-covered hills that made the dawns smell of spice, and he sang again of Malleus the fair, a city of marble spires and gilded domes. He sang to the men of the Blood, "You've been tempered by war so that you are keen and hard as steel, while the men of Incus have grown soft as their golden armor from too much peace. Do you not long to return?"

When the rumormonger finished we paid him the tribute of silence. Then the cheering began, and the men stamped their feet and whistled and struck their open palms against their chests. And I marveled that I too was part of his tale, though he'd never sing of the likes of me—for wasn't I bound to cross the Inward Sea, following the king's army? Soon I'd see the queenmother and her Wolves with my own eyes; I'd see her kingdom and her city. I might live long enough to know the end of her story even before a ballad could be made of it.

But the lowliest bagboy understood the meaning of the song before I did. What mattered the cause of her war? When the rumormonger sang of Incus and held up the beauty of Malleus to dazzle us, every warrior of the Blood and every mudsoldier in camp saw a kingdom ripe for sacking, gold so plentiful it covered the rooftops, women in gossamer gowns to be had for the taking.

The rumormonger put down his fragile dulcet and quenched his thirst with all the wine that came his way. There was singing at every fire, and the men strove to drown each other out. Spiller stood up and sang the song of Iza. He had a shrill falsetto, and before long the rumormonger strolled up and pulled out his little clay pipe, his avicula, and began to pipe along as if he already knew the tune. Spiller sang:

Old Iza she won't lie down,
She won't lie down,
On the blanket, oh.

The rumormonger played high above and then he sang below, but always he knocked his knee drum so the song sped along.

Her jack says I won't keep you,
I can't keep you,
It's home you must go.

Men were clapping and stamping. Noggin began to jig, kicking the coals at the end of the verse to make the sparks dance. He had a rapt look on his face, as if all his meager wits were bent upon his feet.

The mule says she's too bony,
She's too bony,
I won't bear her, no.

Sire Galan tossed the rumormonger a coin—I saw it flash, it was a silverhead—and the rumormonger snatched it out of the air and made a deep bow, and kept the beat. Everyone roared the last verse, for the song had been with us on the road for days.

Old Iza she weeps and wails,
She wails and rails,
As she walks home slow.

It wasn't much of a song, but they made the most of it. They started all over again, and I crawled under Sire Galan's quilt and covered my head. When I woke in the morning, the rumormonger was still there, with his long feet sticking out of a short blanket, his soles toward the embers of our fire.

Villagers came to meet us with fat ducks and round loaves of bread dusty with flour. They tested the coins between their teeth, knowing enough of soldiers to be wary. I had no coin and nothing to trade.

The river ran shallow and close to the road. I forded it on stepping-stones and waded into the tall dry weeds and brambles of a fallow field, for I spied fawn lilies, and I thought the bulbs would do well roasted for supper with a relish of tart rose hips. I foraged whenever I got the chance, and often found enough to stretch or flavor Spiller's bland cooking, and a little besides for the Crux's provisioner. I was glad to do it, as I was glad to tend to the mare that carried me—but it was all I meant to do. Sire Galan's drudges had their duties; if I let them lay their tasks on me, there'd be no end to that road.

I came upon Fleetfoot and Sire Pava's horseboy, Ev, sitting cross-legged on the ground, hidden in the grass. I found them by the smell of roasting meat. They had a fire going, a few flames licking a skinned rabbit on a stick. Ev waved away the smoke with a clutch of straw, so not even a trickle could be seen above their heads.

It was just as well Fleetfoot could fend for himself. I felt ashamed. I had promised Az to look after him, and been a miser with my thoughts instead. I'd not spared one to wonder whether he was cold or hungry.

They had heard me coming, and waited with their ears pricked up. Fleetfoot laughed when he saw me. "Oh, it's you! I feared it was Harien—he always follows his nose into our business. You're just beforetimes. In a moment she'll be cooked."

I sat down with them. "I'm glad to see you both," I said, and so I was. A few days ago these boys had barely known each other, though I knew them both, one from the village, one from the manor stables. Now they sat with their knees touching. They were of an age a few years behind me. I could swear that since I saw them last their cheeks had grown a fine down and their bones had stretched.

Fleetfoot poked the rabbit and Ev said, "Wait." It seemed he'd learned patience from the Dame's old horsemaster, who'd rather coax a colt than beat him. Ev had always lived in the stables; I used to marvel to see him, when he was a small boy, so fearless among the quarrelsome warhorses.

I tucked four or five lily bulbs into the ashes and pushed coals over them. "It's such a small thing," I said. "Not much to share."

Fleetfoot lifted some matted grass under his elbow to show three more rabbits hidden away. He grinned. "There's enough and to spare. I'll give you one to take with you."

My stomach growled and they laughed. They gave me a hind leg, lean but savory. Fleetfoot said the field was full of rabbits. He and Ev had scattered burrs before their warrens and beaten the grass; when the rabbits ran for safety, the burrs stuck to their feet and Fleetfoot caught them easy as you please. "I can always get a few more," he said as he pulled the skin from another rabbit.

"Save the hides," I told him. "I'll sew you a cape if you get enough. Aren't you cold at night?"

"Not so cold. Dogmaster lets us sleep with the dogs."

They were just pups themselves, those two, not yet grown as large as their hands and feet promised. Maybe the war dogs took them for their own whelps.

I had feared dogs since I'd run from the hunters in the Kingswood, and had kept far away from the war dogs. They were huge tawny beasts, short in the muzzle, deep in the chest, long and lean in the back. They could wrestle a horse to the ground by its nose. Their descent could be traced far back, it was said, to two famous boarhounds, Asper and Audax, but they were more massive than any boarhound and more cunning too. They were called manhounds, after their prey, and once unleashed upon it, they were relentless.

"I wonder you're not afraid," I said.

Ev said, with his eyes on the fire, "It's the safest place in the world, once they know you." I'd heard tell that Sire Pava's horsemaster, Harien, had used him for a bedboy until Ev took to disappearing every night instead of sleeping by the horses—and that he got a beating every morning for shirking his duties. I guessed by the look on his face that it was true.

We went back across the river together and I stopped to greet some of Sire Pava's men from the village. Sire Galan was looking for me. Fleetfoot had his last rabbit hidden under his leather tunic; I had the one he gave me by the ears. I held it up to show Sire Galan. "See what I've got for supper!" I said.

"Where did you get it?" He was frowning.

"In the field," I answered, pointing across the river.

"I don't suppose you caught it yourself. Who gave it to you?"

"Why, I could catch a cony if I chose," I said, indignant that he should think I couldn't. "But it was this boy here who gave it to me."

He put his hand on my arm with such a grip the rabbit loosened in my fingers. All his charm had vanished. "Pava's boy," he said hoarsely. He turned to Fleetfoot. "Did he bid you to give her this?"

Fleetfoot stood there with his mouth gaping open, so I answered. "This boy is a cousin of mine," (well, it was almost true) "and he gave it to me of his own will. Am I not to eat when I am hungry?"

"You've no cause to be hungry," Sire Galan said. "I have enough in my stores. You shouldn't come begging around Pava's men."

I laughed in his face, as riled as he was. "I wasn't begging. But if I waited for you to feed me, I should go hungry indeed. Cold pease pottage and onions gone soft and bread as hard to chew as leather. Even a drudge wants more than that."

He pried the rabbit out of my hand and flung it into the middle of the river. Fleetfoot and Ev went after it; Fleetfoot got there first, of course. Sire Galan was stiff with anger. He looked at me with his eyes narrow and his nose pinched, and his grip on my arm was painful. He pulled me along the riverbank toward his men and said, in a voice dangerously even, "Stay away from Pava. There is no hunger you have that I cannot answer for."

"I want nothing from Sire Pava, and I'd sooner see him dead than ask anything of him. But I'll see my cousin whenever I please. And if I look to eat rabbit tonight while you feast on venison and fat pork, I can't see how it does *you* harm. Unless you like me better skin and bones." I jerked my arm from his grip and held it up before his eyes. I pinched the flesh over my wristbone. "I'm not lean enough already to please you?"

He said nothing more, only glared, and we parted company. At first I was pleased that he was a jealous man, for if he guarded me close, it must mean he counted me worth guarding. But that afternoon he did not look back at me once, and as the Sun rolled down and shone her light in our eyes I had a long time to be sorry that I'd governed my tongue so poorly, and to become afraid.

I'd looked to Sire Galan for a shelter, a refuge, but there I was least defended, for he and I rubbed each other raw and laid bare the quick. But I should never have expected safety. The world is perilous; only a fool feels safe. I must rather arm myself, with wit if I could find no keener point, and armor myself with a tougher skin. I'd not be one of those meek straw men soldiers used for practice, poking full of holes till the stuffing is let out; I meant to get in my blows.

Near a hundred men ahorse, another hundred or so afoot, and all like and unlike as river stones: some polished, others rough, some adamant, others no more durable than sun-dried clay. After a few days on the road, I'd begun to sort them.

A drudge who doesn't eavesdrop is deaf indeed, and riding in the troop I overheard plenty. It was loud as a rookery with varlets cawing boasts, jests, and rumors. I learned of the various houses of the clan Crux, and how they were commonly judged, of the rivalries between houses and within them. Crux came to earth once, arrayed as the Sun in a woman's form, ravishingly bright, scorching the ground under her feet. She bore a passel of sons, begotten by various foolhardy mudmen who flamed to ash as she mated with them. Each house of the clan sprang from one of her sons; each sent its headman to the clan councils—nevertheless the houses were not equal in quality or fortune.

I began to know the cataphracts and armigers by the repute their men gave them: who among the Blood had a hasty temper and heavy hand, who was easy prey for a drudge's little frauds, who had earned the fewest complaints. I could tell a man's master from the house crest embroidered on the clan banner he bore, but often as not it could also be read in his manner, for soldiers have a way of aping their betters. If a cataphract was touchy about his honor, his varlets were apt to pick quarrels, seeing insults where none were intended.

Sire Galan had an assurance, which, had it not been warrantable, would have seemed arrogance. As for Sire Rodela, he didn't wear his pride so lightly; it chafed, and made him overbearing with us drudges, and overly familiar with his master. He was always making spiteful jabs—disguised as japes—which Sire Galan countered with ease. When Sire Galan dallied too long with me under his blanket of a morning, Sir Rodela called him Sire Layabout, and said it was time to be riding his horse, not his woman. Sire Galan looked at him hard, saying maybe Sire Roustabout had to mount mares because no woman would have him. They sparred back and forth, and Sire Galan seemed to take it for a companionable jousting. But I thought Sire Rodela's effrontery was a hairbreadth short of offense. He stayed close to Sire Galan, when he was not favoring us with his company.

As for Sire Galan's mudmen, they vaunted him about the camp in little wagers and spats with other varlets over whose master had the best horse or the best seat or the deadliest way with a sword. He was lax with them. I don't believe he noticed that Noggin sometimes laundered his shirts in muddy water, or that Spiller pilfered wine and a few coins now and then. It irked me to see things badly done, but I wouldn't stand between Sire Galan and his men.

Spiller relished gossip as much as any village alewife, and I was his best audience. He told me of Sire Galan's two elder brothers, one dead three campaigns ago, the other of such a light mind a feather outweighed him. Sire Galan stood closer to his father than I had supposed, for Spiller had it that this featherbrained brother might be passed over when it came time to inherit the holdings.

The Crux had only one brother—Sire Galan's father—and only one son, after losing three sons in the usual ways: war, sickness, accident. This son was forced to wait out the campaign safe at home. But if Spiller could make the reckoning, you can be sure others did: Sire Galan stood just four lives away from First of the clan.

I began to see what it meant that Sire Galan and the Crux had the same crest embroidered on their banners—the gyrfalcon emblem of the house of Falco—and why Sire Galan got his way more often than not, more often than he should, perhaps.

The Falco traced their lineage to the eldest son of Crux. Those few times a man from another house had won the title of First by wisdom or boldness or cunning, the Falco had taken it back by the next generation. They never allowed an infant or young boy to become First, as some did, opening the door to rivalry and ruin in house and clan.

They were mountain people, like all the clan of Crux, but their land was rich. Their stronghold, a long way south of the manor where I grew up, was high on a rocky spur driven like a talon into the fat earth of the plain. From this height they surveyed leagues of their own lands, and were less than a day's ride from the capital, Ramus. Sire Galan lived half the year in his father's keep and half in the Crux's palace at court, and Spiller said he was much imitated by the younger cataphracts. When he began to shave his cheeks, others gave up the beards they had but lately grown.

Na would have said I'd done well for myself, and surely it was better than I'd guessed when I chose to lie with a man in a field because he was handsome. A favored son of a favored house of a favored clan. Sire Pava was nothing to compare, and I hoped he was discomfited to see, as everyone did, that next to his cousin he looked a bumpkin.

If I stitched myself to Sire Galan's surcoat and followed him to war and back, what might I gain from it? Perhaps a room of my very own, where I could wait on his pleasure and bear bastards to brawl with his other bastards—of which he had many, Spiller assured me.

Sire Galan had not spoken of his household to me. We had so little time together that we did not spend much in conversation. He'd told me some few small things, such as how much he missed his falcons and the cliffs near his home. He said that when he was a boy he fell one morning while climbing those cliffs to steal eggs, and hurt his leg and lay on a bed of scree until he was found late in the afternoon. There was the scar, see? As he lay there he saw a strange sight: a crow turned on a hawk and chased it all over the sky. I closed my eyes and followed his voice to catch a glimpse of him as a boy, in the morning of his life. It was endearing, I thought, that he should tell me such things in the middle of the night; but it was less endearing to think of his wife and other subjects he never saw fit to mention.

One evening I sat by the cook fire watching the sparks swarm, their lives briefer than a mayfly's. The Kingswood was all around, leagues of it on every side. The fires of the camp kept it at bay, as if each group of men sheltered in a little cave of light. I wrapped myself in silence while Sire Galan's men jabbered. The horse soldiers snubbed the foot soldiers, the foot soldiers, who were naught but shepherds and plowboys, after all, diced for pinecones. The fire burned lower and leaves of flame grew from the logs. In those bright shapes I made out other things: ranks of pennants moving among the coals, a horse galloping, riderless. The images came and went so swiftly I was unsure I'd seen them. But when I closed my eyes, the silhouette of the horse turned black, as if it were seared on my eyelids.

I glanced up to see Sire Galan standing on the other side of the fire, looking at me. His face was bright as a lantern in the firelight, and he smiled. Gods, it was like lighting a torch; I was tinder to his spark, flaring in an instant.

He sat beside me and we leaned shoulder to shoulder.

"It's been long since I saw you last," he said in a low voice.

"I kept you in sight before me," I said.

Sire Rodela came out of the shadows and took a place between Spiller and Flykiller. He demanded food from Spiller, who told him we'd eaten our supper quick as goats loose in a granary, and there was nothing left but roasted chestnuts.

"Peel them for me," Sire Rodela told Spiller. Then he tossed a chestnut at Sire Galan, saying, "Look who's left the First's table early and cheated me of my supper!"

"I don't require your attendance. Go and sup—but you'd best hurry, or you'll be squabbling over scraps with the drudges."

The armiger seemed disinclined to go. He sat staring at us from the other side of the fire. His gaze looked insolent to me, and he wore the lopsided grin he put on when he was up to some mischief. Sire Galan ignored him; he picked up the chestnut and began to peel it. His fingers were deft.

Sire Rodela asked, "Won't you be missed, Sire? It isn't the custom to leave before the sweetmeats are served."

I put my hand on Sire Galan's knee, warmed to think he'd chosen my company. "Let them miss me," he said. "Let them envy me."

"Envy, Cousin? Do you think so? I think they wonder at you, you behave so strangely."

Sire Rodela was forward for a cousin, especially one sired by a bastard. He chided more like an elder brother.

Sire Galan took it lightly enough. "They covet my luck, and Pava most of all. He's feverish because I winkled it out from under his nose. Can I help it he was blind to his chance?" He smiled at me and tossed the pieces of the chestnut hull back at Sire Rodela, one by one. I smiled back. He'd have them think it was all about luck, a warrior's superstition that the god Hazard, in the avatar of Chance, slips her blindfold and winks at those with red hair. Fighting men may worship Rift Warrior, but they hold Hazard Chance close to their hearts, close enough for blame as well as praise.

I was not so vain as to believe I was the object of envy, but I knew Sire Galan was. He shone with fortune like a new-struck coin, and hardly needed me for polish. But I was vain enough to think that if he came back too soon from supper it was not for a bit of luck.

"It's an ill thing to breed envy in camp," Sire Rodela said. He still spoke as if in jest, but like all his jests it had more malice than humor. "Envy begets strife. Perhaps you should give a thought to the good luck of your clan, not just your own. Then we'd all be better pleased, all your cousins."

Under my hand I felt the muscles in Sire Galan's leg tighten. He became still. In that stillness his men grew quiet and raised their heads. In a mild voice, he said, "How so?"

Sire Rodela was so taken with his own wit that he went on heedless into the quiet. "Why, share her favors with us," he said, pointing at me, "and maybe a little good fortune will rub off. A woman's quim is a magic purse; the more you dip in, the more—"

He never finished. In two heartbeats Sire Galan was up and on him, with a forearm leaning on his throat and a knee on his chest. Spiller and Flykiller sprawled out of the way.

"Bastard's spawn," Sire Galan said as Sire Rodela thrashed under him. "Shall I toast your brains or put fire to the soles of your feet? Which would you prefer?"

Sire Rodela's eyes rolled and his tongue hung out. Sounds escaped him, but nothing like a word. By this time I was up and had my hand on Sire Galan's shoulder, shouting in his ear to let go. I did this before I thought, and afterward wondered why. But Sire Galan had a terrible joy in his face, brighter than the fire, and couldn't hear me.

"I think I'll just singe you for now," he said, and he shoved Sire Rodela across the dirt with the arm under his chin until his head was close to the coals. With the other hand he took hold of Sire Rodela's mane and put the ends in the fire. The burning hair smelled foul. "But if you soil her with your dirty tongue again, I'll gladly cut it out."

Then Sire Galan took up a branch with a smoldering tip and burned the hair until it was no more than a finger length all over, methodically, turning Sire Rodela's head this way and that while the armiger tried to scream but could not. When Sire Galan got up, Sire Rodela lay there helplessly, breath wheezing through his windpipe, his head next to the fire. Sire Galan took hold of his feet and dragged him out of danger. His men gawked and never stirred to help or hinder. Spiller smiled broadly.

Sire Galan looked at me, but not as if he saw me. His face was in shadow except for an edge of light around his hair and along his cheek. His brows were drawn down and under them his eyes were dark as water at the bottom of a well. He scowled more now than when he had Sire Rodela by the throat.

I came up close and took his hand. "Let's go away from here," I said. "Let's sleep in the woods tonight."

Now he saw me.

"Are you not afraid?" he asked.

"Not of the woods, no."

I led him into the trees to the breast of a hill, and if Sire Galan marked how surely I found my way in the dark, he never said so. We lay under the branches, under a blanket of night. And I lay under Sire Galan, and watched his face, my own moon rising over, while he looked down upon me. Perhaps my face reflected his light, and he could see more than a pale shape in the darkness, for he kept his eyes open as he rode me; he took his sweet time. When he told me, "You're mine," I didn't deny it.

We awoke, limbs intertwined, and found the Sun up before us. From an outcropping we saw the camp below, on a sandy bank by a bend in the river. Little figures bustled about—more a hornets' nest than a beehive, I thought: all sting and no honey. From the vantage of the camp, surrounded by trees, you couldn't see what we saw: we stood on a last promontory of the forest. The hard foothills of the mountains, stone ribbed, cloaked in trees, met the rolling hills of the plains in a ragged line. The river we'd followed all this way looked like a twisting silver cord; in the distance it flowed into a larger river, braiding into a great skein of water that lay coiled and tangled across the lowlands, catching the light. In the far west the plains were still steeped in the blue air of dawn, pricked here and there by watchfires. At our feet the hills were potbellied with soil, under a dun hide stitched with hedgerows. I counted four villages nearby on high ground, each walled and with a stone tower. Groves and copses cast long black morning shadows over the fields—but these were mere islands of trees. We'd reached the edge of the Kingswood.

When we came down the camp was abuzz with the story of how Sire Galan had burned Sire Rodela's hair and then vanished into the woods. I wished I could become as small as a mouse and ride hidden under Sire Galan's surcoat, above his heart; had I not already broken my promise—my boast—to the Crux that no one would quarrel over me? We'd made them all late; the baggage was loaded. The First of the clan would have no patience for these faults. He seemed a man who would keep his word and not hesitate to feed me to his war dogs.

But no, I misjudged. The Crux was in a good humor. The cataphracts were already on horseback; Sire Galan's black stallion had been saddled and stood by, yanking up grass by the roots. The Crux leaned forward, resting his crossed arms on the high pommel of his saddle, and looked down at Sire Galan. I might have been a mouse after all, for all the notice he took of me. "I heard you took up barbering last night, Galan. But it seems you don't know how to go about it. Shall I send you back to your father and tell him to apprentice you to a barber for the proper schooling? Or do you still plan to be a warrior?"

Sire Galan shrugged and smiled up at his uncle. "Rodela was in need of a trim, so I gave him one. How does he look?"

The Crux laughed and picked up his reins. "Like a sheep with the mange. He won't need to be shorn again for a long time to come. Get to horse, boy. I was just about to leave you behind. Guasca said you must have been eaten by a bear, and Pava said some mountain cannywoman had trapped you in her cave—but I knew better." His voice changed: still a note of indulgence, but under it a rasp like iron on stone. "I've known you for a lazing prankish dillydallier since you were a boy. But I advise you not to try my patience further. You will be schooled or you will go walking—behind us or home to your father, at my choosing."

Sire Galan swung into his saddle in one move, all grace and no effort. He looked not a bit chastened; his shirt hung open about his throat and he wore a few leaves and pine needles on his clothes.

As they rode away Sire Pava said, "I shall call you barber, Cousin, since you've taken up that profession."

"That suits me fine," I heard Sire Galan say. "I can strop my blade so fine and shave a man so gently it will take him an hour to find I've barbered his head from his body."

Sire Rodela did indeed look mangy. He made Spiller trim the burnt ends of his hair with a knife, but it was still uneven and rough. He'd been outfaced when Sire Galan had cropped his hair; he'd been mocked, and yet Sire Rodela shone a little brighter for reflecting his master's glory—for Sire Galan was even more admired in the troop since he'd chastised his man so cleverly. Maybe this was why Sire Rodela bore more of a grudge against his master's men and me than his master. Or he needed no reason.

He knew how to carry a grudge. He'd sucked whey from his mother's teats while Sire Galan had been sucking cream. No doubt it rankled that his grandmother had been a concubine rather than a wife. By the thickness of a blanket—being born on the wrong side of it—he was Musca rather than Falco, for the children of concubines belong to their mother's house. Like all the Musca he took pride in his bitterness. According to Spiller, Sire Rodela claimed his great-great-great-grandfather had been head of the Crux clan before they came to this country. But once here the house of Musca had fallen on stony ground. Ill will had planted them where they could not thrive, and they'd kept tallies of their enemies for these many generations.

And surely Sire Rodela had the look of a man who had been cheated and expected to be cheated again. He'd likely dupe others first if he got the chance, being so sure they'd gull him if they could. I didn't understand why Sire Galan trusted him at his back, before or after he had shorn him. I suppose he took envy for granted, and suspected nothing more.

By the time we reached the lowlands, the wind had changed, bringing with it the smell of turned earth, dung, and smoke from stubble burning after the harvest. The priests called a halt when we drew near a great elm alone in a field of flowering corona. Its branches were black with starlings, numerous as leaves. The birds all sat looking into the wind, and they raised a great raucous chorus.

We waited until the starlings took to the air and wheeled above us two times, black wings against gray sky, swirling like dye stirred into water before they flew away north over the hills. I must have seen this sight a thousand times, but it awed me now, how they moved with one will, how they waited for us before taking wing.

The omen was good, so said the Auspices, according to rumor. I was uneasy; when the gods send messages they must be meddling.

We'd been the better part of a tennight on the road when the little river we'd been following met the great river. We forded where it ran slow and shallow, its marshy verges alive with waterfowl. Low clouds shut out the Sun. There was a new smell in the air, fresh and damp, and a drizzling mist that turned dust to mud. Across the river the road climbed into low hills barren of trees, with fields bounded by knee-high stone walls instead of hedges. Even the ground under our horses' hooves changed, becoming chalky and gray, too lean for much but pasture and heath. The shepherds' huts looked like rubble scattered over the hills.

The Crux had kept us to a pace that wore out the shoe leather of the foot soldiers (those who were shod, anyway), but the morning after we forded the river we stayed long in camp, in the ruins of a fortress built on a mound. The tower was broken, most of its stones pulled down and the timbers lying half burned and rotting on the ground. The wall at the foot of the mound had all but disappeared, the stones carted away for other walls, but a thorn hedge still stood guard, shiny and black in the mist.

The jacks took out their pumice stones, grit and vinegar, awls and laces, and set to work on the armor, so we knew we were close to the Marchfield at last. The cataphracts would go clad in full harness to prove their readiness to the king, and to strut before the other clans, no doubt.

It was a gray morning, between the stones and the mist; even the turf was bleached of color. But I sat with my cloak snugged around me, looking at red, thinking of red. Spiller was helping Sire Galan pull on his underarmor: a pair of leggings and a long-sleeved doublet quilted of heavy linen. This underarmor was sewn three fingers thick where there was most need of padding, and could by itself turn a blow. Many waxed cords, or points, dangled from the quilted cloth, which were used to tie on the plate armor. The linen was dyed red with madder—so as not to show blood, Spiller said.

Sire Galan already had many scars on his body, and I was acquainted with them. Most were earned training with weapons of wood or blunted steel; he'd won a few in duels. I supposed he'd acquitted himself well enough, for he was still walking the earth, and likewise I supposed he'd killed before, though he never said so. The king was said to frown on duels for wasting men, and to wink at them too, for keeping men courteous and in fighting trim. Those who are neither do not live long.

A man in the village once cut himself so badly with a sickle the blood could not be stanched. The Dame had rushed to the field to see what could be done, though it was not her place to heal him. The man was already dead, his skin white, the ground under him red. The Dame told me later there was enough blood in a body to fill a firkin like the ones we used for ale. Man or woman, Blood or mud, it is all the same: once it's let out, it can't be poured back in. Sire Galan and the others had set out of a purpose to spill blood, and it was hard to say whether gods or men were more thirsty for it.

Over the red linen went a shirt and leggings of mail. This shirt, or hauberk, came down to his hips. Some of its tiny links were tinned so they shone, and with the duller iron links they made a feather pattern, which marked him as house of Falco.

This was fine plumage indeed, and yet Sire Galan was only half in his harness. Over all of this went an outer skin of plate, to give him a tougher hide than he was born with. The metal was shaped to his measure and inlaid with silver godsigns for his protection, and each piece was lined in velvet to save on bruises.

It took most of the morning to put it on, and Sire Rodela and Spiller to do it—Spiller with his fumble fingers and Sire Rodela with his curses. Besides the laces to tie the plate to the underarmor and mail, there were buckles and hinge pins and staples and other fastenings.

They started with the leather shoon, wrapped top and toe with narrow bands of iron, for if a man loses his feet, he has nothing to stand on. Next they strapped on greaves for his shins and kneecops for his knees. They tied his prickguard to his leggings with waxed points. Then they belted on a kilt of iron scales laced to deerskin, which covered his thighs and was split for riding. They buckled on his steel cuirass, which was fashioned with artistry to look like a man's torso, front and back; on the chest was engraved a stooping hawk, marked out with silver inlay, and godsigns surrounded the navel. On Sire Galan's right arm, they tied a leather sleeve covered with metal scales, each scale overlapping the next so he could swing a sword with ease. His shield arm had only the mail. Besides all this, there were other sheaths of hammered plate: flaring wings for his shoulders, a gorget for his neck, elbowcops. His gauntlets were fine examples of the armorers' cunning, covering the backs of his hands with strips of metal riveted to give ease of movement, even to each finger, and the knuckles were spiked; the palms were of leather reinforced with mail, so he could grab a blade and not be cut. Sire Rodela hung a baldric about Sire Galan's shoulder and waist to hold his weapons: longsword, smallsword, mercy dagger.

Last they put a little padded cap on Sire Galan's head and fastened it under his chin, and tucked his hair up under it, and put his steel helmet over it. The helmet put Sire Pava's to shame, that he had scraped us bare to buy. It was shaped like a gyrfalcon's head with its beak gaping open; the visor was a silvered mask that covered Sire Galan's face with his own likeness. When he pulled it down, a Galan of metal peered from the gyrfalcon's mouth—a serene face to wear to war. I watched his face as his men armored him, and he looked like the mask: calm, somewhat solemn, somewhat content, the way a child looks playing with a bit of clay, absorbed in the task.

He pushed up his visor and came over to me. He put his shield arm around me and pulled me close. This new skin of his was cold and hard, and I was glad of it. But I wished I could take him by the hair and dip him in metal, so that he was covered all over, for I didn't like the chinks, the way a dagger could find the back of his knee and hamstring him, or a sword find its way through the mail under his arm. We are imperfect vessels. We leak so easily.

CHAPTER 3

Marchfield

We took to the road after the morning mists had lifted, and we'd not been riding long before the Crux sent his men to drive us faster. We spread over the verges of the road into the fields and began to trot and then to canter. Thole stretched into the gait, trying to keep up with the larger horses. The earth resounded under their hooves. We left the foot soldiers and oxcarts and mules behind, and the gold and green banners streamed above our heads. I felt caught up in the spectacle, though I bore no colors but a dark blue dress and the bleached linen of my headcloth.

The road dipped and rose, and we came over the last hill and saw the army encamped over a full league of rolling plain. Beyond the army, the sea. I had imagined the sea would be like a great lake in a bowl of mountains, water cupped by land, but it spilled past the horizon. There was no edge to it; sea dissolved into sky and sky into sea in a gray haze. The surface of the water, green and pocked, reflected the low clouds like an old bronze mirror dulled by verdigris. It was marked by whitecaps quickly scrawled and quickly erased, leaving nothing for the eye to fasten on, a scene absurdly flat and featureless. Yet my eye was caught by it. I looked right past the Marchfield until we were down the hill and riding through a city of sumptuous pavilions and squalid hovels, so swarming with men and horses—and sheep, chickens, boys, dogs, goats, women, and mules—that I was bewildered.

The cataphracts gave a shout and the Crux led us straight in at a gallop, to the crossroads at the center of the Marchfield, where stood the king's hall. As we passed the tents and lean-tos and corrals, the campfires and dungheaps, I saw we were not much of a spectacle after all. A woman looked up from her laundering, a boy from polishing armor; a couple of warriors saw the banners and hailed us. Among so many I thought we'd disappear like a drop of dye in water.

We dismounted and knelt on the beaten ground before the king's hall. From a distance I'd mistaken the hall for a building, and indeed it was larger than any structure I'd ever seen, being the height of four men and wide enough to swallow the Dame's manor and her kitchen garden besides. But it was a vast circular pavilion, framed with timbers of great girth and walled and roofed with painted, gold-stamped leather; a herd of oxen must have given up their hides for it.

King Thyrse himself came out to greet us. The Crux gave him his sword, offering it by the hilt, and the king reversed it and gave it back. He pulled the Crux to his feet and gave him the kiss of peace on his forehead. Then he welcomed each cataphract by name, starting with his own bastard, Sire Guasca, and Sire Galan next, and gave them leave to stand. The armigers remained kneeling, heads bowed, palms flat on the ground. It was not so long a ceremony, but too long for me with my knees on the flints in the road. The horses grew restive behind us, pulling on the reins in the horseboys' hands.

I wouldn't have known him for the king if not for the obeisance we paid him. He was dressed more like some middling-rich armiger in a coarse shirt under a velvet brigandine stained with rust; he wore a plain red cap on his head. He was not so tall, either. I could have looked him eye to eye—except my forehead was to the ground, like the rest of the drudges, and I had to peep at him from under my brows.

I'd seen him before. This was the huntsman who'd brought down the stag in the Kingswood and taken his crown of antlers. His clan was Prey, and he was First of his clan as well as king. No wonder he could summon Prey Hunter and the god would come.

The Crux led us to a bare patch of pasture set aside for his troop. I saw he was as important as they'd said in the village, for we were less than a stone's throw from the king's hall.

The Marchfield, which had looked so sprawling and shapeless to me at first sight, had an underlying symmetry. It was like the divining compass Az had drawn for me in the dirt, with twelve roads, some mere paths, leading outward, from the king's hall at the center to the twelve directions. These roads cut the Marchfield into twelfths, called arcants. Unlike Az's compass, it could not be divided into equal domains for each god or clan, because King Thyrse and his sister, Queenmother Caelum, required half the arcants between them for their troops. The rest of the clans crowded into the other half.

The king had Prey's cataphracts under his command, and also hundreds of well-seasoned horse and foot soldiers, mudmen who gave their allegiance to the king and a daily ration, in something of that order. Queenmother Caelum's army of northerners, her Wolves, had taken four twelfths of the compass, from west-of-north to east, and marked their camp with her pennants of crimson and white. Some had mocked her men at first, saying they were called Wolves for their bravery in harrying sheep—but behind the tents and on the tourney field, they'd taught the mockers what it meant, until their name was spoken with grudging esteem.

The clan of Rift had an entire arcant, between the king and queenmother, to house a large troop of priests who served the avatar of the Warrior. They were so steeped in the mysteries of war, so hardened by its disciplines, that they were said to be more lethal without weapons than other men were with an arsenal.

Each of the remaining ten clans had half an arcant, the boundaries marked by banners around the tents. The king kept his best captains close to his hall; we were south-of-west, sharing an arcant with the clan of Lynx, arrived two days before—but they were farther from the king and nearer the sea. The Dame's husband had been a Lynx. He died before I came to the manor, and the Dame had never spoken of his clan.

We made a better camp than we had on the road. Summons Day, when all the clans must appear or pay forfeit, was still more than a tennight away, and there was no telling how long we'd be there after that. The Auspices blessed the ground with libations of wine and oil, the smoke of candlebark, and the sacrifice of a goat. The Crux marked out the boundaries and divided the space, setting aside the greater part of it for the horses. Foot soldiers were put to work robbing stones from pasture walls to build the corral, a pen for the manhounds, and a great central hearth. After their other work was done, they built lean-tos for themselves against the walls of the corral and dog pen: rough shelters of stone and rope, thatched with gorse brush.

The First's men knew what they were about, and raised his great pavilion quickly at the point nearest the king's hall, and the priests' green tent next to it to serve as both shrine and shelter. This left them free to offer advice (much of it unwanted) to the other varlets as they puzzled and cursed and fussed with ropes and poles and canvas. Sire Pava had bought a round tent of painted leather in Ramus, but he'd left the poles behind; it had never occurred to him that there could be a land without trees. I hid a sneer behind my hands to see him mocked for this by the other cataphracts, until the Crux's bagboy came back with a mule laden with kindling and told Sire Pava's jack, Gaunt, where he could buy wood.

Sire Galan's tent was wider than Az's hut and so high that a tall man could easily stand inside. It was made of canvas patterned with light green and yellow fletches, coated with wax against the damp. The wind plucked at the walls and made the poles and ropes creak. It was more pleasant to me than a house of stone or mud because its walls barred neither light nor air, and yet it was wonderfully dry inside, but for a leak or two at the seams when one of the clouds scurrying by overhead spattered us with rain.

Toward evening I carried two iron pots and a waterskin down the west path, toward the sea. It was Noggin's duty to fetch water, but I was in need of a reason to look at the sea again. Among so many tents, I could only glimpse it.

The narrow path gleamed where feet had worn through the turf to the chalky ground. It twisted around hummocks, through gaps in stone walls, and behind the backs of the tents, before leading me to the edge of a cliff. White seabirds hovered before me in the gulf of air, making small gestures to hold themselves steady, disdaining to overtax their wings. Far below, the sea began.

The path went over the cliff's edge. It was steep, but I was used to scrambling on rocks in the mountains. I left the pots behind, for I needed both my hands, and followed it down, holding on to tufts of sedge and outcroppings of crumbling stone. I hitched up my kirtle and squatted at the water's edge. The sea had a strong smell, not unpleasant. I took a taste and spat it out: saltier than tears. So I learned what everybody knows—that the sea is brine—and was reminded of my ignorance of the world beyond the Kingswood.

I walked north along the shore, and the sea wind pushed at me as if it meant to slip my shadow loose and fling it as high as those white birds. Cold waves splashed over my feet and tumbled the pebbles and shells on the strand. The Sun was low and swaddled in clouds, but she sent a little red light skipping over the water toward me.

Hundreds of ships rode the swells, bare masts as close as dead trees in a flooded forest. I'd never seen sails, so the masts puzzled me. We had boats of bent willow and leather in the village, as clumsy as a barrel unless you had the knack; these ships were bigger than houses, with smooth sides painted with godsigns. Big as the vessels were, it was hard to believe that so many men and horses and wagons could be poured into them and transported over waters so wide you couldn't even see the other shore, much less be assured of finding it.

I'd not been alone for more than a moment since starting this journey. Always in sight, everything I did or did not do remarked on. Not that I was so remarkable, but soldiers are often idle and always looking for diversion. So every man in the troop had a taste of me, my name on his tongue. I hadn't felt how much it pressed upon me, the weight of their speculations, until I set the burden down by the shore.

I dug my feet into the sand and took root there until the Sun had been quenched in the sea. Once I'd known every face in my world. Now I was among strangers, too many to count. I had tied the thread of my life to one of those strangers, and I wasn't sure whether, twisted together, we would make a stronger cord. I felt more myself when we were not together. But Wend Weaver was at work. Sire Galan and I were between her finger and her thumb as she spun, and I feared that if we snagged or tangled, she might get out her shears.

I scrambled up the cliff. The sea was luminous, brighter than the sky and land, as if it held the last light of the Sun. Somehow I'd mislaid the two pots—or they'd been stolen. I feared Spiller would complain of me, and I cast back and forth along the cliff's edge looking for them. After a while I gave it up and made my way on another path toward the campfires and torches, small puddles of light and sound.

Behind the tents a gray shadow detached itself from the other shadows and stood in my way. "What's this?" he said, and he pulled off my headcloth so that my hair came down. He called out, "Come see what I've found! A stray skinsheath!"

I snatched at the cloth, but he held the other end of it. "I'm no stray. I'm of Crux's company."

"You're not," he said, "or you wouldn't be here."

When one farmyard dog starts barking, the rest join in. Soon I had a pack around me, yammering. I reached for my knife and my hand brushed the bag of finger bones hanging from my belt. I didn't need to cast the bones to know the counsel Na and the Dame would have given, for I had them to heart. Na would have said, "All you can do with that little blade is scratch, and scratching will worsen the itch," and the Dame would have advised another use for it, if other means failed—the only sure escape being to turn it on myself. I palmed the knife and tucked my hands into my sleeves. I said again (but my voice was smaller than I'd hoped), "I'm of Crux's company. My cataphract will come looking for me."

The first man mocked me. "Her cataphract will come looking for her—she thinks a cataphract will come looking for his laundress! I suppose she's the only one can keep his dirties clean. Well, will you wash my linens too?" His teeth flashed, and the whites of his eyes. He said to the others, "Aren't I a woman dowser, you laggards? My rod can find quim in a desert!"

I took a step to the side, and he stepped in front of me again.

Another said, from behind my shoulder, "Maybe, but it's such a little stick." A third said, "Trave dowses women all right, but his rod hangs down as soon as he finds one, so what's the use?" They hooted.

Trave replied, "Oh, no. It stands up and quivers; it points right at her. Shall I show you?" He lifted his tunic and began to unlace his prickguard.

The others laughed and shoved each other, waiting to see how far he'd go with this game. I was not about to wait, and pushed between them, toward the king's hall. As if that were a signal, they closed in. So many hands, I couldn't twist free. "She's a slippery one," someone said. "So much the better," said another. Trave was hobbled by his leggings, around his ankles, and he was hopping up and down and shouting, "Wait! Wait!"

The worst of it was that they were still laughing. I stabbed at one man but the blade turned on his thick leather jack. I don't think he noticed the knife before it was struck out of my hand and my arms were bent behind my back. I should have gone for his eyes.

"Get off, you runts, and let me have a look at her!" I heard someone bellow, and then came the thwack of blows landing on skulls and backsides and yelps from the men. I was hauled by my scruff into the circle of tents, into the light of the cook fire and a few torches.

My rescuer was a woman, and an immense one by any measure, up, down, and sideways. Her gown was cut low, perilously close to her nipples, exposing a vast pale bosom sprinkled with moles. The cleft between her breasts was deep enough to swallow a purseful of coins. Her bosom rested on the jutting shelf of an equally vast belly; her dress strained to cover her. She had one hand on her hip; the other held a stout stick of firewood. She looked from me to the men and laughed a derisive laugh.

"Go find yourselves a striped skirt," she told the men. "This little thing isn't big enough to go around the lot of you. You know where the whores are. Go and pay for it. I know Pinch is a cursed skinflint, but what about the rest of you? And if you haven't any coin, you know what you can do? Find a ewe's arse, she won't even notice. Your little dangles won't do more than tickle her. But no, here's better advice—use your hands. It's the soldiers' way, runts: no coin, no cankers. Quick and clean. Have you forgotten how? Come, I'll teach you." She held up the firewood. "Fancy this is your prick," she said. She held up her left hand: "Hand," she said. "You just marry the two like this, see? What a trifling lot of numskulls, forgot what you learned before you were weaned!"

The woman made them laugh, and the air changed, the way it does when a breeze drives away a storm. It made me wonder if I'd been in such danger after all, if she could leash them with a jest. In the torchlight I could see they were but five or six ordinary men. One had the grace to hang his head, but the rest stared at me boldly. I marked Trave at once because his leggings were askew and he still had my headcloth. With my hair uncovered I looked a wanton, so I snatched back the cloth and bound it up again. The blood rose to my face for shame.

The woman hung her fleshy arm over my shoulder and walked us away from the men and the firelight. Her nose and cheeks were broad, with large black pores. Her eyes were kind. "Just come today, I'd guess."

I nodded, finding it hard to speak.

"Don't go anywhere by yourself—take a man with you or you're fair hunting. Otherwise they don't know they're poaching, understand? Even the whores do it, or they won't get paid. I can see you're a country girl, and know no better." With a groan she stooped and plucked something out of the grass. "Is this yours?"

She handed me my little bone-handled knife. She said, "You're lucky these are good boys—they have to work themselves up to do harm, they aren't bred to it like some of the vermin you'll find around here."

I muttered, "I'm lucky you were here."

"That too, dear, that too."

I wiped my nose and eyes on the loose end of my headcloth and gave her a hug. My arms didn't meet around her. When the men jeered I paid them no mind. She was soft, but there was something hard about her under the fat. No wonder they'd scattered at her blows.

I was shaking. She sat me down by the fire and told me her name was Mai, and the runts were not such bad fellows as I might think. I looked at them and thought they might be good lads inside the tents' circle, but behind the tents was another matter entirely.

Mai put on a shawl to cover her bosom and walked me home, with the sheepish man as an escort; our encampments were not far apart. I stepped into Sire Galan's tent without a word to anyone, and found it empty.

Sire Galan had his men out looking for me, without their supper. He rode in after most of them had straggled back to camp, and held up a lantern on a pole. Without getting off his horse, he called, "Have you found her?"

I ran to him, and he slid out of the saddle, handed his lantern to someone, and slapped me hard. I stepped back and he stepped forward, shouting at me in front of everyone. Sire Galan jabbed me with his finger at each step: I was never to go off without leave, never to go alone, never to vex and trouble him again. Was I witless or something worse? Where had I been? In whose tent, whose bed? The Crux watched for a few moments and went into his pavilion. The others stayed to be amused.

I said I was sorry, keeping my voice low. I backed up until I was against the canvas of his tent and could go no farther. When I looked at the ground, he bent and put his face in front of mine and glared, as if he'd turn me to stone. I met his eyes but it was hard to do, hard to stand face-to-face with him. He demanded to know where I had gone, his voice still raised. I mumbled an answer, though I had no good answer to give: I stayed awhile by the sea—the Sun went down and I lost my way (lost, where all roads led to the king's hall, and we were camped in sight of it)—I was sorry I'd troubled him—I'd never seen the sea before.

If I'd said more there would have been blood spilt.

Sire Galan became silent, and that was worse. He turned his face aside and stood there, his jaw clamped shut, his arms crossed, his hands in fists. Then he turned his back on me and walked away.

He saw to it that his men had a good supper and treated them to his private store of wine. His voice was curt, but I heard him laugh when Sire Alcoba said, "High time you broke her to saddle and bridle."

Sire Galan was quick to say, "Oh, but I favor riding bareback."

I went into the tent and lit the lamp set at hand by the door. While I'd been gone his varlets had been working; there were sacks stuffed with heather as pallets for the men and a folding cot of wood and rope and leather in one corner for Sire Galan. This bed had never appeared when we were on the road; it had been folded small in the baggage, so small a mule could carry it. We'd not be sleeping rough. The bed had feet carved like talons, and there was a feather mattress on it, and linens and Sire Galan's quilt besides, which was embroidered all over with bright featherstitching. Perhaps his wife had sewn it. I lay down and pulled the covers over me, wondering if he'd want me in his bed, angry as he was. My face was sore from his blow. I'd have a fine bruise by morning.

I could hear the men by the campfire all too well.

"I don't know why you brought her," Sire Pava said. "I had her once and she was nothing much. I wouldn't have taken the trouble, but she traipsed around with her hair down, pretending she was a maiden when she wasn't."

Sire Galan was silent. Sire Rodela said, "He thinks she's lucky, on account of her red hair."

"Lucky! She's a bit of rubbish picked up on the road. The man who found her—that was Sire Scindo dam Quiesco by Infero of Lynx, my old aunt's husband—didn't find her to be lucky. He got killed on campaign and she came home with the baggage."

It angered me that Sire Pava knew something of my past that I did not, and bandied it about. But his tale made sense of much that had puzzled me, even of the Dame's silences. I'd been sent home with her husband's arms, his armor, horses, bagboy, jack and all, when I was too old for swaddling clothes and too young to be useful. The Dame no doubt thought it a shameful thing to be baggage, loot from some war somewhere. But Na could have told me.

I'd proved more of a bane than a charm, if what Sire Pava said was true. They called me Luck anyway, in the Low tongue. Perhaps some jack had named me, or Na herself. Maybe Sire Scindo's misfortune was fortunate for others; I never heard he was much missed.

Yet to know so much was still to know—nothing: not whether my parents were alive or dead, not where we'd lived. The dream of my father had told me more. I thought I'd recognize those mountains, that valley, if I ever saw them. I remembered how my father had slouched easy in the saddle until he saw the soldiers. Banners of black; what clan bore that color? None I knew.

Sire Galan spoke up. "I suppose you'd call Sire Scindo fortunate if he died in his old age, maundering and sweating and stinking of some fever, so long as he died in his bed. He died as a man should—at war. Maybe you had no luck with the girl because you asked the wrong favors of Chance."

"I wasn't unlucky with her," said Sire Pava. "She's a contrary, hard-mouthed nag."

Sire Galan laughed. "You found her too spirited, did you? Well, I can ride when others are bucked off—isn't that true, Pava?"

* * *

It was a long while before Sire Galan came to the tent, but when he came, he was alone. He flung the men's pallets out of the tent and bade them sleep outside, even Sire Rodela, saying it would do them no harm to stay another night out of doors.

He snuffed out the lamp. He didn't turn me out of bed but crawled in beside me. The wood groaned when it took his weight and I slid toward the hollow he made. The bed was not so wide that two people could lie in it without touching. He lay on his back looking at nothing, his body in a rigor like the one that follows death. He didn't utter a word.

His anger had been hot; now it was cold. And I, being both scorched and chilled, could find no anger to match his, though he'd struck me and, what smarted more, traded jests about me with Sire Pava. For he'd ridden out looking for me, he'd searched the Marchfield high and low. I was humbled by him, and afraid. I feared his silence might go on and on.

I didn't know whether to cajole or excuse or beseech or say he'd injured me with his mistrust, so I did all of these, haltingly, with long silences of my own: small words, but an army of them. I even thought to find a chink in his silence by using the keenest weapon at hand, to tell him some men had set upon me, and where they lived. That would have stirred him; his anger would have found another target. But I forbore. I held my tongue for Mai's sake, and because men should not die over me being a fool. Though I wouldn't have been altogether sorry to see it.

When I gave up and turned my back on him, and tears began to leak and I sobbed, muffling the sound in the quilt, then he softened. His body unclenched, and he rolled on his side, toward me, and I turned to face him.

I was grateful that he'd relented enough to look at me, and I wept some more, covering my face for shame. He put his hand on my shoulder and gave me a shake.

"Where did you go, hmm?" He gave a mirthless laugh. "You made me look a buffoon, riding around the Marchfield whistling for my sheath. This isn't your village. You can't go strolling about wherever you please."

"I never meant to be gone so long, or to cause you worry," I said, as I'd said many times already.

"Mind you don't stray again." He stared at me. The lamps were out, but his face was touched with a wavering red light from the fire in the brazier. I was uneasy under his scrutiny. He said, "Who was before Pava?"

"No one."

"He was not your first, so he says."

"There have been no others."

"Why lie about it?" Sire Galan said. "It doesn't matter to me if there have been two or twenty."

I saw it did matter. I thought it strange that he was jealous of what might or might not have happened before he met me. And then, not strange at all. For to think of those he bedded before me was to wonder if they were fair, bold, sweet, graceful—was to feel plain, shy, sour, awkward. Surely he had no such misgivings.

Yet he was jealous. I smiled and put my palm flat on his chest, resting my fingertip in the notch of bone at the base of his throat. "You don't care?"

"Not a whit." He gritted his words between his teeth, and when he kissed me, he bit. I bit him back. He gathered me up and turned me under him. He hooked his arm under the crook of my knee, and I raised my hips to take him in.

But he tarried to look me in the eye. "I feared I'd lost you. I looked everywhere, and you'd vanished."

"I found my way back."

"I thought Hazard Chance had taken you as quickly as she gave you."

"It was Ardor who brought us together, not Hazard," I said.

"No," he said, taking a fistful of my hair, "you are Chance's blessing on me, to preserve me through dangers and bring me fortune in war. You are my luck."

It was true, then. I'd been taken for a warrior's Chance-given trinket. I'd been wrong to flatter myself that he wanted something more of me than an amulet to hang about his neck. The tenderness I thought I'd seen, the care he'd taken to seek me when I was lost—it was his own skin of which he was fond, not mine. I said, "So you can die in your bed?"

Sire Galan never answered. He buried himself in me, and the sound he made seemed wrenched from him, pulled up by the very root. I lay under him as still and silent and cold as he'd lain not long before. But the more I retreated, the more he pursued. He wouldn't leave me be until I'd turned on him as fiercely as he came after me.

Before he spent himself, he sighed *talisman* into my ear. Then he drifted away into sleep and left me far behind.

When the Sun rose and Sire Galan saw the bruise blooming on my cheek that he'd planted with his blow the night before, he fed me a few honeyed words and promised me a gift. He got sour answers from me. I was in no mood for his charm or his presents. I draped the end of my headcloth to cover the bruise as well as I could.

Sire Galan sent Spiller to look for the pots I'd left on the cliff and took me to the market. Sire Alcoba came with him; he had a purseful of coins that he tossed in the air, saying he'd buy either a blade or a sheath, depending on what caught his fancy first. They were followed by their armigers, Sire Rodela and Sire Buey, and behind them the bagboys, Noggin and Fetcher. Noggin took my arm, for Sire Galan had told him to look after me. I soon learned to keep my distance from Sire Rodela, who nudged me into a puddle at every chance. I walked behind Sire Buey instead. He was a stolid fellow, quite unlike his master, and marched in a straight line regardless of the footing.

The market ran along both sides of the south road, under arcades built of poles roofed with waxed linen, reed mats, or leather. The morning mist turned to a fine rain, and we crowded close under the awnings.

As far as I could tell, everything was for sale in this market except the wind. They even sold water. Half the horizon brimmed with water, yet none in sight was drinkable, so water was hauled in barrels on oxcarts from the wide river a morning's ride to the south, upstream of the delta marshes that soaked alternately in freshwater and salt; drudges lined up with pots and casks and buckets and skins to carry it away. Across the road from the water sellers were the sellers of wood; next to them were drudges sitting on the ground with a few eggs or a brace of pigeons or a heap of turnips and onions on a cloth in front of them. Farmers and goodwives, free to do as they pleased now that the harvest was in, came to sell when they heard that a colewort in the Marchfield fetched as much as a goose would at home—and stayed, turning their hands to laundering or their backs to carrying, only to find their money went faster than it came, no matter how tight they drew their purse strings.

The merchants of luxuries arrived daily from Ramus or from places much more foreign, to judge by their strange faces, with skin very fair or very dark, and their stranger garb. They brought pickled quail eggs, wine from the skirts of the Crags, canopied beds and carpets, a thousand things, just so a cataphract might fancy he ate and drank and slept at home. The Blood spent freely, thinking they would soon be rich with plunder, or else past need of riches.

We stopped at a clothier's stall, one of the best, which had a red canopy over three tables piled with fine-worked cloth. Sire Galan bought me a scarf green as new willow leaves, fringed with gold thread. He wanted me to put it on there and then, and pulled off my old headcloth. I pushed his hands away and quickly tied the new one myself, so it covered the bruise and wrapped around my neck. Now I was marked with his colors. The blue of my dress looked gray against the willow green.

Sire Alcoba leaned on a table, watching us. "I've never seen hair that color," he said to Sire Galan. "Even her eyebrows and lashes are red as fox fur. You should bid her pluck her brows, keep it hid." He raised his own eyebrows as I flushed. "Where do you suppose they breed her kind?"

Sire Galan turned to me. "Do your parents have the same coloring?"

He'd never questioned me about my family before. I was pained that he asked now, so idly, to please a friend; and it was an old wound he struck upon, because there was no answer to give him. "I can't tell," I said, "for I remember neither father nor mother." I'd dreamed of my father in the Kingswood, and his hair was reddish brown—but I didn't see fit to mention it.

"That boy, your cousin, is flax haired. But what of your brothers and sisters, or your other cousins?" This question was not so idle. Sire Galan chased after some scent.

"No one else in the village has red hair, and let that be an end to it!" I said.

"You see?" said Sire Galan, as if I had driven home some point. "Wherever Chance sows lucky ones, there they spring up. They are Hazard's breed, and father and mother have less to do with it than you might think."

Hazard again, and now Hazard's breed. Let him think so. I should be glad he believed I was made of some finer mud than other drudges. But I wasn't glad; I was galled.

The clothier hovered nearby, watching us. His hands alighted first on one stack of cloth, then another. When we'd entered the stall, he had begged pardon of the cataphracts for having nothing fit for them; his cloth was ill made; he knew they were used to better. Merchants always bargain this way with the Blood, claiming their goods are too poor while asking prices too rich. Sire Galan did not seem to notice, as I did, how the merchant grew by degrees less obsequious; he offered us a piece of wool pulled from the bottom of a pile—would do excellent well for a dress, he said. It was dyed a vivid green, much too yellow.

Sire Galan might have bought it, but I shook my head and said, "See how this was woven by a slattern! It's loose everywhere except where it's too tight. And I know this dye. It will fade in the wash like a painted face. It is a bawd's gaud and I will not wear it."

Sire Alcoba said to Sire Galan, "Whether your sheath is Hazard's breed or not, it's clear she was born a vixen. I believe you're outfoxed. You gentled her only last night, and now she bites again."

Sire Galan took my arm. "She's my own sweet vixen," he said.

Sire Alcoba laughed and called him besotted, and Sire Galan smiled back. But when we left the shelter of the shop he dropped my arm and walked ahead again.

To be in such a crowd, and all strangers, was strange to me. We could not help but rub elbows and tread on toes. Low made way for high, low waited upon high, low stood patiently in the mizzling rain while high stood under the awnings. As for Sire Galan and Sire Alcoba, they might have been strolling down any market lane in Ramus. They met friends and stood in the road talking, never mindful that others had to step around us. They met acquaintances, and bowed and doffed their caps; they met enemies too, I suppose, for they doffed their caps with one hand while keeping the other on their swords—very politely. In the Marchfield the clans kept the peace or suffered the king's displeasure, and even a young hotspur took care not to give offense by staring too hard at another man, or walking between two friends on the street, or forgetting to offer a greeting or ask a by-your-leave upon parting, or committing any of a thousand small discourtesies that might provoke an edged answer.

Amidst all these men were many women, more than I expected to see in an army camp. Most would have looked at home around the village well, or scraping pots in the Dame's kitchen: a goodwife selling a few leeks, a worn-out drudge with a bundle of laundry bigger than she was and two children clutching her skirts.

Then there were the whores, enough of them to fill a town of women. Some trawled the crowd, flashing their lures: striped skirts, crude as sacking or sumptuously fine, and all covering much the same wares, no doubt. More harlots could be found down at the end of the market road, across from the armorers and too close to the stink of the tanners. The better quality of courtesans had their own pavilions, set back from the road and well guarded.

Other whores sat on blankets beside the road. When a man came along, they'd close a little curtain hanging from the awning to screen them from passersby—if they bothered with the curtain. One such blanket bawd crossed glances with me as she drew the curtain behind a new customer, who was already fumbling at his laces. I looked down quickly. When I looked up next, the curtain was closed. All the shame was on my part—in her look there'd been nothing but weary indifference. Her pander was there, slouching against a post; he had four or five other women as well, sitting in a row along behind him, wearing his blue and black stripes. He saw me looking and tipped his coxcomb cap, kissing the air at me. I spat on the ground and turned my back.

Such a crop of flesh, such a harvest of shame: I couldn't avert my eyes for long. While Sire Galan saw to the mending of a gauntlet at an armorer's stand, I stared at the whores.

I'd seen a whore only once before. She was a peddler's woman, come to our village on the mountain road. She'd whitened her face with a little starchroot and reddened her lips, but still she was as ordinary as a turnip, neither homely nor beautiful, like half the wives in the village. The peddler carried a big sack of goods for the women, and she had her little one, you might say, for the men. His sack was full of shells such as you could pick up for free along the seashore; in the mountains they are prized for making beads and amulets. Her sack was empty—but which do you suppose fetched the highest prices? The women threw stones at her until she fled. The peddler shrugged his shoulders and hawked a few more trinkets, knowing full well, I imagine, that his doxy would do a fine business in the fields, out of sight of the wives. She left a gift behind too: the canker, which visited many a marriage bed and is stubborn to cure.

I despised whores; but I feared them more, as I feared the bad luck that put them in a striped skirt.

I was surprised to see these women, the drudges and the drabs, but more amazed still to see women of the Blood, arm in arm with a cataphract or an armiger, come promenading down the market road. They couldn't walk unless they had an arm to lean on, because the high wooden pattens they wore strapped to their slippers to keep them out of the muck also made them teeter and mince along.

Sire Pava's wife had not been such a work of artifice. She'd never seen Ramus, and had only hearsay to go on when she stitched her clothes or covered her hair. These dames were from the very wellspring of fashion. Their faces were pale with powder, colorless except for their eyes and the clan marks tattooed on their cheeks; they plucked their eyebrows and hair so that their foreheads should be smooth and white as new-laid eggs, and pinned thin veils to their headcloths to allow a glimpse of this smoothness, this whiteness. Dresses of velvet lined with rabbit fur or of brocade heavy with gold thread hugged their breasts and gathered about their hips to show the curve of their bellies. They held up their skirts in front and trailed them behind in the mud. After my years in the Dame's workshop, I could not help but tot up the hours of spinning, weaving, dying, and stitching in their garments, the labor wrought into every muddy fold.

This, then, was beauty, not some milk-fat cow girl with her cheeks reddened from the Sun like the queen of the village fair. Beauty might flick a glance over me, and find me beneath notice; beauty eyed Sire Galan and found him pleasing.

And beauty was also for sale in this market, it seemed. We met a man of the clan Ardor with his daughter on his arm; she was slim as a reed, but her dress made much of what little figure she had. Her hair fell to her thighs, twisted in a net dotted with pearls. She kept her eyes downcast as her father spoke of her. "She's the last of seven daughters," he said. "Was there ever a man so unfortunate, to sire such an ugly child and have no dowry left to make her face seem sweeter?"

Sire Alcoba said the maiden's skin was as luminous as the pearls in her hair, and Sire Galan said her behavior was perfect in modesty and several other things that I could see were all too true.

Her father said, "To be sure, her skin is fine and her virtue unsullied, and yet I could wish she were not so very plain and so very thin. A man would have to overlook her face and figure. Still, she'll make a fine mate; she will bear."

"It is not her face but her dowry that is plain," Sire Alcoba said gallantly.

She was not plain at all. She peeped at Sire Galan from under her lowered lids, a look both shy and a little sly. I was not the only one to find that no other man in the crowd overshadowed him. His shoulders were wide, his hips were narrow, and his green kidskin surcoat fit well enough to prove it. He wore white linen around his brown throat, and long boots over his long legs. I stood behind him, and couldn't see his face, but I knew what I would see: a smile, not too broad, nor strained, nor insincere—a bit knowing, perhaps, but never enough to be offensive—made by a fine pair of lips, the upper more curved, the bottom more full; a look that alighted, considered, but couldn't be said to linger too long for courtesy or good sense—and burned just the same, igniting a blush on those white cheeks. He knew his sway—had reason to know it well, I could see—but didn't seem to trouble himself to use it. It was no small part of his charm that he bore it so lightly.

His beauty was a blade and we would be parted by it. If he were unsightly, I would not have to see these glances from under lowered lids, or the bold stares, of two or three dames we'd met on the way, that dared him to make a cuckold of the man on their arm; or, worst of all, those looks that spoke too clearly of remembered intimacy. But if he were unsightly, he might wear longer but not so well.

I stared down at my bare feet in the cold mud, wondering: Why, then, had he exerted himself for me? Come back, when we were on the road, to cajole me out of a sullen humor? Barbered Sire Rodela for me? Ridden to find me when I was lost? If I was not mistaken in him, let him turn now and give me a look, a speaking look, for all to see.

Let him give me even a glance.

Sire Alcoba clapped the father on the shoulder and walked him away, with a nod to Sire Galan, saying, "Perhaps you know my wife's cousin? She married Sire Gambade dam Caracoler by Sagitta of Ardor some five years past . . ."

As she was led away, the daughter turned her head, not enough for another peep, but enough to show her profile: a delicate gem.

Then Sire Galan turned and looked at me, still wearing his smile.

"Let's to the cobbler," he said to me. "Winter is setting in and you must be shod."

He would do the same for his horse.

That evening I washed out my old headcloth in a bucket of costly water. The shoemaker had made me wipe my feet before he would take my measure, and offered me nothing to clean them with, not so much as a cup of water to rinse them, so my old linen had to do. The more mud I'd wiped off, the dirtier I'd felt. I hadn't thought to be ashamed of my feet before. My last pair of shoes wore to pieces in the Kingswood, well into winter. I had endured the cold and the chilblains until, slowly, I'd cobbled myself a new pair of feet with soles of horn and toes tough as roots, numb to cold and impervious to stony ground. Now I saw how my feet were splayed, knobbed, cracked, roughened, how dirt had gone under the skin, out of reach of a rag and spit. Unfit for shoes. A drudge's hooves.

Nevertheless, I had two pair of shoes now. The tough brogans would be ready in a few days. The other pair, slippers of red and black leather stitched in a diamond pattern, had caught Sire Galan's eye; he paid an astounding price without so much as dickering. I wore them inside the tent while I hung up my old headcloth to dry. How they pinched! The leather would stretch or my feet would be crushed—there could be no other accommodation between the shoes and me.

I was by myself for a few moments in the tent. I could go nowhere without an escort; even to visit the cesspit I had to take Spiller and Noggin with me, to guard each end of one of the great planks that straddled the trench. There were gangs of boys who would tip the plank as you squatted upon it and drop you into the dung.

This pinched too. And I was not the only one who felt squeezed too tight. When we got back from market, Sire Galan had told Spiller, "If she's not with me, you'd best stick to her like a burr. If she's lost again, I'll take it out of your hide with something worse than a flogging."

I heard Spiller mutter that he had no quarrel with me, but he'd not be saddled by a mare.

"And you're an ill-fitting old boot," I told him. But in truth I had no wish to venture past the clan's tents on my own, being quite convinced it was not safe.

CHAPTER 4

A Wager

'd wanted to see more of the world; here it was, the whole world, so it seemed to me. And what a brave glittering sight, what a hubbub and clamor—what a stink! Even the wind from the sea could not sweep the stench away.

The clans had come to these barren hills and planted a forest of tents leafed with gaudy canvas and leather and blooming with banners. The men were pent up so close in this false forest that they crawled upon each other like wasps. Pent up and idle, idle and restless, they waited for the king to let loose the swarm. In this wood there were but two kinds of game: men and women. Men were hunted on the tourney field. Women were hunted everywhere.

And Hazard Chance was worshiped everywhere, because the cataphracts and their men would wager on anything: who would win a tourney; which stallion would master all the others in the corral; whether a certain dame was with child or no; if one drudge could beat another in a footrace across the Marchfield and back; if a manhound could best a bear; whether a particular flea would jump to your jack or your bagboy if they both sat still as could be.

So it was that Sire Galan made a wager with Sire Alcoba that night, and the next morning I heard about it from Spiller, who had it from Sire Alcoba's jack Rowney, who'd overheard them conversing in this manner:

Sire Alcoba says, "As a wife she would be too cheap—her father spoke truly, she has no dowry at all—but as a concubine she's too dear. He sets a high price on her virtue."

Sire Galan says, "And you already have a wife."

"Indeed, one too many."

"Are you so taken with the maiden then?"

"I like her well enough, but not at the price," says Sire Alcoba.

Spiller and I were on our way to buy water with some of Sire Galan's littlest coins. Noggin should have done it, but he was as likely to bring back saltwater as fresh; he was born to be cheated. The Sun had come up in a miserly mood, giving us rays of lead instead of gold. Rain dripped from low and leaky clouds.

I told Spiller they must have been talking of the pearl-fleshed girl they'd met in the market, draped on her father's arm. I never thought to see a man of the Blood play the merchant—and he did it well, for the more he'd belittled the maiden, the more flawless she looked.

Spiller hadn't seen her. "But listen," he said, "I'm getting to the best part of my tale."

So Sire Galan says, "I wager I could have her maidenhead for free."

And Sire Alcoba says, "I'll take the wager. She'll never do it. She's too modest."

"Not so modest, I think."

"Then she's a fool—chastity is her only wealth."

"If she's a fool, so much the better. And if she's not, I hope she's cunning indeed. A cunning woman will know how to be a maid again by morning, and no one the wiser except the three of us—and perhaps the man who buys her. But he'll not be much cheated, for she'll be more eager after I have done with her."

"How would you prove you've plucked her?" says Sire Alcoba.

"Proof? What proof? My word on it should satisfy you."

"Yet I'd find it hard to believe if I didn't witness it with my own eyes."

"Do you mean to call me a liar even before I've spoken?" says Sire Galan, his hand on his sword hilt.

There was a pause. Spiller said if it had lasted a few moments longer, it would have ended with steel drawn and then blood drawn.

Sire Alcoba says—with a little laugh—"No, no. Of course not. Of course I don't doubt your word."

"It's well you say so."

Another pause, and Sire Alcoba says, "What shall we wager, then? Your black courser against my gray?"

Sire Galan: "You shall have to do better. I already stake my life on this wager. First, she'll be well guarded, and then, if her father comes to learn I've tupped her, he'll try to gore me. Besides, Semental is worth ten of your gray, or you would not always be pleading to ride him."

"Spiller, enough!" I said.

"But Rowney told me more. Don't you wish to hear it?"

Oh, Spiller relished good gossip; he sauced and served it well, too well. I looked him in the face, searching for malice toward me, but found none. Did he truly have such an empty vault under his thatch of hair as to think I might enjoy this tale?

"No, I've heard enough."

"But wait—it's too rich!" Laughter burst out of him. "Sire Alcoba added Rowney to the stakes, and all his upkeep. Sire Galan shall have two jacks!"

"If you don't hold your tongue," I told Spiller, "he'll have no jack at all."

He thought I was joking, but when he saw I wasn't, there was a long silence, sullen on his part, bitter on mine.

We bought water. I tasted it first: one cask was too muddy, another too sandy. A man claimed his water came all the way from the mountains. I swore it did not, but it was still the sweetest to be found.

On the way back to the tent, I thought of how Spiller and I would be harnessed together, for a long while perhaps; I should make amends or he might spit in my food as he did Sire Rodela's. And I had no reason to take affront at him or at his tale—none that he could imagine, anyway.

So I spoke agreeably to him and asked him to tell me the rest, and there was little left to tell except that Sire Galan had three days and four nights to accomplish the feat or lose the wager, and one of those nights had passed already. And Spiller had no doubt he would win, no doubt at all.

The Crux also made a wager. He challenged the clan of Lynx to a tourney of courtesy. It was to be an amiable battle between neighbors, a skirmish fought with mock weapons. The terms were agreed: firstly, one charge with lances of unseasoned pine (easily snapped, and even if the haft didn't break, the point would do little harm, being a three-pronged crownackle made of tin); secondly, combat with oaken swords. They staked nothing more than a dinner on the battle. The losers would feast the winners that same evening.

Sire Erial, a cataphract with more bluster than beard, complained to Sire Galan that it was not a mortal tourney, with unbated weapons. "Does the Crux think we're afraid to fight?" he asked. "Or has he lost his stomach for gambling, that he sets stakes so trifling?"

"Oh, hardly," said Sire Galan. "He's lost his taste for his cook's dishes, and plans to dine at another's expense tonight."

But I heard Cook say that the king had forbidden mortal tourneys, as he had forbidden duels, to save his men for battle; and besides, his master was never born such a fool that he'd risk more than a dinner on untried men. And Cook must have made his own reckoning. He had two calves already turning on spits for surety if we should lose.

I sat cross-legged on the bed watching Sire Galan don his armor all morning long, first the padded red garments, then the mail and plate. He was cock-a-whoop over the battle to come, sure he'd be a victor. I knew little enough of tourneys, being raised in the Dame's household, but I did know that a man could die even in a tourney of courtesy. A lance might catch just so on the helmet and break his neck, or more likely he'd be unhorsed and trampled. Just as clear as I saw him standing before me, with Spiller fastening the latches that held his gorget to his breastplate, I could see him cut and in need of tending, or else past need of anything, mortally wounded. And yet I could hardly wish him to win on the tourney field, as it would give him another weapon in his siege against that maid's virtue—her walls would tumble for certain.

Sire Rodela brought out a wooden box and opened it. Three tourney swords in scabbards rested inside. They may have been of wood, but once unsheathed they shone brighter than steel from the silver leaf that covered them. They were heavier than real swords, being weighted with lead in the pommel and in a channel along the blade so that a man might build up his strength; though they couldn't cut like steel or thrust like steel, they made fine cudgels.

Sire Galan tried one and then another, running his hand down the swords' edges. He nicked his thumb on the second and grinned. "Rift has chosen," he said, and strapped the sheath to his baldric. He looked up from under his brows and saw me wince.

"Oh, you look so grave," he said, laughing. "No fear. I'll bring you trophies if you'll give me a kiss for luck." He leaned over me and claimed his kiss—he took it, I did not give it. I was as ready to curse him as wish him luck, with that other wager on my mind. My fear for him was sullied by fear for myself, for what should become of me if he won or lost; my desire was marred by anger, so that even his smile and his touch came unwelcome. I stayed mute. There was no way to speak of his wager, and no other words could find their way out.

The tourney field was down the east-of-north road beyond the queen's encampment. It was a valley surrounded by low hills, a stretch of scrub grass and gorse rooted in soil so meager the rock bones showed through here and there. Where the ground had been churned into mud, drudges had spread sand and straw for better footing. There were two small enclosures on the field for the jacks, so each could be at hand to tend to his master's wants and weapons and—if his master went down—dart into the melee to pull him out. The fences were made of reed mats strung between posts; they seemed solid to a horse, but the jacks knew how flimsy they were.

I had expected more splendor. But promising or not, this ground was consecrated; as Wend claims pastures, and Eorõe the plowed land, Rift has dominion over the fields of war. The god's priests were there before us, setting smudge pots burning to mark the boundaries of the battle. A warrior driven past those boundaries must yield to his opponent. The smoke smeared more gray over a gray day, but it smelled sweet, for they'd smothered the fires with candlebark.

Canopies hung with colors were set about the hills around the field to shelter the Blood. A good many had come to watch, and mudfolk too, since tourneys were the principal amusement in the long days spent waiting for the army to assemble and set forth.

I went with some of the other drudges who could steal time from their duties. Fleetfoot and I sat together on a rise overlooking the field, perched on a boulder with my cloak over our heads to keep out the never-ending drizzle. Noggin sat nearby, wrapped in an old sack. Since Spiller was needed on the field, the bagboy had been told to look after me. He was as near a nitwit as made no difference, which was agreeable to me. If I had to be on one end of a halter, I'd rather be holding it than wearing it.

I had my eye on Sire Galan. Even in his armor, even in a crowd, even at a distance, I knew him. Of course his gyrfalcon helmet marked him, as well as his painted shield, but after all those days on the road, I could have picked him out just by the way he sat his horse. He was riding the black stallion Semental.

Now he was taking his place in the battle line, to the right of the Crux, wearing his green banner. Sire Rodela was just to his left, for each cataphract rode with his armiger on his shield side. They made a line of thirty-four mounted warriors by my count, but by their reckoning, as always, seventeen. The cataphracts were armed with tourney lances and swords and armored in their second skins of mail and forged iron. Their horses wore bards of sturdy boiled leather marked with godsigns and patterns, and cushions stuffed with straw hung before their chests to guard against lance thrusts and collisions.

All in all, the cataphracts' horses were better protected than the armigers, who wore such motley armor as they could afford. What use was it to an armiger to be called Sire This or Sire That if all his house could provide for him was an old brigandine lined with scales made from horses' hooves? Most armigers are younger sons; perhaps their families could better afford them dead than alive. Sire Rodela's house may have been poor but it was proud. He flaunted a mail shirt, greaves, and a leather helmet strengthened with metal ribs. In some self-mock he'd fastened a lamb's tail to the helmet, saying he would wear it until he'd taken his honor out of pawn by shearing an enemy as he'd been shorn by his master.

The warriors of Lynx lined up near our vantage on the hillside, bearing orange banners. The cataphracts rested their lances upright between saddle and thigh. Each studied the man across from him in the other line. In a tourney of courtesy, it was customary for a cataphract to ride against his own kind in the charge, lance against lance, and for armiger to contend against armiger, for the honor of facing an equal in weapons and armor. In the fracas to follow there would be no such distinction.

The tourney commenced with ceremony. The First of Lynx met the First of Crux in the center of the field, and each gripped a fighting cock by its feet. The birds flapped and lunged, eager to get free, eager to do battle. A priestess of Rift rode out to them, a crone in a red robe and a hat with a great prow and cloth unfurled like sails on either side. It was her duty to shed the first blood that day, and as she sacrificed the cocks, the smell of burning feathers drifted toward us.

The warriors began to shout at each other across the field, great hoarse wordless roars, and they clattered shield upon weapon. They raised this tumult to make their own blood run hot and to chill the blood of the enemy, but it stirred me too, and I found a grin stretched upon my face, the same wolf's grin I saw on other faces.

Silence fell for a moment. The priestess nodded and the two lines of men began to move, as the warriors kicked their horses into a jarring trot that set the pennants bobbing above their heads. The horses gathered speed and the lances shuddered. The cataphracts stood in the stirrups, their weight well forward for the thrust, and when they judged they were close enough they brought their lances down and couched them on the notches in their shields. It seemed impossible they could hit any mark, let alone one so small as a visor—yet how could they miss, with the riders galloping stirrup to stirrup? I foresaw such mayhem when the lines smashed together that I covered my eyes. But then I had to look, and somehow the men rode past each other, and as they passed some struck and most missed. The lines shattered. I felt the sound as much as heard it: the crack of lances breaking came like lightning over the bone-rattling thunder of hooves, and over this rose a greater din from the warriors and spectators. They opened their throats and out came roars and bellows and shrieks, a terrible harsh music only Rift could find pleasing.

Five men were unhorsed—no, six. Their jacks ran out to help them mount. Two had fallen when their mounts collided. A horse thrashed on the ground, grievously injured.

Sire Galan galloped through the charge unscathed. He was near our end of the field when he turned Semental around. His lance had splintered, which meant he'd struck true. He threw it down and drew his sword and rode back toward the melee.

I screamed a warning, though Sire Galan couldn't hear me. He was entangled in a knot of men, only a few green banners amongst the orange ones. He went down and I lost sight of him. His horse reared up with an empty saddle. He was under all those hooves and a tonnage of man and horse and metal that no armor could withstand.

Time was in spate. There was no reckoning how long he was out of my sight. Not long, perhaps, but time enough to imagine a hundred ways a man can lose his life. I'd begrudged him a kiss and now I rued my stinginess. Suppose it was true that Hazard favored me, and because I withheld a kiss Chance turned her back on him? I'd give him all the luck in the world now, if it were not too late.

Somehow Sire Galan mounted again, though he was hemmed in on all sides and weighted down by full armor. His wooden sword began to rise and fall, and the serene silver mask of his helmet made him look as matter-of-fact as a man cutting brush on a hillside. I found myself on my feet, shouting, and I sat down and reined in my tongue.

Fleetfoot nudged and pointed, and there was Sire Pava, unhorsed, at our end of the field. His opponent watched from horseback, and when Sire Pava scrambled to his feet, he knocked him down again with a wallop from the flat of his sword. Sire Pava landed hard, the breath driven out of him. He looked helpless as a turtle flipped on its back. I jeered and Fleetfoot hooted and made the rude sign for a coward, holding up his fist and waggling his little finger like a dog's tail. We knew we were safe from Sire Pava up on the hillside. His helmet had been knocked askew, and he fumbled at its fastenings. He'd get no help from his armiger, Divine Narigon, who was brawling with the other man's armiger nearby.

I looked to Sire Galan and he was still on his horse, still tangled in that group of struggling men. They'd moved as if in one body across the field until they were hard upon the boundary, and each strove to keep his horse inside the ring of smudge pots and to push another out.

Meanwhile Sire Pava's jack, Gaunt, ran to help his master, but the cataphract of Lynx drove him off like a man herding a calf from horseback. Then the cataphract rode over to Sire Pava, where he lay on the ground, and, with nudges and twitches of the reins, he bade his great horse step daintily over him, so that the stallion's forelegs were on either side of Sire Pava's shoulders (which sight amazed us, as horses don't like men under their bellies), and Sire Pava yielded. I shouted to the horse, "Piss on him, piss on him!" and Fleetfoot and I shrieked with laughter until we were winded.

I looked back to see Sire Galan cut a man from the pack, using his stallion, a hand taller than the other man's horse, to force his opponent sideways step by step. The two men leaned toward each other, striking blows that surely must have clattered like hail on the metal of their armor, until Sire Galan drove the other warrior past the smudge pots. Spiller showed himself eager enough then—where had he been hiding when his master was down among the hooves? He should be beaten for shirking, the coward!—running up to collect the man's sword and banners for trophies. Sire Galan trotted off to take another man unawares and I was on my feet again.

Though it was a mock battle, it was a long one, long enough for spectators to stroll about arm in arm to pass the time of day; long enough for the vendors of savories to make their rounds (having no money we were obliged to feed on the smells), and a ragged Abstinent to come begging, who was pelted with coins and stones. Long enough for a rumormonger to sing a ditty he'd made up on the instant about the tourney, praising one man for the elegance and clarity of his form and ridiculing another. I recognized the men he named, but not their deeds, for they were embroidered all over with flowery titles. In the arcane language of combat—a language unknown to me—every attack and counter had its name.

No rumormonger sang of the bravest deed on the field that day. Ev was waiting down by the boundary with the other horseboys and horsemasters of the clan, ready to take a spare mount onto the field if needed. He saw what Fleetfoot and I had missed: Sire Pava's stallion was galloping crazed around the field, likely to trip on his reins and break a leg. Ev was single-minded, and the gods admired it and let him run straight to his goal, underfoot of the horses and past the swinging swords. He caught the stallion's reins and hung on, and after he'd been tossed in the air and dragged along the ground, the horse slowed and stopped, bowing his massive head. Ev was too slight to hold a warhorse with his weight; he barely reached the stallion's withers. He must have calmed him with his voice, a voice the horse had heard since the day he was foaled. (Ev spoke readily to horses; around people he was shy.) There were splinters from a broken lance caught between the stallion's flank and barding, and as he ran, the splinters had been driven deep into his side. The horsemaster, Harien, was quick as a toad's tongue to appear when the danger was over and the boasting began, but it was Ev who carried the scars away that day: two long gouges on his legs from the flints seeded everywhere in the chalky soil.

There came a time during the battle when I had been so buffeted by fear and glee and fear and exhilaration and fear again that I wished only for it to end. How is a tourney decided, when weapons are blunt and armor is strong? One man leaves the field with a broken shinbone, another because his head is ringing like a bell with an iron clapper. A cataphract who yields skulks away and takes his armiger with him. After a while even the strongest man tires of lifting a sword, whether it be of wood or steel. Little by little, man by man, the battle wears out.

Or sometimes, when the king is watching (for he likes to know the stuff and substance of his army), he'll blow his hunting horn and toss a metal cup upon the field, and the man who catches it gets to drink victory. I hadn't known the king was there until his horn sounded and the cup went glinting and tumbling through the air. The Crux caught it easily, so it must have been aimed at him; but I couldn't tell that one clan or the other had fairly won, being ignorant of the arts of Rift Warrior.

But the king is always right. When the tallies were made, the clan of Crux had more trophies and the best of the wager. Rift's priestess filled the victory cup, and when the men of our clan had drained it dry, they galloped their horses around the tourney field, riding uphill toward the spectators as if they meant to run them down, then turning at the last moment and chasing downhill again, whooping all the while. The drudges scattered before their charge, and I ran with the rest, half laughing, half terrified. The Blood stayed unmoved under their awnings. I supposed they'd seen this many times before.

Before one of those shelters, I saw Sire Galan rein in his stallion so hard he set him back on his haunches. He swung his leg over the high pommel of the saddle and jumped down lightly, as if he were not wearing three-quarters of a hundredweight of plate and mail. He took off his helmet and bowed. That maiden of Ardor was standing under the canopy, of course, and her father with her. I was too far away to see her face, but I did see Sire Galan give her a sword he'd taken from a Lynx. He bowed to her, to her father, to her again—it put me in mind of the manor dovecote, how in spring the males puff up their feathers and strut and bob while the females go on pecking.

Fleetfoot saw me looking and started to tease, "Sire Pava has bet against him also, did you know? So Sire Galan is sure to win, because everyone knows Sire Pava and Luck don't get along."

I knew what he meant; there were many in the village still in the habit of calling me by my old name. I said, "Fleetfoot, boy, if you have anything to wager—and I know you don't—I advise you to save your coin. Sire Galan presumes too much on his Luck. He may find she doesn't favor him in this." Oh, I bragged, but I was the only one cut by my wit. I wished I had the power Sire Galan claimed for me of being his luck. I'd bring him this good fortune: that the maid send him away tonight with a no that could not be mistaken for a yes even by the most handsome, amorous, cocksure pricksman in all the Marchfield.

Fleetfoot had heard of Sire Galan's little wager, which meant that any day now the rumormongers would be making up songs about it and singing them in the market. Every wagging tongue added to Sire Galan's danger. If the girl's father found out, he'd likely challenge him to a duel—though for such a dishonorable wager, Sire Galan deserved to be set upon in the dark of night by varlets with staves and given a bad drubbing. If he won his bet, it would call for a mortal fight for certain. Maybe the clan Firsts would put a stop to it before a feud could start; or maybe they'd be the last to find out, along with the girl's father, for who would want to spoil such a fine tale before it could be told?

After the horses were seen to, Sire Galan's men crowded into the tent, even the foot soldiers. Sire Galan could not stop grinning as Spiller and Sire Rodela helped remove his armor. His curls were flattened to his head and dark with sweat, and on his cheeks I saw the impress of helmet straps and rivets of the visor. His men talked all at once, asking one another if they'd seen this act of bravery or that of cowardice. The close air smelled of sweat and horse and ale and damp.

Sire Galan asked me, "Did you see I struck off a man's helmet with my lance?"

I said, "No, the charge was such a muddle. I saw your lance was broken, though."

"I broke it on his head. I took half his ear off."

Spiller spoke up. "I saw it, Sire. It's a wonder he kept his seat."

"I saw it too," said Noggin.

And Sire Rodela said, "You should have aimed lower, then you could have knocked him from his horse."

Sire Galan ignored him. "Did you see me drive a man off the field?" Again, it was me he asked.

"I did. You took his sword as a trophy," I said. "And where is it? I should like to see it."

He took off his padded red shirt and sat on the cot so Spiller and Sire Rodela could pull off his leggings. I crossed my arms and asked again, though I knew the answer well enough. "Where's the sword?"

Spiller sniggered and Sire Rodela smiled his crooked smile. The other men grew quiet.

Sire Galan stood up, naked. Iron plate stops a blade's edge, but the force of a blow will still leave its mark. There were red weals all over his body. He would soon be piebald with bruises. Yet he didn't seem to feel pain. He was drunk on the battle: his eyes shone, his voice was too loud, and his skin had a fine flush everywhere. I judged he would feel it tomorrow, when his blood stopped charging and his heart galloping.

He said to Spiller, "Fetch me my shirt and hose," and then to me, almost on the same breath, "Why, I gave it away." He smiled, but his brows were drawn together. "Did you think I'd forget my promise? I have a better trophy for you."

He found his gauntlet in the pile of armor and pulled from it a small orange bundle. I untied the knot. The cloth was a Lynx banner with a golden cat's eye embroidered as a house crest. Inside its folds lay part of a man's ear: pale, resilient, curved inward like a shell along one smooth edge, ragged and red on the other. There was mud in the hollows. I threw the banner and ear down on the bed and stepped back. The men crowded round to look at it, raising a clamor.

Sire Galan said, "I jumped down from my horse to get it. Did you see? I thought if I waited till after the tourney I'd never find it again."

"I thought I was watching a brave man," I said. "Now I see you're a madman. How could you risk so much for a bit of flesh? I was sure you'd be trampled!"

"Hazard loves madmen, then, because Chance led me right to it. I looked down and saw it gleaming on the ground, and how could I deny her anything? Besides," he said, grinning, "the flesh of an enemy is a powerful charm." He lifted his arms so his white linen shirt could be pulled on over his head.

"He's no enemy, whoever he is, unless you choose to make him so. Lynx and Crux fight for the same king, and you'd best remember it. I'll keep the banner," I told him, "but *that*—that you must return, or sacrifice to Rift, because I'll not carry it and risk a haunting if he should die and be unwillingly tied to me."

Sire Galan sat on the cot and picked up the piece of ear, flexing it between his fingers. He seemed thoughtful and a little amused. He looked up. "Well, I suppose if you don't want it, I'll give it back—tell him that though I couldn't unhorse him, I at least un-eared him!"

His men laughed and repeated the jest, each to the other as if his neighbor might not have heard.

"And what shall I do with this banner?" I asked, under their noise. "Sew it to my dress and go parti-colored like a fool?"

"No," said Sire Galan. "The only colors you will wear will be mine. Hang it before the tent. It will soon have many fellows."

The feast given by the Lynx for the victors went on almost till the Sun rose. I lay in an empty tent listening to the hubbub from the neighboring camp. I couldn't sleep for remembering. I saw again and again the warriors charging us on the hill, after the tourney. They were men I knew and yet, masked by their helmets, they were unknown to me, except for Sire Galan, who wore his own face in silver before him. And they were frightening enough.

But when we ran, we ran from the horses, not the men. The horses: sixteen hands high with hooves big as plates, and their heads masked too and these masks with horns where the forelock should be, and the sound thudding into us as they came closer, close as a thunderclap when lightning strikes your neighbor's house.

We had bleated and scattered like sheep before a pack of wolves. It frightened me more now, remembering, and thinking how it would be to see such a charge in earnest, how I could never face it. How easily they could have run us down. I wondered if I would have heard, under the hoofbeats and the screams, the breath of a blade parting air, and the thought made my back itch from nape to buttocks. This was another thing I'd failed to consider when I followed a warrior to war. Somehow I'd always imagined the face of war turned away from me.

Still awake, I slipped into a dream. In this dream I stood my ground. I roared as they charged. This furor had wanted to get free of me all day, and yet the more I let it out, the more it resounded. I roared and roared, my belly an iron kettle full of echoes.

The horses feared me. They passed on either side and left me standing.

Such a wealth of rage. How could I spend it? When I was not dreaming, anger did not serve.

Sire Galan came back before the others. He sat down next to me on the bed and leaned to give me a kiss. His breath smelled of wine and about his clothes hung an air of smoke and sweat and even a whiff of the privy. When he straightened up, he flinched. Now he was stiff and sore. Now he felt the blows he'd taken that afternoon.

I got up and put on my dress and fetched the lamp burning by the entrance. He smiled at me, as he often did, as if it made him glad to look upon me. I would not show how it weakened me, turning my bones to wax and my bowels to tallow.

I untied the laces of his surcoat. It was stiff with embroidery: glossy holly leaves on a gold field, set here and there with onyx-eyed warblers feeding on clusters of garnet berries.

"You're back early," I said. My voice was hoarse, as if I truly had been shouting. I helped him pull the surcoat over his head. I could see it pained him to raise his arms.

"I'm back late, surely."

"Are we to quibble over this? So late you're early, then, for the Sun is about to show her face. And it's clear as day you're back before the others."

He shrugged. "I grew weary of them and sought better company." He caught one of my hands, busy at the fastenings of his shirt.

Oh, I was sure he had sought better company. Sure he'd left the feast long before this to pay his court to the maiden of Ardor, though how he could do that when she slept, no doubt, cheek by jowl with attendants and kin, I couldn't imagine. I pulled my hand away.

He hadn't won his wager yet. He wasn't smug enough. Nor was he downcast. I guessed he'd seen her and taken some encouragement. I didn't want the lees in the cup, what was left of the wine after he'd gone wooing elsewhere, no matter how he smiled at me.

"I'll make you a tisane to ease the soreness," I said, "and a poultice for your bruises." I was forbidden to touch a man's blood, but where the skin wasn't broken, I could be of some help. The men's healers scoffed at these herbal consolations, claiming a grown man had no use for them. They left them to greenwomen, and many a man was grateful to have a balm for his pains. Soothing is kin to healing, whatever the carnifices say.

I busied myself with the herbs and a brazier and coals, setting water to heat. Sire Galan lay back on the bed with a slight groan, his hose unstrung and an arm over his eyes. I wished I had some dampwick such as I'd tried on Sire Pava—not that it had worked—something like it then. That I'd like to see, that would satisfy me, if he tried his ram against her walls and couldn't batter them down! He'd never breach her then, though her gate be the thickness of a hymen and she as willing as she could be. As willing as I was. As I had been.

By the time the water was hot, Sire Galan was asleep with his jaw hanging open. I was glad of it. I laid warm cloths smeared with a paste of wine, lard, and woundwort on his chest and arms, and still he lay unmoving (though perhaps his breathing grew shallower). I pulled off his hose, revealing a great bruise on his right shin—and at that he did bestir himself. First he smiled, then he uncovered his eyes, then he raised himself on one elbow and said to come lie beside him. But I'd already guessed he was awake, for his prick had stirred before him.

I told him to sit up so I could lay a poultice on his back. He feigned a groan and said, "I cannot sit unless you help me to it," and held out his hand like a child. He was grinning.

I turned my back on him and went to brew the heal-all. I could have laughed, or spat on him, or gone to him—and at the same time too, anger and desire being so compounded together. Instead I squatted by the brazier and watched crumbled leaves and shreds of willow bark color the water brown in the wake of the spoon. When I looked at him again, he was no longer smiling.

I brought over the wooden cup, saying, "This will help with your pains. Have a care, it's hot."

He was still propped on his elbow. I stood there with my hand outstretched, and he wouldn't take the cup. He said, "I think you know a better remedy than this. Or have you already eased some other man this evening, used up all your healing?"

His voice was light, as if he were amused, but I heard something else. He was vexed with me now. How quickly he became jealous, when I was the one with cause.

"Ah, no. You're the first to require any help of me. So take it," I said. "It's nothing much, but it will soothe."

"I still say you know a better remedy."

"You're cross tonight. Everything I say, you gainsay."

"Well, then, don't cross me." With that, he reached for the cup, and grasped my fingers with it. The hot tisane sloshed over my hand and I jerked away. He let the cup drop. It rolled toward my feet.

"Now you've wasted it," I said. My throat was so tight it squeezed my voice small. "It would have helped you sleep. Everyone knows sleep is the best healer."

He sat up on the cot, slowly, stiffly. I met his eyes. I expected to see him angry. But he looked at me straight; he sought me where I hid. This look was like a touch, and it sent a tremor through me. He said, "Firethorn, how can I sleep if you won't lie beside me?"

I might have lost my resolve then and gone to him but for his men returning to the tent from the feast, late but not too late. They arrived stinking, as if they had bathed in ale, stumbling, and singing an old tune with new-minted words having to do with a certain ear.

Sire Rodela was in worse case than Sire Galan, for his armor was inferior. He was bruised everywhere and had a cut on his thigh he had not tended. Spiller poured wine over the wound and tied a rag around it: I poulticed Sire Rodela's bruises (how his hair climbed his back—over his shoulders, down his nape, up from the crack of his buttocks!). He sat quietly under these ministrations, for he was drowned in drink. By then the Sun was truly up. Spiller and I went to fetch water and Sire Galan fell asleep. He slept soundly enough without me, after all.

That was the first night Sire Galan and I had not lain together since we met.

"I suppose you think you did well yesterday," said the Crux to his men as they dined at midday. "You boasted well, it's true. One would have thought you'd won a battle, not a mere tourney of courtesy. But you did not *do* well."

The cataphracts and the priests dined out of doors while the armigers served them. The drizzle had relented at last, though the wind still blew flocks of dirty clouds from west to east and teased at the cloth spread over the table. The air had a chill in it. I was sitting on the ground before Sire Galan's tent, next to Spiller, picking gristle from my teeth. Spiller had found us a mutton shank to go with our pease pottage, but the ewe must have been older than I was.

The Crux did not raise his voice. His men quieted to listen. "If the weapons had been real and unbated," he said, "Lebrel would be dead and Alcoba would be dead and his armiger with him." I could swear the cataphracts stopped chewing, they were so taken aback by his words. Sire Guasca sat with his mouth hanging open. "And Pava would be a prisoner—but he should be dead. He should have died of chagrin, for surrendering without a blow in his own defense."

Sire Erial laughed at this and the Crux rounded on him.

"As for you, Erial, if your sword was as quick as your tongue, you might have done more with it than stick a little jack who came running out to help his master. I don't believe you landed another blow yesterday. But you dodged them well, and for that I praise you."

Sire Erial flushed red and it was Sire Pava's turn to sneer. Spiller snickered and I struck him hard in the shoulder with my fist and whispered, "You've no cause to laugh. I saw you dodging about too yesterday. You were about as much use as a barren cony!" Spiller gave me a cockeyed smile, but if he thought I was just chaffing, he was mistaken. He'd proved a rank coward. I was sure I'd have done better.

The Crux went on, "Guasca acquitted himself well; the king was pleased, I know."

Sire Guasca looked up, closed his jaw, and swallowed. This little bit of praise was water to a parched man. It was said the king kept an eye on all of his bastard sons, highborn or low, and showed them preferment—if they earned it. Perhaps Sire Guasca was more promising than he looked. The king had petitioned the clan for his mother (Sire Lebrel's youngest aunt) because she was beautiful; the clan had gladly given her as a concubine in order to mingle the strength and cunning of Prey, which ran strong in the king, with the line of Crux. But Sire Guasca was lanky where his father was stocky. Nor had he inherited his mother's looks: the skin of his face was pitted and he had a great bobble in his throat that jumped when he swallowed. The other cataphracts had treated him with courtesy but no fondness; he might be well bred but he was still a bastard. I saw them reconsidering: a gangly yearling colt sometimes grows up to win all the races.

"One man unhorsed in the first charge and carried off the field with his shoulder out of joint; that was good. And another fought to a standstill and forced to yield; that was better. But, Guasca," the Crux added, "did you not see that Alcoba was down beside you, and in need of your aid? You could have saved him had you taken the trouble."

He paused too long for comfort.

"And as for Galan, it came to my ear," and here the Crux smiled, just a little, but his voice was vinegar, "that you jumped down from your horse in the midst of battle and jumped back on again, and that is the most heedless, foolhardy, rash maneuver I've seen in a long year, and I care not why you did it or how you did it. You've covered yourself with mud and mistaken it for glory. You took a man, it's true, and you took an ear—true too—and you pleased the rabble and the dames and the whores and the rumormongers, but," he lowered his voice, which had climbed higher and higher, and said through his teeth, "you did not please me." Sire Galan met his uncle's eye, but his hands fiddled with a bit of bread, pulling it to pieces. I'd never seen him look so chastened, but I did not quite believe it. By morning it had been all around the Marchfield that the man whose ear he'd taken had embraced him when it was returned. They were fast friends now. One might have thought Sire Galan had planned all along to return that errant ear to him. The gesture was applauded—except, it would seem, by his uncle.

I admit it made me smile at first to see Sire Galan scolded. I crossed my legs and tucked my skirts more tightly against the chill and had a sobering thought: he would never learn caution, not from his uncle nor anyone else. His quickness was all of a piece with his rashness. As long as he relied on one to get him out of scrapes brought on by the other, he might not live to be a more deliberate man.

Now the Crux stood and leaned on the table, jutting his chin forward. The table tilted under his weight and trenchers and cups and all slid toward him. He raised his voice again. "Am I the only man who saw beyond the point of his sword yesterday? We could ill afford to lose three men. Don't count this as a victory. I measured you against the Lynx and they were weak enough that you stood against them. Against a stronger clan you would not have prevailed. And against our enemy? I fear not one of you would live to cover your wife again if we went into battle today."

He had them in his fist. I couldn't hear so much as a drawn breath. He straightened up and crossed his arms.

"Well, we don't go to battle today, nor tomorrow, nor yet for a while, for Summons Day is a tennight away and after that we must wait upon the signs and the winds—the gods know how long—to take ship and cross the sea. We'll use the time. Now you're blooded, you have the scent. Now I'll teach you. A blade can't be honed without a stone. I'll be hard on you, hard as stone, and the harder I am, the more you'll thank me when you've taken the sharpest edge I can give you."

Then he showed his teeth in his beard and rapped his knuckles on the table. "Eat, if you have appetite. For we've a little skirmish this afternoon with Delve's clan, and I plan to mine some gold from them and a few mares. If you disgrace me less than you did yesterday, I'll be content."

Another tourney. A bruise over a bruise. They'd endure it gladly; I saw their eagerness. They laughed and stretched when he opened his fist and let them go. He was a clever man, to offer them reproof and just enough praise: oil for the whetstone. It was a game to them. They thought war would be much the same, a few more bruises and scars and better trophies.

I would not endure it gladly. It would be easier to be on the field with a reed for a sword than to sit on the hillside day upon day and watch—unless I could teach my tripes not to knot and my blood not to surge through my veins, unless I could watch Sire Galan as if he were any man.

I wouldn't go. I'd stay in the tent.

Staying in the tent was no better, staying and keeping count. Two nights had passed since he'd made his wager. The first night had been peaceful, because I'd been ignorant. The second had been sleepless, and there were two yet to come.

Suppose the maid, if she was still a maid, pleased him so much he decided to take her in keeping, pay her father the fee. If he thought he could bring another woman to the tent and still keep me as his trinket, his lucky talisman . . .

Well, if he did, was he so far wrong?

The maiden is Ardor's kin, carries Ardor's blood, and surely has Ardor's favor. I must have been mistaken, thinking the god took me in hand when I ate the firethorn berries in the Kingswood and didn't die, and then later when Sire Galan and I joined paths. I'd taken too much on myself. Always the same stiff-necked baseless pride. Why would Ardor trouble with me, a drudge of no family, no Blood?

Or if I had not been mistaken, then had the god abandoned me?

Between the pavilions of Sire Guasca and the Auspices was a little dark place, hidden from sight by a tent flap in front and, at the back, an oxcart turned on its side because of a broken axle. I crouched in this little hollow, which stank because men went behind the cart to piss, and I opened the bag of finger bones. I pulled out a few tufts of grass and smoothed the dirt with my palm, and drew the circle and the lines that divided the realms of the gods just as Az had shown me.

The last of the three readings Az had made for me was to determine which gods governed the arc of my life. Three casts and every time the bones had landed in one of Ardor's aspects. I kissed the Dame's blue-dyed finger bone and Na's red one and sat back on my haunches. I heard a man in Sire Guasca's tent say, "Where have you put the hauberk? You've mislaid it!" and the sound of a blow.

I was daring the god. This was arrogance. Still, I would ask only once, cast only once, and if the two little bones did not land in Ardor's domain, I would know I was not under the god's hand—perhaps had never been. I closed my eyes and threw, and when I opened them I saw that Na's bone had landed in Ardor's avatar of the Smith and the Dame's in Wildfire. Whatever other gods were dicing with us, Ardor still claimed me.

Only a fool expects gladness from a god, or gifts without price, or reasons. And this turned out to be the worst thing of all, worse than being mistaken, worse than being abandoned: I was still of some small use to the god, though I could see no purpose in any of it.

I went to the tourney, of course. There was a long wait once we got to the field, for two other clans were skirmishing there already. The Crux had ordered a canopy put up for the clan, and I sat nearby with the foot soldiers and drudges. But the shelter was empty; all the Blood, cataphracts and armigers, were milling down by the field on horseback.

I grew bored and looked at the sky: more low clouds dragging fat bellies from over the sea, like the day before and the day before. At least it wasn't raining. Gray and white seabirds wheeled overhead, joined by a few crows. The sea was to my left, out of sight. Since we'd come here my sense of direction had been rearranged. The sea was a presence, a great gulf of air and wind and water, and I could feel it even when it wasn't visible beyond the hills or the tents of the Marchfield.

I looked at the combat again and realized it was the clan of Prey on the field, the king's own clan, and that the men they fought bore the crimson and white colors of the queenmother. There were twice as many men fighting as in the tourney yesterday.

I looked at the crowd: it was like a festival day. A good many farmers had come with kith and kin, all of them idling on the hills, having found something better to do than the chores that waited at their crofts; they mingled with soldiers and drudges of the Marchfield and the peddlers and whores come to sell them something. The drabs who worked the tourneys were called two-copper whores, after their price. They didn't even have a blanket to call their own, for they didn't lie down, only bent over. It was the cheapest jounce a man could get, unless he got it for free.

I told Fleetfoot I wished to walk all around the field to see the sights and asked if he'd come, but he was spellbound by the tourney. I took Noggin with me, thinking it was for the best. I meant to look for a certain maiden of Ardor, who'd troubled my thoughts day and night of late, and Fleetfoot was no simpleton like Noggin, he'd guess what I was about.

Along the way it seemed that every foot soldier, jack, bagboy, horseboy, or drudge-of-all-work that I passed yapped or clucked at me, jeered or whistled, called me skinsheath or whore, honeypot or little fish, or some other lewd byname. One varlet followed for a while, saying he'd tan the leather of my sheath for me, and suggesting various ways he could do it, some of which were surely impossible, and others bringing Sire Galan too much to mind, so that I blushed even as I pretended indifference. I heard such nonsense whenever I walked with Spiller or Noggin as an escort, or even with both of them at once, but I couldn't get used to it. Men kept quiet only when I was by Sire Galan's side. At first I thought they were mocking me, for I was no beauty to win praises, foul, or otherwise. Soon I saw it was the dish they ladled out to any mudwoman, whether she wore a striped skirt or not, unless she had white hairs enough to prove a grandmother. But Mai had told me, and it was true, that as long as I had a man on my arm they'd keep their hands off. So I took Noggin's arm, I looked straight ahead or at my feet, never meeting a man's eye, for that was dangerous. And I told myself I had armor enough to keep words from wounding.

I walked with Noggin around the field, down one hill, across a rain-sodden bog, up the next hill toward a certain awning hung with the rose pennants of Ardor. Noggin said, "Why do you walk so fast?" and then, catching sight of a man selling fried bread, "I'm hungry." I told Noggin it was no use whining, and he had best bid his hunger go to sleep or find his master and beg from him. I had no coin for buying bread.

"Buy it with a kiss," the peddler said.

"Very well," I said, shoving Noggin toward him. "Kiss him then, if you like his looks so much."

It raised a laugh. We marched on around the field.

"I'm thirsty," Noggin said, and said it again until I heard him.

My mood was fouler than the weather. I couldn't abide having him there with me but dared not go on alone. "Muttonhead!" I said. "Next time carry the waterskin as Spiller bid you. Will you remember?" But what was the use of being angry with such a lackwit? I wondered why Sire Galan had brought him, for he made a poor bagboy. Perhaps it was enough that he knew how to goad a mule with sticks and kicks and curses.

We found rainwater pooled in a hollow on the top of a long stone ridge that cut through the sod. We found food, the bland, crunchy roots of bogbeauty, down by one of the seeps between the hills.

And we found Mai. There she was, no mistaking her. Even sitting on the ground, she was a mountain of a woman. One of her swollen, mole-speckled, blue-veined breasts was bare. A boy of about two years of age with a shock of black hair sucked at the nipple while his hands teased at the fringe of her headcloth and his toes waggled. He was clad in a linen shift too short to cover his dangle.

Though Mai was a mudwoman, a sheath like me, she'd contrived to put a roof over her head, a little lean-to pitched right next to the painted leather awning of Delve. I hadn't marked her clan that night behind the tents, when she'd saved me from the pack of unmannerly curs. Now I saw by the banners it was the very clan the Crux had challenged to a tourney that afternoon. She shared her shelter with a girl of ten or eleven years and a wheezing piebald hound. Three men sat cross-legged beside it, watching the tourney; two of them I recognized. I could not forget those faces. But Mai was there, and therefore nothing to fear.

I stopped in front of her, admiring her audacity. Just to see her raised my spirits.

She looked up and grinned. "If it isn't the country cousin!" she said. "And arrayed in a fine new headcloth and slippers, I see—and a beautiful bruise too."

I put my hand over my cheek. I'd forgotten the bruise Sire Galan had given me until she mentioned it; it must be yellow by now. I said, "The one paid for the others."

"Then you were cheated, girl," she said. "The slippers will wear out sooner than the bruise, over stony ground like this."

I flushed and looked down, sorry I'd tried to make a jest of it. She must think poorly of me already, after the way we'd met. Now I'd made matters worse.

Mai laughed and pushed the dog away. He got up sullenly and left the lean-to, turned round three times, and lay down with his head on her feet. "No harm meant," she said, patting the ground next to her. "Sit here and we'll have a gossip. Who is this handsome fellow with you? Is he the one so generous with gifts?"

I knew from the mockery in her voice that she didn't believe it; still, I was indignant. "Oh, never! This is Sire Galan's bagboy, Noggin."

Noggin smiled at her in his daft way. Mai said, "Well, bagboy, go and see if Cram over there will give you a sip of his ale." To me she said, "I see you've found an escort."

I squeezed in beside her and whispered, "He's a simpleton, you know."

She laughed. "So much the better! Put a ring in his nose and even an ox looks enough of a bull to keep trouble away."

The girl sitting on the other side of Mai leaned forward to get a look at me, peeping through the stringy locks of her hair. When I smiled at her, she ventured a little smile of her own. She was as slim as Mai was stout, thin enough to slip between two gap teeth.

"That's third-daughter, that's Sunup," Mai said, "and this is my littlest, Tobe." She jiggled the boy on her knee until his mouth slipped off the nipple and he began to cry. She bared the other breast and he was content again. "I need to wean him soon, but he makes such a fuss."

"How many altogether?" I asked.

"Nine alive, but just the one boy," she said. "I only brought two with me, Tobe because he's my baby and Sunup to look after him. The rest are home with first-daughter."

"Blessings on them," I murmured.

Mai was the sheath of a cataphract, Sire Torosus. He'd been born landless and luckless, fifth son of a wastrel; now he had a stone keep, rich fields, and six villages in the eastern river valley that had seen as many battles as harvests. What he had was hard-won in bloody service to his clan and the king in every war that had come along for the past twenty years. He'd married well, within the clan, but his wife was of the opinion that she had married poorly. No matter how he pleased his lords, he never could please his dame.

When he wasn't campaigning he lived with his wife and their four sons in the keep, while Mai lived below in the village with her children. Mai had followed him to war for fifteen years, but always before in summertime. This was the first winter campaign, and Sire Torosus didn't approve of it, nor of Queenmother Caelum, who had somehow talked her brother, our king, into this unseasonable venture.

Mai said, "Sire Torosus says this war is what comes of letting a woman rule. She was regent, you know, for eight years before Prince Corvus came of age. But she's ruled longer than that, if what they say is true. While King Voltur had the kingdom of Incus in his fist, she led *him* by the dangle. She couldn't keep the same grip on her son."

"I heard the prince's wife had bewitched him, and that's why Queenmother Caelum must war against him."

Mai grinned. "Well, that's the tale they tell. But his wife is with child now after years of lying fallow. Once the queenmother was sent away, the girl quickened fast." Mai tapped my knee and leaned closer. "So which one do you suppose is the cannywoman? Not the one who was cursed with barrenness. Now Caelum doesn't want the girl to have time to bear the prince's child. That's why she's in such haste, why she sews with a red-hot needle and a flaming thread. King Thyrse has summoned a small army, so she must be counting on half the Blood of Incus rising up with her. They'll not be so quick to follow if the prince has sired an heir."

I gaped at Mai. "You call this a small army?"

She laughed at me. "If the king had need, he could call on ten times as many cataphracts, and better ones too. That's why I told Sire Torosus to stay home. This winter campaign is a fool's errand, I said, so leave it to young fools who don't know any better. We may end up stranded on the wrong side of the Inward Sea with no provisions and no ships to take us home. And suppose we win—you can be sure the queenmother will begrudge us plunder and lands for fear her own people will turn on her. But Sire Torosus says the king must have his reasons, and we'll find out soon enough—and maybe it's the queenmother who's a fool, for letting a man so far into her plans."

It was remarkable to me that Mai gossiped about kings and queens as if they were neighbors in the next croft, and was as quick to find fault. Their doings had seemed far above me, the stuff of ballads, not gossip; but here in the Marchfield, those were one and the same.

Mai sighed. "Sire Torosus says he will go, as he's needed, and anyway he'd just as soon be as far from his dame as he can get. As for me, I'd rather be snug in my croft with that bitch looking down her long upper lip at me than on the road in the winter. But the man won't let me stay home. Says he needs a feather bed for his old bones." She slapped her leg and made the flesh wobble.

I could see how a man might find her soft to lie upon. Her thigh was the size of both of mine.

We were silent for a moment. The baby suckled and Sunup scratched the hound's back until his tail thumped. There was a certain smell of milk and damp dog under the awning, which gave me comfort. The girl peered at me again and smiled.

"She's a rank vixen," Mai said.

"Who is?"

"That Caelum. She should let him win. This is unseemly, to defeat the king before all his clans."

I'd given the tourney barely a glance in my circuit around the field. Now I saw that there were less than two hands of fighters left, and most wore the queenmother's colors. One of the king's men toppled off his horse and lay still as the dead.

I sat up straight, staring at the field. "Is the king down there?"

"Of course he is—there in the gilded armor."

His wooden sword was also leafed with gold, but in the dull light it shone without glittering. He was flanked by two of his clan, the only men of his left on the field. Together they battled twice as many of the queen's party. He lost one man but she lost two. Then his last cataphract fell, taking another with him. King Thyrse fought on alone. A thrust, and one man slumped over his saddle. The king clubbed another to the ground with the weighted hilt of his sword. He ducked, came up on the last man from below, and dispatched him too. Then he was alone on the field, and the sound from the crowd filled the bowl in the hills to overflowing.

I cheered too, but Mai said, "She left it too late. So he'd know she gave it to him."

"But he fought well," I said.

"No one fights that well. Look, here she comes."

Queenmother Caelum rode out on the field to meet the king. Her horse was pure white, caparisoned in unmarked white leather. She wore a crimson gown. Yards of velvet spread over the horse's flanks and trailed to the ground. Her face, in all this crimson, looked pale as a blanched almond. She surrendered a sword, bowing deeply, and the king leaned from his horse to give her the kiss of peace.

The crowd roared, stamped, whistled.

Mai's boy had fallen asleep, oblivious to the noise. She settled him in the valley between her thighs and leaned back on her elbows with a groan. "This one coming is a boy for sure," she said. "He's riding high and he kicks like a hare, right under my heart."

That burden she carried in her great belly was not all fat. I must have been blind not to see it before.

"Every campaign, another baby. I lost the last one bearing it, and so much blood I thought I'd never get up again. I'm afraid this time will be worse, with winter coming and midwives scarce."

"Then why did you quicken again?"

Mai snorted and looked at me in disbelief. She poked her right thumb through the hole in her left fist. "I thought even country girls knew about that. Didn't you watch the bulls and cows go at it?"

"Of course I know how it's done," I said, "but why didn't you take childbane?"

Mai gripped my arm and whispered, "If you know something that stops a baby being planted, you'll be the most sought-after woman in the Marchfield. I thought I'd tried everything—I weaned my children late, I prayed, I put bungs in my bunghole—I did everything but keep the man from my bed, and that I'm unwilling to do! Once I drank a decoction a miscarrier gave me to get rid of a baby when I was three months along. It nearly killed me, but *she* lived." She nodded her head toward Sunup, who was listening to every word. "I guess I'm good fat soil," she added with a coarse laugh. "Plow me and the seed will come up every year. I never go fallow."

I said, "I thought everyone had heard of childbane. All the women where I come from use it if they don't wish to bear. I have some here." I took a leather packet from my belt and unfolded it to show her the gray powder. "I ground the berries so I could put a pinch in my wake-me-up in the morning. It hides the bitter taste. But you can eat them whole."

"How much do you have?"

"Enough for me. Enough for a while."

"Can you get more?"

Mai spoke in a whisper again, so I lowered my voice to match. "Maybe. I haven't seen it around here. It likes wet feet, so there might be some in these little bogs or in the marshes down by the river—I can't believe you don't know of this! Haven't you seen those little white berries with the black eyes? Squirrels won't eat them, nor bears. They cling to the shrub till the next year's leaves come. But they're not so potent after a few months, and you have to take more."

Mai said, "Find some for me. I know plenty who'll pay dear for it. And then you shall be able to buy your own shoes, and with better coin than bruises."

I told Mai I would look out for it, and furthermore that she should send for me when her time came; I was not a midwife, but I'd helped at childbirth and I knew an herb that would slow the bleeding and more than a few for pain. Then I told her I should be going. Our clans were forming their battle lines and I ought to be back with my own people.

"Or what?" she said. "Catch another bruise?"

I shook my head.

"Is it his habit to hit you?"

I said, "No, just the once. That night I met you—because I was off alone and he went looking for me."

"Hmm," said Mai, as if she didn't entirely believe me.

What a mooncalf I was, springing to Sire Galan's defense when he'd dealt me a blow far worse than a slap on the cheek. Her shrewdness—her kindness—touched where I was most sore. Tears began to fall, hot and shameful. I rubbed my face with my skirt, not wanting to sully my new headcloth. Before long my story spilled out too, all about Sire Galan and his wager.

Mai let me talk until I was out of words before she said, "Some would have sold your tale to a rumormonger before you'd finished the telling. I won't—but you're too trusting by far. I hope you haven't come to me for wisdom. I'm more cunning than wise. I know what the wise would say: don't be greedy. What you have is enough and more than you deserve."

I looked at her, stricken.

She grinned back. "Didn't I say I *wasn't* wise? I know a few things, though, and some to the purpose. I know a hexwoman. She sells curses at tourneys—you know, those little men made of lead that you name after some fighter you're wagering against and throw into the fire. But I heard she had something more potent in her cat-skin bag—something like invisible wasps that sting your enemies and make them ill. She could send a curse to take the bloom off the maid."

I made the ward sign. "Never. I don't hold with ill wishing. It's a foul thing—and besides, it comes back to you, they say."

Mai shrugged. "Some say. Well, there is something else—but a curse would be cheaper."

She said I should not try to stop Sire Galan from his course. He was bent on it, had staked more than a horse, more than his life on it—had staked his pride. He'd have the girl if she could be had, without reckoning the consequences. What I could do was to make sure that Sire Galan, whether he won the wager or lost it, would cleave to me and take no other (or if he did, not for long, she said). And she told me how I could bind him, what to do and when to do it.

Before I left Mai passed me a waterskin. "Wash your face, if you must go. You don't want the clods to know you've been crying, do you? It's plain as the dirt on your cheeks."

She was there under a canopy, that maid of Ardor. She sat on a little stool of wood and leather with her skirts spread about her. The gown was of a fine iridescent silk—rose if you looked at it one way, blue another—that I'd only seen pictured in tapestries before. She was not quite as beautiful as I remembered: face as pale, yes, but aided by a little starchroot, which failed to hide the smudges under her eyes. Though she watched the warriors line up on the field below, her thoughts seemed far away. She yawned and lifted a hand over her mouth. There were rings on every finger, even the thumb. Weren't those jewels sufficient to buy her a husband? The neck of her bodice was cut low and bordered in ermine. The thin gauze of her underdress made a pretense of covering what her gown revealed. Egret plumes were braided into her hair. The sea wind ruffled the plumes, lifted locks of her hair, and set the banners flapping above the canvas roof. I didn't see her father, but there were other men of Ardor's Blood standing under the shelter, and jacks and foot soldiers on guard around it.

The maid leaned toward a dame sitting next to her whose garments were severe in comparison: an unmarried aunt, perhaps, kept like a farmyard dog to guard the hen coop. She said something and the woman nodded and beckoned one of the jacks to her.

She sent the jack over to us. He pushed Noggin and put a boot to his backside, saying, "Get, get, get!" as if he were chasing a goat out of a garden. Noggin squawked and dodged out of his way. The jack took a little more trouble with me. He unslung his baldric and struck me across the back with his leather scabbard—the sword still sheathed in it—saying, "And you! Keep your eyes off your betters. Mend your manners or your skull will need mending."

I spat on the ground and he cuffed my ear.

She never turned our way.

I didn't presume to think the maiden had recognized me from the meeting in the marketplace, when I'd stood behind Sire Galan stealing glances at her while she stole glances at him. She had us chased away because we marred her view. We should not be allowed to occupy even the corner of her eye. Whereas I'd set out to fill my eyes with her, maybe in hopes she would prove older and uglier than I remembered. Now I knew she was fair. "Scratch an itch and catch a fever," Na used to say when I was too curious for my own good.

Before I saw the maid again, I had pitied her. She was stalked from a blind and didn't know she was hunted for a foul wager. She was young and slight and I didn't see how she would bear up under a woman's sorrows, for she was bound to suffer—as I was suffering now—if Sire Galan hit his mark and stopped courting as quick as he'd started. I'd even had a little notion, which I'd kept in the back of my mind because it did not bear a closer look, that I might go to her on the sly and warn her about the wager. I'd fancied her grateful and Sire Galan the loser and no one else the wiser. But I quailed fast enough when I saw her in her finery with her guards about her. No warning would be welcome if it came from the likes of me.

To be sure she was well guarded—from the likes of me. Her jack had hit me just hard enough for show, but I smarted all the same.

And then I thought: even if she knew of the wager, she might still let Sire Galan come courting. She was gambling too, staking her reputation against his hard heart that a smooth brow and round cheeks and all the rest of her beauty, what I could see and what was hidden, would tangle him in such a net he could not escape. Who was quarry here, after all?

I had not hated her before this.

Whore. What was she but a high-priced harlot, and her father a pander?

It was just shy of dishonorable for a woman of the Blood to contract as a concubine if she did not have the dowry to get a husband. But such arrangements should be made quietly, not flaunted like this, paraded about the Marchfield. Her offspring would be bastards; they would carry her name, not her mate's, and if they inherited anything, it would be at their father's whim. But they could claim God's Blood; they'd be part of a clan. Unlike any children of mine.

Mai had told me how to bind Sire Galan, but it was not until that moment that I made up my mind to do it. The Dame had always scoffed at such arts. But she never had need of love charms, and I did.

There was no feast that night and no boasting. The clan had lost the tourney and captured but a single sword. The Crux was strangely full of gaiety, as if he did not care, or worse, was glad of it. He taunted his men, saying he'd expected no more from a herd of geldings.

Sire Galan had been unhorsed in the first charge and forced to yield; in the tent he was tight-lipped and grim. Divine Xyster, the priest of Crux Moon who served as the men's carnifex, pronounced one rib broken and nothing to be done but bleeding and binding. The priest left after drawing a bowlful of blood with a cut quill. I poulticed Sire Galan's bruises, both new and old, and Spiller wrapped him tightly round the ribs in a long sheet of coarse linen.

I was as glad as the Crux seemed to be, but didn't show it. That Sire Galan had lost was good: surely the maiden would scorn him now. That he was injured was better: perhaps he would not go roaming that night.

But he called for his best surcoat; he strapped on his sword. He left the tent, taking Sire Rodela and Spiller with him as if he expected trouble might lie in wait on his path. And he didn't return till sunrise.

The binding charm Mai had taught me would have to wait till dark-of-the-Moon, when Crux Moon is somnolent and lazy. When he is full he's apt to turn spells and wishes topsy-turvy. But I was already preparing. I'd plucked three hairs from Sire Galan when I cleaned off the sticky poultice: one hair from his head, one from over his heart, and one from his groin. He'd yelped and cursed me for clumsiness, but I'm sure he suspected nothing. I'd saved the hollow quill the carnifex used to take his blood. Mai said these things, along with a few strands of my own hair, thread spun of lamb's wool, and a womandrake root, would be sufficient to plait a strong binding.

I knew well enough what the womandrake looked like and the kind of place it liked to grow. We named it bryony and used it several ways in season: the spring shoots for eating, the fall berries for a weak dye, the stinking fleshy root to cure gravel in the piss. When the root is forked, as it sometimes is, it's called womandrake because it resembles nothing so much as a naked waist and thighs, dirty yellow in color and wrinkled as if with folds of fat. I thought I might find it in the bottomlands by the river, if I could get there. Its vines had grown rampant by the river near the Dame's manor, sending out tendrils to strangle shrubs and saplings.

That night and the next were long. Of the day that passed between them there's little to tell. I waited upon the outcome of the wager. There was nothing to do but wait, until it occurred to me that it could do no harm to pray. I asked Sire Galan's leave to go to the public shrines that flanked the king's hall. I told Sire Galan I'd pray for him; if he was surprised by my piety, he showed no sign of it. Perhaps he thought my prayers were his due.

Each of the twelve gods had a shrine marked by a small standing stone set under the wide eaves of the circular hall. Before this stone another was laid flat for an altar. Each altar, tended by priests of the god's clan, held a brazier and bowl for sacrifices and carved images of the avatars. I visited them in turn and made obeisance, but at the shrines of Ardor, Hazard, and Crux I offered such sacrifices as I could afford, burning locks of my hair to ash and pricking my arm with thorns to let a few drops of blood fall into the bowl. It seemed to me that these three gods held sway over the wager and its outcome, and further, that they were at odds with one another and we were caught up in their rivalry. There could be no way to propitiate them all, if that were true. Still, I tried, and with my paltry offerings and poorer prayers, I asked for their favor, though all I truly desired of them was that we should be left out of their quarrels. I also sacrificed to Wend Weaver, for the Dame's sake, though I no longer felt her hand on the threads.

If the Blood need an oracle, they go to the priests. Drudges must rely on filthy god-bothered revelators who squat on their heels in the marketplace, killing songbirds or lizards and reading their entrails for a fine fee. Any man trying to catch his wife with a pricksman can scratch the itch of his suspicions there, and any maid can learn whether her swain-yet-to-be is dark or fair and what manner of clothes he wears, so she can recognize her good fortune when he walks by.

I stayed away. I had questions enough, but no trust in the answers and no coin to buy them. I tried the bones again, but they didn't speak to me; or if they spoke, I didn't know how to listen.

On the fourth and last night of the wager, I could not bear to stay in the tent with the stench of men and mildewed heather. I wrapped myself in my cloak and lay down before the door flap. Light rain fell on and off and low mists drifted over the ground, mixed with the smoke of banked fires. The air smelled of the sea and the turning of the year.

I kept thinking of what the Crux had said, how I was nothing but a bit of mud that Sire Galan could scrape from his boot any time he wished. I thought also of how the maid had looked in her ermine and her egret plumes. I slept a little, but it was no better than waking, for my dreams were addled and disquieting.

Sire Galan returned an hour or two before dawn, accompanied by Sire Rodela. He asked why I slept in front of the tent and I told him it was warmer outside since the bed had lately grown cold.

Sire Rodela gave me a look that spoke clearly, a smirking half smile that showed how he looked forward to my comeuppance. He stared at me long and boldly even after the lamp was lit in the tent. I could see he thought his master was ready to cast me off and that I would fall into his grip as a matter of course, like some hand-me-down mail shirt.

Spiller was awakened with a kick. He ministered to Sire Galan, unwinding the cloth from around his chest; his whole right side had gone livid with a plum-colored bruise over his cracked rib. Sire Galan sucked in his breath while Spiller rubbed on a salve he'd gotten from the priest. It smelled like horse liniment. Spiller wrapped him again, pulling the bandage as tight as he could.

The tent was quiet. Sire Galan said nothing much, his jaw being clamped against the pain. Sire Rodela told Spiller to fetch this and fetch that and scurry for it, you clod! and other orders so that the jack, brimming with questions, didn't dare spill any. And I kept my peace, if you can call it peace. I felt such a pain in my chest, such a shortness of wind, it was as if my own rib had broken. I could read the signs clear enough. Even if Sire Rodela had not smirked so, I would have known Sire Galan had won his wager by the disarrayed laces of his hose and by the very smell of another woman that rose from him when Spiller pulled off his clothes, a cloying scent of rose attar and lavender and also, I swear, the musk of her quim.

Sire Galan lay down on the cot like an old man, with a grimace and a groan and a sigh. It might have been a sigh of satisfaction. I took it for one.

I snuffed out the lamp and lay down beside him, thinking he'd leave me alone that night, bruised and sore as he was—and spent, no doubt, after his many exertions. He rested his head on my shoulder, as he often did, and his leg and arm lay across me and his breathing slowed. I thought he slept. His arm weighed heavily and I pushed it off. He put his hand on me again, on my belly and farther down. I could feel his prick against my thigh. I turned away, saying, "You should rest."

He pulled me toward him and said, "It's not rest I want."

When he hoisted himself over me, I saw him wince. I turned my face to the side and his shoulder pressed into my cheek. His flesh, his bone, the cords of his neck were wood, polished with sweat. If he was wood, he was a flail, and I was grain on the threshing floor.

I was a thousand grains, my thoughts flown like chaff. All that was left was the taste of salt.

After daybreak Sire Galan sent Spiller for Sire Alcoba's jack, Rowney. "And tell him to bring his belongings," he called after, as Spiller hurried off with a grin about to split his face in two.

By the gods, they were smug, every man of Sire Galan's and the man himself, smug as cats. They went about their duties of the morning full of cheer and louder than usual. They had a new trophy to boast about and a new man to serve as the target of their jests, though they aimed old taunts at him, having no wit to think of new ones.

Sire Galan left the tent. I pulled the blanket up over my head and saw no reason to stir, ever. Someone sat down at the end of the bed. "Don't you want to know how it was done?" he said.

It was Sire Rodela. I uncovered my face and reached for my shift, but he was sitting on it. Noggin dozed on his pallet in the corner, so we were not alone; I was not much reassured by the sight. I tugged at the dress. Sire Rodela grinned instead of moving.

"I marvel at him," he said. "I admire my cousin's stamina, though I fault his taste. He spends himself on high and low, makes one woman moan and the other whimper, and all in the same night. Any man with bollocks might do that, I suppose—but not with a broken rib. That makes him something of a wonder."

"Your manners have grown worse," I said. "Perhaps you need another trimming."

In truth, the coarse brown hair that started below Sire Rodela's bald crown was more close-cropped now than after Sire Galan had shorn him, because he'd gone to a real barber in the marketplace to even out the patches. He'd made up for this lack of hair by growing a heavy beard that covered his cheeks and throat, shaving just enough to show the clan tattoos on his cheekbones.

He said, "I don't know why he wants to wallow with a sow like you, when he can find better so easily."

"And you never *shall* know!" I said, and I pushed him off the cot with my foot while I yanked my dress out from under him.

He stood and looked down at me and started to talk. I pulled my dress on under the covers and stood up, the bed between us. I wrapped my headcloth, pulling and knotting and tucking it tightly: I'd done it countless times without a thought, but never so clumsily.

He was saying the girl had been willing enough after the first tourney when she'd had another look at Sire Galan. The puzzle was how to do it, with her aunt on the pallet next to her and her handmaid on the other side and her father and a dozen men stretched out and snoring in the tent. During the day was no better. She was always under someone's eye.

So she feigned the squirts, which had her running to the privy tent all night. You know the privy tents?

I knew. Women of the Blood too delicate to use a chamber pot in a tentful of men or to squat over a ditch with their skirts hitched up would visit their own small tents, pitched for the purpose near the sea and away from the common dungheaps.

Back and forth she ran to the tent all night. First the aunt and handmaid went with her, and three men. By the fourth time the aunt was too tired, so just the handmaid went with the men. The fifth time there were only two men. The sixth time, past the middle of the night, only one—and the handmaid, of course, who'd do as she was told. The maiden stayed long in the privy and her guard dozed off, and Sire Galan started whispering to her from behind the tent.

I fumbled for my brogans. The cobbler had brought them the day before, and they fit me well, much better than the slippers. One lace had a knot I couldn't untangle.

Well, in the day she was much recovered, but by nightfall she felt the flux coming on again. The same thing happened except this time Sire Galan slipped inside the tent toward morning, still whispering, and he dandled her on his knee until she grew faint from the stench and fevered from the kisses, and he promised he'd come back.

"And last night," Sire Rodela went on, "he cured her!" I heard him laugh as I ran from the tent.

CHAPTER 5

The Binding

ow can a drudge be humbled? We should start humble; we can go no lower than to be what we are. But I was cursed with pride I should not have owned. I had misjudged twice, thinking the favor of one of the Blood had raised me up: first the Dame, then Sire Galan. I had step by step walked into this snare; I couldn't gnaw off my foot as badgers are said to do in order to get free of it.

Mai had warned me that the binding spell she gave me could not be undone, and furthermore it had a price: the tighter I bound Sire Galan to me, the more I myself would be bound. "If I knew a way to tie one without the other, I'd have more coffers of gold than the king. There are those who claim it can be done—but never believe it," she said. "That's not the way of things."

Now I understood her. I'd have given my right foot if he felt everything and I felt nothing, if I could snare him and set myself free.

Only three days till dark-of-the-Moon and I waned as the Moon did. Sire Galan never mentioned the maiden or the wager in my hearing. We were skin to skin in the bed and he gave off heat like a brazier, as always, but I stayed cold. I lay under him while he used me according to his mood: one night urgent and unsparing and the next coaxing, tender, breathing endearments into my ear, such as *my heart* and *my flame*. No doubt he'd said as much to the maid; his words were worthless coins, to be scattered anywhere. I minded his lies, but more I minded his lying kisses, how he could seem so fond and be so false.

I slept poorly, but hated to rise. By day I was sluggish and stinting of words. I was worn out from thinking the same few meager thoughts. One led to another, another, then back to the first, no room for anything else. Of these thoughts the only bright one was the binding Mai had taught me. If

I couldn't get free, I'd make sure Sire Galan was caught with me. Despite Mai's warning I bound my hopes to this, hour by hour. Yet I feared dark-of-the-Moon would pass and I'd have no chance to plait the charm. In another month it might well be too late.

Flykiller said Sire Galan's horses would be catching glanders soon if something wasn't done. He lived next to the corral in a thatched lean-to with other horsemasters and horseboys, and kept one eye on the horses even as he slept. The mounts of the troop were crowded at night into a field the size of the Dame's kitchen garden, mules and nags mingling with warhorses. There had been many battles in the corral (and wagers on them) until Semental had won the title of First among the horses, a title he maintained against all challengers with nips and nudges and an occasional fierce charge. The warhorses, better treated than the others, had a ration of grain and daily exercise, but the crowding made them cross or listless according to their natures. Only a goat could live on what was left inside the fence: prickly furze, saw grass, and nettles. The pale soil underfoot was fetlock deep in mud after all the rain. Flykiller asked Sire Galan's leave to take his horses to the river to cut green fodder, a ride that would take the better part of a day there and back.

Sire Galan's rib was healing well; it hardly troubled him at all. A ride to the river was such a fine idea, he thought, that he'd come along and do a little hunting if the Crux would give him leave. And if he came his new friend must come—Sire Erizo dam Morada by Erne of Lynx, the same man whose ear he had partly removed—for he'd married into the clan of Carnal and had hunting privileges in their lands by the river. And if they hunted, they must try for boar, for it was the season when boars grow fat on beech mast and acorns. Sire Alcoba said he'd come too; he never could resist a hunt, however much it pained him to see Sire Galan ride on the gray stallion he'd lost to him in the wager. If Sire Alcoba was coming, Sire Erizo thought he might also bring his cousin, Sire Caulicle. And of course each man must have his armiger and jack, his horsemaster and horseboy and spare mounts.

And if Sire Galan took all his men, then I would go too. I didn't ask his leave. Sire Galan's horseboy, Uly, saddled Thole, and I tied my rolled-up cloak to the cantle, and I was ready.

By then the morning was nearly gone. We set out with eighteen men on horseback, Dogmaster and a pack of manhounds (also in need of exercise), twenty mounts on leads, and me on the mare. We took the south road out of the Marchfield, and the whores in the market called out to us with lewd words and gestures to bring them fresh meat.

Past the second hill south of the encampment, we came upon the king's works and had to ride out of our way around them. King Thyrse had ordered a road built to bring his army from the Marchfield to the sea. Quarrymen had cut away the cliff in giant steps down to the beach; now drudges were using pounded rubble and mud to smooth them into a great ramp. The gap in the cliff had been spanned with a gate of wood and iron guarded by two towers. Great wharves were moored out to sea. When the army moved, the wharves would form a roadway to the boats in the harbor.

We paused on the crest of the hill to watch the men toiling below us, breaking up rocks and moving them with barrows and sledges and ox teams. Most of the workers were foot soldiers; each clan sent a score of drudges to serve the king three days out of every tennight. The men grumbled, saying if the work didn't kill them the rock slides would.

I'd heard the talk, but it was only when I saw the great scar of muck and rubble that I understood that a mountain could be moved at a king's command. Sire Galan and the others looked upon this sight with satisfaction. Progress so swift meant that war was coming apace.

Past the king's works, the south road ran along the edge of the cliff. The cataphracts ignored the narrow track and rode abreast, talking of hunting; I heard Sire Galan say he missed his peregrine falcon more than anything—more, even, than his cook. Next time he wouldn't fail to bring both of them, the one to hunt and the other to prepare the game. Sire Alcoba asked if he didn't miss his wife; I couldn't hear the answer for the laughter.

All afternoon the Sun followed us on her slow drift toward the pewter-gray sea. Behind the constant mists, she looked more like the pale disk of the Moon. The shingle at the foot of the cliff was covered with streamers of black sea hay and drifts of shells. Tall rock sentinels stood in the breaking waves; tufts of pale grass grew from their summits like hair. Gulls stalked up and down or rode the swells past the foam. I saw one dive headfirst from the air, disappear into the sea, and come flying out with an eel twisting in its beak.

I remembered how happy I'd been on the road to the Marchfield—quite forgetting the troubles and pains we met on the way—and thought I should never be that glad again. But sorrow is tedious and even anger palls in time. When Sire Galan turned in his saddle and looked for me twice or thrice, as he used to do, I answered his smiles with my own.

It was good to leave the stink of the Marchfield, good to be on Thole's back again. She'd lost her chestnut gloss and her winter coat was coming in dull and patchy. I promised her I'd try to take her out of the corral more often. The confinement didn't agree with either of us. She snuffed the air as we went along, and reached for any patch of green. The trampled heather smelled sweet.

We reached the river before dusk and made our camp near a stretch of pebbled shore where shallow-drafted riverboats beached to unload their cargoes. The nearest ford was five leagues upstream; this close to the sea, the river was both wide and deep. It looked placid, but out beyond the swamp rush and the drifts of yellowing duckwort, swift currents moved under the surface. There was no one in sight save for a man fishing from a coracle midstream. When we hallooed to him, he paddled off and disappeared into the brush on the other bank.

It cheered me to see trees again, after looking so long at the barren hills around the Marchfield. Here were alders clinging to the riverbank, willows trailing tattered leaves in the water, dark stands of cedar, and thickets of red-twigged osier. We'd even left behind the foul weather of the heath. The Sun dropped her veils and sent a ruddy light slanting through the branches and across the brown water, kindling white tassels of swamp rush that flickered in the wind like flames. Horses stood patiently in the shallows while the horsemasters and boys poured water over them in silver streams and groomed them until they shone.

The cataphracts and armigers left on foot with the dogs to look for signs of a boar worth the chase. I went hunting too, alone. I hitched up my skirts and took off my shoes and set off west along the riverbank, toward the sea, for the men had gone east. In no time I was covered in mud to my knees. The earth underfoot was black and soft, held together by the roots of rush, reed, and bracken. Small muddy streams threaded through the tussocks.

I needed to find a womandrake by nightfall. While I looked I filled my gather sack with haws and rose hips, cloudberries and dewberries, and anything else that came to hand that was good to eat or use. I moved inland, for the ground near the river was too wet; there were bryony vines in plenty, but when I dug around the roots with a stick, none were forked.

I came upon a stand of childbane bushes by one of the many rivulets that come down from the highlands to feed the great river. I took handfuls of the white berries in haste, thinking of Mai, wishing I had time to take more. I marked the spot in hopes I could come back the next day.

By the time I found my womandrake, sunlight was coming straight at me, over the ground between the black trunks of the trees. The root grew so deep, it took till long after sundown to dig it out. It was heavy as an infant and its pale, wrinkled legs were as long as my forearm.

I did and said everything just as Mai had instructed me. The night under the trees was darker than night in the Marchfield with its fires and torches burning under open sky, but I saw enough from the corners of my eyes to do what needed to be done. I was filled with purpose, and when I invoked the gods who meddle in these matters, I felt their gaze turn to me. I didn't shrink under their attention, but was enlarged, stretching and leaping like a shadow when a torch is lit. At last I bound the womandrake in the cord plaited of lamb's wool and of Galan's hair and mine, and I buried her again in the damp earth and stamped the dirt down.

Then it fell quiet. For days my head had been filled with clamor, a constant gabble and hiss that had drowned out sense and goaded me on. That noise was gone. I found myself bereft, my purpose fled.

I heard wind sigh through the branches, saying *hush*; I heard the river running and the trickle of smaller waters making a way to it and the call of a curlew and the rustle of a mouse in the undergrowth.

I thought: *What have I done? I've done a foolish thing.*

Later, Rowney claimed he'd heard the shade of a woman sobbing by the river. But that was me.

I made my way back to camp with the river on my right. I thought it likely I'd be missed, likely I'd get a slap or worse for staying away so long past dark. Yet Sire Galan hadn't missed me, for he was not in camp. The man in the boat on the river had reported to his master, and his master had sent his steward to find out who the travelers were, and when the steward found out that Sire Erizo was one of the party—the husband of his master's niece—why then the Blood must come to the manor for the night to eat and sleep in ease, and tomorrow they'd all hunt boar together. Before sundown they had sent a ferry for the cataphracts and armigers and their jacks to attend them, and left behind a cask of ale, a pig, and a quantity of moorhens: unlooked-for hospitality for the drudges, who'd been making merry ever since.

Rowney and Spiller had diced to see which would accompany Sire Galan, and Rowney had lost. He was singing by the fire. He had a sweet voice, but the song was foul; the horseboys joined him on the chorus. I offered cloudberries from my gather sack, so no one would question my muddy hem and the scratches on my skin. I was suddenly ravenous, and nothing—not pig cracklings and a moor hen baked in clay, not ale and roasted onions, nor even berries and cream—could fill me up.

The next day the boars were wary and the hunting party had to settle for a fox, run to ground by the dogs up by the ford on the other side of the river. I had better luck, coming back to the camp by midday with my sack tied in knots around handfuls of remedies for wounds and fevers and flux, and my old headcloth full of childbane.

I'd found time to sit for a moment on a fallen log, under two branches that clacked like a couple of old gossips, and ask myself why I'd given up my chance to wander like this, answerable to no one, beholden to no one. I remember looking down at my hand splayed on the log. There was black earth under my nails from digging. All around my fingers grew a forest of moss, tiny spruce trees on a mountain of rotting wood. A beetle bumbled through this forest, away from the shadow of my hand. One yellow leaf drifted down from the branches overhead. I began to wonder if I'd be able to tell from Galan's face or manner that the binding was working its way with him. Perhaps he was already caught. How would I be sure of it?

Maybe at that moment, even after the binding, I was free to choose another way. If so, the chance passed unrecognized. I gave no more thought to being alone.

Was it a sign when Galan slowed to ride abreast of me on the journey back to the Marchfield? All he said at first was that it was a shame the fine weather had not lasted.

I agreed, and he looked sidelong at me and asked if I'd slept well without him.

"Oh, very soundly," I said. He frowned and cantered ahead; I smiled to myself.

My tides started to flow the evening we returned. Usually I don't bleed until a few days after the Moon begins to wax, but I was glad to find the bloodstain, glad to know the childbane was working. That night I wrapped myself in my cloak and lay down on the floor beside Galan's cot, explaining that I was unclean.

After an hour or so he said, in a whisper, "I can't sleep," and I said, "Hush! Now you've awakened me," though I was not asleep either. I was well satisfied he should go as sleepless as I had gone during the long nights of the wager. If he didn't stray for the next five nights, during my tides, I'd be sure of him.

I'd learned deceit in a good school, under Sire Pava and Dame Lyra and their steward, and now it was ready to hand when I needed it. Early in the morning, while Galan still lay abed, I sent Noggin with a message to Mai: a twist of cloth marked with Hazard's godsign, wrapped around a few berries of childbane. I didn't trust him with any words that he might forget or repeat to the wrong person, trusting Mai instead to understand that she should meet me at the shrine of Hazard by the king's hall.

I brewed Galan some wake-me-up. While he was rubbing the sleep from his eyes, I asked leave to pray at the shrines that morning. It was raining again, a hard rain that pelted the canvas of the tent and seeped under the walls to soak the heather-stuffed pallets. Spiller and Rowney sat polishing Galan's armor with grit, scritch-scratching the rust off the iron.

Galan said he'd give me leave so long as I'd sacrifice a dove to Hazard for him; he rolled over in his blanket to fish a copper coin from the sack he kept under the bed. He said, "Keep what's left over to buy yourself a trinket."

I tossed it back to him, saying, "You owe Hazard more than this for all her favors to you. Too slight an offering will slight her."

Galan sighed and got up, pulling on his hose. He took the key to his strongbox from its hiding place in the scabbard of his dagger and unlocked the box. He pulled out a coin of silver and I shook my head.

"Even an old ewe fetches gold in this marketplace," I said. "And a jenny ass costs as much as a fine warhorse at home. Prices climb day to day. This morning the water and wood cost a silverhead—didn't Spiller tell you?"

Spiller looked up and pursed his lips. Nowadays the vendors came to us; I knew as well as he did that he'd paid three-quarters of a silver piece and pocketed the three coppers left over. But I wasn't going to say so.

"Do you take me for a fool?" asked Galan. "It's raining casks and noggins out there. Water is free for the taking."

"It's tainted," Spiller said, glaring at me. "It tastes like gull droppings." The roof flaps were devised to catch the rain and direct it to barrels, but rain wasn't all they caught.

"It will do well enough," said Galan. He grumbled about knavish jacks and spendthrift drudges. But the truth was, he spent coins as if his strongbox was bottomless.

He pulled out a gold coin from the box and dropped it into my palm. He said, "Is this what you're looking for? Go to the market and pick out a fine goat for Hazard—for I suppose it's wise counsel never to stint the gods. But while you're about it, I don't doubt a little gold will stick to your fingers. The milkmaid skims the cream."

I bristled at this. "I've never asked for a gift from you, nor taken anything but what you wanted to give. If you don't trust me, make the sacrifice yourself. It would be more welcome to the god if you did."

I tried to give the coin back but he wouldn't take it. He pulled me toward him.

"Why not?" he asked.

"Why not what?"

"Why not ask for a dress, a coin, a bauble? Every woman expects such tokens."

Now he mocked me. I looked down, flushing. I could think of no reason why I hadn't asked for what I needed. Like one of his men, or his horses, my needs were in his care.

"You could use a dress. This one is a rag."

I looked him in the eye. "It's nearly new."

"Then it began as a rag." He picked up the copper coin and the silver coin and opened my palm to put them next to the gold. "Is it so hard to ask? Indulge me, then. I'd like to see you better clad."

I closed my hand on the coins and he wrapped his hand around mine and stroked his thumb over my wrist and I knew my pulse was jumping under his touch. He smiled and let me go. I tucked the coins into one of the pockets hidden in my belt. I didn't need to be told the cloth for the dress should be green.

"See if you can find Hazard a goat with a rusty beard," he said. "Chance favors that kind."

Galan insisted I take Rowney as well as Noggin, since I was going to the market. I liked Rowney well enough: he was shy and soft-spoken, and stumbled over his words so much, except when he sang, that he chose to keep silent most of the time. For all his stumbling, he'd made few missteps since Galan had won him from Sire Alcoba, showing just enough deference to Spiller, staying well away from Sire Rodela, and thinking of what Sire

Galan might need before he thought of it himself. He'd been courteous to me. But Rowney might winkle out my business; therefore I didn't welcome his company. Not that I had a say in the matter.

Mai found me near Hazard's shrine, standing under the roof of the king's hall, out of the rain. Some of the ox-hide flaps that made the walls were rolled up, opening the pavilion to those who had business with the king as well as those who came to gawk. Tapestries figured with battle scenes hid the king's private quarters. I wondered if the Dame had woven any of them.

Mai had two escorts, Trave and Pinch. They walked on either side, holding up a canopy to keep her dry. The rain, blown by the wind, had nevertheless doused her. The wet wool of her dress clung to her buttocks, and men turned to watch her go by, gaping at her heft shifting from side to side. Tall as she was, she was taller still that day, standing a head above me on thick wooden pattens that kept her above the ankle-deep mud as if she were one of the Blood.

Mai embraced me, called me Coz, and asked if all was well.

"Well enough," I answered.

The goat bleated before his throat was cut. When the sacrifice was properly done, I gave the priest two costly lumps of myrrh, the resin bled from amber trees, precious for its scent, healing properties, and because—it is said—there's only one grove of amber trees in all the world, and it's guarded by quarrelsome three-headed serpents. I saved one last lump for Ardor. And so the gold piece was spent.

Mai and I stood together under the eaves. She sent Trave and Pinch off with two copperheads to fetch fried bread; I sent Rowney after them with my copper so we could snatch a chance to talk. That left Noggin with us; he gaped so wide at the passersby I wondered his mouth didn't fill with rain.

I gave Mai the childbane wrapped in my old headcloth. Some of the berries had been crushed, and though they were white, they left a dark stain on the linen. I told her they ought to be properly dried if they were to last for a few months, but I couldn't do that for her, not in Galan's tent. It would be noticed.

When I said there was enough in the bundle to last three women a whole winter, or one woman until childbane ripened again next autumn, she embraced me. With my face against her bosom, I could feel the great laugh rolling up out of her belly. "Coz, we'll be queens among the whores—especially the whores who go by the title of Dame," she said.

"I don't know if I'll be able to find more," I said.

"No matter: the scarcer it is, the more it's desired. And it needn't last the winter. A tennight or two will do. When the army moves, most of the women will stay behind and have no use for childbane for a while. The whores will have earned enough to roll up their blankets for a year. And you, do you go with the army or stay?"

"I'll go."

"I'll be glad of your company," she said. Then she asked, "How goes that other matter? Did Sire Galan win his wager?"

"He did," I said.

"But you're still in his bed."

"I have my tides just now."

"A pity," said Mai.

I smiled at her. "He hasn't strayed from the tent at night."

"So you did as I told you?"

I nodded. "This morning he gave me this without my asking." I showed her the silver coin. It was something I could hold in my hand. How could I speak of his other tokens—a look, a touch—that I counted the greater treasure, when they were so fleeting, so easy to counterfeit?

She plucked the silverhead from my fingers and dropped it into a purse she had hidden between her breasts. "Never show coin in a crowd of cut-purses," she said. "I'll care for this awhile, and just you watch—it will breed in my little pouch."

The men came back with the fried bread and we ate together, watching the rain drip from the leather roof and run over the sodden ground. I pulled my cloak tight around me, grateful for its shelter, as I had been many times before. I tried to ignore Trave and Pinch, for I couldn't forget how they'd laid hands on me behind the tents. Trave had not forgotten either; he leaned forward now and then to leer at me.

Mai said, "That maid you told me about—the one who's a maid no longer—I hear she's fallen ill."

"Are we talking of the same maiden? From the clan of Ardor—I don't know her name. Rumor said she had the squirts, but she was cured."

"No, she's getting worse. She has the wasting sickness."

I wiped my mouth on my sleeve. "Even today she's sick?"

"Oh, yes. They say she's like to die."

"How do you know this?"

Mai popped the last morsel of bread into her mouth. Still chewing, she grinned and said, "I know this one who knows that one. I've never paid a rumormonger yet—they pay me!" And she laughed.

I didn't believe the maiden was sick. I thought she was feigning, as she had before, so she could go to the privy tent and wait for Sire Galan. And when I thought of her waiting and Galan keeping to his own bed, I was well pleased.

Mai insisted on taking me to the market to spend my silver, swearing that without her help every rogue, diddler, and gouger in the place would descend on me like flies on a stink. I was vexed she thought me so easy to cheat, yet soon I was glad of her help. She knew all the clothiers, if only by reputation, and they knew of her as well. Much of the cloth was no better than I could weave myself, but at last I found a length of fine wool, green and soft as moss, with the nap raised for warmth. The merchant asked three silverheads for it. Mai chaffered him down to two, but I objected that I had only one and couldn't afford it. I turned to leave, my eyes stinging. I'd denied I wanted a new dress, but once I saw the cloth, I wanted it badly.

"Tut," she said. "Such a fuss." She pulled the purse from its hiding place between her breasts and took out Sire Galan's silverhead, and sure enough, the coin came back with two offspring, also of silver. Those were the first coins I ever called my own.

I took the wool in my arms, could not resist the touch of it.

"And the thread too," Mai told the merchant.

When we parted she told me she visited Delve's shrine daily, just after sunrise. "Perhaps we'll chance upon each other again," she said. She winked at Rowney and pinched Noggin's cheek and swayed away.

The very next day was Summons Day, come at last. We'd been in the Marchfield for twelve days, and more had happened in those few days than in a twelvemonth when I'd lived with the Dame.

The clans assembled under a gray sky and the eyes of the king and Queenmother Caelum. Each clan strove to outdo the others in the magnificence of their armor, weapons, and horseflesh. Every soldier, down to the least kitchenboy, was mustered out and given clan banners to bear on poles, and their colors spread over the tourney field and the hills around it like a great gaudy shawl.

Galan made his bagboy accompany me. Noggin and I stood in the crowd of onlookers: farmers, harlots, peddlers, and thieves, mostly. I craned to look between heads and shoulders, eager to see everything. I thought back to my first glimpse of Galan's company, how we'd all been bedazzled. It was far more splendid and more fearsome to see the denizens of the Marchfield, high and low, armed and massed in their ranks so tightly a child couldn't slip between them, to see them transformed from so many gamblers, gossips, fops, brawlers, rowdies, swordsmen, prickmasters, catcallers, idlers, and drudges—that is to say, so many men—into an army. Mai had called it a small army, but I thought surely that once it began to march it could overrun the world—having, at the time, but a small idea of how big the world is.

King Thyrse stood on a tiered platform at one end of the field, and one by one the clans came before him to offer him their oaths and make sacrifices to the gods. So the morning passed. In the afternoon there was a farcical battle between the jacks, wearing armor of plaited straw and wielding weapons of swamp rush. The priests of Rift cast off the solemnity of the morning and joined the battle, riding donkeys so small their feet dragged on the ground. It was done for Rift's amusement, perhaps, but when six jacks were borne injured from the field (for they soon began to fight with blows and kicks), the crowd bellowed in delight.

After this false battle there was a real slaughter. The king ordered a herd of fallow deer driven onto the tourney field, and his war dogs loosed on them. The dogs, being kin to gazehounds, hunt silently; the deer leapt high and the dogs streaked low after them and pulled them down. After the manhounds had tasted blood, the king and his clansmen of Prey rode onto the field to finish the hunt. There would be venison for the Blood that night. There was meat for the rest of us too, from the sacrifices; what we offer to the gods they share with us in turn.

When my tides ran dry, I came back to Galan's bed. He might have gone elsewhere when I denied him, but he had not. The binding had worked and he was mine as I had been his. I meant to take possession. I'd invoked Carnal's avatar of Desire when I bound him, and now she came at my call. I wanted her to give Galan a craving only I could satisfy. But it was hard to tell—he was eager enough, but he'd never failed to desire me, even when he dallied with that maid. It was me Desire scratched deepest, scratched where I'd gone numb, leaving behind a fiery itch.

CHAPTER 6

Greenwoman

ummons Day had passed and still the king kept the army waiting. At times I forgot we'd soon be going to war, forgot that the Marchfield wouldn't outlive the year, for it seemed as though this city might endure as long as one built of stone.

Prices climbed day by day and the weather grew colder. The Sun hid behind mists and a constant drizzle. The king hanged a few men for fighting out of the tourney field; deserters had their toes cut off so they could run no more and thieves had their fingers cut off so they could pinch no more. It made a show, and kept our minds off the cold water that seeped into our blankets, the fever running through the Marchfield, the insults that flowered into feuds.

The Crux kept his promise to work his men hard. In the stony hills north of the camp, he set them against each other on horseback and on foot, with real weapons, so they could learn to master their arms, their horses, their own fear and pain. They had to vanquish their appetites too, for they were fed scantily at midday on bread and jerky; instead of an after-dinner nap they spent most afternoons at the tourney field, skirmishing or watching. Often the Crux challenged opponents who dealt his men harsh lessons—lessons he thought needful. The cataphracts and armigers had battled since they were old enough to play sticks-and-stones; the Crux showed them they knew less than they thought. During the tourneys I could see his training taking hold.

The horse soldiers drilled too. Though they had little to do in tourneys, in war Spiller and Rowney, Flykiller and Uly would fight at Sire Galan's side. All the men returned to the tent at night exhausted and bruised, but the jacks cleaned muddy armor and the horsemaster and his boy tended to the mounts while Sires Galan and Rodela took their ease at supper and after.

The foot soldiers weren't taught how to war; when the time came, they'd be sent into battle to be an obstacle over which the opposing army might stumble. They had their duties, digging and hauling or emptying pisspots or any other chore a jack disdained to do, and now and then they were called to serve in the king's work gangs. When they were not worked too hard, they were too idle. They waited, huddling in their lean-tos under rain that dripped through the thatch, and they muttered about the stony ground and the foul weather and the fouler food, and they quarreled. But if you didn't listen for it, you might have thought them as patient and mute as cows in a pasture with their backs to a snowstorm.

As for Sire Galan, he never lazed abed in the morning as he used to do. He woke every day when the Sun was a mere notion to ready himself for fighting. Skill with weapons and horses had always come easily to him, perhaps too easily; now I saw him striving, pushing himself hard. He'd been bested in a tourney and it rankled. His broken rib had healed more quickly than his pride.

An edge is made as much from the steel taken away as the steel that is left. Just so Galan was growing keen; I could see it as I tended to his bruises and pains at night. He lost his sleekness, the smooth roundness under the skin. His sinews and muscles grew tough as hempen cords, knotting ribs to spine, limbs to trunk. His hands hardened, learning the fit of the lance and scorpion, sword and mace the way a farmer's hands know the sickle from the scythe. He bore his carapace of iron without complaint, as if it were no more of a burden than a surcoat of velvet stiffened with gold thread. Some of the cataphracts grumbled at such drudgery, but Galan wore his weariness out, teaching himself to be tireless. He hung five more banners before his tent and propped the weapons he won as trophies inside the doorway.

There were other women in the clan's tents now, other fodder for the men's gossip. Some lived there and some came and went for a night or so. The Crux tolerated us, knowing that when the troop left the Marchfield for war, most would stay behind. The only woman of the Blood was Sire Farol's wife, Dame Hartura. Being prone to jealousy and hoping, so I heard, to catch Sire Farol doing something he shouldn't, she'd persuaded her father to let her accompany his troop from the clan Growan. Sire Farol was crestfallen when she arrived. She kept to his tent with her handmaid and her own cook, except for tourneys, when she could be found under the awnings of Crux, screaming until she was hoarse.

There were mudwomen too, sheaths like myself. One crept about in a brown rag and never raised her eyes from the ground, and everyone knew she was shared by the men in Sire Erial's tent, down to the bagboy. I pitied her. Once I offered her some childbane, but she scurried off with a sideways look of distrust and fear and avoided me after. Sire Guasca had found a pretty sheath named Suripanta. She plucked her brows and forehead like one of the Blood, and though she lived in the tent next to ours, she had no use for me once she saw the cut of my clothes and learned I wasn't from Ramus. I detested her and her wandering eye; she liked to start fights among men who weren't allowed to touch her. Sometimes at night she screeched at Sire Guasca and we could hear her and the thumps that silenced her. If they quarreled too loudly, the Crux would send his armiger over to bid them be quiet. Sire Pava had a sheath too, for two days of every tennight. She was a whore of some repute, and he couldn't afford to buy all her favors.

Since Galan was busy all hours during the day, I was no longer constantly under his eye. I had few duties, and those few I'd taken on myself: tending the fire, making poultices and tisanes to ease the men's bruises and sore muscles, a bit of cooking and sewing. In the evenings I worked on my dress and a cloak for Fleetfoot with a hood lined in rabbit fur. Galan seemed incurious about how I spent my days, so long as I was in his bed at night. This suited me well, for idleness chafed, and I'd found other occupations.

I went to the shrines around the king's hall just after daybreak—to pray, I would have told Galan, had he asked, but he'd already risen, armed, and left for the hills and his exercises. I took Noggin, for Sire Galan couldn't spare his jacks to go about with me. I felt Ardor had naught to do with me anymore, being the god of that maiden I counted my enemy. But the bones had said otherwise, when last I'd thrown them, so I burned a lock of my hair at Ardor's shrine.

After, I found Mai at the shrine of Delve, where she paid her respects every morning.

"I have some visits to make," she said. "Would you care to come with me?" She looked me up and down and clucked at my old dress and battered sheepskin cloak. Mai herself wore a gown of gray velvet with split skirts that fell on either side of her great belly, showing a red underdress. Her headcloth was piled high and wrapped with a silver chain. She courted a beating, for there were some armigers in the Marchfield who did not like to see a drudge dress too well—better than an armiger could afford. She said, "A pity your gown isn't finished. Well, we must make do. Can you be wise, I wonder?"

"What do you mean?"

"I need you to be wise today. I think it would be best if you kept your lips sewn tight. The less you say, the more you'll be taken for a sage."

"Am I so foolish when I open my mouth?" Indeed, I felt the fool, for longing to see Mai again and forgetting how her teasing was apt to chafe.

She gave me one of her hard hugs and laughed. "It's not that you're foolish, Coz. But for certain you're greener than a pintle shoot. It's been a long time since I was as green as you."

There is a world of women that men never see, and Mai was one of the powers in that world. I knew her for a canny—how could I not, when she'd given me the means to bind Galan?—now I saw her ply her trade. And she hardly needed to tell me to keep quiet, for my tongue was in a knot when she took me to the pavilion of a certain dame of Prey, the king's own clan. We left Noggin, Pinch, and Trave to hunker before the tent while we went in. The dame dismissed her guards and kept her handmaid. Soon we heard the men dicing outside.

The tent was crowded with heavy, carved furniture of a sort more fitting to a manor than a campaign. No doubt it would all be carted back again when the men left for war and the women of the Blood went home. The dame sat before a table with her face shadowed by a great horned wimple draped with gauze. I could see the tip of her sharp nose and the arch of her nostrils, reddened as if she'd been tippling or sniffling.

Mai took from her girdle a small wallet, and from the wallet an oilskin packet, which she unfolded on the table with delicacy, despite her swollen fingers, to reveal a handful of shriveled white berries: childbane. Enough for a tennight, at most. She said, "This comes all the way from the spine of the world, the Interminable Mountains. It can't be found in these parts—it's precious, very rare." She gestured at me. "When Firethorn first brought it to me, after a long and arduous journey, I thought of you at once, my dame." I was not sure where the Interminable Mountains might be—each of our mountains had its own name, and none went by that one—but I nodded as if she hadn't just lied uphill and down.

The dame craned her long neck and looked down her nose to see what lay before her on the table. "What is it?"

Mai grinned and leaned toward her. She lowered her voice. "Childbane, my dame. It will preserve your figure and your reputation. Once before, you came to me, to make sure that your husband would sleep soundly at night and annoy you no more. But a cold bed grows stale after a while—don't you think? Now you can find another man to warm you—a comelier man—one who is neither so old nor so fat, one with an upstanding prick instead of a flabby old dangle. And he won't have to unsheathe before you've had your fill, eh? Or make you suck on him instead (though to be sure, a swallow of white blood now and then is good for the complexion). Chew a few of these afterward and never fear your secret will show in a few months."

The dame's nose grew even redder, and I blushed myself. I was shocked to hear Mai broach such matters so boldly, so coarsely, as if she spoke to another sheath or a whore, and not a woman of the Blood. I expected the dame to call her guards and have us driven off. And besides, I'd heard talk of pricklickers, but I'd taken it for a jape, a by-name soldiers used to insult each other. Spiller called Noggin one at least twice a day. Mai caught my eye and winked.

The dame sat demurely with her hands folded on her lap, her eyes downcast. She said, "How much?"

Mai said, "Five blondes."

Five gold coins! I found my mouth gaping and closed it tight.

Most of the Blood scorn bargaining, which is why they're easy to cheat unless their servants bargain for them. This dame said, "Give me whatever four will buy. I can afford no more."

"A pity," Mai said, "to give up even a little pleasure."

"There's something else I need of you," the dame said, and hesitated.

Mai leaned closer and waited.

The dame said abruptly, "Can you give me something to make men desire me? A charm, something . . ."

"You don't need one, a fine dame like yourself! There are many as would be willing—Sire Celoso for one. Haven't you seen him stare? Blink at him and he'll come running."

The dame looked up at Mai for the first time. She'd gazed down at the table before, or to one side or the other, or to the hands in her lap. Daylight coming around the edge of the door flap fell on her face. No starchroot could cover the burning of her cheeks. "It's Sire Brama I want, and I want him to grovel."

I'd never heard of the man, but I recognized the need. It was shameful to see the dame lay bare a thought that should be kept hidden—and to recall

I'd done the same not long ago. Mai had a gift [illegible] secrets, for she appeared to understand any folly witho[illegible] In truth, she did judge, but she hid it well.

I looked to the dame's handmaid, sitting on a stool behin[illegible] She had a hand over her mouth to hide her smile. She looked bac[illegible] her eyes were merry.

Mai said, "Ah, I see. That's a different matter. You need a specific. But you say you have no money?"

"For that I can give another goldhead."

"Usually it costs two," said Mai. "But for you, my dame, I will strive to do my poor best. Can you get a lock of his hair?"

The dame shook her head.

"It will be less certain. But I'll do what I can."

After we left the tent, Mai said, "I should have asked for eight; she's rich enough. One of these blondes is yours, you know."

I thought, *Only one?* I'd found the childbane for her. Yet it was an astonishing fee. She made me rich, even as she made herself richer. I whispered my thanks, and then I asked, "Will you make a binding for the dame?" Perhaps it wasn't as great a favor as I'd thought when she'd told me how to bind Galan, if she'd do as much for anyone. Still, she'd taught me for free. I wondered why, now that I knew it was her trade.

She didn't answer. Instead she said, "Did you hear who she was after? Her stepson, that's who. She was too young to wed such an old man. Her parents should have chosen better. Sell that to a rumormonger! There'd be a few silverheads in it—now, don't fret, don't purse your lips at me! I'd hardly sell her secret when it's worth so much more locked up in my strongbox." She tapped her forehead. Then she cupped my face in her hand and her fingers dug into my cheeks. "It's true you held your tongue in there, but you have a very speaking face. I can read you like an omen. You nearly made me laugh. Had you never heard of sucking a prick before?"

I was abashed, the more so that her men and Noggin were behind us, and could hear what she said. But I'd been puzzling over something, so I whispered to her and she inclined her head to hear me. "Mai, I don't see how you keep from biting."

I was sure she'd mock me for my ignorance, but she just shook her head and looked at me with pity. "You learn fast or get your teeth knocked out, don't you? You don't want to end up like those toothless old whores they ucklers—all gums. Their quims have dried up and they're good for nothing else." She laughed, and there was a bitter sound to it. "Now your ears are burning! Stay with me, Coz. I'll teach you not to blush."

After midday, while many were sleeping off their dinners, Mai took me to see some whores of her acquaintance who lived down the market road, in a tent striped red and rose. Trave wanted to come inside; he said he had coin for it. Mai gave him a shove and told him these whores were not for the likes of him. We left the men outside again and went in.

Seven whores lived in that tent with an old crone and two or three girl children to haul slops and cook and launder—and a pander, who had little to do by my reckoning. When we went in the pander was lying in bed. He got up and pulled hose over his skinny legs and tucked his dangle into a huge leather prickguard that hung to his knees. Mai said, "If only your prick was that long!" and he smiled and said, "Oh, it's long enough when it stands up, even for a great big woman like you—just try what I can do with it!" And he waggled the prickguard and turned his grin from Mai to me.

When he'd gone out, Mai sat on one of the beds, which griped under her weight. She asked the whore lying under the covers, "What *does* he do with it?" and the whore replied, "Not as much as he thinks," and that set them all to laughing and piling one quip upon another.

I stood stiffly just inside the doorway. I'd never yet spoken to a whore. A wooden statue of Carnal's female avatar, Desire, the benefactor of harlots, stood face-to-face with me. She was naked, as always, save for her cap shaped like a foreskin. Her hips were as wide as Mai's, and her round breasts and the folds of her belly were polished from the hands of the women and their patrons who rubbed her for blessings on their way in and out of the tent. She held her lamp high, casting a golden haze within the dim tent. The daylight that seeped through the striped canvas walls behind her was tinted red. The whites of her eyes were inlaid with mother-of-pearl and her pupils were onyx.

I owed Desire a debt and I wondered how she would make me pay. I should sacrifice a dove to her before it was too late. But she'd already exacted my homage—hadn't she?—when she made me so greedy for Galan, when she made us both so greedy that we brawled and battered against each other, stealing the breath from each other's mouths, until Galan shoved me half over the edge of the cot, and I was hanging on, saying things that shouldn't be said aloud, and the cot juddered and rocked under us as if it might give way.

I felt Desire's touch on my cleft, and the shock of heat from it. She reminded me that she presided here, where whores coupled for coin. She outstared me and I looked away from her.

Some of the whores were still abed; some sat about clad in sheer underdresses, breakfasting or applying their paints at tables laden with half-eaten birds, bread crumbs, apples, and walnuts, with wigs, paint pots, powders, mortars and pestles. Their beds were crowded close as the boats moored down in the harbor, each with striped gauze curtains draped from bedposts tall as masts. The curtains, like their clothes, hid very little. The air was ripe with the commingled smells of musk, smoke, sweat, chamber pots, and too many perfumes. And under it all, the stink of the tannery farther down the market road.

Mai beckoned me and I came a few more steps into the tent. She gave them my name and told them I was Sire Galan's sheath. Their names were easy to remember, being all flowers, though I was hard put to match the flower to the doxy.

"Sire Galan?" said one. "Is he the prickmaster who wagered against a maiden's virtue and won?"

"I'd like to meet the fool who bet against him," said another, who went by the name of Corncockle. "He must be easy to cozen if he laid money on a woman's chastity. Maybe he'll believe I'm a maiden too." She sat with her eyes closed and her head tilted back, wearing little more than a sly smile, while a short, wide-bottomed whore brushed her long black hair until it fell straight as rain down her back.

Rumor must have jumped like a flea from one gossip to the next. How else could Galan's wager be known here among the whores? And how long before the maid's father knew?

"I heard the maiden's pining away for Sire Galan now that he's done with her."

"That's because he's better than other men—they say he has a bone in his prick, that he stands always at the ready. Is it true?"

They all laughed at my offended expression, and Mai laughed the loudest.

A towhead harlot—she was called Corona—came up close to me. She touched my eyebrow, saying, "Is your hair truly red like this? Or is there a dye for it?" There was something odd about her. She had lean hips and a bobble in her throat like a man's. Was she a eunuch? I'd heard tell the whores hadn't much use for boy children, but some chose to cut the sacs off their baby boys rather than leave them to die on some hillside.

I said shortly, "I was born with it."

"May I see?" she asked, and she tugged at my headcloth.

I pushed her hand away.

"Oh, why not?" said Mai. "We're all women here. Come, sit here and I'll give your hair a good brushing." She patted the bed beside her.

I let myself be coaxed. Mai had tickled my vanity, for my hair was the only beauty on which I prided myself. Besides, to be admired, even by a whore, was better than to be mocked. I sat on the tumbled quilts and took off my headcloth. The bawds came around, cooing and wrapping my curls around their fingers, and I ducked my head and tried not to smile. Mai took up a brush and tugged it through my hair until my scalp stung. "Such tangles!" she said, but soon the brush went freely, and I was as content as a cat having its chin scratched.

"Your hair is very shiny. Do you wash it with piss?" asked a whore called Cowslip.

I wrinkled my nose. "Water of maythen is better, and doesn't stink."

Cowslip said, "Can you get me some of this maythen?" Her own hair was lank.

"You'd be better off eating pig knuckles and bone marrow, if you can get them. It will make your hair grow thick."

Mai gave me a nudge. "Bring her some of this water, next time we come," and she yanked my hair for emphasis.

"Surely," I said. "I'll make some up for you." Already I knew where to go for maythen, for I'd seen a place on the sea cliff where it spread among rocks, in a carpet. The flowers were dry now, but still smelled sweet when they were trodden, a sign that they kept their strength.

And so, slowly, we arrived at our purpose. We dawdled so long I'd begun to think Mai visited only as a friend, but these were customers too. She brought out an amulet she'd made for one of the whores. It was in a leather pouch with a thong to go around the neck. Neither said what it was for, but I saw six silverheads (graybeards, the whores called them) go into the purse Mai hid between her breasts.

Then Mai brought out the childbane and named her price. She boasted that she meant to make the miscarrier go a-begging; not a woman in the Marchfield would have to trust her life to that bloody butcher again, now that a quickening could be stopped before it started. Then Mai swore that childbane grew only on the peak of Barren Mountain, in an ice garden patrolled by bears walking upright and dressed as men, and that I—a renowned greenwoman—had braved wolves and storms and bears and all to pluck the berries from under the very noses of the gods. The tale was riddled with nonsense, and yet the whores didn't go astray, trusting her. I knew myself that childbane worked, and furthermore that Mai was no mountebank. Hadn't she given me a potent cure for jealousy?

Corncockle, the black-haired whore, chaffered with Mai over the price until they settled on less than the dame had paid, for a good many more berries. Then Corncockle said, "Mai, I need you to make a virgin for me."

Mai laughed. "Why bother? There's none of you could pass."

Corncockle waved her hand and called, "Come here! Come on!" in a sharp voice, and a naked girl came out from behind the beds. She was thin save for a belly round as a porridge pot. Her breasts had yet to swell, and there was no woman's beard to hide the smooth lips of her quim. She didn't try to cover herself; I supposed she had no use for modesty, living in a whore's tent. She stood beside Corncockle, resting one foot on the other, and I could see the resemblance. Her hair was black, in a long plait over her shoulder.

"Your daughter?" Mai asked.

"Yes, and just look at her! She's been sulking ever since she lost her maidenhead. What a pruneface! Who'd want her now?"

The girl did have a sullen look, and dark pouches under her eyes like an old woman's.

"She's young, isn't she?" Mai said.

"She's been on my tit for ten years. It's time she earned her keep." Corncockle gave her daughter a shake, and the girl scowled at the floor.

I'd been lulled, thinking the harlots were amiable women—forthright enough to blister my ears, but harmless nevertheless. Here was the harm.

I asked the girl her name and she wouldn't look at me.

Her mother said, "I'll call her Prune if she doesn't mend her ways—but for now she's called Catnep. She has firepiss, or so she says, and she's shirking—aren't you, my heart?—but soon we'll have her good as new."

"No wonder she's sour," Mai said. "What did you expect? A big pestle in that little mortar, grinding away. Of course she has firepiss. Many a grown woman catches it after her wedding night. It would be worse for a little one like her."

Corncockle said, "It's that crone, Hobblen. She aimed a curse at me, because she has a fancy for Sire Trasera and he fancies me instead. I'm shielded, so it struck Catnep instead." She touched the tattoo she wore at the base of her throat.

Mai said, "No need to look so far for cause, when the cause is she's too young."

"No younger than I was when I started," Corncockle said.

I went to the girl and took her hands in mine. Her palms were dry and her fingers cold: no fever, then. She let me hold her hands as if they had nothing to do with her, and Corncockle didn't object, though she rolled her eyes at me when the girl looked away.

I asked Catnep, "Does the piss burn on its way out? Do you have to use the pot many times in the night?"

She nodded and looked at me from the corner of an eye.

"Is the piss cloudy or clear?"

Catnep shrugged. I leaned closer. She smelled frowsty, like unaired sheets. Her pulse quickened under my fingers and I let her go. She sidled away and put the bed between us. I asked her which pisspot she used and she pointed to a cot in the darkest corner.

Corncockle spoke up. "Well, as you said, Mai, plenty of women get firepiss when they're first broken to riding. And they get over it."

I stooped and found the chamber pot. An acrid smell hit me when I raised the lid. There was a milky look to the piss, but no sign of blood.

I was angry and didn't trouble to hide it. "No more men," I said. "I'll make a tisane for her that should help—but no more men." I looked at Corncockle straight. "It's true that most get over it, but sometimes after the burning goes away and a woman seems cured, fever sneaks upstream and brings a pain deep in the kidneys, and before you know it, the fever has carried her right off. So have a care, will you? I'll come back, and meanwhile you must sacrifice to Torrent, who rules the waters of the body. Ask the priestess of Wellspring, she'll tell you what's owing. And feed Catnep coddled eggs and a mash of parsnips—parsley root too, if there's any to be found—to strengthen her kidneys."

I took up my headcloth and hid my hair again. "Give her plenty of warmed wine, very much watered, with a spoon of honey and verjuice in every cup. She must drink and drink until her piss runs clear." Honey was good for almost anything, but more than that, it would keep the girl drinking and make her mother (or her pander) fish deep in the purse.

They should pay, and pay dear. "Make sure it's honey from the linnflower tree," I added, for that was the hardest to obtain.

Catnep stared at me openly now; they all stared. Corncockle looked to Mai, saying, "She has costly notions, your friend. Does she suppose we sleep on sacks of coins?"

Mai said, "Spend a little now to earn a lot later."

Corncockle answered just as quick. "Spend a lot, you mean—to earn a little."

Mai cocked her eyebrow. "Do as you please. But I shan't make the girl a new maidenhead until she's cured. And I expect you'll find Firethorn gives good advice. She may be a bit country in her ways, but is it a fault in a greenwoman to be green?"

Outside the tent I said to Mai, "Do you think Catnep has even had her first tides?"

"Likely not."

I thought Mai was vexed with me, because her voice was curt. We walked on in silence with our attendants following behind. Then she sighed. "They'll sell her three or four more times as a maiden. Each man will pay a steep price to be the first, and never know his prick has drawn pig's blood from a little bladder hidden up her quim. No doubt one will give her the canker, and her price will fall. But she's blessed, you see, to have a mother to look after her, and so many aunts. And I've heard their pander is too lazy to beat them; he lets his whores do as they please."

"You call that blessed?"

"In a manner, I do. And when you've gone to war and back, then you can judge—for you'll see worse, much worse. But blessed as you or me? No. Desire smiled on me long ago, or I'd still be a whore and not a sheath. As for you," she said, beginning to grin, "all the bawds have been clamoring to see you, for you've won a notable victory in the war between the sheaths and the dames. Sire Galan may think he won the wager, hmm? But we know better."

I'd spoken up boldly in the whores' tent, but that night, lying awake while Galan slept, I wondered if I'd misspoken. I feared I didn't deserve the trust I'd demanded of the whores, of Corncockle and her daughter. The Dame was in my thoughts. All day she'd been there, as if her tiny shade perched on my shoulder. I felt her scorn to see that dame with her hunger so naked, and all those whores, to see me take money for childbane, which had always been free for the finding. Now I wanted her in the flesh to tell me what to do. I felt between the feather bed and the cot to find the pouch of bones I hid there, and clutched it in my hand.

The Dame used to say that the gods send no malady without also sending a remedy, and they're not to blame if we fail to discover it. But neither are the gods to blame for every ailment. We bring some on ourselves by way of folly or neglect; we wish them on others out of malice, or they're sent by shades who have their own reasons for plaguing the living. So with Catnep's illness. A man's lust may have caused it (and that was Desire's domain, and therefore her busywork), but it was the mother who sold her daughter to that man, who opened the gate that affliction entered.

Surely Corncockle hadn't set out to hurt her daughter for spite. Yet she'd caused her injury, and now she blamed Catnep, as if the sickness were her fault, even as if she were to blame for being born. So the mother did further harm. No need for a curse to burrow under her daughter's skin—such a cloud of ill feeling must make it hard for the girl to breathe, make her weak and her ailment strong. What remedy for that?

I wished I had some oil of savin. Twice I'd helped the Dame distill it from the dark blue berries of the evergreen shrub. It was sovereign for cleansing the waters. The girl would need but a few drops a day for a few days—yet those drops were impossible to come by here in the Marchfield. Even if I could gather enough berries, I had no alembic for distilling, no charcoal, no fresh running water . . . Perhaps oil of savin could be bought? There were herb sellers in the market, but I distrusted their wares. How could I be sure an herb was picked when the signs were right and prepared properly if I didn't do it myself?

Tomorrow I too would make sacrifices on Catnep's behalf: to Wellspring, the avatar of Torrent who lies sleeping underground, who let the girl's waters get muddy, and to Ardor Wildfire, who brought on the burning. Water and fire, fire and water. These gods were opposed in their natures, not their wills. In striving against each other, neither strove to get the upper hand. Victory was in the balance, and there I'd find the cure.

And Carnal Desire, she must be mollified too.

I should have demanded some greater sacrifice from that whore Corncockle. In the village, to be called a whore had the sting of a slap, but how could it sting her when it was plain fact?

Perhaps she would mind, at that. Mai had told me that such quality of whores, with their own tents and beds, called themselves queans or joybirds and the like, and prided themselves on their many accomplishments, such as singing, dancing, playing instruments, and conversing. Still, they'd lie under any man with enough coin—so long as he was of the Blood. Corncockle and her sisters were particular.

I knew what Mai meant when she called us blessed. I knew my good fortune, he was lying beside me, and I wouldn't quibble over which god had shown me favor: Hazard or Ardor or—for that matter—Carnal. I turned into Galan's warmth and he stirred and pulled me closer, tucking me between his arm and his body.

"You're restless tonight," he murmured. "All elbows." He stroked my back. I could feel the light scrape of his calluses and my skin quickened in the wake of his touch.

I nuzzled the corner of his jaw and put my knee over his legs. "Your pardon, Sire. I didn't mean to wake you."

He turned his face toward me and I felt him smile. The featherweight of his breath brushed my temple. "Indeed?" he said.

When Wellspring wakes, which she does rarely, she makes the earth shake. While she lies sleeping under blankets of rock, she dreams and visits us. So she came to me as I dreamed, and in the way of dreams, she came disguised, for even gods must take other forms when they visit Sleep's domain.

I dreamed of Mai's lazy piebald hound. He was standing before me and I reached out my hand to pat him on the head and he shook it off. I reached out again and he shook his head and snarled, and the next time he tried to catch my hand in his mouth, and I couldn't tell if he meant to play or fight. He frightened me so that I woke up. I thought, *It's only Mai's old dog,* and I went back to sleep.

He was still there, and this time I understood when he took my hand in his mouth and tugged. He wasn't menacing; he was insistent. He trotted off and I followed, out past the Marchfield, over the hills and down to the sea, where part of the cliff had crumbled into hillocks covered with stiff brown grass. The dog lay down with his tongue lolling and I sat beside him.

When I awoke I had a line from a song in my mind, one the Dame had taught me: *Seek it by restless waters, shun it by still waters.* And I knew—of course I knew, why hadn't I thought of it at once?—that the girl could be helped by the roots of dog grass, so called because dogs eat the green shoots to make themselves spew when they're sick. And that I'd find it growing somewhere by the restless sea. The roots would be beneficial in any season, for the song said: *In Wellspring's larder it keeps year 'round.*

Before dawn, while Galan was arming for the day, I went to the dog pen to find Fleetfoot. I knew I'd have to catch him early or he'd be gone, for he was always running about the Marchfield doing errands or making mischief. I hated to go near the manhounds, though they were penned behind a stone wall, a thorn fence, and high netting, and sure enough they started to clamor when I went to the gate. Fleetfoot came when I beckoned, walking among them fearlessly. I asked him to inquire of Dogmaster where dog grass could be found.

Fleetfoot said, "Oh, I can show you. I've often fetched it when the dogs needed a purge." He wasn't a dogboy yet, but before long I thought Dogmaster would claim all his time, for he was willing and quick.

"Is it far?" I asked, and he shrugged.

Not so far. Before the morning mists had cleared, we found it down by the shore, above the highest tide but below the cliffs, on a hill of sand and gravel very like the one in my dream. Then I saw through Wellspring's disguise and gave thanks.

Back in the tent Noggin groused about having to walk such a long way before breakfast, but as soon as he ate, he went back to sleep. I swear he could sleep anywhere, even standing up like a horse; his wits were always dozing. Fleetfoot stayed with me—for I fed him well—and I put him to work pulling maythen flowers from their stems. Maythen had been underfoot when we walked along the top of the cliff, the flowers gone brittle, dried to a dull gold, and the sweet smell had reminded me of the rinse I'd promised to Cowslip for her hair. On the way back I found new shoots of stinging nettles, bright green at the foot of the old faded stalks. Juice pressed from the stems would strengthen the rinse. I marveled at how all I needed was in my path that day.

I stripped and scrubbed the dog grass roots. I'd come back with a sackful of them. They are of the sort that runs sideways underground, with clumps of rootlets growing down and stems growing up. Fleetfoot and I talked of the village and the Marchfield—or rather, Fleetfoot talked and I listened with one ear. In the other I heard the tune of that song I'd risen with in the morning.

My dream had shown me where to look for the dog grass roots, not how to prepare them. I put them to steep in water just off the boil, asking Hearthkeeper to bless the fire and Wellspring the water. But how much root, how much water, how long to steep? I went on by taste, by smell, by guesswork, until I'd made a weak infusion that Catnep might drink by the glassful. It was slippery on the tongue and tasted worse than boiled turnip peelings, so I added some sprigs of esdragon and some spoonfuls of honey. Later I'd boil the infusion to make a decoction strong enough to take one spoonful at a time, but for now it was best that she drink plentifully.

The task was familiar. The Dame had shown me all manner of preparations. How I missed her stone basins, her distillery, her drying room, with its pungent smells and warm hearth in winter! I felt her beside me, a guardian. What I did seemed fitting and I didn't fear error. A god had favored my work. And the roots themselves seemed to have their requirements, and to make them plain to me.

When I returned to the whores' tent, I made sure to go with Mai. Fleetfoot had found her after searching half the Marchfield; he was an excellent messenger, for he'd never walk when he could run, he took such joy in going fast. She met me by the shrines around the king's hall, where I'd turned some of my gold coin into sacrifices: two doves for Carnal, one on behalf of the girl, one for me, and a vial of precious thymoil for Torrent. I gave Ardor three fat candles that would burn a day and a night.

Catnep made a face, but she drank down a cupful of the medicine straightaway. She was clothed today, but to little purpose, being in a gown so filmy her dark nipples stared out like eyes behind a veil. The tent was hot from many braziers and the heat of bodies.

It was late in the afternoon and Corncockle had a customer. Her long black hair was spread over the pillow. She'd raised her legs so high they were over the man's shoulders and next to his ears (which I'd never thought to do), and his buttocks were going up and down and she was moaning. She saw me and nodded and kept on about her business. When the man was done and gone, Corncockle pulled on a gown without tightening the laces and came over. Her forehead had the sheen of sweat, but her breathing was calm.

She greeted me and said, "Catnep had a hard night—up twenty times and whimpering. It was all the drinking that did it." There was worry in her eyes I hadn't seen yesterday, and accusation.

Catnep said, "It burns, it burns."

"I know," I said, "and I'm sorry for it, but it must be done."

Catnep let me take her hand and draw her to one of the empty beds, and when I asked her to lie down, she did. She still had a sulky look; it was so habitual with her, it was graved on her face. I drew her gown up about her waist and couldn't help but think of the man who'd done so before me. Catnep squirmed and tried to push my hands away, but Corncockle sat beside her and took her hands to keep them still. I pressed on the girl's abdomen and then turned her over and pressed on the small of her back, above her narrow haunches. I asked if she was sore anywhere—for I feared the firepiss might enflame her kidneys.

She mumbled into the bedclothes, "No, but your hands are too cold."

"The better to put out the fire," I said.

I glanced up and saw Mai standing there with her arms crossed and her head tilted. A quizzical stance, but her face was sober.

Catnep's flesh was firm and warm under my hands, but she began to shiver. I bade her turn over again, faceup, and I laid my palms over her groin and spread my fingers over her belly. I trusted that infusion I'd given her to drink, but medicine alone will not cure, if the gods do not relent, or better yet show us favor.

There is no healing without prayer. Prayer is in the herbs, in the harvesting and preparation; prayer is in the healer's soothing touch. But I'd never before presumed, as I did now, to lay my hands on someone and call upon a god to heal her. I was no priestess, to send prayers on strong wings. But surely my prayers and my touch could do no harm, and might do more, in all humility—for I prayed to the god who'd once favored me enough to save my life.

So I sang over Catnep the wordless song the firethorn tree had taught me, and underneath, in silent counterpoint, I prayed to Ardor Wildfire to take the burning away and to spare her the scourge of fever. When I was done my hands were hot. I pulled Catnep's kirtle down and helped her sit up, and I put my arm around her shoulders. She was crying silently, still shivering. She stiffened against me and wouldn't take my comfort, so I let her go, and she went to Corncockle and stood clutching her mother's skirts like a much younger child.

Stillness had gathered round us in the tent. The whores were all staring. I broke the quiet, saying to Corncockle, "I've done what I can for now. Send word to Mai if she worsens, especially if she catches a fever, and Mai will get word to me." I put my hand on the ox bladder I'd filled with the infusion of dog grass root and stoppered with a wax plug scribed with Torrent's godsign. "Mind she drinks from this thrice a day—and that she goes on drinking the watered wine too."

Then Cowslip came forward, asking for her maythen water and wanting to know what she owed me. I shrugged and looked to Mai, and Mai said, "A graybeard," and I was content with it.

There was no fee for the healing. How can a healer charge for what the gods have given? But Corncockle made me a gift of a tortoiseshell comb, and showed me the best way to tuck it into my headcloth.

Then one whore asked for something to banish lice, and another for something to keep her awake, for she was working so hard she was falling asleep under her customers. "A man comes to a joybird for flattery," she said. "If he wanted a woman who found him tedious, he'd have stayed home." It was heady to be deemed wise.

Before I left I saw Catnep sitting back in the dark corner on her bed, wrapped in a shawl. I was sure the remedy was sound. Hadn't Wellspring come to me in a dream? But the sooner the girl was healed, the sooner her mother would sell her again.

Mai had her vocation, and I began mine. She was a follower of Carnal Desire, and practiced in her arts. She knew how to kindle a man and how to hold him, how to cool him and how to fool him. She could make a woman seem a virgin, just as Corncockle had said, with a pessary for a new hymen and pig's blood to stain the sheets. She had a potion, rather costly, that made you dream of coupling with the one you desired. She never lacked for patrons, high and low.

As for me, I gained a name as a greenwoman. Afflictions were as rife among the women as rats in a midden: the canker, the squirts, shakes and fevers, thrash, weeping sores, boils, and the flaming itches. And there were the wounded women. In the village too, some men beat their wives, but I'd seen nothing like this before: the whore with two ribs broken by her pander, and still he made her bear the weight of customers; the goat girl whose father took after her with a scythe; the sheath tickled by her cataphract with the point of his dagger because his jack had looked at her too long; the laundress caught out alone on the north-of-east road by a pack of foot soldiers, who took her by force and then battered her face with a stone.

I met the boneset, the midwife, the stancher who could stop bleeding with a touch, and the canny who healed the cursed by turning the hex back on the one who sent it. I learned from them, and I did what I could for the women who needed my help. But wisdom lies also in knowing what can't be done. There were times when I left well alone, for patience was the only medicine, and times when I could do no more than ease the journey with fare-thee-well, for the Queen of the Dead had already called on the shade to depart the flesh.

Catnep had taught me caution. I never again promised a cure before I'd devised a remedy; Wellspring's dream was a blessing, and one should not take blessings for granted. Still, I healed this one and that, and they were grateful. When they gave me gifts, I shared them with Mai. What I kept I hid from Galan, along with the coin I earned outright from selling childbane and bloodbright, soothe-me and wake-me-up, powders to blanch the skin and tints to bring a false blush, maythen water and the like for the hair, and a salve of my own devising to kill lice. Even Sire Guasca's sheath, Suripanta, sent for some of my tincture of wart-begone to rid her of spots; I counted it a victory, though a petty one, that she took care to greet me pleasantly now. Fleetfoot became my runner, and he prospered too, spending his earnings on meat pies and honey cakes. He ate all day and never grew fat.

I used up most of the herbs I'd brought from the Kingswood and gathered by the river. I'd carried enough for myself, not thinking others would have need of them. So I'd ride out of a morning on Thole, with Noggin on a mule beside me, to watch Galan and the others at their exercises—riding up and down hills at a gallop, jumping stone walls, vaulting into the saddle, and fighting as if they meant to kill each other in earnest—and I'd dawdle on the way, looking for remedies for this ailment or that. Or we'd go to watch the tourneys in the afternoon, and while Galan was well occupied, I'd circle the tourney field with Noggin, wandering farther and farther afield until we'd left the crowds and battles behind, and found ourselves on some quiet south-facing hillside, where a rivulet issued from the rocks and made a hospitable place for plants to root and grow. I was used to the bagboy now, and never minded he was there. While I filled my gather sack, he'd yawn and doze or amuse himself by catching flies or lying on his back to watch breezes chase the low clouds.

Just as I'd done in the Kingswood, I made trial of new plants by way of smell and taste, and learned which to use and which to avoid. And I sought out herb sellers in the market, and while some were miserly with their lore, others shared freely. Their most potent cures grew in the forests under the sea and were all unknown to me.

I hung bundles of herbs from the tent poles to dry—though it was too damp for proper drying, and much went to waste—and when Galan asked why I cluttered up the tent, I'd say this one was for poulticing bruises, and that one for a tonic to keep chills away, and another for flavoring Spiller's watery stews, and none of it was a lie. But there was much I didn't say. Spiller complained of having to stoop his head, and Rowney looked at me more and more askance; but both were grateful for the lousebane.

One morning Mai told me, "I was up before you today. I was sent for in secret to attend Maid Vulpeja. She complains she's sick to death from longing, and it's true she's wasted away."

I asked indifferently, "Well, have you cured her?"

"You're cold as a canny's quim!" said Mai. "The girl pines to death for Sire Galan, and it seems you don't care one way or the other."

"Ah," I said. "So that's her name. I never knew it."

Mai and I had met, as usual, by the shrine of Delve. We put our heads together and whispered.

"Is it true she's dying for him?" I asked.

"I've seen countless sick from desire but never one yet who died from it. She pines, yes. She's inconsolable. He sent no message, not a word since he tumbled her, and she, being a pigeon and unfledged besides, had believed his promises. I can give her a charm, but I'm afraid it won't cure her. Something else is amiss."

"How can you give her a charm, Mai? With the right hand you gave Galan to me, with the left you take him away!"

She grinned. "Never fear, it's only an amulet to help her forget. I would try nothing more, for my reputation. You know *she* could never bind him."

"I know no such thing," I said. "She is beautiful—of pure Blood—has many graces. I'm none of that."

Mai waved her hand as if dismissing a servant. "Oh, nonsense! She's a pudding, a mere pudding. But still, I pity her, she's been brought so low. What illness is it that causes cramps and retching and weakness but no fever? She can't keep food down; she pisses in the bed, poor thing, and her skin is like tallow, and clammy too. And she's not too clear in the head."

"How long has she been like this?"

"Well, it was before Summons Day—remember?—I told you she was ill. Now she's so thin she'll leave naught but bones to burn. She'll be dead in a matter of days, I should think."

"Is her heart strong or weak? How does her breath smell?" I asked.

Mai snorted. "I didn't get close enough to find out. And besides, we met in a privy."

"Of course," I muttered.

"And there was a stink all around. She'd been borne there on a litter. Her father's sister came too, to keep an eye on her. She's a pursed-lip, pickled dame if ever I saw one. The girl summoned me without her leave and the aunt tried to send me away again as quick as she could; but I saw enough. Tell me, what malady would you guess from those signs?"

I shrugged. "I'm not certain. It's odd she has no fever, for a fever often brings weakness and clamminess and such derangement of the senses. Haven't they called for a healer?"

Mai leaned closer, dropped her voice even lower. "The aunt is nursing her, and therein lies the affliction, I suspect. If I asked you what poison could cause these signs—what then would you say?"

"Poison?" I asked, much too loudly.

Mai said, "The little fool confided in her dear aunt, and her aunt told her dear father. It looks to me they fed her something that didn't agree with her. Better a dead maid than a deflowered one. They think to hush it up."

I couldn't forget how the maiden had sent her manservant to chase us off like dogs. Yet when I searched my heart for pity, I found a scrap. I said, "It could be dead-men's bells, I suppose, or four or five other things. I've never seen anyone poisoned, but I know that if you use the leaves of dead-men's bells against dropsy—for it brings on pissing, which cleanses the body—you must have a care with it. It can kill if you're too free with your measure. Many have mistakenly given more and more of it, thinking to purge an illness, and thereby caused the very illness they sought to cure. I've heard it's used against madness too. Perhaps they didn't mean to hurt her."

Mai gave a cynical grin. "No more than a priest means to hurt the sacrifice. But is there a remedy for it, if it is poison?"

"The obvious remedy. She must take no food or anything but pure water from her aunt or father, or anyone she lives with, even those she trusts. If she hasn't already taken too much of the poison, she might recover."

"If she doesn't starve first," Mai said, "for who will feed her?"

"She's better off starving. It kills more slowly."

Mai said, "Couldn't I slip in a cure with the charm? That might get by her aunt."

I said, "I know only so much of poisons as touches on healing: how to prepare a safe dose of a dangerous medicine, or what to do for an adder's bite or when a child eats too many dillyberries. If you want to know more, ask a poisoner. Surely you know one, Mai. You know everyone."

Mai spat on the ground and made a warding sign. "I know of one, indeed. But I don't doubt the aunt consulted her first."

There was a long pause. Then I asked, for this had puzzled me, "Why take such pains? Why does it matter to you if this Maid Vulpeja lives or dies?"

Mai shrugged, raising her hands as if to say, *Who knows?* But then she gave me reasons, laughing at some even as she said them: pity, for the girl was young; because she'd never yet lost someone to lovesickness and wouldn't have it said that she'd failed in this case. Furthermore, the old dame made her hackles rise; she didn't like her face or her demeanor, and she meant to hinder her. They ought to be crossed, it was a vile thing they did; and besides, it would be a pleasure to tweak the dame's long nose.

"Enough," I said. "I'm convinced you have reasons, though every one too weak to stand on its own legs. And I'm sorry I can't be of help. I know of no way to save her but to starve her, if it is indeed poison."

"Well, think on it. And think on this as well: Sire Galan is not safe. They are willing to poison their own blood so the shame dies with her; they won't attack him outright, lest their dishonor be told, but he should ward against treachery. He should have a care."

We did no further business that morning. I went back to the tent, and as I sat sewing my dress, I thought long about what Mai had said. I had some pale green thread, and I stitched leaves on the bodice, and among the leaves tiny flowers made of shell beads. I stitched my thoughts like this: hard to believe she was dying—Mai had seen her, it must be so—she shouldn't die for a wager—I wouldn't mourn if she did—if she dies he'll be blamed for it—nonsense, he'll be praised, for being a man for whom a maid would die of longing—even if rumor praises him he'll have to die, the father will see to that—is there more danger for Galan in her life or her death?—he should be warned—he wouldn't listen to me—if I saw her, I might know what to do—perhaps the dead-men's bells could be rinsed out in the urine—or mustard and vinegar to make her spew it up—better not meddle—maybe I should use dwale—it's strong enough to help her but it might kill her instead—they'd think I poisoned her, having cause—how strange it would be if I saved her—I could be burned for trying.

Stitch by stitch the pattern grew. My hands knew their work. As my needle jabbed I had time to grow angry with Galan all over again and to scorn him: heedless—brash—arrogant—reckless—feckless—fool! I'd bound myself to this man for good and forever, and didn't that make me as much of a fool? There had been jealousy twisted in the binding, a wish to give pain where pain had been given, the need to own where I was owned, and desire, of course, grasping, insistent desire. An appetite for his touch. Though I craved the sight of him too, and also his words, his sighs, his smiles, the timbre of his voice, the way he looked at me, the taste of his salt. Mai had given me the cure, and I'd been eased for a while. I'd even brought to our bed tricks I'd learned from listening to whores, and when I was forward, he did not hold back. I'd been lulled into thinking the wager was forgotten and the danger passed, and I'd tried to put it out of my mind, as Galan seemed to have done. But he had trifled with a maiden; men can die for such trifling. As the maid was likely to die.

Maid Vulpeja. I found I didn't have the stomach to hate her thoroughly. Suppose she *had* fancied herself a match for Galan. Well, she was but a 'prentice in these wars. Many a veteran had made the same mistake, if rumor spoke true. It was pity she deserved, being, like me, another fool for Galan's charm. Only I was the one lying in his bed at night, while she lay dying. How could I deny her healing if it was within my powers?

And Galan must be warned, though I dreaded breaking the silence between us on the matter of the wager and the maid. I feared what he might say and even more what I might say, once I started talking. I'd have to find words vehement enough to make him listen, but not so hot as to kindle his anger.

So stitch by stitch and thought by thought I made this resolve: whatever I could do to mend this harm, I should do.

CHAPTER 7

Tourney of Courtesy

rux and Ardor were now at odds; Hazard, who set one against the other, made mischief with all of us. The gods trample our resolves.

Evening passed and morning came, and still I hadn't found the words to warn Galan. He rose before cockcrow, as usual, to don his armor, and I heard him conversing with his men about the opponents he'd face that afternoon in the tourney. I listened with only one ear, having heard such talk daily: this one was of no account, that one had some metal to him; Sire Rodela saying beware of a certain Sire Voltizo; Galan laughing and saying he feared him as much as any mouse.

Still I didn't understand. But when we got to the tourney field that afternoon, and I saw the rose-colored banners of the other clan ranged against ours, I realized Crux was to fight Ardor. Then I was uneasy. Ardor had more men: twenty-three cataphracts to our seventeen, not counting the armigers. The fighters would not pair off neatly, one against one. When a clan is outnumbered, and the lines are uneven, a man can't be sure how many will ride against him.

The clan leaders had chosen the scorpion rather than the lance as the weapon for the charge, with the sword to be used after, at will. The scorpion has a wooden shaft not much taller than a man, topped by a head that combines sting, claw, and venom. The sting is the thrusting point, shaped like a short sword. Near the base of the sting is the claw, a wide sickle, sharpened on both the inner and outer curves; it could be used to hook an opponent from his horse or prune one of his limbs. Across from it is the so-called venom, a small heavy spike capable of piercing a helmet. On horseback, the scorpion is wielded with one hand while the other holds the reins. Afoot, it is most often used two-handed, like a quarterstaff. The men adorned the scorpions' shafts with fluttering pennons and tassels, as they did their lances, for the sake of show and to confuse the eyes of their enemies. These being tourney weapons, the scorpion hafts were of pine instead of ironwood and the blades of oak instead of tempered steel.

When the clans charged I forgot to be uneasy. I lost myself in the crowd; we drew in our breath at the signal, and as the charge commenced the breath rushed out with a shout and we were caught there, in the instant of greatest tension and greatest beauty, as the men urged on their horses and the banners streamed in the wind of their riding and the noise shook the air.

I drew another breath and the moment was flown. Galan had let Semental get two strides ahead when the lines met. It was a bad habit they had, both man and horse altogether too eager, and surely the Crux would scourge Galan for it later. The horses with heart will strive to be first, and the ones that lack courage will dawdle, and it is on every man to keep the line straight and strong and tight.

Now they made fine targets. Two men charged Galan: one cataphract aimed high, using his scorpion as a lance, bracing it under his arm to put more force behind the blow; another aimed lower, at Semental, though it was foul to aim at a man's horse in a tourney of courtesy. Their armigers went after Sire Rodela.

I saw Galan rock in the saddle when the first cataphract's scorpion glanced off his shoulderguard. The impact should have broken the soft wood of the shaft, but it remained whole. As Galan galloped on he managed to sweep his weapon sideways at the other man, but the blow was feeble and he failed to hook him with the claw. Semental easily outpaced the other horses, leaving Sire Rodela to fend off Sire Galan's pursuers. Near the edge of the field, Galan turned and rested the scorpion across his saddlebow. In the few moments he had before his attackers closed the distance, I saw him flex his right hand, as if to make sure of his grip. He leaned forward and plucked a scorpion with a splintered shaft out of the padded cushion that protected Semental's chest. I hadn't seen that blow go home.

He picked up his weapon again and joined the melee. Now three cataphracts set upon Galan at once while their armigers went to work driving Sire Rodela away from his master's side. Sire Rodela rarely used the scorpion or the lance. He could afford only one tourney weapon (and that one borrowed from Galan, since the armiger had won two trophy swords but lost three), so he kept to the sword, being more skilled in its use. It told against him this time, as one of the armigers against him had a scorpion and harried him while staying well beyond his reach. Sire Rodela held his shield up against the drumming of their blades. Soon his sword wagged slower and slower, like the tail of a beaten dog. The armiger with the scorpion stayed to finish him and the other two joined the fight against Galan.

Sire Galan had been singled out in other tourneys; it made sense to disable a strong fighter early if it could be done. There was no doubt that this time they intended to make him yield by main force rather than by driving him past the boundary. They crowded him on all sides. Semental lashed out with hooves and teeth, pivoted and struck again. Galan knocked an armiger half senseless; the man bounced like a sack of turnips as his horse took the opportunity to trot off the field.

The riders urged their horses closer, until Semental no longer had room to turn. Galan had lost his shield. A cataphract jabbed at him with the sting of his scorpion while the others tried to unseat him by hooking his armor with their curved claws. Galan held his scorpion like a stave to parry with the shaft and strike with both ends. Perhaps he forgot, in the heat of the fight, that the shaft was of pine and couldn't withstand a heavy blow. When it broke he kept the short end, with the blade. There was no time to draw his sword.

I was watching Galan, only Galan, yet I missed the blow that found its way under his breastplate and severed the belt of his scaled kilt before slipping through the skin and muscle of his belly. I thought Galan had lost his balance when he leaned sideways in the saddle. I thought he'd right himself again. Then he slid. Then he toppled.

I hadn't seen any blood. Nevertheless I was on my feet and running down the hill pell-mell, cursing in both the High and the Low, and praying too. I ran because I hadn't been afraid enough, given that the men of Ardor had reason to do him harm, and now I was too afraid. He'd fallen like a dead man.

Galan was half hidden by the legs of the warhorses trampling all around him. Semental did not run; Galan had trained him to stand steady on the battlefield if he was unhorsed. The stallion's head was down, as if he was blowing hard. An armiger dismounted and cut Galan's banner from the pole and took the weapon from his grip. The Crux rode up, and Sire Alcoba followed with their armigers—why did they come so late?—and while they engaged Ardor's men, Spiller and Rowney came running. The jacks picked Galan up, one at his head and one at his feet, and carried him hastily toward the enclosure on the field. His rump dragged along the ground and his head lolled.

I had the sense to stop short of the smudge pots, for it would have been sacrilege for me to enter the field during a tourney. The priests of Rift who patrolled the boundary would have cut me down.

The tourney went on and on. I waited for it to end, watching the jacks' enclosure instead of the battle as a priest of Rift hurried there, followed by two more, and close on their heels came Divine Xyster, the Auspex of Crux who served as carnifex. They stayed hidden behind the reed fence with Sire Rodela and Spiller and Rowney, and all the while I didn't know if Galan was dead or mortally wounded or merely scratched and dazed.

One clan or another won and I didn't care. Galan's men bore him back to the camp as gently as they could on a stretcher made of two lances and a length of canvas. Sire Rodela, Divine Xyster, and I walked along beside. They'd taken off Galan's helm. His face was pale. His eyes were half shuttered, showing more white than dark pupil. He kept his face turned toward me. He said, "The whoreson bastards have scratched me, haven't they?" and nothing more. His breath came in gasps with frightening pauses, and his cheeks were streaked with sweat and runnels of tears. Sire Rodela had taken off his own padded linen shirt and stuffed it under Galan's breastplate. The blood didn't show on the red shirt, but it left a trail of spots behind us on the muddy road.

They took Galan straightaway into the pavilion of the Auspices of Crux. When I tried to follow, one of the priests' varlets stopped me with a shove, for fear I'd taint Galan's wound with my touch. I wished I were his jack and not his sheath, because Spiller and Rowney were allowed to care for him. When one or the other came out of the tent to fetch something, I pestered them for news.

Spiller said Sire Galan's abdomen had been sliced from his right rib to a handsbreadth past his navel, on the left. He and Rowney agreed the cut had been made by the point of a scorpion, which had found its way between Galan's cuirass and his kilt, punctured a hole in the mail and linen underarmor, and raked across his belly. Just the tip had gone through; the hook of the scorpion had caught on his breastplate and stopped the blade. Galan also had the mark of hooves on his thigh and forearm where a horse or two had trodden on him, and a bad bruise on his shoulder where he'd taken the first blow. No bones were broken. It was the belly wound that worried them.

The wound could easily have been mortal. It was meant to be by the man who dealt it, the father of Maid Vulpeja, the same Sire Voltizo they'd talked about that morning. But Sire Galan did, after all, have luck with him. Divine Xyster said the blade had cut to his tripes but not laid them open. A little deeper and he'd have spilled his guts and that was death for sure. He might die anyway if the wound went bad, of course, but the carnifex had sacrificed a dove and read the entrails, and the omens, on the whole, were good. He would treat him. No healer will risk his good repute on a useless attempt to cure a doomed man.

Spiller was not forthcoming about how the priest cared for Galan's wound. He was brusque with me, as if he was far too busy to attend to my questions. Rowney, on the other hand, told me a few things. He said Divine Xyster used spiderwebs to stanch the flow of blood, which came from a chest full of small reddish spiders brought along for the purpose. The priest had only to reach in a stick and twirl it to bring out a handful of the stuff. Rowney was made to pick the spiders out carefully and put them back in the chest so they could go on spinning in the dark.

Divine Xyster had put some sort of greasy salve on the wound. Rowney could tell me nothing of its ingredients except that it smelled like horse piss and contained verdigris. The priest had fetched a tarnished copper disk from a tall pot in the corner, and scraped the surface of the disk with a knife to produce a green powder that he mixed with the salve.

He'd painted godsigns and charms onto strips of linen, using more verdigris bound with egg white as pigment, and covered the wound with as tidy and intricate a bandage as one could ever hope to see, according to Rowney. Last of all he'd fumigated the tent by burning sage, candlebark, and dried flowers of consolation—the latter tending to produce a dreamless sleep; I could smell that for myself.

Rowney had said a lot, for a man who liked to be silent. I promised him a pigeon for his help, and some hen's eggs if he'd bring me a bit of the salve. I put my faith in the priest's lore of spiderwebs and verdigris, so different from anything I'd learned from the Dame. Both his lore and his prayers were bound to be more potent than my own. I was eager to know his secrets, as if in knowing I could have some share in Galan's healing. In truth I was helpless, and it was hard to bear.

I went to crouch between the Auspices' tent and Sire Guasca's, in the small and stinking hiding place I'd used earlier when I'd cast the bones. I leaned my head against the wall of the priests' tent. I heard nothing from Galan, not even a moan, only Divine Xyster droning a chant. It was evening. It occurred to me to wonder why the others hadn't come back from the tourney field. The camp was empty except for Sire Galan, the priest, his men, and me.

It was more than a feat for a wooden blade to get past iron plate, a mail shirt, and padded underarmor to find flesh. It was impossible.

After we left the field, the priests of Rift went circumspectly to the king. They had examined Sire Galan's wound and garments and they accused the clan of Ardor of bringing real weapons to a tourney of courtesy. The clan's weapons were seized, but only one, that of Sire Voltizo, proved to be of keen-edged steel, masked under silver gilt.

It was an affront to the king, to the clan of Crux, and worse—to the god Rift. Though the king had forbidden mortal tourneys, warriors still brought their private quarrels to the tourneys of courtesy. But it was uncommonly rare to flaunt the rules of battle, and rarer still to be caught doing it. No one would have objected to the man killing Galan fairly, but even Sire Voltizo's kin, who had gladly helped him humble an enemy on the tourney field, disappeared from his side when his base cheat was discovered. He wouldn't say why he'd done it (though there were some who already knew), and he claimed no one had helped him do it; he was only sorry he hadn't given Sire Galan mercy when he'd had the chance. Everyone understood this to mean giving him the point of his mercy dagger through a slit in his visor.

The Auspices of Rift consulted the entrails of a bull. Rift, as expected, demanded blood for the desecration. The king and the First of Crux also asked for recompense, the one for breaking the king's peace, the other for the craven assault on his cataphract, whether the injury proved mortal or not. The parties were long together under the king's canopy. The Ardor no doubt pled for leniency and the many-mouthed crowd spread rumors, most absurd, some with the stink of truth. Such as that Sire Voltizo had offered up his daughter to Rift in his place, but was refused.

It's best not to dally when gods are offended. Sire Voltizo was given a choice: a warrior's death or a quick one. To no one's surprise, he chose to die like a warrior.

It was agreed that Sire Voltizo would never have committed such an offense—for he was known to be reasonably sober minded and free of blasphemy—if offense had not been given to him. If he wished to keep the nature of the insult secret, that was his affair. But as Sire Galan had offended him, and in so doing caused him to offend Rift, Sire Galan must also pay forfeit: his best warhorse, Semental. Rift was known to appreciate an offering of fine horseflesh. Of the two condemned to die, everyone knew the horse was more gallant than the man. The stallion was to be given the same chance as the man—not a fighting chance, for there was no way to win—but a chance to die well.

Galan knew nothing of this, for he was lying in the priests' tent, pale, cold, and trembling at first, and later pale and sweating. I made barley water and took it to the tent, but the carnifex sent me away, saying brusquely that a man with a belly wound should—of course—take no food or any drink except a purge to empty his guts. "Of course," I said, and went to sit, shamefaced, inside Galan's tent, where I could watch the comings and goings. At least I was spared the company of Sire Rodela. He'd ridden back to the tourney field to tell the Crux of Galan's condition.

The execution was a fine spectacle, I heard that night when the crowds came back from the tourney field. Sire Rodela wouldn't speak of it. Neither would Flykiller, who had trained Semental from colt to yearling to the age of three, when Sire Galan himself took him in hand. I heard it from Fleetfoot and Ev, who'd stood on the back of Sire Pava's spare warhorse to see over the crowds.

Some days at the Marchfield it was hard to tell nightfall from bad weather. This was one of those days. A brief rain squall hid the sunset. Crowds of drudges huddled on the hills. Those who'd missed the tournament had come running when they heard the news. They watched as a wall of men of the Blood surrounded the tourney field: priests with torches, cataphracts and armigers on horseback with weapons in hand. It was a somber sight in the gloom, but there was great joy afoot among the mudfolk at the prospect of an execution.

Sire Voltizo had the choice of weapons; he picked the scorpion and sword. They gave him Semental to ride. Four priests of Rift were sent against him, but only one of the four rode out to take him on. They judged that would be enough. The priest wore no armor at all, not even a helmet, which the crowd took as an insult to Sire Voltizo.

The vanished Sun gave just enough light for the sharp-eyed to see what was happening on the field. The chosen priest cantered toward Sire Voltizo. The condemned was overmatched from the first blow and parry. His seat was poor, he slewed in the saddle as Semental danced away, and when Semental felt his rider slipping, he helped him fall. He was not the sort of horse to be patient with a bad rider.

In a moment Sire Voltizo was sprawling on the ground. In another moment the priest leaned over and dispatched him, driving the scorpion's point into his armpit through mail and underarmor and ribs. He was commended for making such a forceful blow with only one hand (that being the sort of thing that brought renown to Rift's priests). The priest had to dismount to pull the scorpion out, it was lodged so deep. As was proper, his hand never left the shaft of the weapon. Sire Voltizo expired with a jerk and an exhalation of blood, and so died quickly after all.

If not for Semental, the crowd would have been sorely disappointed. The black stallion made a better show than Sire Voltizo. He'd been trained to stand by Galan, but the man at his feet was not his master. He ran. Ev could not say a word about it, for it cut him deep, so Fleetfoot told me how it was. Semental was penned on the field by the men surrounding it; no horse is fool enough to charge a wall of lances unless a man he trusts is on his back, whispering lies in his ear. As the last light faded from the sky, the priests chased him around the tourney field. He galloped back and forth, he dodged, and three times he neighed a challenge and turned on one of the men who harried him. He ran in and out of torchlight. He was a black horse, and in his green-dyed leather armor he nearly disappeared in the darkness. But they could hear him. The crowd around the field was that silent. They could hear his hoofbeats, the creak of leather and the jangle of metal trappings, and they heard him grow more and more winded until every breath rasped through his windpipe with a harsh grunt and a strange high-pitched whistle.

It required one priest to dispose of Sire Voltizo; it took all four stinging Semental with their scorpions to ride him down. They had to change their mounts twice, for he wore out their horses. He endured thirteen wounds before the one that finished him.

By the time the pyre was built and the sea wind had carried most of the smoke and ash of Sire Voltizo, Semental, and a heap of dry gorse west toward the mountains, everyone in the crowd knew the tale of Sire Galan and Sire Voltizo's daughter. Some blamed Galan; more blamed the dead man, on two accounts: that he had displayed her too freely and guarded her too poorly; most blamed his daughter for the disgrace she had brought on her house and clan. It won her no pity that she was supposed to be dying of love. The sooner the better, they said.

The Crux came back to camp after most of his men, after the tale had been told and retold. He came galloping and stopped in a puddle, splashing mud. He dismounted and thrust his reins at Thrasher, his horsemaster. He strode to the priest's tent and jerked the tent flap closed behind him.

Inside the tent the priest held a lamp in his hand as he talked to the Crux, by Galan's pallet. The flame spilled just enough light to stretch their shadows on the tent wall. I crept back to my hiding place to listen. I was not the only eavesdropper. The cataphracts around the hearth fire paused at their late supper.

"How is he?" asked the Crux.

I could see his shadow kneel. The priest brought the lamp down by Galan's face.

"Fortunate," Divine Xyster said.

"So he'll live, then."

"For yet a while—though I never venture to predict how long any warrior will live. His bowels are still whole, and that is the best omen we could ask for in a belly wound."

Sire Galan spoke up, saying, "I'm glad to hear it." He startled me—yet how good it was to hear him speak, though his voice was small and strained with a pitiful bravado.

The Crux stood up abruptly and walked away from him. The priest followed. They lowered their voices.

"How long till he's healed?" the Crux asked.

Divine Xyster answered, "If the wound doesn't fester, he'll be ready to ride in less than a tennight. Ready to fight in two, I should guess. He mends fast, judging by his broken rib. If the wound turns noxious, of course . . ." He didn't finish the thought. The Crux was already on his way out of the tent.

The priest followed, saying Galan was in his right mind and could be spoken to. The Crux said, "I'll speak to him tomorrow," and he bit his words so hard they barely escaped his teeth.

I peered from my hiding place behind the tent flap. The priest stayed in the doorway of the tent, looking at the sky. I couldn't tell what signs he might be reading there, in the heavy clouds that covered the crescent Moon and stars. Perhaps he smelled omens in the chill sea wind. He stood there a long time, while the Crux took himself to his own tent and called for his supper.

Around the fire, the cataphracts had fallen silent when the Crux passed them by. Every one of them had felt his anger from time to time. He used it well, nipping their heels to make them run where they should go. This was anger of a different order, and they feared the Crux all the more because he mastered his wrath and made it wait on the morrow, until he had considered what was owing and to whom. There was blame enough to go around. He'd learned of Sire Galan's wager somehow. Not one of them had seen fit to warn him of it, though it touched on the honor of the clan.

I heard Galan shift on his pallet and gasp and curse, as if the pain had caught him hard. I crawled back to sit as close to him as I could with the tent wall between us.

It was not much of a wall. It was merely a sheet of heavy waxed canvas, though it forbade me the other side. From thought to act was quick: I took out my little bone-handled knife and cut a slit crosswise. With one eye I saw Galan lying on a pallet under a blanket of fleece. He was no more than a stride away from me. They'd set a low screen of mats about him, but it wasn't enough to keep out the drafts from the doorway, which made the flame of the oil lamp beside him stretch and bow. In the shadows behind the screen, I saw the altar of Crux, with the blue bowl of the Heavens and the statues of the gilded Sun and the silver Moon in their places upon it. Galan's left arm was outside the covers. His hand was a fist and his face was like a fist, forehead knotted, jaw clenched, nostrils pinched. He stared upward. His skin was chalky and his lips were blue. He might have been a man of stone.

"Sire Galan," I whispered.

He turned his head toward the sound and whispered back, "Is that you?"

"How do you fare?"

He made a smile that was half a grimace. "Marvelously well. It seems I'm to live a while longer." His breath came shallow and fast, and made his voice uneven.

"Is the pain bad?"

He denied it, but I could see for myself he lied. I asked just to hear him speak.

"I suppose we lost the tourney," Galan said. "The Crux seems vexed. I suppose he wagered something he didn't want to lose."

He was right to fret over the First's mood, but so far wrong about the cause, it stopped my throat. Already we were on dangerous ground. I said in a low voice, "I don't know who won or lost."

"I can't hear you," said Galan.

"I said I don't care who won or lost. Once you were wounded, I stopped watching."

"Well, fetch Rodela then. He can give me the tally."

He thought so little of my company he preferred Sire Rodela and his surly tongue. I got to my feet without another word, my eyes smarting. I knew what he'd learn from Sire Rodela would wound him again—and he was sore wounded already.

Then I heard him say, "But stay. No need for hurry. Stay awhile with me."

I sank down again and looked through the hole in the canvas. He was still turned toward me. His brows were drawn together, and I could see the faint luster of his eyes in his shadowed face. It took a moment for me to master my voice. "I'm here, and I'll stay as long as you bid me." Even as I spoke I cursed myself for a dog that would cringe one instant and grovel the next.

Galan's brow smoothed and he closed his eyes. I looked away and rested my head on my knees.

I should speak to him but every word led to Semental.

After a while he whispered, "Firethorn?"

"Yes?"

"I'm thirsty."

"I'll fetch the carnifex."

"No, no. Give me one of your tisanes. I'd drink it without complaint now."

"The priest will have something better. Shall I get him?"

"Stay," he said.

Another pause, and he said, "You must sacrifice to Hazard in the morning, for my luck is still with me."

"It's sure you'd be dead if Chance hadn't turned the blade." I looked through the peephole again.

"Yes, my Luck keeps faith with me." A faint smile crossed his face and was gone. "She should sit right here, inside the tent. What harm in that?" His eyes closed again, and before long he slept.

I knew he spoke of me, not Hazard. I'd never told him that I was called Luck most of my life, and yet he made me wear the name again. I thought I'd bound him tightly to me, but more than one thing can tie a man to a woman. If that was all I was to him, his luck and nothing more, what was to stop him from turning on me in the morning when he found out he was not as fortunate as he supposed?

But I was not his luck. He'd stored up trouble for himself; now it came upon him when he was weakest. It was none of my doing and so how could I undo it?

As for Hazard, Galan presumed too much on the god's favor, forgetting the god has three avatars, and only one seemed fond of him. When Hazard is female, she is blind Chance, and she has a weakness for bold and reckless men. If she puts a finger on the dice for a man or tips the odds in an even wager or makes his enemy's horse stumble, why then she is his luck, indeed. Like most fighting men, this is what Galan counted on. Warriors court Chance with prayers and sacrifices, and they woo her the more faithfully that she's so fickle.

Hazard's male avatar is Peril. He's owed respect and even fear, but warriors don't love him, for he is too impartial. The god's third aspect has no face, no body, no manifestation aside from a deep thrumming sound that only a few have been blessed—or cursed—to hear. This is Fate, a most unyielding avatar.

Some of Hazard's Auspices worship Fate alone, and claim that even the lowliest drudge walks a preordained path, from which it is impossible to stray. These Fatalists preach that Chance and Peril are merely masks for Fate's workings, nothing in themselves, and moreover that all the gods move at Fate's bidding. Their followers take comfort in thinking that their every deed is meant to be; it excuses all manner of meanness.

These zealots are much opposed by other priests, who say instead that Fate is a realm; it lies as close to ours as tongue to teeth. Kings and queens are born in it. The rest of the Blood should pray their paths never take them inside. The temples are filled with such wrangles, as if the priests believe they can, by disputation, lay bare the nature of the gods and their manifold powers, and resolve for all time why everything that takes place does and must take place.

Let the priests argue. I took the finger bones of Na and the Dame from my pouch and held one in each hand. In daylight I might have cast them and asked for guidance. But I was too intent on the dim light from the lamp that glowed behind the canvas wall of the tent and spilled through the slit. I looked through the hole again. Galan slept, but he was not restful. I could see the sheen of sweat on his skin. He'd pushed the fleece away as if it stifled him, baring the neat crisscrossed bandage under his ribs, and yet he was shivering. Where was the carnifex? Galan needed tending.

I would sacrifice to Hazard in the morning, but I'd not send my prayers by way of Chance and her blind priestess. I'd bid the priest of Fate make the kill. The more I thought about it, the more I was sure Galan had been spared for Hazard Fate's purposes, and not because Chance had winked at him.

Sow one bad seed and reap a hundred, and you are in Fate's realm. Just so with Galan's wager. All these consequences begotten by one careless coupling—the maid dying, her father and Semental dead, and Galan nearly so—didn't they show he had unwittingly trespassed? And yet, who can say he crossed into Fate's domain there and then? If the Fatalists are right, maybe all his steps were meant to lead to that act and no other.

Divine Xyster came in with one of his varlets, and they woke Galan. They bathed his face and limbs with water, and he went from shivering to shaking. Then they purged him, first with an emetic of mustard seeds, then an enema. I watched all this and cursed them in silence, for I could see it was a torment to him. Spasms wracked him. The emetic brought up a thin dark vomit; the enema not so much substance as a foul smell. He lay on his side facing toward me and stared at nothing at all.

The carnifex was nearly silent, save to tell Galan to turn or swallow. Galan was also silent, I think for fear that if he opened his mouth, moans would come out of it. He shook and shook, even after the priest and his man covered him against the cold.

The other two Auspices of Crux came in with their servants. They unrolled their beds—no heather for the priests; they lay on feather beds heaped with quilts. A boy went around to snuff the lamps and candles, but left the candlebark and consolation burning in the brazier on the altar.

I listened to Galan's breath, how it limped, halted, stumbled. He was the worse for their care. He had puked and shat until there was nothing left and opened his wound with the strain of it; the bandages were spotted red. Then they went to sleep and gave him nothing for the pain but the smoke of consolation. Perhaps the purging was necessary; it must be so. But I could have given him more ease.

My own guts ached. They were strung tight as catgut strings on a dulcet and quivered as if they'd been plucked. If the priests of Fate are right, we all of us, all the time, resonate to Fate's thrumming, even though the note is too low to hear. It frightened me to think of it.

I became aware again of the finger bones in my hands, gripped so hard they scored my palms. In one hand was the Dame. She had never honored Hazard, in any form: despised gamblers and those who craved danger, and scorned anyone who mistook their own faults and foolish choices for destiny. I flushed with shame to think how she would have condemned Sire Galan for his folly and me for being his sheath.

I had been selfish and kept her finger bone. That meant she knew my state and must be grieved to see me come step-by-step to this stinking ground between the tents.

Then the Dame spoke up from my right hand. I knew that tone of voice. There was nothing in it so soft as sorrow or weak as sympathy. Instead vexation, impatience, and a tinge of weary disappointment, as if she feared that, after all, my clay might not be fit to mold. She said she'd never raised me to be willful and wayward, and yet I was. And even though I had by my own recklessness strayed into Fate's realm, I should be wise enough to know there was more than one way to cross it. That was all she said.

I'd displeased her, a thing I always feared to do. Even so, I felt her care. She was a long way gone on her journey and had traveled far to speak to me. I kissed her finger bone—such a tiny thing, the last joint of the chiefest finger of the right hand—and saw the Dame before me, not her face, but her hands at rest upon the taut warp of a newly strung loom. Every other thread was raised by the heddle, and her hands lay on the shining strands without weighing them down. Her skin was reddened and scored by tiny cuts from the warp thread. Her knuckles were chapped, no matter that every night she'd rubbed her skin with lanolin; it was cold in the weaving room in winter and she needed the shutters open for the light. The square fingernails were trimmed close to the quick to keep from snags while she worked. I couldn't remember ever seeing her hands lying this still, for they were never idle when she was alive.

She turned her hand upward, and before me in the lines that criss-crossed her palm, in the folds and swellings of her hand, I saw Fate's kingdom. It was like a map with every path marked and every crossroads and all the floods and precipices that made the ways treacherous. I saw how we'd arrived here, how we'd chosen one road above all others; those byways faded into the Dame's hand even as I watched, until they were nothing more than faint lines, and only the way we'd taken was plain, a deep crease across her palm. Yet from this moment on, nothing was clear. The crease branched and branched again; there were many ramifying ways, and paths crossed in confusion.

But I searched, and at last I found a way that led out of Fate's domain. The path was narrow and precarious. Galan had been spared so he could go forward. He might choose to go on as he had been, blind and rash, reaping a crop of ill consequence; or he might make amends. He must make amends.

He should pay for what he'd stolen. He must take the maiden who was no longer a maid to his tent before her aunt could kill her entirely. I would nurse her back to health so Galan could send her home. Then let his wife care for his concubine, let them suffer the sight of each other.

A strait road, a hard one. I could refuse it. Couldn't I heal her in the tent of her kinsmen—wouldn't that be enough? But I saw that path too on the map in the Dame's palm; it led to the maiden's death, and mine for meddling, and no end to the feud. She must be brought under Galan's protection; even that was a chance, not a certainty, a way beset by hazards. I saw it now, and saw it plain, that this was a burden laid on me. This was surely why Ardor had chosen me in the Kingswood, saved my life, bound me to Galan, and brought me here: to save one of his Blood. If I gave Ardor the maiden's life, I'd be quit of my debt and god-bothered no longer.

But it was cruel that it should fall to me to make her bloom again, in Galan's tent, in his bed. It was more than I could do.

It was all that I could do.

The Dame closed her fist, and she was gone. I was on my knees rocking beside the tent, still clutching the finger bones. There was a scorched taste in my mouth and I was cold, cold, cold.

Through the slit in the tent wall, I saw Galan lying awake, the whites of his eyes gleaming like shells. How could I convince him of what must be done? I needed no omens to foresee he'd be hard to persuade.

In the morning I'd try. In the morning. For now the priests and their men were sleeping, and it was better not to quarrel, not to rouse them. To let Galan know I still kept vigil there, I began to hum, low and quiet. He turned his head toward me and smiled. Bits and pieces of melodies came to me, songs the Dame had sung at her loom, the reapers' chants, Na's lullabies: somehow the tune the bird had sung to me in the firethorn tree twined around the others, made of them one song. It eased me; I hoped it was some comfort to Galan.

Before dawn Divine Xyster got up to see to him. He asked Galan if he slept, and Galan said no, a bird kept him awake. A while after the priest went back to his bed, Galan whispered, "I thought if a bird was singing, it must mean dawn is near. Isn't this the longest night ever?" I thought to myself, *Long as it is, you may wish it never ended,* but I said, "Morning will come, it always comes."

And so it did, a gray morning with the Sun in hiding. On its heels came the Crux, with his burden of bad news and ire. He dismissed the priests and their servants. I wasn't the only one listening with cocked ears outside the tent walls, but with my eye at the slit I could see what others could not. It was darker inside than without. Smoke from the brazier hazed the air. The Crux came and stood by Galan's pallet, looking down at him. His face was grim, but his voice, when he began, was mild. He told Galan the blade that cut him was made of steel, and Galan unwisely said he'd wondered if it was.

"And why did you wonder?" asked the Crux, in a reasonable tone. "Did you think the man might have cause to bring steel to a tourney of courtesy?" Out of respect for the dead, the Crux avoided using Sire Voltizo's name.

Sire Galan held his tongue.

The Crux waited. While he was waiting he began to pace, and the silence grew heavier until it could not be borne.

Galan said—hesitating, as if he had some doubt about the matter—"I thought he might."

"You thought he *might,*" said the Crux, turning to face Galan.

Galan said, "Perhaps he didn't welcome my courtship of his daughter." He thought he could banter with his uncle, as he often did, that he faced nothing more caustic than a little sarcasm. He should have listened harder.

The Crux came three steps back and crouched by Galan's head. He leaned close, as if to make sure no words could escape on their way from him to Galan, and he spoke quietly, deliberately, and his voice shook for being held so strictly in check. He said, "As sure as you are lying on your back with your belly opened, you are lying with your tongue. The man would have welcomed courtship, but you took his daughter's virtue, and for no other cause than a wager. And here's what's come of it: your precious Semental is dead, and the maiden's father is executed, and last night someone caught Sire Alcoba's armiger out alone and stove his head in, and now Alcoba is hot to spill Blood for Blood. Do you see an end to this?"

"Semental is dead?" asked Galan. I could barely hear him.

"Yes, dead." The Crux laughed harshly. "But I'm sure it will solace you to know he accounted well for himself before he died. Which is more than I can say of the maiden's father." He stood, and from this greater height said to Galan, "The carnifex says this is not a mortal wound; see to it that it doesn't kill you, for I have other plans. I told you this once already, Nephew. It seems you didn't listen. I said if you tried my patience too hard, you would go walking: home to your father or behind me. If your wound isn't healed by the time the king is ready to go to war—and that time is nearly upon us—I'll send you back to your father, and I'll have your word on it you'll walk every step of the way. If you're well enough, you can follow me. But you'll come on foot, you'll fight on foot, and if luck is with you and the gods permit, I'll be able to tell your father you died as bravely as your horse."

The Crux turned and left the tent. I heard him say curtly to the priests waiting outside, "Let him be for a while."

While the Crux had spoken to him, Galan had lain on his back, stiff and unmoving. Now everything that was rigid in him bent. He turned on his side, face to the wall, and labored hard not to make a sound, but failed. Such moans and sobs tore from him that I could not bear to see or hear, and I sat rocking on my haunches with my hands covering my ears.

When he was spent he quieted. I took my hands from my ears and heard him turn on the pallet. He said, in a voice rough from misuse, "Are you still there?"

He could only be speaking to me. I whispered, "Yes."

"Did you know all this?"

"Not all of it."

He said bitterly, "I called you my bird. I should rather have called you a carrion crow. All this long night and you didn't think to give me one word to warn me of what was to come."

"I thought it kinder not to tell you."

"Did you know Semental had died—and the man too?"

"I had heard. I wasn't there to see it, I was here in the camp waiting for news of you."

"And yet you didn't tell me."

"It wasn't my place to tell you."

"That's a cowardly lie," he shouted. "Your place? Were you ever so chary of overstepping it? You seem free enough to me. You have a ready tongue when it pleases you to be insolent. It is not your *place,* as you say, to keep anything from me that I have need to know."

He railed so loudly that the priests hurried in to see what troubled him. They must have feared his wits were wandering, to be disputing with the air itself.

He shouted again, "Go fetch me Sire Rodela. I'll have no more of your lullabies today!"

I stumbled away from my hiding place, around the upturned cart and behind the tents. All that had seemed so clear last night was muddied now. Had I wronged him? It was true: I had been a coward not to tell him. He'd not had time to don armor against the Crux's blows, and all because I would not be the one to hurt him. All the same, he'd earned every blow.

Spiller met me outside Sire Galan's tent with raised eyebrows and a thumb drawn across his throat. Inside, Sire Rodela stood while Rowney knelt to fasten his greaves about his calves.

"Look who comes, tail between her legs. I thought you'd wandered off for good," said Sire Rodela, smiling. As he spoke he turned a ring on the finger of his right hand, and before I guessed what he meant to do, he stepped forward and slapped me so hard across the cheek my ears rang. "Where did you lie last night, while your master lay wounded? This is how you repay his favors: you stray like a bitch in heat. Can't you go one night without a pricking?" he said, and he made to come after me.

I dodged away, my hand pressed to my cheek, while Rowney—bless him—clasped Sire Rodela's leg and said, "Please hold still, Sire. I'm not done with these buckles."

I spoke up for myself in a shaking voice, "Sire Rodela, your master summons you. Best go quick. And if you want to know where I was last night, ask him and trouble me no more." My hand came away from my cheek smeared with blood. "Look what you've done. You suppose wrong if you think I'm so out of favor you can mar me and Sire Galan won't fault you for it."

"I've marked you," he said, holding up his hand to show the family crest on the ring he'd used to cut me. "It's a mere scratch—a little remembrance from me not to stray again. And here's your leash and collar." He hauled Rowney upright by grasping his ear and said to him, "I know you've finished with my greaves. You took long enough. Now bring my helmet, and see she stays here until I say otherwise."

"But I have errands in the market, Sire," Rowney said.

"Errands must wait. Have you forgot whose armiger was killed last night? No man leaves the tents without four or five others and his arms and his wits about him. We have Sire Galan to thank for this." He turned to me again. "I'll go pay a visit to my cousin. And if he doesn't know where you were last night, I'll cross your face with stripes and I daresay he'll praise me for it."

When he was safely gone, I lay facedown on the cot with my head on my arms and thought how swiftly events unraveled, more swiftly than amends could be made. Now Sire Alcoba's armiger was dead, and no one owning up to his killing. Sire Buey had probably been set upon by a mob. He'd been a good fighter too. Durable, more ox than bull. His wits plodded but got where they were going. He had steadied Sire Alcoba, and the Crux was right: it was hard to see an end to this feud now that it was openly begun.

In the light of day, I still didn't know how I could convince Galan to purchase what he had already enjoyed for free, especially since he was angry with me and likely wouldn't welcome me near him. There was much I should be doing and nothing I could do, so I lay there disconsolate, my forces spent.

Spiller and Rowney chattered and clattered about the tent. They put on their heavy leather jacks and armed as if they were readying for battle. For Spiller, I think, the feud was a fine way to pass the time until the war began. Rowney took it more to heart. Before Sire Galan won him in the wager from Sire Alcoba, he'd served with Sire Buey and liked him well. He was eager to go trawling for vengeance with his former master—whatever he was told about keeping to the tent.

Sire Rodela came back sooner than I expected. I stood as far from him as I could, wary of him, but he didn't concern himself with me. He sent for Flykiller and told him to curry Sire Galan's warhorses, braid their manes and tails with green ribbons, and gild their hooves. Sire Galan had said that if he couldn't ride them, the gods should have them. Rift had already taken his best horse; let Crux have Melena, the bay, and Hazard the gray he'd won from Sire Alcoba, and maybe then the gods would be content.

"Yes, Sire," said Flykiller. He was a silent man, and now his face spoke for him, how grievous it was to see his charges and all his care of them day and night, his pride and delight, wrested away in a moment.

Oh, this was a fine gesture for Sire Galan to make, perhaps a wanton one. A passingly good warhorse is worth more than a crofter's household can scratch out in a year or two; fine horses like these were worth half a village. Semental had been priceless. I wondered if the gods would be appeased with a gift offered from spite instead of reverence. Nothing given to the gods is wasted, but an ox or two would have done as well, would have been generous. Two warhorses came perilously close to squandering.

Sire Rodela called Spiller and Rowney and Noggin to him and said, "Your master comes home on the morrow. Make everything ready for him; turn the tent upside down if you must." He took the key to Sire Galan's strongbox from the purse at his belt and gave Spiller some silverheads (and it cost me a pang to see him so free with Galan's key and Galan's silver). "Get enough stores at the market to last a week. Sire Alcoba and Sire Lebrel are sending their men this afternoon. Go with them and be wary, do you hear?"

I spoke up. "I should go too. Sire Galan will need soothe-me for his pain, and I have none left."

"The priests will see to that," Sire Rodela said. "You're not to leave the camp." He came closer with his crooked smile. "The scratch is not so bad, is it?"

As soon as the men had left the tent, I went back to my hiding place. I peeked and saw Sire Galan asleep at last. I would not wake him. I wrapped myself in my cloak and lay on the narrow ground between the tents and watched the clouds roil by in the patch of sky over my head. Thoughts drifted into dreams. I tried to dream that all would be well, as if that would make it so, but the dreams changed shape as readily as the clouds and as little obedient to my command.

The priests woke Sire Galan at nightfall, when it was time for the sacrifices. They put him on a litter and carried him the short distance to the altars around the king's hall. When we had arrived at the Marchfield, the king had honored the clan by placing our camp near him. I wondered if he regretted that now. How far had the clan of Crux fallen in his estimation? There were always rivalries among the clans, and feuds that came and went; this feud promised to linger.

The Crux himself led Melena, and Sire Alcoba the gray. Flykiller had prepared the horses well. They wore only bits and bridles and they'd been brushed until their coats shone, and without their heavy caparisons anyone could see how well they were shaped from forelock to fetlock and what fine horseflesh would soon be carcasses. Behind them came the Auspices and Sire Galan on his litter, followed by the cataphracts, armigers, and jacks, all bearing torches. Men and women from other clans joined us as word spread, and their foot soldiers and drudges too, until a multitude had gathered at the king's hall. The clan of Ardor stayed away.

One man whispered to his neighbor, pointing out Sire Galan. The next must perforce speak a little louder to be heard over the first, and so on, until solemn voices became a clamor. They hushed again when we stopped at Hazard's shrine. Three priests waited there, droning a chord of ill-fitting notes. One of them—Fate's Auspex—played an instrument with one string that made a low, throbbing sound under his thumb that set my teeth on edge. On the stone altar stood statues of two of Hazard's aspects: a blindfolded wooden Chance, wearing a gown of red paint, and Peril, cast in bronze, with armor of silver. Fate was not represented. A bundle of dried sess, smoldering on the three-legged brazier, gave off a drugged smoke to lull the sacrifice.

The gray went to his death unknowing. Not docile, because a warhorse isn't bred for docility, but unafraid and willing to be led, which was counted a good omen. The priestess of Hazard Chance held the knife. She had no need to wear a blindfold like her mistress, for she had long ago sacrificed her eyes. Fate's priest had to guide her hand to the gray's throat. Still, the cut was swift and clean. The Crux kept Melena turned away from the altar so he wouldn't see the other horse die. The bay's nostrils widened when he smelled blood and he snorted. But he was not much disturbed. Warhorses are inured to that smell when they are colts, made to stand by while a butcher does his work.

Galan stood up for this, although he couldn't stand straight or alone. He leaned on Divine Xyster's arm, his face even paler than it was before. His stare was fixed and glazed, as if he couldn't see what was before him. He never blinked or wept. He'd shed his tears for Semental and had none to spare. It made him seem coldhearted, but I could see what it cost him to stand and watch; he spent his strength, his stubbornness, his will. After the horse that had been Sire Alcoba's foundered and thrashed and lay still, Sire Alcoba turned and gave Galan a bitter look.

Galan looked down. His knees gave way and Divine Xyster caught him under the arms and lowered him to the litter so he could be carried to the altar of Crux, on the other side of the king's hall. The crowd came too, some ahead, some behind, all around us. It was no longer a procession but an eddying current that bore me along, a mote among other motes who jostled and pushed and dinned gossip and nonsense in my ears.

Melena was restive now; he pranced and sidled and jerked his head. The blood smell, the crowd, the noise meant a tourney to him and he was ready for it. He wouldn't stand still at the altar. Two men had elbowed their way in front of me, but over their shoulders I could see Melena's round eye, his ears pricked forward, his tail whisking, the muscles bunching in his hindquarters as he backed away, pulling against the reins the Crux held. I saw his bewilderment when the Crux jerked hard on the curb bit and Flykiller came up on the bay's right side and took hold of his mane and threw his weight over his withers to keep him steady for the knife.

Galan stood again. Divine Hamus, the Auspex of the Sun, made the cut, but it wasn't clean because Melena was tossing his head and had to be cut twice. Blood spattered over the gold statue of the Sun and the silver statue of the Moon, over the Auspices and the Crux and the spectators and on Galan too. But enough was caught, in the blue glass basin that represented the Heavens, for the priests to use in divination. Melena staggered. A shudder ran over his skin. His left hind leg gave way and he fell sideways, toward the Crux, and in a little while the kicking stopped and he was dead.

The crowd made a loud murmurous sound around me, like the sea, but I moved in silence, as if the noise had deafened me. I listened for another sound, for the low thrum of Fate. I knew it was there, beyond my hearing. I could feel it under my ribs, in the pit of my belly, in my womb. Torchlight chased shadows over the glossy hide of the fallen horse and the gray standing stones of the altars. Galan wavered in this light, half a shade himself. The hair rose on my nape and I felt, for better or worse, that the eyes of the gods were truly upon us.

Many stayed for the butchery, the search for portents in the entrails, and the other blood rites of the Auspices. And they stayed for the feasting after. The mudfolk would dine well on the sacrifices that night—all the better because the Blood are forbidden to eat horseflesh. I followed Galan's litter back to the tent. He had slumped and lost consciousness, his wound bleeding freely again. He'd already lost so much blood. How much more could there be?

This time I watched through my peephole as Divine Xyster tended Galan, and if that was sacrilege, I didn't care. I saw everything the priest did. He bade his servant to come quick and spread his hands over the wound and press down. The blood welled up between his fingers, but in time it stopped flowing. Mercifully, Galan was still in a dead faint. Then the cobwebs and salve, a clean bandage and more smoke. Divine Xyster had a short temper. He cursed Spiller and Rowney for standing about in the way, struck his varlet for bringing the wrong salve, and muttered about Sire Galan's idiocy. But his hands were precise and sure and kind.

Galan groaned and opened his eyes and Divine Xyster said to him, "Did you mean to offer up your own blood too? I shall have to keep you here until I'm sure you won't do yourself further harm."

Galan made no answer except to close his eyes and turn his head away. The priest sat back on his heels and eyed him for a moment. Then he got to his feet and rinsed his hands in a basin of water. He told Spiller and Rowney to stay with Sire Galan and come running for him if he took a turn for the worse or began to bleed again; he'd be with the other priests at the altar.

When Divine Xyster was gone, Spiller and Rowney exchanged a look. Rowney checked the tightness of his belt and the looseness of his sword in its sheath and said, "You watch. I'll be off." Spiller grinned and wished him good hunting, and I knew that it wouldn't go well with any man of Ardor, from bagboy to cataphract, found roaming alone tonight. I hoped none would be that foolish.

Spiller settled himself on the ground with his back against a wooden chest and his legs stretched out before him, and before long his head nodded and jerked as he wrestled with sleep and lost.

So I kept watch on Galan, and as I did I marked how his face had changed. I could never have fixed my eyes on him so long if he were well; when he caught me looking, I'd blush and look away. Now he could not defend against my gaze.

His skin had slowly lost the brown tint of summer while we were at the Marchfield. He rode out all day, but under clouds and usually under armor. Still he had shown a ruddy health, but tonight his face was pale as vellum, and on this vellum was written, in inky shadows, the shape of his skull. I saw the fever creep upon him again until his hair was matted to his brow with sweat and red bloomed high on his cheeks. He turned his head from side to side. Muscles twitched in his arms and hands.

I kept vigil in my place beside the tent, by night and by day. Galan slept more than he woke. In his sleep he mumbled and cried out, but when he woke he was silent, his mouth an obdurate line. He said nothing even when Divine Xyster gave him a foul emetic to drink each day, forcing him to retch from the bottom of his belly when there was nothing to bring up. Afterward he'd lie back stricken with weakness, and I'd see his eyes glinting through slits, his hands restless and shaking among the bedclothes. His wound would seep again.

Divine Xyster burned herbs and chanted over Galan, and consulted with the other priests of Crux over the omens. Galan himself had made his wound more grievous, but the gods were troubled too. The Auspices were much alarmed by Crux Moon on the night of the sacrifices. He had squatted low in the sky, a baleful yellow, and the part missing from the full was on top, giving him an ungainly look. On the other hand, they'd seen a great many hawks circling over the Marchfield, a sign that the ancestors of the House of Falco were near—whether to guard Sire Galan, or to guide him through his dying, it was hard to say.

The Crux didn't come to see Galan; nor did Galan's former friend, Sire Alcoba. Sire Rodela came often. Sometimes he squatted by Sire Galan's pallet and told him the news, while Galan stayed unspeaking: Had he heard that Sire Limen's best horse had broken a leg? Or that some of Sire Alcoba's foot soldiers had trounced two of Ardor's drudges out behind the cesspits and left them for dead? And Sire Lebrel's bagboy had disappeared—killed in the feud or deserted, no one could say. Sire Rodela said the whole Marchfield was in a commotion and every man, even the lowliest foot soldier, had taken to wearing clan colors, a ribbon or a feather in the cap. The king's own clan, Prey, strutted about in force to keep the peace, as if their Blood was purer than the rest, and it wouldn't be long before such offense was given as would have to be answered.

And Sire Rodela told Galan, "Your sheath didn't come home again last night. Where do you suppose she's got to?" The armiger knew full well where I was; all Sire Galan's men knew by then, though they never discovered my peephole. Galan turned his back on Sire Rodela, and the armiger smiled.

But I also saw Sire Rodela sit by Galan's side while his master sank into Sleep's ocean and was visited by dreams that startled him into speech. The words Galan uttered in his sleep were thick and mangled, incomprehensible. The armiger had worry on his brow as he listened. He fidgeted at his beard, rolling his jowl and bristles between his thumb and finger, a habit he'd taken up after Sire Galan had burned off his hair, when he left off following Galan's clean-shaven fashion. His dark eyes fastened on Galan or somewhere beyond him.

I'd often wondered what Sire Rodela felt for his master, aside from envy, which seemed a kind of thwarted admiration. They jested and mocked each other harshly in a way that, among men, sometimes masks fondness. But if there was fondness, they hid it too well. What did affection matter, so long as the armiger was loyal? I thought he was; I hoped so. Now in the dark I saw something unexpected on Sire Rodela's face. It surprised me that the bastard's son showed such care for his better-born cousin.

Sire Galan had other visitors, but they went away unsatisfied. He wouldn't break his silence.

I too found nothing to say.

* * *

On the second morning Mai swept boldly as you please into our camp on her high wooden soles, Trave and Pinch on either arm. She sent Spiller to fetch me. When she saw me she clucked and fussed and swore she could hear my bones rattle. I admitted I had forgotten to eat much. It nearly undid me to see her. If I could have I'd have laid my head on her breast and wept like a child. There was no place to talk without being overheard, so we stayed in the tent feeding twigs to the brazier and spoke softly while Galan's men were near.

"I saw Sire Galan at the sacrifice," said Mai. "A feather could have knocked him over. They're laying odds against him in the market. Some give him a day; some a week."

"He should never have got out of bed. He was mending, before. But he'll mend yet, you'll see." I believed this too, for no cause but one: I couldn't imagine anything else.

"It was the first time I had a good look at him."

"He has looked better," I said.

Mai grinned. "Even so, I can see he's cut from good cloth."

I swallowed the knot in my throat before saying, "He's cut to my measure, anyway."

"I wouldn't mind taking his measure myself," said Mai.

I answered quickly, "That would finish him for sure."

She laughed that rumbling laugh of hers from deep in the belly, the one she had when the jests were especially pungent. "Never fear," she said, holding up her hands. "He has troubles enough without me."

I leaned close and lowered my voice to ask, "What do they say of him in the Marchfield? Do they think the sacrifices ill done?"

She said, "He never puts a foot wrong. If he'd taken it meekly when the Crux made him a foot soldier, he'd have lost all repute. Instead, he tied the Crux's beard to his mustache and the old man had to stand still for it—he couldn't very well say the gods didn't deserve such a generous propitiation."

"But surely every man of the Blood who envied Sire Galan before will scorn him as soon as they see him walking."

Mai shrugged. "Maybe. Or maybe he'll start a foolish fashion and the young men will jump off their horses and go strolling after him." She paraded two fingers down the hill of her thigh. "Of course the *sober* men, the careful old miserly men—Sire Torosus for one—they say the Crux was too lenient and Sire Galan too extravagant. But what of it? The whores love Sire Galan, the hotspurs love him—it seems the gods love him. *I'd* never wager against him."

"To be lauded by fools is no great feat," I said, "and no great comfort to me, either. He'll be killed with his first step on a battlefield. As well fight naked as without a horse."

Mai sighed and took my hand between her own. Her fingers were warm and mine were cold. "Didn't your mother warn you when you were on the teat to stay away from warriors?"

I shook my head and couldn't say a word. We sat a moment in silence and I thought of what would become of Mai if Sire Torosus should die, leaving his wife high on a hill with no reason to love her husband's sheath and her husband's mudchildren. I squeezed her hand and said, "Good advice often falls on deaf ears, doesn't it?"

I looked around the tent. Noggin was sleeping behind some sacks of grain; perhaps he thought he was hiding, but his wheezing gave him away. Sire Rodela and Rowney were out. Trave and Pinch diced near the doorway. Spiller sat nearby with the leather tack and bards of the warhorses spread all around him. He was oiling the leather and polishing the metal fittings. The caparisons would be sent back to Sire Galan's home, as they were no use to him now.

I chose my next words with care, for Spiller could hear us. "Mai, do you remember that—that harlot you told me about—the one with the wasting sickness? How does she fare?"

"Well, she's not dead yet, though I can't imagine why not. I visited her yesterday and gave her a bit of medicine: barley water mostly, and the cleanest mountain water I could buy."

"Barley water should be good for what ails her," I said. "And what of her sour old aunt? Does she still tend her with such—devotion?"

"She's much distracted with other affairs. The whole brothel, you might say, is in an uproar."

I lifted the grate on the brazier to feed the flames. We sat in a small puddle of heat. Day by day, the air by the sea grew more chill, the brazier more welcome. As I broke a branch, I hid my voice in the crack and rustle and said, as if indifferently curious, "I suppose the whore could be got cheap now. She looks worthless, but someone who could cure her could get quite a bargain."

Mai laughed. "Do you plan to take up pandering?"

I rolled my eyes toward Spiller to caution her and said, "No. I just wondered what price she'd fetch these days."

Mai looked at me askance. "Hasn't she cost enough already?" was all she said. I knew she took my meaning, even if my reasons puzzled her. She'd find out for me what price Ardor asked for a concubine now that she was used and had not worn well.

On the evening of the third day, Sire Galan asked for water in a grating voice. I sat up to put my eye to the peephole. I'd been lying under a bit of awning I'd made from two old sacks. A mizzling rain, driven sideways by the wind, stung the bare skin of my face and neck. Drops clung like sandflies to the fleece of my cloak.

Inside the tent was a haven of light and warmth. They'd put three braziers around Galan, for he had wandered from fever to chill and back again many times. Rowney jumped up with alacrity and took him a cup of water; he and Spiller had watched by turns. Divine Xyster squatted beside his patient to watch. Galan couldn't sit up by himself, so Rowney lifted his head and put the cup to his lips. Galan gulped three or four times—I could hear the dry working of his throat—before he began to cough. Divine Xyster rolled him on his side until the fit passed, then let him lie on his back again. He pushed Rowney away and gave Galan water himself, but slowly, one sip at a time.

When Galan had drunk his fill, Divine Xyster took his arm away and asked gruffly, "Are you with us now? I began to fear the shades would take you."

Galan shook his head on the pillow. "The shades would have none of me," he said. "They turned me back."

Divine Xyster said, "It's just as well. The Crux would have clipped my ears if you'd died. But it wasn't your fatal hour. I thought you'd live—it was a clean wound for a belly wound. It will make a fine scar."

"Just my luck," Galan said. He turned his head toward the wall, toward me. His eyes closed in the sleep of a man so exhausted another word was beyond his strength.

Divine Xyster claimed he knew all along that Galan would live, but I'd seen the carnifex when he hadn't looked so certain, when he'd gotten up in the night to touch Galan's forehead and peer under the bandages, when he'd bidden his varlet to bathe him with cool water or Rowney to bring coals and furs and be quick about it.

When Galan had asked for water, I'd taken my first unfettered breath in days. Fear had so beset me during my vigil that when his breath came short, so did mine, and when he shivered, so did I. My neck was crooked, my back bowed, as if I'd been trussed up in my own sinews. The thought of that maiden—Vulpeja—stayed with me while Galan lay helpless. She was helpless too, surrounded by her loving enemies, and he was to blame for it, as he was to blame for the feud that had already taken lives. Beneath the fear, there was rage. The more I tamped it down, the more it gained strength.

How could I speak of her when he was downcast already? And I dreaded his fury. He'd brooded these last days away; surely he'd had time to contemplate how I'd failed him with my silence.

If I didn't speak now, I'd fail him again.

Deep in the night I heard Galan turn on his pallet from one side to another, and on his back again, and I guessed from his breathing that he was awake and suffering. All those men sleeping in the tent—the priests and their drudges, Galan's jacks—and yet Galan was alone. Pain is always borne alone.

I leaned my cheek against the tent wall and sent my whisper through the canvas. "Sire, you'll be coming home soon. On the morrow or the day after, I heard Divine Xyster say."

"Are you there? I thought I heard rustling outside the tent, like a mouse in the wall, these last few days. Yet it wasn't like you to hold your tongue."

"Nor like you, Sire."

"You should have spoken."

"Would you have answered?"

There was silence. I was so afraid he wouldn't speak again that I held my breath.

"I dreamed you were here," he said at last. His whisper was just above a sigh.

"That was no dream."

"So did you truly lie beside me in the tent, and wrap yourself around me, and give me a fever against the chill?"

"I fear I wasn't so bold."

"I also dreamed you left me," he said.

"I never left."

"But I seem to recall I sent you away." His words were sharp but the voice was wry.

Joy was rising in me. He didn't speak of my transgression; nor would I. Maybe the fever had burned his anger to ash. So his jealousy too had sometimes passed, quickly as a summer storm raking across the mountains.

Now that I was sure of his answer, I dared to ask, "Do you mean to banish me again?"

"No," he said.

"Just as well. I wouldn't have gone."

"Stubborn," he said. I heard fondness in it. "That's a flaw in a woman."

"You have the same fault," I said.

"It's no fault in a man."

One of the priests stirred on his feather bed and I waited until he was quiet. "I say it is. You were so set upon the sacrifice of your horses, you got up from your sickbed beforetimes and it nearly killed you."

"Ah, but I'm too stubborn to die."

My lips near the canvas, I murmured, "Then I'm glad of it. If the shades won't have you because you're mule headed, I suppose it's some use after all."

I heard a muffled laugh that stopped short with a gasp. "Less chaff, please," Galan said. "I haven't the stomach for it tonight."

Our whispers made free of the dark, went where we ourselves couldn't go, as if lips brushed against an ear, as if sound were touch. And if we talked nonsense, what of it? It eased me to spar with him. Yet we crossed wits near a precipice; one misstep and we might fall.

I put my eye to the slit. The lamps were out, but his face was clear before me. His cheek and jaw were shadowed by beard; the rest was white as bone. He turned on his side, toward me, and cradled his head on his arm. To turn made him wince, but he smiled when he said, "I have a chill. Come and warm me."

I did imagine creeping in to lie beside him on the pallet, and the thought burned. But I said, "Divine Xyster doesn't sleep as soundly as you suppose. You have only to stir and he'll come running."

"I'll risk it."

"I will not."

There was no smile on his face now. He labored to sit. The covers slid down, leaving his torso bare save for the bandage crisscrossing his midriff. He bowed his head and his hair fell over his face; his breath came harsh and quick. He began to hitch himself across the floor toward me. Only days ago he'd have covered the ground between us in one stride.

"What are you doing?"

"If you won't come to me, I must come to you," he said.

"Then you're reckless, and a fool besides."

"Fool, is it?"

"What would *you* call a man who throws everything away on a whim and a wager? Even his life—for you'll lose that too if you're not careful." I was reckless myself. I hadn't meant to speak so bluntly, but my anger was hasty, and wouldn't tarry for wisdom.

He reached out his hand and touched the wall between us. "Hush," he said. "I've had time and enough these last days to reckon how much of a fool I am, and of what sort. I don't need you to tell me. But tell me this: *have* I lost everything? I dreamed I lost you too. Is it true?"

I said, "I know why you want me, why you keep me. It's for luck, only for luck. You've said so yourself. Now your luck has turned, what use am I?"

"What use?" he asked. "What use is breath?"

I answered, "None, to a dead man. So lie you down and rest." But the words lingered between us and now I heard them better: *What use is breath?* I'd sought this when I bound him, that I should be as necessary to him as air, water, and bread. Yet I had reason to mistrust his words.

He wouldn't lie down. I had the advantage, for I could see him where he saw only darkness. I searched for omens in the furrows of his brow and the corners of his mouth. I should be able to interpret him well; I'd studied his signs, since we'd met, as carefully as any priest studied auguries. I'd taken his long silence as a token of sorrow and of rage that he'd been cast down. Nor did I forget his anger at me. Had I misread him? There was both sorrow and rage, I was sure of it; but if he was contrite, it meant he'd turned his fury most of all upon himself.

I traced the line of his profile from brow to nose to lips, and there I tarried. I could barely hear him. "You'll leave me now, sure as Chance has abandoned me."

He turned away, and by the hunch of his shoulders, the angle of his nape, the curve of his back, this much was plain: he grieved, and yet refused to weep. What could I say to ease him? I had nothing as precious to offer as what he'd lost—Chance's favor, horses, the regard of his fellows. I'd already given what little I had, and as far as I could tell, sweet words aside, he didn't value that little so highly.

In a while he turned toward me. His eyes were narrowed and his mouth was grim. "You'll leave me, sooner or later. Well—you may try—but you'll find you don't have my leave to go."

"It was a dream," I said.

"It was a *true* dream."

"It was false. Why say this? I've been steadfast. *You* are the one who dallied elsewhere." Vehement words, constrained by a whisper.

"And perhaps I will again. That means nothing." He was jealous of the breeze touching my skin; a sheath hadn't the same prerogative.

"You paid dear for that nothing."

"And if I lose you too, I will have paid too much."

"Fine words. If you mean them."

"Do you willfully mistake my meaning? I have been plain as I can be. I've tried to please you, haven't I? I thought you were content."

"With a headcloth, a length of wool, and a pair of slippers."

"If it's gifts you want—if that's all you want—you shall have them. What rare and precious thing do you lack? I'll get it for you. You forget my uncle left me something when he took my pride. He left me my money."

I pressed my cheek against the tent. My face was wet. A torrent of words had carried us this far, farther than I'd meant to go. Yet not far enough—I should speak of that maiden now, and how she too had paid for what they'd done. But I was afraid to speak of it. And I was selfish; never had bitter words sounded so sweet.

Galan said, "I gave you something I thought you wanted more. You're a hawk by nature; very well, I let you slip your jesses and hunt about the Marchfield with your fat friend amongst the dames and the whores, and make a few coins. Maybe I misjudged. I see I got no thanks for it."

"So you had me watched." I thought of Noggin, simple Noggin, always at heel like my own shadow. I should have guessed he was carrying tales.

"If you keep one secret from me, you may keep many. I may be a fool, but I'm not foolish enough to take a woman's word for how she spends her time," he said harshly.

"Then judge me by my deeds, not my word—as I judge you by yours. What cause do *you* have for mistrust? Why accuse me, say I will leave? Is it because you want me to go? I'm just a sheath, and when the war is over, you'll put away your sword and cast me off. If that time has already come, tell me quick and have done with it." I looked away from the peephole, from his face and his blind staring eyes.

"Enough," Galan said. "Is this your revenge for a few nights away from your bed? You'd mock me to death."

"I'm not mocking you," I whispered.

"Maybe I deserve it of you. I've laid waste to all I've touched, even this, even what I hold most dear."

"Now you mock me."

"No, never."

There was a long, long silence. In that silence much noise that I hadn't heard before: the wind, the spatter of rain on the tents, dogs barking, a man snoring. I'd been so intent on Galan, I'd nearly forgotten the priests and their drudges asleep in the tent. I'd followed his voice deep into the quiet between us, where we could speak no louder than a breath and be heard, and no other would hear us.

When he spoke again I felt he had picked his words with great care before he let them go. "When I first saw you, you caught my fancy; maybe for the color of your hair. I thought a tumble or two would suffice. But the more I had, the more I wanted. On the third night, when I asked you to come with me, I asked myself why I should be so content to lie beside you while you slept. And yet—you agreed too readily and that made me wonder, and I was not the first and that made me jealous—and so I was discontent. On the fourth night I thought: what appetite grows the more it is fed, and finds no surfeit? I asked the same on the fifth night and the sixth and every night thereafter. I thought that the little maiden might cure my craving; I wagered on it, you might say. But all she cured was my doubt." He paused. In a voice less than a whisper, he said, "If you truly don't know this—if you don't know I'm starving now for the sight of you—I fear it's not mockery but something worse: indifference. It means you don't feel the same want."

If a woman can be unmanned, I was. Unmanned and disarmed. I leaned on the tent and put my palms against the canvas and my eye to the slit and saw him sitting still and tense with his head cocked, as if he listened for something—for me.

"Galan," I said, and went no further. I had never called him Galan without "Sire" before it. I started again. "You sent me away, but here I sit. Why else would I be here?"

He smiled faintly. He said, "To torment me, I suppose," but he breathed freer.

"Because we are bound, you and I," I said truthfully. If I could believe him, he was tied to me even before I buried the womandrake. Now we must be twice bound—but this I forbore to say. "It's a tight knot. Only a blade can undo it."

I pressed against the wall between us. Under one finger I felt a seam that held together two lengths of the canvas, running up and down the wall. Wax was thick over the seam to keep out rain, but the stitches were coarse and long.

"Galan, do the priests still sleep?"

"So it seems. Like bears in winter."

I put my knife to the heavy thread of the seam, cut it through, and with knife and fingertips began to unpick the stitching. I cursed under my breath that I had not thought of this before, how I might unseam a bit of the wall and sew it up again before daybreak, and none the wiser.

Galan laughed a short, breathless laugh. I heard him drag himself closer. "And you call *me* a fool," he said.

CHAPTER 8

Honor

ivine Xyster was true to his word, sending Sire Galan home to his tent on the morrow. Those who'd wagered on Sire Galan dying paid up and made new wagers on whether he'd go home or go to war. A few fools bet that the Crux would relent and let him ride. A race was on between Sire Galan's mending and the war beginning.

The king's men had finished cutting their road to the sea, leaving a wide white scar behind them, paved with chalky rubble. The sledgehammers were silent. But down by the boatworks, the thump of caulkers pounding tow between the cracks with heavy mallets echoed off the cliffs; the armories in the market sent up a thudding, ringing, clanging, tapping, rasping, hissing din from the various hammers, large and small, and from the files, chisels, bellows, and hot metal doused in cold water. All that would go on until we departed, and after; such work was never finished.

Why, then, did the king dally in the Marchfield with winter coming on? At night our breath clouded the air and some mornings there was a rime of frost on the gorse bushes. It was not the cold alone that people feared, but the damp that came with it; those two companions roamed the encampment, spreading ague and other ills, making mischief. From our own tents a two-day fever called the burning carried off Sire Limen and left the Crux with the unlucky number of sixteen cataphracts; it also took Sire Erial's jack, Ware, and five foot soldiers. One of them was Dag, from my village. The carnifex bled the sick in the tents and dosed them with some kind of fever-soothe, and left the foot soldiers to fend as best they could. They said Divine Xyster could tell a man was likely to die by the color of his blood, for it would be nearer black than red. Most who got the burning recovered from it as swiftly as it had come, whether Divine Xyster bled them or not. As for the others, the soldiers shrugged and said Chance wanted their bones for dice.

But restlessness too was catching. "Sow out of time and reap a poor harvest," the drudges said, meaning war had its seasons and winter was not one of them. The longer King Thyrse waited, the more we'd suffer for it, food and fodder and shelter all harder to come by. The rumormongers claimed he had a reason for delay, but no two agreed on what it might be, or when we might leave. The Crux, who spent hours closeted with the king, said nothing, and time proved rumors to be lies.

Once I asked Mai why the king tarried. She shrugged and told me I must learn to love the waiting. She said it was a soldier's lot to wait and wait and never know why, and the rest was dust and mud and a hard slog followed by a sudden sharp poke in the eye, and if a man lived through that, there'd be more of the same. Much like a sheath's life, she said, only we didn't mind so much when we got poked.

Sire Galan was determined to mend fast. He aimed to go to war even if he had to walk. He promised to obey Divine Xyster, to sleep when he was bidden and to lie abed until he was bidden to rise, to eat and drink as he was bidden and in everything be more biddable than I'd ever found him.

I hoped he might be as obliging to me, for I must try him on the matter of Maid Vulpeja; already I'd waited too long. At times I'd doubted she was poisoned, but then I'd think how a slow poison was better disguised. Nearly a tennight ago Mai had said the maid had no more than a few days to live, and yet she lingered. But I had no doubt she'd die soon if she didn't leave her clan's tent for better care. That was a race too, though no one wagered on it.

That first night Galan was back in his own bed, I pinched the wick of the last burning lamp between my fingers and bent over him.

"I'll lie on the floor," I whispered, "for your comfort."

"I think not," he said.

We were alone in the tent save for Noggin, asleep on his pallet by the grain sacks. The rain had moved on, east toward the mountains, and fog had come in its stead, settling on the camp near evening. The Blood had taken their supper outside and now most of them sat up late around the common hearth, a ring of blackened stones. Sire Guasca's jack brought out his pipes and another man a pair of gourd drums, and they played melancholy tunes at first and then the raucous songs that follow too much wine. The fire waxed and waned as it was fed a bit of driftwood, damp gorse, or one of the bundled sheaves of salt hay that could be gotten cheap; the firelight hollowed out a vault within the white fog.

I untied my headcloth and shucked off my dress and crawled in beside Galan. I was afraid I'd hurt him. The cot had never seemed so narrow. No room to lie unless we clasped tight, or one turned when the other did. Galan didn't smell sweet; he had the sour taint of fever sweat still on him.

I hadn't tied the door flap and it snapped in the wind. A draft of cold air found its way inside, fraying the ribbon of smoke rising from consolation flowers on the brazier. A faint red glow breathed from the coals. I would have gotten up to fix the door, but I was grateful for air that carried the smell of the sea.

Galan and I lay face-to-face. His skin burned against me except where the bandage covered him. I put my arm under his neck and he tucked his head between my shoulder and cheek; he sighed and I sighed. Then he began to shake, and after a moment I realized he was laughing silently. "Oh," he said, "I'll never forget it, how you opened a door in the tent last night where none should be. You're a clever seamstress."

"Maybe. But don't boast about it or the Crux will throw me to the dogs. He promised to do it once if I got underfoot, and he's a man of his word."

"Ah, yes. My *amiable* uncle . . . ," he said, and there was a freight of bitter pride in those few words. He claimed the Crux had taken his pride when he'd disgraced him, but it was there regardless—and no small part of it was pride in his Blood, his house, his uncle, and his uncle's favor. But Galan had spent that favor lavishly, spent it until it was gone. There'd be no leniency from the Crux, no kindness beyond the one mercy he'd already been offered.

Thinking of this, I moved my head so I could look him in the eye, and said urgently, "Galan, you must take your time mending. Or feign sickness, if need be. No one will blame you if you're not well enough to go to war. Accept your uncle's charity and go home. Why should you cast your life away? You won't please the Crux—he's past pleasing."

He laughed. "You've not met my father. It's no safer at home."

I was vexed that my fear amused him; I'd not show it again. I mocked him, saying, "So your father frightens you?"

"More than any army," he said, and took a kiss before I expected it.

And soon he had one leg between my legs and a hand traveling down my back, and his mouth was on my neck and the question I'd thought of asking was flown. And then I had my leg on his waist and the blanket slipped down, and then his teeth on my lower lip and his arm under my knee and yet some sense enough left to both of us to know he couldn't take my weight on him nor should he lie on me, so we stayed side by side and it was awkward until we found our fit. Then I opened my eyes and found Galan watching me with a narrow smile. He moved a little and no more, gave a little and no more, my hips a cradle for this rocking. My breath caught at the intolerable sweet torment and I closed my eyes against his smile. Then he grasped my shoulders and his hands tangled in my hair and he pulled me down hard.

Afterward he lay sighing against my neck and there was honey in my veins. My limbs felt full and heavy and warm even as cold air licked sweat from my skin. He asked if I was content and I was sorry he'd spoken, for I was content, and wished I could remain so, side by side with him through a peaceful night. I waited too long to answer, making excuses to myself that Maid Vulpeja would keep till the morrow, and if perchance she didn't outlive the night, the gods could hardly fault me for it. Knowing all the while that my courage was failing and all the speeches and words I'd mustered against this moment had run off like so many deserters. He pressed me and still I hesitated and he pressed me harder, thinking I kept a secret from him. By then I had so vexed him with my silence I might as well speak up, and I told him I'd be content if he would pay Maid Vulpeja's price and bring her to his tent as his concubine and save her life. He surprised me by laughing long and hard.

"I'm in earnest. Why do you laugh?" I said.

"Save her life? Do you suppose she dies of lovesickness, and I'm the cure?"

"She lies closer to death right now than you lay these last nights. I've heard that her kin have poisoned her, and all because she let a certain pickpocket at her maidenhead, a light-fingered, ungrateful thief. A fickle thief. You've forgotten all about her—haven't you?—though she dies for you."

He said, "Her father showed her about like a whore. He shouldn't have been surprised she turned out to be one."

I'd stifled my fury a long time. Now, as it rose, my voice rose with it. I said that if she was a whore, he'd made her one, and now she was dying for it, as her father and Sire Alcoba's armiger and Semental too had died for it, and for his honor he should do something to make amends.

There was a long wait before Galan spoke, and when he did his voice was low, and where my words had rushed, his had a deliberate pace. "My honor is not in *your* keeping," he said, and he turned on his back and stared at the ceiling of the tent.

"How good is your honor—to a woman? I wonder what you said to Maid Vulpeja in the privy tent, what promises, what swearing up and down, what oaths on your faith and by your word?" I had one arm over his chest and I felt his breathing change and his muscles stiffen. I moved my arm away. Suddenly I felt it was dangerous to touch him, though we lay so close.

He turned a look on me that held my voice in my throat. When he spoke his mouth twisted, as if the words tasted sour. "Do you think I have to forswear myself to get a maid to lift her skirts? I said no more than I needed to say, which was that she was fair and I wanted her. Which was not a lie. And since she is the seventh of seven daughters and without a dowry—and within reach of any old man with a purse of gold who thinks a virgin's blood and a tight sheath will polish up his rusty prick—do you wonder she didn't require much persuasion? She gave her maidenhead away for a good jouncing, and what she gave, she gave freely."

He made me see it again, he meant me to see it as I had pictured it too many times unbidden since he'd won his wager: Maid Vulpeja astride his lap in the privy tent, skirts rucked about her waist, his hands gripping her hips, his voice in her ear.

I said through my teeth, "You are a notable prickmaster, I'm sure. And I'm sure you've gotten in and out of many beds and many scrapes before and never felt it touched on your honor, though you dishonored those you touched. But this is different, isn't it? Her maidenhead, which you claim you got for free, cost you your health, your horses, and will probably cost you your life before long. The rest of her will come cheap—because she *was* fair. She's not fair any longer. Now her face, which pleased you so much, looks very like a skull. Three chests of linens and fifteen good milk cows toward a sister's dowry and she's yours. Or anyone's."

"Let anyone have her then. I owe her nothing."

"But you dishonored her. And try as you might to gainsay it, you are dishonored too."

He rolled toward me and his hand was over my mouth, pressing hard, and his face was so close I felt his breath on my cheek. It was then I recalled how he'd let Sire Rodela say too much before he burned off his hair. So he had let me condemn myself, word by word. But it was too late to unsay any of it.

In a hoarse voice he said, "I would kill a man for saying less than you've said tonight. And you—a mudwoman—presume to teach me what the honor of my Blood requires. It's true what they say: 'Smite a drudge and he will favor you, favor a drudge and he will spite you.' I should have beaten you long ago. Maybe then you wouldn't despise me."

He took his hand away and I drew breath to say I didn't despise him, I never despised him. He put his hand over my mouth again and whispered, "Be still! I'd get no joy of thrashing you, but I'll do it if you try me further." And with that he pushed himself away and lay with his back toward me.

I wondered at his forbearance, why he hadn't struck me for the things I'd said. How could I have spoken of his honor when I knew he was so jealous of it? I'd blundered my way into this quarrel with unguarded words and lost my chance to win it. There was no shelter in his bed, so I got up and pulled on my dress; I put the blanket over Galan and he shrugged it off. Then I sat on the ground next to the cot and bowed my head.

It was beyond my ken how if a man looked at Galan sideways he'd have his hand on his hilt, ready to draw for honor's sake, and yet he had come from the privy tent with his honor intact while Maid Vulpeja's was as broken as her hymen. The Blood claim mudfolk have no honor worth the name, and it's true we prize fertility over virginity and lay no blame on bastards for being fatherless. And we steal from our masters and cheat our masters and shirk our duties, so the Blood say, and it's not all a lie. Why shouldn't we, for the Blood tax the bread right out of our mouths? But we shun a man who steals his neighbor's sheep or his neighbor's wife. And when one man promises to pay another a weight of grain when his crop comes in and they spit in the dust to seal it, sure enough the one will pay the other. If there are a few stones mixed into the wheat, why, the second man should have sifted.

I knew something of honor, though I had none to call my own. In the Dame's household, honor had to do with a certain fastidious honesty and touchy pride. No man could ever find fault with her good name or good husbandry, despite that she lacked a husband.

I'd thought *that* was a woman's honor until I'd come to the Marchfield and met Mai. She had many patrons among the dames of the Blood who wore their good repute like gilding; a scratch would uncover any manner of wantonness. Maid Vulpeja would be untarnished still if only she'd kept her secret from the wrong ears.

Men also had honor of various qualities. Galan was not one to value his lightly. It came to me too late how I'd insulted him when I accused him of making false promises to part the maid from her maidenhead. It cut him deep that I rated his word so shallow. He might have forgiven the rest. I thought bitterly that he was more scrupulous of the wager than the woman.

I wiped my eyes and nose on the blanket. Galan lay awake; I knew it from his breathing. Sire Rodela's stuttering laugh came from Sire Alcoba's tent, and Spiller joined in at a higher pitch. Sire Rodela laughing meant trouble for somebody. He'd left his mail shirt in our tent, but I took no comfort in that, for I'd seen him earlier and he was wearing a borrowed jack with metal rings laced to leather, so he could move quietly. They'd go hunting tonight, for they'd set a price on Sire Buey's life and wouldn't be satisfied until one of Ardor's Blood had paid it.

I kept thinking about what I could say now that I'd said too much. I tried one phrase and another and found them all wanting. All wanting. My thoughts scurried and made reckonings and bred doubts and meanwhile my body suffered. The cage of my ribs closed tight and I could hardly breathe. My throat was scraped raw.

The gods had meddled, that was the difficulty. Otherwise I'd not be carrying the burden of Maid Vulpeja's life. But soon I began to wonder if I had read the gods' signs right, and before long I was in doubt that Ardor and Hazard had shown me any signs at all. Perhaps I'd made much of a few scraps: firethorn berries and two finger bones, a daydream that came untimely in the night—and my pride, my temper, my unruly tongue.

I doubted Galan most of all. He'd told me plainly what would happen if I tried to talk to him. If Galan and I came to blows in hot anger, it would not matter so much, but a cold beating—a methodical beating—and after it, more of this cold silence—that would be hard to endure. The silence hardest of all. It gave me a chill to think how I'd bound us together. Suppose the binding held, though he despised me now and never troubled to speak to me again?

I shouldn't have risked so much as one of his frowns for the maiden, for she'd done me nothing but harm. As for the harm she suffered, she'd chosen it. Let her die quick and trouble me no more.

Still sitting on the floor, I turned toward Galan and watched his back. His curls were dark against the nape of his neck. The neat bandage that wrapped him from ribs to hips was disarranged and twisted. We'd done that in our recklessness. Last night, tonight even, I had been inside his keep; now I was outside. His back was obdurate, a wall of flesh and bone. I would make myself small enough to crawl through any chink in the mortar—if I could find one—and chance a beating if need be, for I would not be walled out.

"Sire, give me leave to speak," I said.

He didn't stir, though his breathing changed pace. He didn't forbid me. I took my leave from that. I spoke low and asked his forgiveness. I hadn't meant to say he was dishonored or forsworn, never that; my ignorance was to blame for choosing my words so poorly. He was right, I knew nothing of honor and should have held my peace. It was just my unbridled tongue—a fault of mine—I often had cause to regret it, but never more than now.

All this I said to his back, and meant it too, much of it, but even to my own ear, my voice sounded false, no matter how earnestly I spoke. False and craven. The voice of a drudge to a master, for so he'd named me and so I was. Last night he'd sung a different tune. But wasn't it the same song with which he had tickled Vulpeja's ears? *You are fair and I want you*. I'd heard more because I wished to. I clenched my fists on my knees and rested my forehead on them and fell quiet. He'd let me talk without raising a hand to stop me, but I took no comfort in it; I had buzzed in his ear like some fly he couldn't be bothered to swat. He didn't even look at me. Speech was fruitless. I would wait him out.

In the end, though I waited half the night, sitting by the cot and lying by it and sitting again, I couldn't outwait him. His stubbornness outweighed mine. I had tried placating him and failed. He wouldn't let me back out of this quarrel; there was no way through but forward. I couldn't rid myself of Maid Vulpeja after all, because whether the gods toyed with us or not, as long as there was a feud every man and jack of Ardor would seek Galan as a trophy. It was fear that drove me, not courage, when I lit the wick of the oil lamp and brought it around the cot and knelt where I could see him face-to-face, within his reach. He glared and I faltered.

I set the lamp carefully on the ground before looking at him straight. "Galan, do you think I want that whore in your tent? Do you think I'd risk a beating for her? It is for *your* sake I spoke."

He raised himself on one elbow abruptly and I held out one hand, palm toward him, to fend off the threat in his eyes.

"Why should I help her, if not for you?" I asked. "Do you think she'll be grateful to me if I cure her? She'll likely spit in my eye—and if she dies I'll get the blame. But I've *seen* this. Hazard Fate showed this to me the night you were wounded."

He was still as a cat daring a mouse to cross its path.

I went on in haste. "Everything has gone amiss since your wager. This is not Chance, just as it wasn't Chance alone that you were spared. You're in Fate's domain now. As I kept watch by the tent, I saw the paths as clear as I see your face before me now, as clear as the lines on the palm of my hand, and there is but one way out and it's a narrow road indeed. You must save her life to end the feud."

At that he cursed and lay back on the cot, staring upward. His face had paled. Then I knew why he listened, why he held his hand. He was frightened.

I pressed on. "If you wait—even another day—it may be too late. The paths in Fate's kingdom do not stay in one place."

He said, "Hazard sent *you* a vision. The gods don't soil themselves with mud." Despite the scorn in his voice, I counted it a victory that I'd made him speak.

"The gods made us first and found us fair, or you'd have no ancestors."

"Oh, you're fair enough. But mud is mud."

Mud is mud. I rose up from my knees and walked away from the cot, out of his reach.

I said, "Once you called me Hazard's breed. Have you forgotten?" No matter that I didn't believe it, if he did. "Perhaps, if Hazard sent me to you, it was to tell you this. But now I know my words are wasted. You'll never take her as a concubine, for what would the hotspurs say? You'd rather affront the gods than have it said you lost your wager and paid for her after all. Why the gods took offense, I don't know, for there's nothing remarkable in a plucked maidenhead. You made amends—sacrificed unsparingly to Rift and Crux and Hazard, to every god but the one you most offended. You begrudged Ardor, and Ardor will hound you."

Galan sat up abruptly and put his feet on the ground as if he meant to stand, but pain waylaid him and he went no farther. He gripped the edge of the cot, hard. The look he turned on me was still full of rage, but it was shadowed with fear and hurt and something more—disgust. "I'm weary. I'll take no more taunts from you," he said, and paused to catch his breath. "It's your spite I can't stand. One minute you seem fond and the next . . ." He shook his head and looked away. I could see the weariness in his face, in the ashy skin and the bruised flesh under his eyes and the gaunt cheeks.

He went on. "I don't care where you sleep tonight, but you'll not lie beside me. If you still want a thrashing in the morning, ask me then." And he bent down and snuffed the lamp's wick, and settled on his side with his back to me again and the blanket over him.

The night was at its lowest ebb when I went outside and sat by the deserted hearth and stirred up the coals. The fog was thinning, dark patches streaking the white, but it was still hard to see from one side of the common yard to the other, much less anything beyond our tents. I'd learned to rely on shadows to see in the dark; in the fog I was as blind as everyone else. The fog blanched the night and smothered the eye. It begot wraiths that moved among the tents, and I was afraid if I looked too long I might recognize them.

I shivered under my cloak and put a handful of salt hay on the fire to make it flare up. I would begin the night over, and when he asked if I was content, I would say yes and yes again, and a curse on Maid Vulpeja and all her kin for coming between us.

I heard a rumbling growl and looked up and forgot to breathe. A great manhound bared his teeth no more than ten paces from me. A man behind the dog said, "Who is it?" and I breathed again, seeing it was Dogmaster and the beast was chained.

I said, "It's me," and a moment later thought to add, "Firethorn."

He came closer and the manhound loomed over me, his hackles up, still growling. Dogmaster put a hand on his ruff and said to the dog, "Be still! No danger." To me he said, "What are you doing out in the middle of the night?"

I shrugged. I couldn't recall he'd ever spoken to me before.

"Best go in," he said, and turned and walked past the tents and into the fog. He was patrolling and I was a lackwit, for I'd never stopped to think that if Sire Alcoba and Sire Rodela could go in search of trouble, Ardor could also bring trouble to us. The weather favored raids.

They'd know Galan's tent by his banners. They'd know he was in there wounded. Thank the gods they didn't know he was alone save for Noggin, who was worse than useless.

I went to Sire Alcoba's tent and peered inside. The tent was empty, as I feared. I stood, and when I turned around, there was Sire Alcoba with his sword point at my breastbone. He raised one black eyebrow and said, "Looking for someone?"

"Sire Galan's men, Sire," I said, my eyes on the ground. "He lies unguarded."

Sire Alcoba motioned and Rowney came out from between his tent and Galan's. From the corner of my eye, I saw another shape move, and that was Spiller on the path that edged our camp. Sire Alcoba with Galan's men: well, that was fair, as he'd lost his jack and his armiger too through Galan's wager. Fetcher was Sire Alcoba's jack now, raised from his bagboy to replace Rowney, but he'd found no armiger to take the place of Sire Buey. Perhaps he must avenge him first.

"I thought you'd gone hunting, Sire," I said.

He pointed to Galan's tent. Rowney took me by the elbow and pushed me inside. When I turned to protest, Rowney put his finger over his lips and squatted down outside the door flap with his bare sword before him. I scrabbled under Galan's cot for my belt with its little knife. Not for the first time, I wished for a longer blade and the knack of using it.

I sat inside the door, facing into the tent. I knew how easy it was to cut another doorway in a canvas wall; Ardor's men could come from any direction. A plague on Galan, sleeping soundly after our quarrel. He'd sleep through his death if he wasn't careful.

So I waited through the night, cold and shivering, until I heard a noise—and there was little to hear but the manhound sniffing around the tent, the clink of his leash, the scuffle of Dogmaster's footsteps—and then heat would flood me and sweat would seep from my skin. Stomach queasy, mouth dry, heart thumping. My thoughts skittered away from the danger, and once I drowsed, only to start awake more afraid than before. After a while I thought to draw Galan's sword. It was folly. What harm could I do with a blade against a trained man, unless he chose to fall on it? The sword was heavier than I expected. But my hand was soothed by the feel of the hilt.

A dog barked. The other war dogs sent up a clamor, and I jumped to my feet and hissed to Rowney, "Are they here?" and discovered he was no longer on the other side of the tent door. The fog was more like gauze now than uncarded wool. Rowney stood near the tent with his head tilted. He saw me and shrugged. The dogs quieted, but not before they were answered by others around the Marchfield, and those by others.

I heard someone ask, "Anything?" and Sire Alcoba said, "Nothing."

"The gods send us a quiet night," said the Crux, moving away.

Sire Alcoba didn't answer.

Rain came instead of dawn and pelted the fog away. When it cleared there were still dark clouds in the east, hiding the Sun, but over the sea there were more scraps of blue in the sky than we'd seen for many days. Spiller was the first to come back to the tent, and I hurried to sheathe Galan's sword as he entered.

He grinned when he saw it and asked if I'd slept well.

"About as well as you," I answered.

Rowney came in and Spiller laughed, saying he looked like a drowned rat. Spiller had no call to talk, with his thatch of hair matted to his forehead and water dripping from the eaves.

Noggin had slept through the disturbances of the night. Spiller rousted him out of bed and sent him off, sniffling and coughing his morning cough, to empty the chamber pot and fetch water. "Lazy sod," he called after him.

Galan still slept, so I kept my voice low. "Did you really think Ardor would attack our tents last night? Break the king's peace?" In the night it had seemed so likely, but now that it was day and nothing had happened save for dogs barking, I had my doubts.

"Aahh!" Spiller said with disgust. "The Crux is too careful." He unlaced his heavy leather jerkin, which was stiff with tow padding and sodden from the rain, and hung it from a tent pole. "He caught us leaving camp and put the hobbles on us, made us keep watch instead."

Rowney dried his sword and dagger on a blanket. "Too bad Ardor didn't try us. The Crux planned on it, I think. He had fifteen men on guard besides us, waiting for them. If they'd come, we'd have spilled their blood and caught no blame for it."

Noggin set down the water bucket, saying, "You should have waked me," and Spiller snorted.

I said, "The Crux has too much sense to want this feud. More sense than you. I wager he expected more trouble from Sire Alcoba than from Ardor last night, and had you standing guard against yourselves." I laughed at how the Crux had outwitted them, but the jest pricked me too. I hoped I'd never live through another such night.

Yet I would. Wasn't I on my way to war? I wondered if I'd have the strength for it.

Rowney shook his head as if he disagreed with me but couldn't be bothered to argue. Spiller said, "Huh. The Crux spits on Ardor's name. He must be planning something to requite the murder of our armiger."

I said, "No matter how carefully you measure out the blood spilled on each side, the scales never balance. They tip one way and then another—it's easier to start a feud than end one."

Spiller scoffed and gave me the old saying: "A coward's wisdom is as easy as a whore's virtue—and just as little to be trusted." Rowney shook his head silently again and took out his oil and whetstone.

I lit a fire in the brazier and set about making a strong brew of wake-me-up. When I looked up Galan was watching me. I flushed, wondering how long he'd been awake.

His stare slid past me and he said to his men, "Where's Rodela?"

Spiller gaped.

"Well?"

"I don't know, Sire," Spiller replied. It was plain he had an idea where Sire Rodela was, and wouldn't say.

"Get over here," Galan said, "and help me to the pisspot."

Spiller and Rowney jumped up and helped Galan to sit on the edge of the cot. A rank, foxy smell came from the bedclothes. One jack grasped him under the arm to keep him steady, while the other held the chamber pot. When Galan had pissed he shook them off and sat with his shoulders hunched. In a while he said, "Bring me clothes," and Rowney fetched a linen shirt and eased it over his head. It was not a simple matter to put on hose but Galan insisted on it, though we could tell it pained him. Next he stood and next he walked, Spiller and Rowney on either side, a few paces across the tent and back.

I asked, "Is this wise?" He ignored me, except his lips tightened and I could almost hear his teeth grind together. "I'll fetch Divine Xyster," I said. Then he looked at me and I stopped halfway to my feet and sat back down on the ground.

He called for his boots and his surcoat. To put on his boots he must sit and stand again, and by that time his face was haggard. He left the tent with one hand on Spiller's shoulder and the other on Rowney's, and I watched him walk past the tents of Sire Guasca and the priests to the tent of the Crux—not many paces, but every pace costly—and as he walked he straightened his back and seemed to steady.

A few cataphracts were already at the hearth. I guessed that most of them had been up all night; they were boisterous, pestering Cook and his drudges as they went about their work, cawing at every little gibe. They hailed Galan when they saw him. He lifted his hand and smiled and ducked into the Crux's pavilion. Rowney and Spiller stayed outside, squatting on their heels and pitching stones at a puddle. Before long the Crux's men came out of the tent, leaving Galan alone with him.

I was sitting on the ground eating porridge and watching the Crux's doorway when Sire Rodela came back. He sauntered up as if he'd been out for a stroll, wearing the borrowed jack stiffened with iron rings, a sword, and his usual crooked smile. Wherever he'd been, the rain had caught him, for he was wet through. His arms were crossed, which seemed odd until I saw that one arm cradled the other and there was blood between his fingers. He jerked his head to bid me follow him into the tent.

He sat on Galan's cot and started to unlace the jack one-handed. The leather thongs were swollen tight from the rain; he impatiently called me to help. He had a habit of ordering me to do this or that for him, and I of pretending not to hear. Spiller too was often deaf to his commands. The jack and I were allies in this, at least, our private war with the armiger, and though it was risky, we were practiced at reading his moods; his smiles often foretold more trouble than his frowns. This morning Sire Rodela was well pleased with himself, warmed by some secret cheer, though his left hand curled uselessly in his lap and he dripped blood on Galan's bedclothes. I told Noggin to help him and busied myself with the cook pot at the brazier.

The armiger scowled and asked, "Where is Sire Galan?"

"He wondered as much about you, Sire," I said.

"Well, here I am," he said sharply. "Where is he? I thought he'd be safe in his bed."

"He's with the Crux."

"Oho, so that's how the wind blows." He didn't seem perturbed. I wondered if he knew why Galan had gone to see the Crux; not that it mattered, as Sire Rodela was ever one to tell me what I didn't wish to know and hide the rest.

He grimaced as Noggin pulled off the jack and the padded red shirt. He bent his left arm at the elbow and inspected it.

Noggin sucked air between his teeth and I took one look and said, "I'll get the carnifex quick." I'd expected a cut, but this wound laid bare the meat in a slice along the back of Sire Rodela's hairy forearm, from his elbow halfway to his wrist. Blood welled from it.

"No," said Sire Rodela, looking at me. "No need. You bind it."

"I won't touch it. Divine Xyster would have my hide. It's bleeding badly." I wondered he was so willing to risk defilement by letting a woman touch his wound. Did he mean to trap me in a transgression so he could turn the priests on me?

He set his jaw and said, "This is not so bad; I've had worse. Now clean me up and be quick about it—and you'd better keep quiet about it or *I'll* have your hides."

Noggin stood there slack-jawed until I snapped at him to find some linen—a shirt, anyone's shirt—and hold it over Sire Rodela's wound. "Press hard," I said, "even if he curses you." I fetched rainwater from the barrels. It was none too clean, but would do. What else? Spiller had poured wine on a cut once. That was all we had, lacking Divine Xyster's cobwebs and foul-smelling salves. If he were a woman, I'd have put a paste of woundwort on it and maybe even stitched it closed, but I wouldn't risk so much for Sire Rodela. And Noggin was too clumsy; I'd seen his mending on Sire Galan's shirts.

Sire Rodela's eyes met mine over Noggin's shoulder. He didn't even flinch as Noggin pressed. "And the other man?" I asked. "How did you leave him?"

He smiled one of his dangerous smiles. "Shorn," was all he said.

I asked Noggin to lift the cloth; the bleeding had lessened, but the linen was mostly soaked. I could see something white that looked like bone. I said, "This is deep. If you won't let me get the priest, let me fetch Spiller. He'll keep quiet."

Sire Rodela said, "He couldn't hold his tongue unless I plucked it out and handed it to him."

"You think Noggin can? He tells Sire Galan everything," I said. The bagboy seemed too daft to be sly, but I'd not overlook him again—and if I made trouble for him with Sire Rodela, I didn't mind. "Let me get Spiller."

Spiller was reluctant to come at Sire Rodela's bidding until I whispered why he was needed. On our way back to the tent, under the eyes of the cataphracts, I asked quietly if he could hear what Sire Galan and the Crux were saying to each other. "For I know you were listening," I added.

He claimed he hadn't heard a word.

Spiller set about tending Sire Rodela's wound. The jack had a little smirk fixed to his face as he poured wine over the wound, and Sire Rodela yelped and called Spiller's mother a sow and said he'd render his whole family for lard. Then he told Spiller to stop dawdling and tie it up quick and have done with it.

"Who did this, Sire?" Spiller asked, as he tore a strip of linen from Sire Rodela's only bedsheet to wind around his arm.

Sire Rodela said, "See if you can guess." He loosened the drawstring of the purse at his belt and pulled out a handful of brown hair. He dangled it before us. For a moment I failed to understand; then I saw that the hair sprouted from a bloody piece of scalp about as wide as my palm. I looked from this thing to Sire Rodela, so vain of his prize, and felt the skin tighten on my own scalp. Noggin tittered.

Spiller said, "Where's the rest of him?"

"In the sea."

"What was he, a jack?"

"Sire Bizco."

Spiller crowed and I asked, "Who?" I didn't repeat the name, for it would call the dead man's attention to us.

Noggin said, "The armiger to the man who wounded Sire Galan, of course." As if everyone knew. He was jiggling from foot to foot in his excitement.

I turned to Sire Rodela. "Do you mean to tether this armiger here by his hair? He'll haunt you for it."

"I'll haunt *him*. I mean to see to it that he stays close to the living long enough to savor every one of his regrets. Then I'll burn this and send him on his way." He tucked the swatch of skin and hair back in his pouch and sneered. "His first regret will be that he thought too well of himself and not well enough of me."

We had the rest of the tale from Sire Rodela by the time Spiller had finished bandaging his arm, for he was a sufficient braggart that he couldn't keep it quiet. He used the dead man's name freely, as if he delighted to think his shade could overhear. Spiller asked how he'd caught the armiger, and Sire Rodela said he'd come at his call, trotting to him like a hound. Both armigers had reasons to pursue the feud between Ardor and Crux privately, for their masters and on their own accounts too. In the tallies of shame and honor, it is not enough to have an even score; one must better the other. I remembered how Sire Rodela had been harried and overmatched by a man with a scorpion—Sire Bizco, no doubt—in the same tourney that ended with Galan injured and Sire Voltizo disgraced. But Sire Bizco had two other armigers helping him, and he'd thought to prove he could do the same on his own; Sire Rodela had planned to teach him otherwise.

They met before dawn at the foot of the cliff below the end of the south-of-west road, and walked far out on the strand, for the tide was low, and they fought between the tide pools, churning up the sand and pebbles on the beach. High tide would smooth out the marks of their battle, and if two men's footprints went under the waves and only one man's came out, it was unlikely to be noticed. Sire Rodela had taken the wound on his forearm from Sire Bizco, but he'd dealt him a worse one in return and a fatal one soon after. They'd started in the fog and finished in the rain.

Sire Rodela called for Noggin to bring his helmet. He cut off the lamb's tail he'd attached to it after Sire Galan had shorn him. His honor was out of pawn now, he said with a lopsided smile, and he wrapped a lock of Sire Bizco's hair in a leather cord and tied it to the crest of his helmet.

"I don't think you should flaunt it like that," I said, "unless you want all the world to know."

"They'll take it for a dame's favor," he said. He looked at each of us in turn. "Not a word on this to anyone, not even Sire Galan."

I said, "You can't think to keep it from him, Sire. He's sure to see. What would you have done if he'd been here?"

"A lucky chance. And I intend to stay lucky." He fixed his eyes on me and his smile was vicious. "If you tell Sire Galan or anyone else, I swear by my two sacs I'll skin a piece of your pelt too, and not from your scalp. From under your skirts." Spiller sniggered as if it was a fine joke, but I didn't take it for one.

CHAPTER 9

Concubine

hree days later Sire Galan came back from a visit to the Crux and told his jacks to clear a corner of the floor and to hang his linen bedclothes as curtains to make a private room within the tent. His cot should be set up behind the curtains.

"Where should I put the baggage?" Spiller asked, for we were crowded in the tent already, with pallets and chests and sacks, pots and barrels, weapons and armor and horse tack.

"Stow it well or stow yourself outside," Galan said. His manner forbade further questions. He turned to me. "I'm bringing a concubine to the tent. She is in your charge and I expect you to care for her well, as you said you would."

He'd not said so many words to me at one time since our quarrel over Maid Vulpeja. In all that while I'd fed my famished hopes on husks, such as a smile when he forgot to frown, an unguarded word, a look more hurt than angry. Now that he spoke to me, between the heat in his eyes and the chill in his voice I found myself with nothing to say. He'd heeded my counsel about Maid Vulpeja after all. But what did it avail me to win the argument if I lost Galan for it? Rue is ever a tardy caller, always too late, always unwelcome. There is a reason the bitterest herb is named for it.

Galan's jacks stared at him, but Sire Rodela contemplated me. Whatever he saw on my face amused him. He sat leaning against his saddle, with his cloak of felted wool wrapped around him to hide his arm, which had swollen to the size of a thigh. The night before, Spiller had cut away his bandage after Galan went to sleep, revealing flesh streaked red and pus stinking of corruption. Sire Rodela had complained of a touch of ague to explain away both the cloak and his fits of shivering. Rowney had not been fooled but Galan hadn't seemed to notice.

It was not like Galan to be so incurious, but after coming home from the priests' tent, he'd retreated to his cot, there to lie asleep or brooding, rising only to pace a little farther and a little longer each day until he was worn enough to rest. His men had fast learned to be wary of him, not to laugh or prattle, not to risk the edge of his temper. He'd not been above chaffing with them before. They were used to an easier master and had an idea who was to blame. The Crux, for one; they all took Sire Galan's part in this, and though their master never once complained of his punishment or said he didn't deserve it, his men said it for him when he was out of earshot. Me, for another. They knew Galan and I had quarreled. Impossible they shouldn't know, when I slept beside his cot instead of beside him, when he fended off my touch. The silence between us had filled the tent.

Sire Rodela spoke up and I marked how he didn't trouble to hide his insolence from Galan. "Has someone new taken your fancy, then?"

Galan rounded on him. "Maid Vulpeja is coming. You shall show her due courtesy or answer for it."

If Sire Rodela was surprised by this news, he hid it well. I suppose he reckoned quickly and what he reckoned pleased him. He raised his thick eyebrows and smiled at me. "Oh, we'll make her welcome, won't we?"

Consort Vulpeja—she was a maiden no longer, now that she was a concubine, and she'd never be a Dame—was borne to our tent that afternoon in a closed litter carried by four jacks from the clan of Lynx, which had served as the go-between in the transaction between Ardor and Crux. Besides her disgrace, she had nothing but a chest of clothing to her name. Her clan had packed her off without a proper escort, handmaid, or horse. It was the makings of a shabby peace, if peace was what they wanted.

The same Lynx men who set her down inside Sire Galan's tent picked up a heavy sack and bore it away with most of his gold in it. I heard later from Mai, who had it from a rumormonger even before the song was all over the Marchfield, that the Ardor had raised Maid Vulpeja's price when he found out who'd come to offer for her; raised it and laughed, and when Galan met the new price, asked for more. He demanded a colt of Semental's get. There were few of these and no more to come now that Semental was dead, and Galan wanted to keep the two he owned himself. He wouldn't give in and the negotiations almost foundered. In the end the Ardor accepted two warhorses of lesser lineage to be sent from Galan's keep to her father's. Each would be sufficient to dower one of her unmarried sisters.

The Ardor never mentioned that Maid Vulpeja was ill. That was widely known already. No doubt he thought it a fine jest that Galan would pay such a price for spoilt goods. As for Sire Galan, he let himself be mocked and cheated and never said why.

Rowney and Spiller lifted her from the litter to the cot in the curtained room. I could have done it myself. She weighed little more than a dame's gown of velvet. She didn't know where she was, perhaps didn't know who she was. Her eyelids were half open, but her eyes were glazed, the whites grayish. Her long hair, the gold of ripe wheat, was now lank and dull. Where the top of her forehead had been plucked, a fine down had grown over the slope. Her skin was pale over a tracery of blue veins. She was cold to the touch. The only sound she made was the scratching of her breath as she labored for air.

I bent over her and pulled away her cloak: another sign of her clan's contempt, for it was made of wool as coarse as sacking. Beneath the cloak she wore a stained underdress of muslin, thin enough to reveal the bent sticks of her limbs, her narrow bird-chest, her slack breasts, the shadows of her nipples and the triangle of hair over her quim. Whatever else was wrong with her, she was starving. Galan stood by with a frown, and when I met his eyes this time, his anger was not aimed at me. He asked his men if they did not have chores to be about, and they left us alone with her.

Her breath smelled sweet, not sour. I knelt and put my head over her heart and listened for the faint beat under the louder sound of her gasps for air. The rhythm was uneven and so slow I could scarcely believe it. I felt for my own pulse and my heart made nearly two beats for every one of hers. I looked up at Galan and shook my head. "I'm afraid. She is—to hear she was dying was one thing, but to see it . . ."

He came a step closer and said, "I didn't quite believe you, till now. Are you *sure* it's poison?"

"I wouldn't call it lovesickness, would you?" I said. "I'm certain of nothing, except that she has wasted away in—how long has it been?—near a month since your wager. It's hard for me to believe, even now that the signs are before me, that a woman would poison her own brother's child. I'm glad I have no kin, if kin will do this." I pulled the cloak up to her chin, weary of the sight of her. I put my hand on her cheek. She was so cold. Her eyes did not blink. I wondered if she heard us.

"What signs?" Galan demanded. "Have you proof?"

"This has an unnatural look. It might *seem* to be the wasting sickness. It's like enough. But if it were, she'd have a fever, her skin would be yellowish, and her breath would smell of carrion. I think they might have given her dead-men's bells, a little at a time, to make her waste away slowly—for that would raise fewer questions than a quick death. Dead-men's bells would harm the heart, and her heart is surely weak. It beats uneven and slow, and then sometimes runs a few steps and slows again."

"You know too much of poisons," he said harshly. "How is it you know so much?"

"Dead-men's bells is a medicine too—but dangerous in the wrong hands." I hesitated, then stood up and met his eyes. He deserved the truth from me. "I'll do everything I can, but I'm not sure I know how to cure her. I might kill her instead."

He gave me a bleak look. "You should have thought of that before."

There was no answer to that. When we had quarreled I'd pretended certainty, after certainty had flown, laying claim to a god's counsel, and he'd trusted me enough to act upon it—and now perhaps I'd led us straight into one of the snares hidden across the paths in Fate's realm.

He turned to leave.

I said, "There are herbs to strengthen a weak heart, but I must search them out. I have none to suit such a dire condition." I didn't tell him that the most potent remedy I knew was also a poison, the herb called dwale. I'd hoped I wouldn't have to use it, until I saw her and heard her laggard heart. At this time of year, it should still bear its inky black cherries, less baneful than root and leaf and perhaps easier to use, sweet where the leaves were bitter. "And I'll need help," I went on, "to watch her day and night. Let me send for a girl I know to sit with her while I sleep. We'll need a goat for milk, and plenty of honey."

Galan looked back over his shoulder. "Fetch what herbs you need, but go with Spiller and Rowney both. There is a truce, but it's still not safe."

"And the rest?"

"Send for anything you require, but careful what you spend. I've almost emptied my purse for this . . . ," he said, pointing at Consort Vulpeja, "this *bargain*."

The concubine wouldn't eat or drink, no matter how I coaxed her. I knelt by her side, holding a dug of cloth sopping with goat's milk to her lips. She turned her head away, her mouth drawn tight, and the milk ran down over her chin. I tapped her cheek with my finger and whispered to her, calling her name, but though her eyes were half open, I couldn't see a glimmer of sense in them.

I bustled about that afternoon, sending Rowney to buy a goat and Fleetfoot to ask Mai to send her daughter Sunup to help with the nursing. I had Noggin and Spiller running back and forth for a brazier, a blanket, water for bathing, and things to entice her to drink: goat's milk, mare's milk, mulled wine, stomach-settle tisane, rainwater strained through the finest weave, ale, and on and on. Galan stayed away. But when the bustling was done and she was bathed and I'd chafed her bony limbs to warm her and rubbed her skin with scented oil and combed her hair and found a decent clean shift to cover her—and I was alone with her again—then the matter remained. She would not eat or drink.

She must have gone wandering somewhere and left her body behind, commanding it to refuse everything. I'd grown impatient with her and then angry, but how could I stay angry when this stubborn refusal had likely saved her life? It was my advice she'd taken, my advice given carelessly to Mai and passed on, and I couldn't fathom how she had enough strength to cling to it even in this strange state between sleep and waking. It had saved her, but it was killing her now.

If she would only eat, I might not have to resort to dwale.

I'd told Mai I knew of poisons only where they touched on healing, and that was true as far as it went. But sometimes healing and harm were so close a hair couldn't slip between them. I'd learned from the Dame that every poison had its twin, each an antidote for the other, but of these twins only a few were known to mankind: such as dead-men's bells and dwale. The one could cure too much of the other; either could kill.

Rift ruled poisons. Rift, of all the gods the one I feared most, terrible in every aspect: the Queen of the Dead, the Warrior, and Dread. And dwale was in the domain of the Queen of the Dead.

To start a heart or still it, so the song of dwale went. It was a jaunty tune, such as Rift Queen favored. And why shouldn't she be merry? The population of her realm grew day by day, and never diminished.

The song was all riddles. *Search here and there and I'll let you be, search high and low and you might find me*. The Dame had sung it for me once, on the day we'd come across dwale growing from the stones of a ruined tower deep in the Kingswood. The tower had been built on a rock outcropping, and the slope below it had been so overgrazed that the trees had never grown back, though the herds were long gone. She told me dwale liked rocky ground such as ruins and quarries, lands disturbed by man. It thrived in poor, spent soil. But she also warned me away from it, saying most of its uses were ill ones. I asked what it might be good for.

She said, "Dwale has its uses in extremity, for a failing heart; I'd not chance it for anything less. Look for a languor close to death and most of all a laggard pulse. If the heart is very weak and very slow, dwale will strengthen it. But give too little and it slows the pulse even more; give too much and the poison kills." I'd asked her then, "How much is too much?" and she'd leaned on the pommel and said, "I don't know. I've never had cause to use it. Sowmaster had two children who died of it. They ate a good many berries before they got sick, and it took them three days to die."

If I used dwale I'd likely kill the concubine. Yet she'd starve if I couldn't rouse her.

There, by the cot, I opened the bag of finger bones. I would ask the Dame to tarry for me, though I had no claim on her of kinship or obligation. When she was alive she'd told me what she knew of dwale, and it was little enough. But they say shades grow wiser on their journey and see farther. Perhaps she could help me now, as she'd helped the night she showed her palm to me.

I pulled out the drawstring and flattened the pouch and there was the compass of gods Az had embroidered on the leather, smaller than the one she'd drawn in the dirt. It would do for the purpose. I smeared charcoal on my eyelids, as Az had done, to help me see. I blew on the two tiny bones to warm them, and I threw them down on the circle, asking the Dame and Na to bless me with their counsel if ever they were fond of me.

I left the concubine in Sunup's hands. Mai's daughter was thin enough herself to need a good feeding, and she was shy and hid behind her hair, but she was also gentle. She began with a grave air to coax Consort Vulpeja to suckle the warm goat's milk and honey. She patted the woman's arm and hair as if she were a child; I'd seen her do the same with Tobe, her little brother.

Galan was standing in the doorway of the tent when I came out from behind the curtain that concealed Consort Vulpeja's sickbed. I told him I'd take Spiller and Rowney to look north of camp for the remedy she needed, and that I'd return as soon as I could but I wasn't sure how far we'd have to go to find it. We couldn't afford to waste another day.

I sounded more sure than I felt. The bones had spoken; I'd understood only a little of what they'd said. I'd been given a direction and a sense of urgency. By that I knew I must chance the dwale or lose her.

Galan nodded and stood away from the door so I could get by. His looks were unforgiving, when he looked at me at all. Often, as now, he looked anywhere else. Sire Rodela watched us from the corner. He was lying huddled on his side with his cloak about his ears, too miserable, for once, to enjoy another's misery.

Galan's silence wounded me. He was such a miser he wouldn't grant me one word, not even fare-thee-well. I wanted to answer his silence with a scream; a harridan's shriek was pent up in my throat, and it was for Consort Vulpeja as well as myself. I swallowed it down and ducked my head and stepped past him.

The afternoon was gone. The air was chill but not so damp as it had been of late. The year was on the wane and bit by bit night battened on the day. I could see the Sun already heading seaward behind the high clouds. If we hurried, I might find what I sought before dark.

I guessed Spiller and Rowney would be dicing behind the tents with some other jacks, as they often did when they had an idle moment, so I set out across the compound to look for them. Sire Pava saw me and called me over. He was sitting in front of his tent on a folding chair of leather and wood. His legs were outstretched before him and crossed at the ankles and he appeared to be admiring the toes of his boots. I went, thinking it was gossip he wanted; not that I'd oblige him, but it was unwise for a drudge to ignore a cataphract completely, and too late to pretend I hadn't heard him.

When I didn't come near enough to suit, he beckoned me closer. He turned his gaze from his boots to my face and smiled. "It seems I misjudged you," he said. "Surely you must be . . . charming . . . after all, for Sire Galan to take so long to tire of you."

I felt my blood heating and cursed my thin skin for showing a flush so readily.

He sat up and leaned toward me. I took a step backward. He said, "No need to be skittish. I just want you to know that if you find yourself without a bed, I can give you one." He opened his mouth and laughed until I could see down his gullet.

The whole camp knew Galan had turned on me, and thought I'd be looking for a new blade to sheathe. What else would they think after Galan took a concubine? No matter that she was near a skeleton. Probably by tomorrow there'd be a song about how she was dying of desire until she got a bit of his cure-all. He'd charm his way out of this too if she lived.

I'd have liked to stuff my fist down Sire Pava's gullet. But I did nothing and said nothing. I hurried away with his laughter coming after me.

Spiller and Rowney got the rough side of my tongue when they complained about leaving the camp so late. By the time we had the horses saddled and I'd kicked Thole into a trot—while Spiller muttered that a woman who brays like a mule should be beaten like one—the light was yellowing and the shadows were long.

I'd followed the east-of-north road before, hunting for herbs with Noggin. Past the tourney field and the scattered crofts of shepherds, the road came to the battered face of a long escarpment running roughly east to west. There Noggin and I had always turned back, but the road went on, climbing up among the rocks to reach a plateau people thereabouts called the Hardscrabble. I hoped to find dwale up there in the heights.

Thole was ready to run and I let her. At least Galan had spared some of his horses from the sacrifice, and we were free to ride though he was not. We made good speed once out of the Marchfield, past the befouled air and the crowds. I'd been mewed up in camp since Galan was wounded, at first because I didn't want to leave his side, and then because—though he wouldn't speak to me—he also wouldn't let me go beyond the clan's tents while the feud threatened. His care had prisoned me for days; his anger made that prison comfortless.

Even beyond the Marchfield I did not feel free of it. I carried the taint with me, the stink of my own thoughts. I couldn't bear Galan's silence. Or to be cast out and prey to the likes of Sire Pava again. Or to nurse Consort Vulpeja back to health so she could take Galan from me. Or if she died and I was at fault and I lost all for nothing. I rode in a daze until Thole stumbled and I caught her mane between my hands, and I looked around to find we were already climbing the escarpment.

Thole and I were in the lead. I saw how sweat darkened her coat and how she thrust her way up among the rocks with her neck outstretched and her head bobbing, breathing hard. She was a drudge and bore what had to be borne. As I would, having no other choice.

Switchbacks took us across the face of the escarpment, and as we climbed, more of the sea came into view, burnished gold by the setting Sun. The Marchfield was a blotch of color below us, with banners of smoke rising from the cook fires. Close at hand I saw jillybells and goat's ears and gallwort and other herbs growing among the boulders and rock shelves of the slope, but passed them by. There was no time.

When we reached the top of the plateau, we paused to let the horses breathe. The highlands before us were bleaker than the lands around the Marchfield, and I'd thought those barren: here there were no hedges or fields or pastures, nothing to keep even a shepherd alive. Pale rocks lay everywhere, boulders the size of houses, stones round as loaves of bread, drifts of gravel and grit. The bedrock broke through the soil, like backbones, along the low ridges. Everything that grew was stunted. A mat of low creepers, sedges, and mosses grew underfoot, and here and there a shrub had managed to take root in the shelter of a boulder, the branches reaching eastward, shaped by the hard winds from the sea.

Spiller took one look about him and pointed west to the Sun, which was red and half drowned in the water. "We'd better turn around right now. I don't know what you think to find up here, but it's an ill-favored place and I don't wish to take that road down in the dark, do you?"

It wasn't that I disagreed with him, but I'd had enough of his grousing, all the way up the hill, about greased-stoat chases and high-handed women. "So, are you afraid to be out after dark?"

Rowney eyed us both but stayed out of it.

Spiller scowled. "It's witless to go down that hill without even a moon to see by."

"There's plenty of light yet. We'll make torches if need be."

"Sire Galan won't be pleased if you break your neck."

"I'm not so sure of that," I said.

Spiller snorted. "Kill yourself if you like, but leave me out of it." He yanked the reins and turned his horse away.

I called after him, "Sire Galan knows I'm only doing what is needful."

Spiller twisted around with his hand on the cantle of his saddle and looked at Rowney. "Are you coming or not?"

"You go," I said to both of them, "if you're so frightened. Stay at the foot of the scarp and wait for me. If I don't find what I seek by last light, I'll turn back."

Rowney spoke up at last. "I'll stay with you," he said, and Spiller glared at him and hunched up his shoulders and kicked his horse back down the hill.

I met Rowney's eyes, feeling sheepish at my show of temper. "I'll try to be quick, but I don't know this country or if what I need can be found here."

"Let's be going, then," he said, shrugging. He looked unconcerned, though while Spiller and I had argued, the Sun had gone under the sea, leaving a red pool in her wake.

In the twilight we trotted along the road, which was wide and deeply rutted. From time to time I'd turn Thole toward a bush or a pile of rocks that harbored green life in the crannies, and lean from the saddle to examine a plant more closely. Nothing came of it save scratches from the thorns of a spiny dog rose and some rose hips I took in payment for the scratches. I gave a few to Rowney. They were a tart but welcome refreshment. In summer this land would bloom. Now it offered scant hope.

We'd ridden perhaps another full league before Rowney said quietly, "Do you think we should light some torches?" and I saw that night had fallen. I hadn't noticed before, because the road was wide and paler than the lands it crossed and the crescent Moon gave a soft glow to the clouds, and to me everything was as clear as daylight. But Rowney did not have my eyes. He'd stayed close as the darkness grew, riding knee to knee with me, without a word until now.

I reined in Thole and turned to look at him. Rowney's face was pale and I could see a tightness about the jaw that belied his calm voice. I was stubborn to go on in the dark. But I couldn't give up yet, and he wouldn't ask me.

"Very well," I said, getting down from the mare. My legs shook. I hadn't ridden so far in many days. I gave Thole's reins to Rowney and told him to wait. In a short while I had the makings of two torches: bundles of gorse branches wrapped in bindwort, tipped with clumps of moss and grasses. I lit one with the coal I carried in the copper fire flask on my belt, praying to Ardor under my breath. The torch was crude and made more smoke than light. It wouldn't last long.

"We'll ride till this burns out," I told Rowney. "Then we'll turn back."

I couldn't see as far with the torch. The light moved with us, past boulders like great sleeping animals, and the road moved under us. We went down one long hill and up another, and on the other side of that hill the road came abruptly to the edge of a great pit and turned to go around the rim.

I dismounted and walked to the very edge, and Rowney gave a yelp, saying, "Have a care!" I looked back to tell him not to worry and a few pebbles went over the brink and splashed far below.

I leaned forward to see where they'd gone. "It's an old quarry, I think."

Rowney said, "The torch is almost finished. Shall we turn back now?"

"No. If I'm to find what I'm looking for, I'll find it here." I told him to lead the horses away from the ledge and let them graze, and that I'd be back before the second torch burned out.

He offered it to me, saying he could make another, but I shook my head. "I'm better off without it," I said. He stared and said nothing.

I trudged along the road as it followed the rim and turned downward, becoming a wide ramp cut into the quarry wall. I ran my hands along this wall, which was white and smooth, made of a much denser rock than the porous chalk of the sea cliffs. The white gleamed in the dark. I could see the stone had been cut into great steps and ledges, some still perfect and others broken and fissured. Soil had collected there, away from the brunt of the winds, and rain had filled the bottom of the quarry like a cistern. Trees had taken root all around this pool and in the cracks in the walls. Somehow their seeds had winged their way to the Hardscrabble, where no forests grew or ever had grown as far as I could tell. And I went down into the murmuring of those trees and the shadows streaming from the bare branches, marveling to myself as I laid my hand in greeting upon their trunks, here the smooth hide of a beech and there the rough bark of an elm, here a quick beam and there a silver birch. None of the trees had attained great size, but I felt nevertheless that they were of a great age.

And there, in a jumble of massive blocks chiseled from the wall by ice, or perhaps cut by man and discarded for imperfections, I found dwale: two bushy plants, one nearly my height and the other smaller, with sturdy stalks and the leaves all dry and stiff in this late season. I recognized it, even in the dark, by its own particular darkness. Under the leaves I found some of the black berries, and then I was sure of it.

It was well the Dame had lessoned me in remembrance, for we'd spoken of dwale just that once, and never had another occasion. She was impatient of repetition, and rarely had to tell me twice when it came to plants, though I never could keep in mind how to weave the summer-and-winter pattern or the loveknot, no matter how often my knuckles were rapped with the shuttle.

I'd put my trust in what she'd told me and in a song and two finger bones, and I'd searched both high and low, and my steps had led me straight across the Hardscrabble to this quarry and this plant.

A gift from the Queen of the Dead, for a dead woman had led me to it. But I didn't feel the Dame with me. I must do this alone.

One plant would be enough—more than enough. I wrapped my gather sack around my hands to protect me from the poison and pulled up the smaller plant, and gave thanks to Rift as I pulled. The dwale came from the soil reluctantly at first, and then quickly, as if a hand had let it go. I took one of the berries and dropped it in the hole left by the roots, and watered it generously with blood from a vein in the crook of my elbow, and pushed the muddy dirt over it so that it might be reborn next year, tall and deadly. All the gods welcome blood as a sacrifice, but Rift requires it.

I cut the plant into lengths with my knife and bundled everything into the sack: root, stalk, leaves, and berries. Then I washed my hands and arms in the cold, cold water of the quarry pool.

Halfway up the ramp I stopped to rest. I wondered what buildings this white stone had gone to make and whether those buildings lay in ruins or still stood somewhere. I took a deep breath and smelled damp, fallen leaves: the scent of late fall. As we'd lingered in the Marchfield, autumn had passed me by—for what was autumn without trees to mark its passage?

And then I heard the fluttering of many wings. The bats came out. They came from the caves in the quarry wall like a black wind gusting through the air above and below me.

Rift Dread came. If it was in answer to my prayers, it was a gift I never sought. The swarm is Dread's manifestation, swarms of insects or birds or bats; sometimes too the avatar shows itself in clouds of dust or ash, in waterspouts and whirlwinds. Otherwise it is bodiless, unless we give ourselves up to it. Dread is Rift's most intimate aspect, for it inhabits us.

I knew full well that bats were harmless; the manor had a bat tower for keeping down the insects, next to the dovecote—and yet I cowered on the road with my arms covering my head, in a blinding, mindless panic. Possessed by Dread. An endless time before the terror passed and I found myself queasy and faint and soaked in cold sweat.

The god had left behind a little seed of fear. I should have been afraid all along to go down into the quarry in the dark. Anyone would be. Instead I'd gone fearless and even glad, to be among trees again, to be among the shadows.

I'd left the Kingswood long ago. What had it made of me?

When I came back from the quarry, I found Rowney had built a fire and busied himself making torches better than the ones I'd made. He was uneasy with me when I returned. His glance was shyer and his silence warier.

He rode a little behind me and not by my side. The road was wide enough that we risked cantering, and the torch smoked and cast a poor, jerking light before the horses' hooves. At that pace the escarpment's edge proved to be not so far, after all.

We returned in the dark to find the cataphracts had guests from another clan, someone's sister's husband and assorted cousins, no doubt. They'd finished dining and had progressed to the sweetmeats and nuts and drinking songs around the hearth. Armigers stood behind them, supping on the tougher cuts of mutton when they were not attending to their masters' wants.

Galan was not among the cataphracts. He was in the tent, stretched out on a pallet with his hands behind his head. His supper—the bland boiled greens and barley porridge allowed him by Divine Xyster—was untouched. When I came in alone, having left Spiller and Rowney to see to the horses, Galan sat up. He moved gingerly. Sire Rodela lay face to the wall, and judging by his grating snore, he was asleep.

"You're late," Galan said, looking at his food as if he'd just noticed it. He picked up the plate and put it down again with disgust. "Faugh, it's cold."

I crouched in front of him and still he looked away.

"I expected you sooner," he said.

"We had a long ride."

"I hope it was to the purpose." His voice was hard, but his gaze, when it finally crossed mine, was not.

I nodded. The silence between us tugged, a strand so delicate a breath could part it, and I feared even to smile, and it was my turn to look down.

But when I looked up, his face was grim again and I sighed and stood, saying I must see to Consort Vulpeja, and I took the bundle of dwale with me to her curtained room. Yet I felt the silence stretch between us, strong as a rope.

Consort Vulpeja seemed to sleep with her eyes half open. Her breathing alarmed me. It hurt to listen to the sound; there was something trapped and desperate in it, though it issued from a listless body.

I tried to rouse her. I pinched her wrists and cheeks and called loudly in her ear, and though I woke Sunup from a doze, Consort Vulpeja didn't stir. I shook her; I tried to pry open her mouth. I sent Sunup for hot wake-me-up and waved the steaming cup under the sick woman's nose, and I thought I saw the first hint of an expression cross her face—revulsion. After I had so exerted myself in tormenting her, I felt for the pulse at her neck and it still beat slow slow slow, her heart a funeral drum.

Sunup watched as I did all this, her mouth somewhat ajar. When I turned to her, she cringed, as if she thought I was about to shake her too. I sent her from the room, telling her to find something to eat and to sleep as much as she could, for I'd need to wake her later in the night to take my own rest. She settled herself just beyond the curtain on a nest of old sacks and dirty linen.

I sat back and stared at Consort Vulpeja. I was tired and hungry and most of all uncertain. I'd planned to make a weak tisane of the dwale berries, and give it to her sip by sip—but how to make her swallow it?

The bones hadn't pointed to Ardor. If only I knew for sure that I did Ardor's bidding, that I had the god's help to do what needed to be done. But one god had aided me already that day, and instead of gratitude, I felt dread. To be obliged to Rift was a terrible debt.

My gaze turned to the brazier. I thought of how Ardor's priests are said to read the future in fire; I saw nothing but a single flame scampering along a charred branch. Even so, I took my small knife and reopened the cut in my arm, and I sprinkled a libation of blood on the brazier for Ardor, for Consort Vulpeja's sake. The flame dodged and spat at me. I added another branch and shreds of candlebark to sweeten the smoke.

I wrapped my hands in old rags and emptied my gather sack onto a cloth spread on the ground. I set aside the berries first. There were only eight, fewer than I'd hoped for: somewhat shriveled, but still with a gloss on their black skins. I pulled the brittle leaves from the stalk and a whitish milk that smelled as sour as whey seeped from the stems. I left the root alone. It was thick as two fingers, branching, with a grayish bark. After dividing the plant I put the berries in a stoppered gourd and wrapped each kind of part in separate bundles, for each had its own strength. I made sure that not one berry or leaf or stem was left on the ground.

It was the candlebark that gave me the idea. She wouldn't take food or drink, but she could not forgo breathing. No obstinacy was strong enough for that.

I crumbled three leaves of the dwale into a shallow clay bowl. I took a coal from the brazier and dropped it into the bowl and the leaves began to give off an acrid smoke. I leaned over Consort Vulpeja and gently blew the smoke into her nostrils. Each time I took a breath, I turned my head away. When the leaves had burned, I paused to listen to her chest. Her breathing was somewhat eased; it didn't make such a clamor going in and out of her chest. Her heart still lagged.

My eyes watered and I rubbed them. Smoke hazed my vision, smearing everything with gray, more smoke than I'd have expected from those few leaves. I took off my headcloth and fanned it to clear the air, and looked out from behind the curtain to ask Rowney to open the door flap. Galan eyed me strangely but did not forbid it. On their side it smelled more of onions and coleworts and wood smoke than of dwale and candlebark.

Then I waited. I didn't know whether she'd breathed too little, too much, or enough of the smoke. The dwale might need time to do its work; or just as likely its power had already been exhausted. I could do nothing but wait awhile. For yet a while. But patience came hard. Tired as I was, my limbs itched as if I would be moving.

They had lit many lamps in the tent. I could see the shadows of Spiller and Rowney moving on the white curtain, and hear Spiller cracking bones and scraping them for marrow soup, and saying he could eat his horse tonight, he had such an appetite. Sire Galan spoke up and asked how far we'd ridden. There was a silence before Rowney answered, saying we'd gone into the Hardscrabble as far as the quarry. So they all knew that ground; I should not have been surprised. The Crux had ridden his men hard to make them hard.

She *was* breathing easier, I was sure of it. Yet now her breath slipped in and out so quietly, I could hardly tell she was alive. I put the fingers of my left hand against the great vein by her throat and at the same time I felt my own vein, and was not reassured. The river of her blood flowed sluggishly, while mine coursed swift and strong, the vein leaping under my hand.

I looked at her closely. The tattoo of Ardor's godsign was dark blue against the pallor of her cheek; it had the stroke above it that marked the aspect of the Smith. She would never, as a concubine, wear the sign of Crux. Her eyes gleamed under the lids, a fixed stare. Where was she? Where had she gone, if she was not here?

The smoke hadn't roused her. She needed more. I crumbled three more leaves and this time I draped a blanket over us both so the smoke couldn't escape, lifting a corner every time I drew breath.

I knew it was dangerous; I couldn't avoid the smoke entirely, it stung my nose and gathered in my hair. When the leaves were ash, I ducked out from under the blanket and held it over her like a tent. My arms shook. I was panting and my mouth was dry as lint. My tongue felt strange and thick, it no longer belonged in my mouth, and my face too did not feel like it belonged to me. It was numb, a mask of flesh.

I dropped the blanket on the floor and staggered to the tent wall and leaned upon it. The canvas stretched around me, pulling against the ropes and stakes, and I sagged against the wall and slid until I was sitting down. I leaned over, or fell over, and my face was near the wall, and a little cold air threaded its way between the canvas and the ground. I gulped it in, along with the smell of seawater and mud and cesspits too, but it was not enough to banish the smoke, which hung in the air like chaff above a threshing floor or flour in a mill, but did not dance like chaff or flour. This smoke lay over and around everything, thick enough to rub between the fingers, quiescent as long-settled dust.

I crawled back to Consort Vulpeja. Her heart was beating stronger, harder, faster than before. I leaned against the cot, on my knees. There was elation somewhere, and if it wasn't mine, nevertheless I felt it lap through me like a warm tide. There were shadows in the smoke, in the corners of my eyes. I wasn't afraid of shadows, I greeted them as old friends and felt myself slipping out of my skin and I began to laugh at being free of it again, but no sound came out and I was bending forward at the waist, rocking and laughing soundlessly, giddy with it, slipping sideways. Instead of becoming light enough to fly, I was heavy and lying on the ground, my eyes open and full of shades, and I could see Na and see right through her to the curtain hanging from the ceiling of the tent. Na was laughing too and rocking back and forth, her mouth cracked wide, her teeth worn and yellow. I wanted to ask what amused her but couldn't utter a word, and it didn't matter because the laughter was catching, like a yawn I gave to her and she gave back to me. My ribs ached from this gaiety, I wheezed and gasped. After a while Na stopped laughing and came closer and stooped over me as I had stooped over Consort Vulpeja, peering at me, and she told me to hold fast and then she was gone.

I wished to see the Dame. I thought if Na was here she must be nearby too. I saw a figure in the distance carrying a candle and I was gladdened, thinking she came to me; then I found it was I who carried the candle. I wore Consort Vulpeja's dirty muslin shift and my feet were bare and the ground was freezing. I was unsteady, stumbling. The candlelight was too bright; it hurt my eyes. I snuffed it out and then I could see better, shades all around me, multitudes of shades, yet each was solitary. I searched for the Dame a long time before I realized it was Consort Vulpeja I sought and I began to call her name. My voice was the only sound in a muffling silence, and when I found her she was sitting upright upon a stool in a gown of rose and blue silk, as haughty as she'd been at the tourney field—so long ago, when she was still a maid—and she wasn't glad to see me, not at all. She rebuked me for disturbing her peace.

I shouted at her with no regard that she was of the Blood and I was not. I called her a whore and a fool and a weakling and a coward and when my insults failed to rouse her, I began to plead. She turned to walk away. I struck her with my fists then, and grabbed her by the hair and dragged her behind me though she wailed at me to leave off.

But I didn't know where to go. All directions were the same in this dark and barren place that never saw the Sun rise or set. I stopped, and the concubine twisted in my hands and tried to get away, and I did hold fast, as Na had told me to. And I prayed, though I didn't know where I was or whether any god could hear me.

There was a sound, a humming, a wordless tune that came from somewhere behind me. Dwale's song. It didn't sound jaunty now, but rather forlorn and stately, and I thought, *So that's how it's meant to be sung.* I turned and heard it before me and I had a direction again, and I set out toward the song, and as I walked, pulling Consort Vulpeja by the halter of her hair, the melody became a path. She screeched at me so loudly I could barely hear the song, but I followed it note by note, step by step. When it climbed, we climbed, though the plain was flat, and when it descended, we went downhill. The way seemed longer going out than coming in. We tired, and Consort Vulpeja stumbled after me silent as a sleepwalker. At last I saw the white curtain in the distance, like a flag, and went toward it, and Galan was there bending over me, calling me by name. My fist was caught in Consort Vulpeja's hair and he disentangled it gently and pulled me to sit up. He gripped my shoulders hard, shaking me, shaking me.

"What have you done?" he asked over and over, and between the shaking and the shouting, my ears rang.

I said, "Stop!" and grasped his sleeve, and after a while he heard me.

"By the gods," he said, "what have you done to yourself?"

My head lolled upon my neck. His face was right before mine and yet I could hardly see him. The light was painful and I closed my eyes and tears leaked out.

"This is foul," Galan said. "You've spewed all over yourself." He called for a kettle of water and when Spiller brought it he sent him away, he sent them all away. He pulled my dress over my head and took a rag and cleaned my face and hair and limbs. I couldn't sit upright by myself; he propped me against the cot while he looked for something clean for me to wear. "Haven't you another dress?" he asked. "I told you to get one." I wanted to say that I hadn't finished the embroidery, but my tongue was thick and in a moment I'd forgotten the question. He opened Consort Vulpeja's trunk and took out a gown of rose wool. We were much of a size, the maiden and I, before she began to starve, except I was the taller. He dragged the dress over my head and guided my arms through the sleeves. I tried to help, but my limbs were heavy and unwieldy. He left it unlaced in back.

I found my voice and asked for water. I couldn't summon the spit to swallow, my mouth was so dry. When I'd drunk most of a cupful and the rest had spilled down my front, I said, "Take me outside."

Galan lifted me and I heard him gasp. It crossed my mind that he would hurt himself carrying me, but no thought could stay long in my mind except one: I had to remember to breathe. If I forgot to remember, I'd suffocate. I clung to this surety as other thoughts darted by, quickly past recall, such as Consort Vulpeja, such as dwale, such as Galan. This even while Galan carried me outside and sat down with me beside the tent. I sat between his legs, leaning back against his chest, held upright in the circle of his arms. I squeezed my eyes shut and sucked in air. He pulled a blanket around both of us and bowed his head against the nape of my neck. When I began to shiver he tightened his arms.

I forgot to remember to breathe and yet I went on breathing, and in time the shaking subsided.

He asked me again, and now I heard his anger, "What have you done to yourself, hmm? Tell me."

"It is the dwale," I said.

"Dwale? What is dwale?"

"The bane," I said. "The remedy."

He gave me a shake. "What do you mean?"

Words eluded me, except one. "Smoke," I said.

He pulled back my damp hair and hissed into my ear. "If you have harmed yourself—for her—" He took a breath but didn't go on.

"I will be well. In a little while."

"You'd best be well," he muttered.

I could feel my swollen heart and my blood in spate pounding in my ears like the sea against rocks, wave upon wave. The waves came too fast. I wondered that Galan couldn't hear them, they were so loud. And I could not see clearly. We'd left the smoke behind in the tent and yet it hung before my eyes—or it was in my eyes—a smudge, a shadow. But my mind was clearer.

"What of Consort Vulpeja?" I asked. "How is she?" I wouldn't have been surprised if I'd killed her with my cure. Somewhere there was fear and remorse, but it was distant and had no sting.

He said he didn't care, but I persisted. Presently he sent Sunup to look at her, and soon she came back and said, "She's awake, Sire."

Glad news, but I didn't feel it. "I'll see to her," I said.

"No, you will not. Tell the girl what needs to be done."

Sunup stood waiting with her head bowed, glancing at us sideways. She looked dim and insubstantial.

"I must listen to her heart. Let me up," I said, for his arms were locked tight around me.

"You can't even stand," Galan said, "so be still and let the girl tend to her."

His anger didn't daunt me this time. I leaned against him and turned my head, and his breath was on my cheek.

I whispered, "If I can stand, will you let me?"

"Try," he said, but didn't loosen his arms.

But I didn't try; I had neither the strength nor the will to stand. I told Sunup to give Consort Vulpeja water, as much as she would drink, and the girl went away. I said to Galan, "Let me lie down. I must lie down," for I was overtaken by dizziness. I lay on the earth and it reeled and turned under me, and I felt the immensity of it, the expanse of fields and forests and mountains and seas reaching beyond the circle of our horizon to the horizon only the gods see, the very rim of the world; I felt also how small I was, borne on this wheel. And yet we were at the center, as if the Marchfield was the hub of the spinning world. The sky above was a luminous gray, brighter than a full moon would have made it, and it was only when the east began to blush red that I understood the night had passed, the hours unaccounted for.

Galan's head was fringed with light. It was hard to see his face against the dazzle above. "Never, never, never," he said, and once he said, "Fool," and with each word he pushed and I made way for him and I thought he could not go deeper but he did. When he was done he lay on me without moving, his face against my neck. It was the sky that spun now, but slowly, and the earth stayed in its place. I couldn't breathe for the weight of him and I told him so, and he raised his head.

"Swear by Crux you'll never do such a foolish thing again."

"I thought it necessary," I said.

"What, for my honor?" he asked bitterly.

I shook my head; I'd not speak of his honor again. He lifted himself off me and lay on his back with his arm over his eyes and his hose disheveled. I sat up, which took no small effort, and straightened my skirts and looked down at him. My pulse resounded still, thudding through my body, but the beats came more slowly than before. "No harm was done," I said, "and maybe some good. I took a chance. You gamble yourself, you should understand."

He took his arm away from his eyes and looked at me. "I wouldn't hazard one hair of your head for her, not to save her life." There was nothing tender in his voice but rage.

I couldn't help it: I laughed in his face. I plucked out a hair and dangled it before him. "Take one, take as many as you like. A hair is nothing. You cost me more than that when you wagered that the maiden was a whore." I let the hair go and it glinted as the wind took it. I struggled to my feet. The earth started to move again and I balanced unsteadily. "I'm going in," I said, and walked away.

There was still too much smoke in the tent. I wondered that no one else noticed it. There was another smell too, a stench, and it came from Sire Rodela. Spiller and Rowney were both kneeling by him. He had a leather strap between his teeth and sweat on his furrowed brow. The stinking bandage was in a heap on the floor. I could see his swollen forearm had darkened around the wound.

Spiller had a knife and Rowney a bowl. I asked what they were doing, and Spiller said, "Bleeding him, of course."

I said, "You should call the priest—I've said it before."

Spiller said, "Divine Xyster would just bleed him too. Now leave us be and see to your own charge."

I fumbled my way from the door to the curtained room. There were obstacles everywhere: the baggage and pallets and Noggin grinding meal. Sunup was perched on Consort Vulpeja's linen chest with her back straight, keeping watch. It shamed me to see her so constant in her duty.

"Did she take water?" I asked.

"A little," she said in a hushed voice. "I think she's sleeping now."

"And you? Are you sleepy too?"

She shrugged.

In this room the smell of dwale was pungent; the smoke had clung to the curtain and the bedclothes. And I had sent Sunup in here without giving it a thought. I said hastily, "You must go out now, go right outside the tent and stay there awhile. Get Noggin to give you food and water. Sleep if you can, and I'll send if I need you."

She looked at me round-eyed and scurried away.

I took out my knife and cut the threads that held together a long seam in the tent wall, and opened a window where there'd been none before. I should have thought of it last night—for I knew how easily it could be done—but my head had been as befuddled as the air in the tent, and needed a wind to clear it.

Then I turned to Consort Vulpeja. I'd delayed so long, fearing to look at her.

There was a scarlet flush on her neck and creeping up her cheeks. I put my head on her chest to listen and her breath was quiet but her heart was loud. I couldn't measure her pulse against mine because mine was still galloping and yet hers was trotting at a good and steady pace. I lifted my head and she was staring at me. Her eyes looked strange. I'd never seen eyes so black; her hazel irises were thin as gold rings. I could see myself peering in, reflected in the devouring pupils.

"I think you might live after all, Consort," I said.

Her eyes followed me as I stood.

"That's my gown," she said. Her voice had rusted from disuse. "Who are you?"

"I'm Sire Galan's . . . ," I hesitated over the word, ". . . his sheath."

She squinted at me. "Take it off. Burn it."

I laughed. "You are better indeed, Consort. I rejoice to see you restored to yourself. I'll take the dress off, and gladly, but I'll not burn it. Your kin have left you poor—you can't afford it." I fingered the wool of the skirt. It was light and finespun. The weave was plain, the only ornament being flamestitch embroidery that ran up the front of the bodice and around the neck, in thread the color of gold, but not of gold wire. No doubt it was meant to be worn under an ornate surcoat and over a gauzy underdress. But the Ardor hadn't seen fit to send those. This was the best garment left in her clothes chest.

The flush spread until her whole face was red.

I went outside the curtain to fetch my green dress from the bundle where I kept my things. I hadn't finished embroidering the vines. When Galan had been wounded, I'd put it aside and forgotten it. I came back and stripped off her gown and folded it neatly and put it away. My breasts and haunches were round, compared to hers, and I didn't care if she knew it. My dress was of wool nearly as fine as hers. Her gown fastened in the back, and she needed a handmaid's help to dress. Mine laced up the front. It fit well; Mai had seen to that.

I looked at her and she'd turned her face away. Her cheeks were sunken, her jaws clamped. I rued my temper already. If she'd not been so weak, no doubt she'd have made me improve my manners. The trouble was, she put me in mind of Dame Lyra, and I remembered *her* manner too well.

I softened my voice. "Will you take some nourishment, Consort Vulpeja? I have goat's milk, very soothing, or broth if you like. Either will give you strength."

"Whose tent?" she asked. It tried her strength to speak; she hoarded her words.

"Sire Galan's, of course. You can see by his colors." I gestured to the tent wall with its stenciled pattern of green and gold fletches.

I thought she'd be glad to hear this, but she shut her eyes and a few tears leaked out.

"He'll be here by and by. Meanwhile, you should drink something. Or do you think you could eat?" I poured a cup of the goat's milk and honey we'd prepared last night and took it to her.

She shook her head.

"Water, perhaps?" I said, bringing a flask to her lips. "It's only water. It can do you no harm."

Still she refused, her mouth and eyes tight shut. I sat down wearily by the curtain and poured myself a cup. I was thirsty, even if she wasn't, but there was a tinny taste in my mouth that water couldn't wash away. The dwale was almost finished with me. My pulse had quieted at last and my limbs obeyed my bidding. What lingered was grit in the joints, lead in the bone, and, in the belly pit, unease. My eyes burned in the light.

I had seen many things last night, but little clearly. I remembered Na, I remembered seizing Consort Vulpeja's hair, but half the night had dissipated with the smoke. I must have been wandering in the lands between the living and the dead when I brought Consort Vulpeja back against her will. I'd never imagined those lands were so vast, so populous. The shades I'd seen, were they the recently dead, reluctant to depart on their journey? Were they waiting to be born? Maybe there were others as ill as Consort Vulpeja, unable to travel toward life or death. I couldn't recall, and perhaps it was for the best. I'd found the one I sought among the many, and that should content me. I wished to learn no more about it.

She'd breathed more of the smoke. Thank the gods she'd lived through it. And, by the gods, she was stubborn. I could admire her for it. She lifted one hand and began to pluck at the neck of her shift as if it bothered her. I was glad to see she could move. She had lain so still since she arrived.

"Bid Tousle to come," she said.

"Who is Tousle?"

"My handmaid. Fetch her!" Her voice was shrill, the rust taken off the edge.

"You have no handmaid."

"Don't lie. She was just here."

"Ah, that was Sunup," I said. "But she's not yours. Shall I send for her? Will you drink then?"

Her head rolled back and forth on the pillow, no and no again. She said, "You lie. You lie."

I leaned over and put my palm against her cheek to keep her head still. "I'll fetch Sire Galan, then you'll see. You're safe now."

She stared, her eyes too black and too suspicious.

Beyond the curtain the tent was crowded. Sire Galan was sitting on two sacks with his shirt off and Divine Xyster was tending to him and grumbling, for the wound had bled a little in the night and required a new bandage. The carnifex did not like to change the bandage often; the wound cured better undisturbed. He fussed that Sire Galan was too careless and would never heal.

When he was done with Galan he asked, "What of your new concubine? I heard she has the wasting sickness."

Galan stood, using a tent pole to pull himself up. "I'd be obliged if you would look upon her and tell me what can be done for her. I fear she may die. She's a meager thing, thin as a bone, and she hasn't spoken since she came here—stares without seeing and doesn't move. It's as if she sleeps with her eyes open. Will you come?" He gestured to the curtain.

I spoke, keeping my eyes lowered. "Permit me, Sire Galan, but I think she's better today."

"Is she?" Galan said, looking at me in disbelief.

"May the gods be praised," said Divine Xyster. "It's a good omen."

I followed Galan and the priest into Consort Vulpeja's chamber. They stood on either side of her cot, gazing down. She looked from Sire Galan to Divine Xyster and back again, and tears welled up and she began to sob: great sobs from such a slight body. She cried with all the abandon of an infant, except she covered her face with her hands.

"Why does she weep?" Divine Xyster asked.

Galan shrugged and frowned in distaste. "I beg your indulgence, but I'm sure I don't know; I thought this was what she wanted."

I thought it plain enough it was hope that overcame her. Could he be blind to it? Against grief and fear and spite she was better defended; hope had breached the walls.

"No matter. The only thing harder to divine than the mind of a god is the mind of a woman." The priest shook his head. "The Ardor should have demanded less than half the price he asked, for she's more than half dead. An ill wish could carry her off."

Galan said, "Yet it's remarkable how much she's mended in a day. Yesterday I'd have wagered that she'd never wake up—not that I'd wager on such a thing, of course," he added in haste.

I said, "She won't eat or drink, Sire. Have you a cure for that?"

Divine Xyster did not allow that I had spoken.

When Consort Vulpeja's sobs had shrunk to the size of hiccups, I gave her a cloth to wipe her face. She said to the men, "Please turn away, I beg you—don't look at me. I've never been fair but now I'm sure I'd affright children."

Galan did look away, chewing on his lip. Divine Xyster stooped and patted her shoulder. "What's this I hear? You must eat. It's your duty. You must put on flesh and regain your comeliness, for you owe it to Sire Galan as his concubine."

"Am I? Am I his concubine?" she asked, and the joy on her face was more to be pitied than all her sobbing.

She looked to Galan for an answer but it was Divine Xyster who said, "Indeed. Don't you remember?"

"I recall nothing since my father died."

"Then they've sent you here against your will," Galan said. The gods know, many parents have traded their daughters into concubinage without consent, and married them off without consent too, but Galan was too proud for it. That was for older and uglier men.

"Of course I'm willing. Of course," she said, and tears rained down even as she smiled.

After a pause Galan said awkwardly, "Will you promise to eat? You must be strong, for there's much traveling ahead." Though his voice was gentle, his face was stern, as if she'd displeased him.

She said, "Yes, Sire," very meekly, all her stubbornness hidden for the moment.

Divine Xyster and Galan left. I heard the priest say, outside the tent, "We'll steal the laugh from between the Ardor's teeth, Galan. We'll polish her till she shines, and then see who made the better bargain."

When they were gone she asked for her mirror. I searched through her chest but didn't find one. She didn't believe, at first, that it wasn't there—it was of bronze with gold relief of the Smith at his forge, was I blind?—and then she seemed to think I'd stolen it, judging by her glare. So I did what any drudge would do, lacking a mirror: I filled a black kettle with water and set it on a footstool, and when the water was still I turned her on her side so she could look down and see herself. She was too feeble to lift the weight of her own head, so I supported her and brought the lamp close to her face.

It was cruel of me to obey her. She let out a small moan and I felt her recoil. She closed her eyes and turned her face into my shoulder. I laid her down again and she didn't open her eyes for a long while.

When she did she began to find fault. The goat's milk was sour and the beef broth salty, the wine was vinegar and the porridge too thick. It all made her gag. She gained strength the more she wore me down. It took till after midday to find something to suit, something she'd demanded at an expense of coin and trouble because her grandmother had once commended it: a fresh egg stirred into broth made from the hen that laid it. At last she slept.

I left Sunup with her and went to lie down outside her curtained chamber. I courted sleep. I could hear Rowney at work refurbishing the brigandine, a vest of stiff green canvas lined with iron scales that Sire Galan, when he trained, wore on occasion instead of the heavier mail shirt and cuirass. Rowney rubbed rust from the iron with pumice and tapped at the rivets that held the scales in place, and sang "Will Ye or Nill Ye" under his breath. It seemed he only knew the chorus, which he sang over and over.

It's not the dreams we crave of Sleep, but the nothingness. That I knew from a winter in the Kingswood; every drudge knows it, when to live is to suffer. *Will ye or nill ye,* Rowney sang, *I will have my way.* What is it we forget when we wake?

I had supposed that I'd found Consort Vulpeja in the borderlands between our living world and the realm of the Queen of the Dead. But maybe those were sleepers I had seen. Maybe I'd found my way to some bleak shore in Sleep's ocean, where our shades go wandering during that brief death every night when we are asleep past dreaming. *So lay you down a-smiling, for tears are not beguiling*. If so, it's a pitiless place; there's no welcome there. No woman greets her child or man his wife, though their bodies may lie sleeping side by side, clasped tight. *And I will be long gone*, sang Rowney, *before the break of day*.

And yet sleep is a better healer than any carnifex or greenwoman. If Consort Vulpeja could sleep a true sleep—and no more of that strange state, that absence—I'd see her mend soon . . . *For tears are not beguiling*. Gods, she'd been undone; it had shocked me to see her give way like that before Galan. It had done her no good—I had seen his look. She was not cunning after all. *And I will be long gone before the break of day*. How well would she mend when she found out he didn't desire her? She must nurse on false hope until she's strong enough to wean.

Will ye or nill ye, Rowney sang, as he scoured rust from the scales. I'd have told him to hold his tongue except I couldn't bestir myself to wag my own. I couldn't even twitch. My heart tapped willy-nilly, and sleep did draw me under, and the song darted among my dreams.

Of all the dreams there was only one I could remember after I awoke. But that one left me richer by one word: *fedan*. I knew it was in my native tongue, the language I'd forgotten. Fedan—father.

I was standing between my father's knees and he was pulling on my wool cap and knotting under my chin the yarn ties of the ear flaps. His rough hands snagged my hair. I was filled with a pure joy, the joy that belongs to children, because I was to ride over-mountain with my father to sell the colt. Not that I wanted to sell the colt, because I was fond of him. But my father said he needed my help to drive a hard bargain, and I was too young to imagine he was teasing me.

I asked him questions: Fedan, will the colt be gelded by his new master? Will he grow up to be as fast as Ganos? Fedan, can I have a fry cake when we get to market? Fedan, will the colt fetch a good price?

His name didn't come to me in the dream. To me he was always Fedan.

I can't remember a room, a window, a chair, only my father's presence, the solid strength of his legs in leather britches, his hands. The smell of horses; the smell of the tangy sourpottage that was always on the hearth. My cap of a blue felt so dark it was almost black, embroidered with red and yellow checks. My red vest, my market finery. I was so small my shoulders came just to above his knees, but I was old enough to ride with him to market on my sorrel pony, a bright sorrel to match my hair. My pony never cantered except uphill, and then only for a few paces, no matter how I kicked.

Twice now I had dreamed a true dream of my father. I needed no revelator to tell me what it meant. By my father's rough hands and patient touch, I knew him, though I couldn't recall his face clearly. He was a farmer, a horse breeder.

As a foundling I'd been free to fancy any parentage, and there were times I thought that if the Dame was fond of me, it must be because something in my blood called to hers; perhaps I was better born than I seemed, a bastard of the Blood—this hope so secret that after I reached a reasoning age, I hid it even from myself. But the kernel of the fancy was still there, and now I rooted it out. I was no bastard. I had a father and a mother too, though I'd never dreamed of her—who else would have embroidered my cap and vest so finely? I had them and lost them.

I was dear to my father. In my dream I was dear to him.

"Sire Galan must be told *now*. He'll blame us if Sire Rodela turns up a corpse one morning." That was Rowney, whispering.

"He's not dying," Spiller whispered back.

They woke me from my last dream. I wish I could have lingered there. I kept my eyes closed and my body still.

"He is," Rowney insisted. "See, it's turning black."

"Men get over the blackening."

"Most don't. And it isn't just the blackening. It's that dead man. Have you forgot Sire Rodela has a piece of you-know-who's scalp? You can be sure his shade is nearby and angry—and making the wound angry." Spiller was silent. Rowney went on whispering, after a pause. "And what do you suppose Sire Rodela did with the body? What of that? I doubt he burned it. He's made trouble for all of us."

The shades of the Blood are known to grow more and more malicious when held here against their will and against custom. Sire Bizco's body was probably rotting underwater, and until the waves ground his bones to sand he'd stay for vengeance. And if we left his body behind, left the

Marchfield and crossed the sea, and Sire Rodela still carried his prize of skin and hair—why then, the shade could follow.

"Sire Rodela dam Whoreson by Pigsticker," said Spiller, and I heard Noggin cackle. "Tell me when he did *not* cause trouble for us."

"So let him die, I suppose!" Rowney said.

"I'm doing what can be done for him—the priests could do no more," Spiller said sullenly.

"Not so. The priests could ward against the dead man and that you cannot do."

"Anyway, I'm not telling Sire Galan," Spiller said. "If he's too blind to see what is under his own nose—or smell it, for that matter . . . He'd just beat us, or worse, for not telling him sooner. He's in a foul temper these days, and I for one am not fool enough to stick my head in a hornets' nest and call it a hat. And suppose Sire Rodela heals—and I say he will—he'll think up something even nastier to punish us for telling tales on him."

"An angry shade will afflict you worse than Sire Galan or Sire Rodela or a swarm of hornets."

"I'll take my chances with the dead. The living worry me more."

"That's because you're a dolt," Rowney said with some heat.

I expected Spiller to take offense, but I should have guessed better, for I knew him to be a coward. He muttered something and was quiet for a while. Then he said, "Suppose we ask the canny?"

Rowney said, "Ask her what?"

"What to do about the shade, you clodpate!"

There was another pause.

Rowney said, in a very low voice, "Very well. You ask her."

"Well, I will," Spiller said.

"Well—go on then."

I heard Spiller get up and cross the tent. He shook me.

A canny. They thought me a canny! I opened my eyes and he drew back, startled. My eyes must have turned black from the dwale, like Consort Vulpeja's. The gray shadows that had dimmed my sight were gone. The tent was full of light. It was like being inside a lantern. My eyes watered and I blinked.

I opened my mouth to quarrel with him and thought again. I sat up and waited for the dizziness to pass. I felt threadbare as two-hundred-year-old linen, bleached and scrubbed too many times.

"Help me stand," I said. "I must see to Consort Vulpeja."

"She's sleeping," Spiller said. "I looked in on her just now. You both slept an afternoon and a night and a morning and half the next afternoon away."

"So long? Truly?"

He nodded.

"Why did you wake me then, if not for the concubine?" I asked, though I knew the answer. "My dreams were more pleasant than your company, I assure you."

"It's about Sire Rodela. He's not getting better."

"You'd best not be waking me unless he's dying." I held my hand out to Spiller and he hesitated a long moment before he helped me to my feet. I looked to Rowney; he was closemouthed, though he'd been bold enough before.

I knelt beside Sire Rodela. He was deep in a fever dream and his legs jerked; his breathing was rough. He'd thrown off his cloak. Under it he wore only his plain shirt, and it was soaked through and twisted around his chest, leaving his body bare below. Spiller had made a loose bandage, having learned that a tight one became embedded as the arm swelled. Now the swelling reached from Sire Rodela's forearm to his shoulder; his fingers were thick and red as sausages. I can't say I pitied him and yet it was hard to think of him as a threat, he looked so slack with his hairy legs sprawling and his dangle sleeping and his face pallid under the beard.

I laid one palm on his burning forehead, the other on his chest, and silently I asked Ardor for help. All in a moment I felt my hands grow hot and the warmth travel upward, and I drew a little heat away from him. But there was a fire hidden under the bandage I was forbidden to touch. I'd seen the blackening before, how it spreads as flame spreads, leaving charred flesh in its wake. "Have you bathed him in cold water? No? Well, bring some and quickly!"

"It's the shade of that armiger he killed who's at fault for this," Spiller said. "We wondered what to do about it."

"Shade or no shade, I've already told you what to do: get the carnifex."

Rowney and Noggin dragged a cask of water toward us. "Now you'll need a rag," I said to Spiller. "Wash him with the water and do it again and again till he cools down. I've seen you take better care of your horse when he's overheated! And make him drink water too, as much as he'll take. I'll go fetch Divine Xyster myself."

"Not so hasty," he said. "We don't need the priest if you'll just tell us what to do about the dead man."

I laughed at him. "What do *I* know about that? No more than you—no more than any fool knows. Why don't you burn his little trophy? Then the shade won't find him so easily."

"That won't be enough." Rowney spoke at last.

"No, you're right. You need the carnifex. The blackening will kill him if the fever doesn't." I knelt down and began to search among Sire Rodela's clothes. "Still, let's burn it. Perhaps it will help—and it can do no harm. Where is it?"

I found the pouch locked away in the small iron-bound box where Sire Rodela kept his valuables. Spiller showed me the key, for he'd spied it out long ago. It was cleverly disguised: the tongue to the buckle of Sire Rodela's knife belt. I loosened the drawstring of the pouch and pulled out the scrap of scalp by a few of the silky hairs, fine as a woman's, fine as Consort Vulpeja's. Surely Sire Bizco had been her kin, a distant cousin at least, if he was her father's armiger. Touching it made my skin creep. "Rowney, fetch his helmet."

I dropped the grisly thing on the brazier and it began to scorch. I added a handful of candlebark and another of salt hay and the fire flared up. Rowney squatted by the brazier and threw on the lock of hair from the helmet and watched it shrivel to ash.

"Gods, what a stink," he said.

"Like when the master burned Sire Rodela's hair," Noggin said.

"Have you ever smelled a drowned man burning?" asked Spiller. "That's the worst."

"Shouldn't you say something?" Rowney asked me, looking a trifle shamefaced.

"Such as what?"

"I don't know—'Begone, Sire Bizco, and a curse on your living kin if ever you return again.' Such as that."

"Well, you've just said it."

"You say it too," he said.

I began to laugh. Soon Noggin was giggling and Spiller joined in. Rowney did not. When I saw his face, the laugh stuck in my craw. I said, "I'm no hex, Rowney. I'm a greenwoman, no more than that. My curses are no more potent than yours."

He wouldn't meet my eyes. This had come of our expedition in the dark. He was a brave man but I'd frightened him. I stood and steadied myself by gripping Rowney's shoulder, digging in my fingers. He flinched but bore it.

"Tittle-tattle I may be, but I'm going for the carnifex," I said to Spiller, and my voice came out hoarse. "Sire Rodela was left to your solicitous care and see what has come of it. You'd let him die before you'd own up that you kept something from Sire Galan he should have known."

"Why blame me?" Spiller said. "We all kept it from him."

"Not anymore," I said.

"What is it you aren't hiding from me anymore?" Galan asked, pulling the door flap closed behind him. We drudges had been speaking among ourselves in the Low. I hadn't known he understood so much of it.

He gave us a thrashing, all of us. He laid on with a girth strap about our shoulders and backs and we stood still for it, one at a time, except for Noggin, who rolled on the floor and whimpered. But first he summoned Divine Xyster, who took Sire Rodela away to the priests' tent, and then he waited until I'd fed Consort Vulpeja what little she could eat—a mash of white bread and milk—and it was nigh on suppertime by then.

Sire Galan gave me no more licks than anyone else, nor any fewer: exactly fifteen. I was the last to get my share. When he finished he said we should be grateful he didn't have his strength back, or he'd have peeled the skin from our ribs, which he would do if we ever did such a thing again. Sire Rodela might order us about and it was our duty to obey him, but not if it meant crossing him—Sire Galan—who was, he should not need to remind us, master of us all and Sire Rodela's master too.

Sire Galan stalked out and we could hear the cataphracts outside whistle and cheer him. They were just back from the training field and had been diverted from their own aches and pains by the sounds of the strap against flesh and the groans Galan had wrested from us.

Spiller put on his shirt, wincing, saying we'd gotten off lightly—but wait till Sire Rodela was better, we'd wish we were never born. We'd wish he was dead, anyway.

I eased the bodice of my dress over my back and shoulders and pulled the laces, but not very tight. Galan could have chosen to hit us harder. As it was we were striped with wide welts and just a few thin lines of red where the skin had broken. The dress was new and now it would be bloodstained, but I'd nothing else to wear, for my old dress was still filthy from the dwale sickness. Rowney made the avert sign with his fingers and I realized I was cursing, steadily cursing. I made my way to Consort Vulpeja's chamber, for I'd had enough of Sire Galan and his drudges.

She was no better. She greeted me with a false sweet smile and said, "You have a lenient master, I think. Too lenient. He should have given you a hundred strokes."

I glanced at her and went to pick up my soiled dress from the corner where Galan had tossed it. I filled a pot from the cask we'd put in her room and built up a fire in the brazier to heat it. It hurt to move: not just from the strap, but from the horseback journey and some last touch of the dwale smoke, which left me stiff and aching everywhere.

"Are you disregarding me? Because if you are I'll make sure you get another thrashing." She lay on her cot with her hands folded at her waist and turned her head to watch me.

"No, Consort Vulpeja. What is it you need?"

"You must answer when I speak to you."

"Yes, Consort."

Sunup was sitting in the corner by the tent pole sucking on a hank of hair and watching us talk.

"Poor girl," I said to her. "You shall go home soon. Would you like that?"

She took the hair from her mouth and said, "My mother said I should stay as long as I'm needed."

"I want her," said Consort Vulpeja. "She minds me well and I need a new handmaid. Sire Galan will give her to me."

"She's not his to give," I said.

"So you are to be my handmaid, I suppose," she said.

I dunked my dress into the pot, though the water wasn't hot yet—would it never boil?—and I began to scrub the cloth with a scour stone and wood ash.

"*My* laundry needs doing," she said.

"I'll get you well, Consort, if I can. The rest I'll not undertake."

"That's up to Sire Galan, surely."

I shook my head and sat back on my heels and stared at her. "No, it's not," I said. "For true, it's not."

CHAPTER 10

Feud

he next day was Peaceday and, as it happened, a neap tide. And when the sea went out and out, farther out than we'd seen it go before, leaving the strand bare and sparkling with pebbles and shells and rivulets of water, and uncovering great rocks with hides of salt hay and barnacles, why then there was one rock that did not belong there. Someone saw it from the cliff and there was no mistaking the shape of a man sprawled on his back, legs akimbo.

Soon everyone knew it was Sire Bizco, and knew his clothes had been stuffed with stones. There was sand in his nostrils and mouth and salt frosting his eyelashes. His body was bloated and his skin was puffy and strangely mottled, and a piece of his scalp was missing.

The Ardor himself clambered down the cliff path to see the body. His clan fetched Sire Bizco and burned him with due ceremony. It was said his face was too misshapen to make a good death mask, so they sent his helm to take its place in the clan's Council of the Dead. The rest of his armor was burned with him, for he had no son, but his arms went to the clan. A warrior who dies as a warrior should—on the battlefield instead of in his bed—leaves much of himself behind in his arms and armor; his sons and clan can claim that strength, though it makes the shade's journey harder. Just so, a man will try to take his enemy's equipage for a prize, to be a victor twice—once over the living man and again over the dead. If the battle has been bitter, he'll hang the trophies in his hall for daily mockery and take no ransom for them. This keeps memory long and wars hot.

Sire Rodela had hidden the body and taken for his prize something closer than armor—the man's own skin. The Ardor didn't know who had killed Sire Bizco, but he had no doubt which clan to blame for both the death and the desecration.

It is forbidden to fight on Peacedays, but on the morrow the dormant feud awoke. One of Ardor's cataphracts was leaving a harlot's tent just as one of ours—Sire Ocio—came to call on her, and the brawl that followed yielded a few sword cuts and a cracked pate. Sire Ocio was slashed across his cheek, which would improve his looks, everyone agreed; but the Crux scowled and set men to stand watch every night.

So Sire Galan's sacrifice of his pride went for naught. He'd gained only Consort Vulpeja, who had one face for Galan and another for me. Toward Galan she kept her voice high and her eyes low, as if she were still a maid. Perhaps she didn't realize how unbecoming this was to a starveling. Perhaps she thought she'd fascinated him once and would again. It showed how little she knew him. She'd had a brief acquaintance with his charm and his prick and knew his reputation for wielding both, and also the renown he'd won for his somewhat insolent bravery on the tourney field. But how could she know him?

He would have respected her courage, if he'd seen it.

She set out to make herself well. She'd been slender before, but smooth and clean limbed. Now there wasn't enough flesh to fill a pinch, and her skin was papery and loose on her frame. She forced herself to eat, though food disgusted her. Half of what she ate came up in retching and much of the rest was purged by the squirts. She was so weak that sometimes she fainted from the exertion of vomiting. But she took some small nourishment despite this: enough to live, enough to gain ground.

The concubine had no more command over herself than an infant. We had to borrow linens. When she soiled herself I washed her with water steeped with sweet-smelling herbs and orris root to chase away the stench and bedsores. Sunup helped. We'd turn her this way and that, and Consort Vulpeja would submit in silence, keeping her eyes closed, as if she pretended we were not there.

All this put me in mind of the Dame, my own dame, wasting away before she died, and how I'd washed her and cared for her, how her slow dying was a torment to us both. I could muster no fondness for Consort Vulpeja. The best I could offer was pity—which she scorned—and patience, and a touch as gentle as I could make it.

She was afflicted by strange moods, one moment lethargic, the next raging or laughing or crying at nothing. But most often she was possessed by a peevish restless will. Oh, how she irked me then, pouring vinegar on my sores. Without the strength to stir from her bed, she could only speak, and speak she did. She wanted what she couldn't have and if by some great exertion I got it for her, it no longer suited.

She asked after Galan's wife: Was she beautiful? Was she of good temper, sweet, docile? How big was her dowry? I couldn't answer her questions, knowing nothing of his wife; she called my silence impudent. Yet when I spoke she also took offense. Either way she swore she'd have Galan thrash me again.

She asked what Galan had paid for her. The prestige of a wife is the dowry she brings to her husband, but that of a concubine is the price she fetches. This I could answer. It was all over the Marchfield how Galan had beggared himself for her. The news put flesh on her bones. What else could she suppose except that Galan was besotted with her?

He came once an evening. She prepared herself for his visits like a man donning armor. I plucked her forehead as she asked me to do, and she squeezed out some tears from the pain without making a sound. She'd dismiss me when he came, but the wall of her chamber was merely a sheet. I heard. We all heard. Galan would inquire after her health and she'd say she was mending. She'd ask after his health and he'd answer he did very well. (Neither would mention her father, who had caused both their injuries.) He might say that the weather continued to be foul, but the priests claimed it would change for the better soon. This was the substance, along with the silences. You'd think he had his tongue lashed to his teeth.

After such a conversation Galan would leave the tent without a glance at any of us, and I'd go to Consort Vulpeja and find her exhilarated, to judge by the flush on her cheeks and the pulse at her neck. If I spoke I might be cruel, so I reined myself in and chewed the sour metal of the bit. Galan's visits were a better elixir than anything I could have made for her.

We were, the concubine and I, still tormented by the dwale. Rift Dread visited her in her sleep and followed her into daylight. She'd shriek that ants were crawling all over her. She cowered away from thieves and packs of black dogs. Her dead father visited her in a rage and called down curses on her head. She begged me to unbind her, thinking her ankles were tied. She swore I was poisoning her. I learned to wait until these confusions passed and she mastered her fear. She took food from my hands despite her mistrust—watching askance all the while. I could hardly begrudge her these suspicions, for she had indeed been poisoned by those who should have cared for her. And she knew that I, as Galan's sheath, had no cause to cherish and much to spite her.

It was Rift Warrior who visited me. I dreamed of death. Not so much of dying but of killing. I'd wake from dreams of fire and a knife in my hands and blood on the blade, wake because I was shouting in my sleep, wake to find I hadn't made a sound.

And Galan, who once would have gathered me up and lulled me into a gentler sleep, was no longer by my side. I was unwelcome in his bed. I slept on the floor by his concubine and suffered her to preen herself about it.

Had I imagined the tenderness in the way Galan had cared for me after the dwale? The welts on my back said I'd dreamed it. I couldn't trust my memory, for it was shiftless and a liar besides, every day a different tale since I breathed the smoke. I was still unsure what realm I'd visited, and what god ruled there. I hoped I'd never journey in those lands again, awake and alive. It seemed a fever dream now, and no more to be trusted.

I hardly saw Galan. He was away from the tent as much as he could be. He was sometimes in the Auspices' tent to see Sire Rodela—who'd mend, the carnifex said—and sometimes in the Crux's tent for various councils. But mostly he was off with his jacks and his horsemaster, beyond the Marchfield in some secluded place, making trials of his strength, what was left to him, and trying to win it back. He'd spent much of his life training to fight from horseback; he'd mastered vaulting on and off in all his armor and other such accomplishments. Without a horse he'd lost the better part of his weaponry. Now he gave up his mail hauberk and leggings, and most of his plate as well, and went lightly armored after the fashion of the priests of Rift. The better to dodge, Spiller said. Galan must learn new tricks, or invent them.

At nightfall Galan would come back to the tent on foot with his men on horseback beside him: an odd sight, and he got some chaff for it from the other cataphracts. He kept his helmet on with the visor down until he was inside the tent, and when he took it off, his face was pale and hard as ivory and shiny with sweat. When he stripped I could see his wound was healing, leaving a thick ridge of scar that twisted under his rib and past his navel. I worried that the sinews of his abdomen, so newly knit together again, would pull apart from his exertions. And every day he took new blows, new bruises, new cuts, which must have come from his men. I thought he was reckless, though I didn't say so; my advice hadn't served him well and I'd lost the taste for giving it. And for him to go alone and afoot through the

Marchfield—alone but for his horse soldiers, and one of them a liverless coward—was to dare the clan of Ardor to take him.

Galan had won back his men. Spiller and Rowney were his again, as if they hadn't been creeping about the tent for days like curs looking to be kicked, as if they'd never wronged him and been whipped for it, as if he'd never taught them constraint.

All the constraint was between us.

Mai came the third morning after Peaceday. She carried her boy Tobe on her hip and was flanked by her usual escorts. They were armed with longswords and Pinch had a manhound on a choke chain with the little piebald cur trotting free beside. Mai took a risk visiting our camp, since the clan of Ardor made note of our friends and took them for enemies.

Sunup saw her first and called me out of the tent. Tobe crowed to see his sister and held out his arms to her, and Mai let him go and we stood watching as the boy tottered across the common yard on his stubby legs and Sunup chased after him, pouncing. They giggled until they shrieked. The dogs started to bark at the goat tied outside our tent and the goat replied, and Pinch cursed and dragged the manhound away, and I laughed at all this commotion until I marked that Mai was watching her daughter with a frown.

Sunup darted about, her bare shins flashing under the ragged hem of a skirt that suddenly seemed too short for her. I saw how quickly she'd brightened and shed her grave and watchful air. It made me think I'd done wrong to keep her by me, so long away from home.

I said to Mai, "She's a dear one, your daughter."

"What have you given her to eat?" said Mai. "She's grown too much."

I took it for a jest, but when I saw she was still frowning, I said, "Daughters grow. Is that so sorrowful?"

"They grow foolish. They grow disobedient."

"Not Sunup, surely."

Mai shrugged and put aside her frown. "Sire Torosus is vexed with me for lending her. Says the Sun doesn't rise properly without her in our tent."

I was taken aback by this. I'd seen Sire Torosus and he was not so sobersided as Mai had painted him, but rather lean where she was fat, hard as ironwood, and quick in deed and speech—altogether a man. Yet somehow I'd never imagined him or any man of the Blood taking notice of his mud-children, much less missing one of them. I told Mai, "Consort Vulpeja is fond of her too, wants her for a handmaid."

"I need Sunup, or I'd gladly give her in service," Mai said. "She'd be well out of it, for Consort Vulpeja will not be coming to war with us, will she?"

I shook my head.

"Does she know this?"

"Not yet."

"Does she want to, do you think?"

"She expects to. Didn't you give her a charm for forgetting Sire Galan? I can't say it worked. She lives on hope, from one of his smiles to the next."

Mai snorted. "And I suppose you don't."

She had a barbed wit sometimes.

"Well, has she a hope?" Mai asked.

I forced a smile. "None. False hope in plenty, though. I'm sure she thinks there will be ballads written about the two of them."

"Oh, there are. You're not about the Marchfield much anymore, or you'd have heard them. The first made Sire Galan out to be a dupe for the price he paid for a bag of bones. But now there's a new song that couldn't have been bettered if Sire Galan had written it himself—and perhaps he did, at that, or paid a rumormonger to write it. Shall I sing it for you?"

"I'm sure you sing like a crow."

"Not so," she said, with her rumbling laugh. "I'm a very sweet singer. Sire Torosus himself likened me to a goose, last time I sang for him." She began to honk out a song and I covered my ears and cried mercy.

She left off and lowered her voice. "You have been missed. You promised Naja an ointment for her chilblains, remember? And old Mullen—the one who sells clay amulets—she has a cough like to burst her bellows. The concubine isn't the only one ailing in the Marchfield."

I shrugged. "I'm afraid to leave her. She's still weak—she has yet to sit up on her own."

"I thought she was supposed to be better. Mark this: she'll need to be shown off, and soon, or the hotspurs will learn a new tune."

"She is better. See for yourself."

Mai put her hand on my arm. "Be forewarned: I've brought a little charm for her, something to keep her in hopes."

"And what will it do to Sire Galan, your charm?" I asked her.

"Not a thing, dear heart, not a thing."

When Mai went to the sickbed, Consort Vulpeja took her hand and kissed it, which I never expected to see. But then I thought of how Mai must have looked to the maiden as she lay sickening: Mai braving the wrathful eye of the aunt, bringing charms and hints and warnings.

Consort Vulpeja said, half weeping, "Mai, I'm so very glad to see you!"

Mai looked down from her great height, made greater by her wooden soles, and said, "I'm pleased to see you so much better."

The concubine pressed Mai's hand to her cheek and wouldn't let go. "I wouldn't be here if not for you. And yet I can't show you my gratitude as I should. My clan has left me without the means."

Mai tugged her hand away and went to sit on the linen chest nearby. She lowered herself with a grunt. Her gown wrapped tight around her belly and the skirt rode high in front. Her ankles were swollen, and thick blue veins had risen under the skin. "No matter," she said. "It's enough for me to see that you live, that you're cared for well. And how's the food? Better than your aunt served, I should think." She grinned and flicked a glance at me.

Consort Vulpeja would not admit so much. "It's not tasty, and besides, it makes me sick," she complained.

I said, "It's just that her stomach is still tender."

"The food is wholesome," Mai said to the concubine firmly. "You must eat as much as your bowels can bear."

"I do try," she said, and tears ran fast as snowmelt. Then, through gulps and sniffles, she lamented that Sire Galan would never desire her again—how could he?—she was hideous, she was withered. Better that he had never seen her again than to see her so—and he'd given so much for her and she'd never please him—and he made her weak with just a look, made fire run through her (and here she tugged at the bedclothes as if she felt the heat)—yet a look of pity was not what she craved.

I winced, not wanting to know so much. It reminded me of the way I'd wailed over Sire Galan in Mai's ears. Is that how I'd sounded?

Mai leaned forward and patted the concubine's hand, saying, "Soon you'll be yourself again. He'll not remember you as you are now. A man's desire feasts on what's before him, not what he saw yesterday—isn't that our usual complaint?" She laughed. "But here it's all to the good."

"You're right, I'm sure," Consort Vulpeja said, wiping her face with the bedclothes. "He sent for me, after all. I must take heart from that."

"I've brought something for you," Mai said, taking a cloth-bound packet from the purse on her low-slung girdle. "If you bathe in this daily—

just a pinch in the bathwater—you'll be desired. But you mustn't expect it to work right away. It will take some little time."

Consort Vulpeja said, "What can I give you for all your help? It's a heavy weight to be so beholden. Look in my chest, the one you sit upon. Take anything you want and still I'll owe you more, for I owe you my life and my place."

Mai said, "It was Firethorn who saved your life," but the concubine didn't seem to hear. She wouldn't rest until Mai had taken a gift—anything—everything, if she wished, as much as she would take.

Mai was at last persuaded to open the chest. She bent over it with one hand on her back, as if stooping pained her, and the other hand fingering what she found inside. A rose-colored gown, two muslin shifts, a rough woolen cloak that a jack might wear, a wimple, hose and garters, a leather girdle with an empty purse, two fur cuffs (merely rabbit), a tippet of fox, a small wooden box containing a comb, a silver chain, a few loose pearls. Mai looked at me, cocking an eyebrow at these paltry possessions; we both knew harlots and handmaids who owned as much. Nevertheless, she straightened up with the cloak in her hand.

After we left the tent, I asked Mai, "Are you my friend?" I had begun to wonder.

She grinned and rested her heavy arm on my shoulder. "Coz, you invited the cuckoo to your nest; are you so amazed, now, to see what hatches? She's here and you must make the best of it, and the best you can do is mend her and send her off to Galan's keep and out of your way, as quick as can be."

Tobe came running and buried his head in Mai's skirts. She hoisted him up to sit on one hip and he tugged at her dress, wanting to nurse. She gave his hand a little slap. Sunup came and stood by my side, watching the two of them, solemn again. Mai tossed her the cloak she had gotten from Consort Vulpeja, saying she'd done well, and when she came home—and that would be soon, she hoped—she'd make her an overdress from it against the winter winds.

I said, "Mai, can you give me some of what you gave Consort Vulpeja?"

"You think you have need of it?"

I nodded. I would not wail like Consort Vulpeja. I would not.

"Why, has Sire Galan's dangle lost its prick?"

"It's not that."

"So you've quarreled, I suppose. It's nothing. You've bound him and he'll not get far before he feels the leash. Besides, I told you the charm would not move Sire Galan. It's to ease her mind, for the desire she needs is the desire to live. I'll send you something better if you like, but I still say that if you'd whistle, he'd come to heel."

This made me laugh; it was a bitter jest that she supposed Galan was on the leash when I felt the collar tight around my own throat.

That same day Consort Vulpeja had another visitor: Sire Farol's wife, Dame Hartura. Though she lived just across the common yard, I hadn't seen a hair of her hide for days. She only left the tent to go to tourneys and I'd stayed away from those since Galan was injured. She came carrying a gift and sly reminders that she was a wife and Consort Vulpeja wasn't. The gift was handsome: enough fine lawn to make an underdress, with an edging of white embroidery over white. It's true there was a stain on it, but nothing to trouble a good seamstress.

Consort Vulpeja made me prop her up in bed for the visit. I stayed at hand, fearing she might faint. At first they went back and forth to determine if they had kin in common, which they did, of course, somewhat distant. The Blood parse blood ties to a fine degree and to many generations, whereas we mudfolk reckon just enough to keep from coupling with those we shouldn't.

Consort Vulpeja got a pinched look about her nostrils when Dame Hartura mentioned Sire Galan's son, a stout boy, a very healthy babe—he had the exact stamp of his sire—whom she'd seen before she left Ramus for the Marchfield. Consort Vulpeja hardly needed to be told there were two sides to a bedsheet and any boy Galan begot of her would be born on the wrong side.

As for the gift, she took it hard but hid it well. She drooped her head and said she was humbled by Dame Hartura's generosity; she was unworthy to wear such fine cloth, unworthy to receive it, and from such a very gracious hand at that! She praised the gift as highly as if Dame Hartura had brought her cartloads of velvets and miniver, and belittled herself, saying she was beneath the notice of her exalted visitor. All this was properly said and to be expected, as it was expected that, in turn, Dame Hartura would say the gift was nothing, was less than a token, she didn't mean to insult her with it but it was the best she could give from her poor linen chest. Then she added that Consort Vulpeja's beauty was spoken of widely and she was grateful to be given the chance to adorn her. This last jab, it seemed, she couldn't resist.

After this visit Consort Vulpeja's temper came untethered and she raged at me and everything I did, from afternoon till evening. She struck me too, but with such feeble blows I made nothing of it, thinking it was no wonder she was tender from Dame Hartura's show of charity. But when she screamed at Sunup and frightened her, I swore I'd sit on her if she didn't quiet down, and I turned my back on her and set about brewing a tisane to bring on drowsiness.

Sire Galan came home while she was shrieking that I was a hoof-handed sow, a clumsy, verminous, stinking drudge, and moreover a slut with a cankered sheath as big as a harbor, commodious enough to berth three ships at once—too loose a fit to please a man. He pushed aside the curtain and stood looking at her from under the visor of his helmet. When she caught sight of him, she stopped short and her reddened face blanched.

He said nothing to her. To me he said mildly, "Firethorn, come and help with my armor."

I ducked under his arm and he let the curtain fall behind us. He sent his varlets off to the armorer to have a new grip put on his buckler and the dents in its face hammered smooth again. They all had to go on every errand because of the feud.

There was a multitude of fastenings, buckles and points and latches, and just as he was armored from foot up to head, he was undressed the other way, from head to foot. He pulled off the helmet himself and untied the padded cap. The smell of sweat was sharp.

He wore a grim face. "Is it her custom to revile you so?" he asked, as I worked at the buckles of his neckguard. "I never thought to hear such foulness from her mouth—it's like the stink coming from a privy pit."

"She's out of sorts today. She had a visitor and it was too great a strain."

"What visitor?"

"Dame Hartura. She gave her a fine length of cloth for an underdress. Can you afford a seamstress to have it made up?"

I kept my voice cool. His was colder. "Call for a seamstress if one is needed and don't trouble me with it. And don't trouble yourself over my money; what I have left will suffice, and if it doesn't, I'll borrow against what the war will bring me."

"Then shall I have the seamstress make a velvet gown, as well, and a brocade surcoat? And a warmer cloak too, I think. The clothes your concubine brought with her are not fit to be seen. Besides, she lacks anything in your colors."

At that he grew heated. "Is your heart made of flint? How can you ask and ask and ask in such a . . . such a stony way, when she repays all your care with ill use? How can you ask it of *me*? I never wanted her in my charge, and I'll not have her wearing my colors."

If my heart was flint, it was as quick to strike sparks as his. I said, "You wanted her enough, once."

"As you remind me at every chance. I tire of this dispute, of you instructing me in my obligations with a tongue as keen as a mercy dagger when you are apt to forget your *own* duties. I've not found you so trustworthy of late."

I didn't protest. How could I? I applied myself to the fastenings of his brigandine, under his left arm, and kept my face averted.

He put one hand over mine to stop me working. "Most of all," he said, and his stare scorched even though I didn't meet his eyes, "most of all I tire of you sleeping by her side instead of mine."

I looked at him. "I didn't think I was required there any longer."

"'Required'? Must you be required? Do as you please," he said bitterly. "I'll not *require* you."

One word misplaced and offense was given yet again. "I meant—you didn't seem to want me there."

"Well, you were mistaken. Not for the first time."

Off came the brigandine and the scaled kilt and the greaves. The quilted underarmor came off too, in more haste, and he was down to his bandage, and we didn't stop there, not until he had untied my headcloth and undone my laces and pushed the dress off my shoulders and down over my hips. When he felt the raised welts on my back, he grew gentler. He lay on the pallet and pulled me down to him, but I was not so gentle. I sat astride and rode him hard and spurred him on. I scratched him a few welts to remember me by, as I'd remembered him these past nights.

We tarried too long and were asleep when Galan's men came back with the repaired buckler. Spiller and Rowney woke us when they came in and lit the lamps. Galan rose and dressed, in no hurry, and went out to take his supper with the other cataphracts. Spiller waited until he was gone, then made a show of sniffing the air and said, with a sly grin at Rowney, "Say farewell to sleep. She's in rut again and will be caterwauling every night." Rowney looked at me sidelong.

I was in no mood for Spiller's japes but couldn't let it pass. He was the kind to tickle a bull with a switch until the bull gored him. I finished knotting my headcloth and said, "If Rowney can sleep through your snoring, he can sleep through anything, for you bray like a donkey." Noggin snickered and I turned on him. "As for you, Noggin, your snore is more of a whinny—all mixed with snorts. Sometimes I'd swear there was a horse in the tent."

Noggin maintained that he never snored; if he did he'd wake himself up, for the slightest noise disturbed him. This was such a bald lie that Spiller and I got to chaffing him, and there was some hooting and loud laughter. But Rowney didn't laugh.

I made Consort Vulpeja's soup of broth and coddled egg and took it in to her. The only light in her chamber came from behind the curtain. Sunup had dozed off on her nest of rags and forgotten the lamps. When I went to light them, Consort Vulpeja said, "Leave it dark."

"I have your supper," I said. "You must see to eat."

She turned her head away and said, "Leave me be."

I recognized the sound in the concubine's voice and the unyielding line her lips made pressed together. It had taken no longer than the hour of dusk, while the light colored and faded from the sky, to undo every gain she'd won in the past days.

Galan did not rise as early as usual the next morning, for when he woke, there I was next to him. I was in his bed again after a long exile, but by the ardency of his welcome, you'd think he was the one who'd been banished. He was not a man to forgive an insult; it seemed he meant to forget, instead, that I'd taken him for a man of dubious word and tarnished honor. Not that we spoke of it. And I'd forgive him anything to be home. He was all the home I had.

In time he got up and put on his armor and left with all his men except Noggin.

Consort Vulpeja wouldn't take a morsel of food, not even from Sunup's hand. Her courage had failed, but her stubbornness was steadfast. Mai told me once that she never yet saw anyone die of desire. What of despair, then? For Consort Vulpeja seemed fixed on dying.

All morning I wheedled, and she replied with silence and a glare that spoke loud and plain. In the afternoon I prepared a bath for her with a pinch of the herbs Mai had brought, which smelled sweet and a trifle musky. She knocked the basin from my hands and screamed that I'd exchanged Mai's herbs for some which would do her harm—make her skin blister, likely—and used Mai's on myself. This raging left her with red cheeks and a white circle around her mouth. Then she fell into a stupor and spoke no more.

I had not one true word of comfort for her. She'd overheard Galan say he'd never wanted her. She'd overheard more than that. I kept on offering her food and drink and something to ease her rest, with a coaxing voice and soothing hands, but all the while there was this buzz and thrum all through me, an exultant—even vaunting—singing in the blood. I was dismayed to feel it, but I did, nevertheless. I did, forgetting the sting of the cloth rubbing against the welts on my back. Is this what a man feels when his enemy lies in the dust with the sword at his throat and he savors the question: whether to bear down or no? Jealousy is wont to give no quarter.

CHAPTER 11

Armiger

here was a cold, dry wind that afternoon, blowing down from the Hardscrabble. Gusts rattled the canvas against the poles and made the ropes creak. Noggin had gone off with a few of the Crux's kitchenboys to gather fuel. These days a stick of wood wasn't to be found, and charcoal from the mountains was so dear it was sold by the handful, not the sack. We burned dried horse dung, gorse twigs, and salt hay, and plenty of each, for the chill in the air and all the sheets that needed boiling. It was as if Ardor Hearth-keeper had withdrawn her favor from the Marchfield, making our hearth fires flare and stink and sputter out too quickly. Or she warned us not to take her for granted.

I would gladly have traded errands with Noggin, to be outside and let the wind blow through me, but I stayed in the dim tent close to Consort Vulpeja. Was this the change of weather they said the king awaited? There had been good omens in the Heavens, according to the Auspices of Crux, such as lances of geese heading west across the Inward Sea instead of south, and a raven, struck dead by a fish eagle, that fell at the king's feet during a tourney.

I'd looked for signs myself, casting the bones again for Consort Vulpeja. But in three throws they had pointed every which way and might as well have been mute, for all I could hear them.

I ground barley: another handful of grain, grit between the rough, shallow mortar and the round stone of the pestle. I thought of Az and that led me to Fleetfoot and how I'd seen less of him of late, having no need for a messenger. I had but one patient now, and her malady was beyond me.

Sire Rodela ducked under the door flap. He looked down at me with that smile of his that was close kin to a sneer.

I was amazed he'd come on his own shanks. I thought we might not see him again until he was carried from the priests' tent headfirst on a bier. His cheeks were sallow under dark whiskers. His hair was thin on top of his pate and thick everywhere else; it had grown past his ears and nearly to his shoulders, and by the length of it I measured the time passed since Galan had shorn him. When he took off his cloak, I saw his bandaged forearm was near its right size again. He sat down in the accustomed spot on his pallet and stretched out his legs and propped his back against his saddle. He didn't speak for a while and I went on grinding under his regard, my head low as I knelt before the mortar. He'd been in the priests' tent a hand of days, half a tennight, and I'd grown used to his absence. Now that he was back I recalled too well the sullen weight of his presence, the affliction of his gaze.

"I thought you'd be gone," he said.

I said nothing.

"Does Galan still have a use for you? You'll do as a nursemaid, I suppose, for him and his new bedmate too, until she's better. I saw her when she was brought in—it will be some while before she's fit for a pricking again."

Yesterday, before Galan took me back into his bed, this taunt might have found its mark; today I was proof against it. I kept on grinding and said, "She can hear you, Sire."

"Ah, then it's true she's roused from her long faint. Shall I go beg her pardon?"

"Leave her be, Sire. She has no strength to spare for visitors."

He'd spoken his gibes lazily, as if amused, showing his teeth in his beard. Now his voice grew harsh. "That's not for you to say. Go and ask if she'll receive me."

I never could tell what his fancy would fix on, and was relieved it had passed over me for the moment. I went behind the curtain. Sunup was plaiting green thread into Consort Vulpeja's hair, many little plaits around the crown of her head. The concubine's eyes were closed.

"Does she sleep?" I whispered to Sunup. Sunup nodded yes just as the concubine opened her eyes and squinted at me.

"Sire Rodela is here, Consort," I said. "He begs leave to come and visit you."

"Who is Sire Rodela?" she asked.

"Sire Galan's armiger." Likely they'd met before, but not so she'd remember his name.

"No," she said, frowning.

I waited awhile, but no more was forthcoming. "You don't wish to see him?"

When she answered, her voice shook and began to rise in pitch. "Tell him he has no cause to ask such a thing. Does he think I'm some wanton who would see a man alone? Let him ask his master for leave when he gets home. Then I might receive him, in company with Sire Galan—or I might not, for he has put my modesty to the question. And if *you* were any better than a two-copper harlot yourself, you'd know better than to sully my ears with such a message!"

This stung, for I was indeed too ignorant of the courtesies of the Blood; I suspected Sire Rodela had sent me in on purpose to collect just such a rebuke.

I thought he'd mock me when I came out. Instead his brows came down and he roared, "Does she think I don't know what her modesty is worth? I stood guard outside the privy tent while she bared her buttocks and bent over for a tupping, and now she pretends she's a maid still? A curse on all her stiff-necked clan. Look at her father—how he covered his infamy with silver gilt. She'd do the same if she could. But it will not be enough to cozen me."

She shrieked from behind the curtain. "I'll tell Sire Galan of your insolence. He'll see to you. He'll cut off your sacs and stop up your mouth with them!"

He rose to his feet and went to stand just outside her chamber, jeering. "If she doesn't learn—and soon—manners to befit her new station, if she goes on looking for insults behind every courtesy, she'll get Galan killed dueling over an honor she's already squandered. A concubine cannot be so mincing about every little thing. I merely wished to pay my respects, nothing more, and see how she rails at me!"

"I know my place, but you don't know yours," she cried. "The bitch who whelped you must have got loose from the kennel to breed such a mongrel. Whoreson jack! Mudborn!"

I hid a smile behind my hands to hear her berate someone else for once, but when I looked to Sire Rodela's face, I stopped smiling.

"The concubine should know," he said, speaking clearly, "that my Blood runs cleaner than hers, for I've never tainted it with a drop of dishonor."

He waited for an answer with his hand gripping the curtain. It was well for her that she curbed her tongue at last, and made none, else I'm sure he'd have gone into her chamber without leave and what he might have done then I couldn't guess. Instead he put on his sneer and turned away. "She has a sweet disposition, doesn't she? Sire Galan must be pleased. Now he has two shrews in his tent, gnawing at his sacs, eating his grain. I wish him joy of the both of you."

I went in to Consort Vulpeja and found her weeping into her bedclothes. The sight of me didn't improve her temper. It was too much a reminder that she'd gambled away her place in her house and clan for a man who didn't welcome her. I left her with Sunup, who lay down beside her on the cot and clasped her tightly. The concubine did not push her away; neither did she seem to take the comfort offered.

I hoped that by the time I left her chamber, Sire Rodela would have gone to seek better company elsewhere. But there he was, sitting by his strongbox. He'd opened it to find his purse was empty, save for his coins and a few hairs from Sire Bizco's scalp that had tangled in the laces. I stood dead still when he looked up at me, as afraid as if I'd just come upon a viper underfoot and didn't know which way to step.

He barked, "Where is it?"

I didn't pretend to misunderstand. "Burnt, Sire," I said, and took a step sideways, toward the door.

"Who did it? Was it you?"

"It was done to save your life, Sire, to placate the armiger's shade. He was giving you the fever." We should never have done it. Spiller was right, we should have let him die.

He got to his feet. "To save my life? It was maggots saved my life, nothing but maggots. Do you see this?" He pulled the bandage from his forearm and bared his wound. The blackened crust was gone, and in its place was the pink of a new scar growing between the lips of the cut. "The priests put blowflies to breed on me and left the worms to work. They're very clever, the priests. And the maggots are clever too, to eat what's dead and leave the rest." He turned his hard laugh on himself. "Nibble and gnaw all night and all day. I could feel them from time to time, tickling."

I sidled toward the door but he saw me and was there in two strides.

"Do you know what comforted me while I lay in the priests' tent? It was the thought that Sire Bizco was miserable too, that he had time to count over and over those he had wronged and those who'd wronged him. That I'd be the chief amongst them all, a stone in his craw. That he was not quit of me yet nor I of him. So who was it robbed me of this? Was it my cousin, my fortunate cousin? Was it you who told Galan?"

I opened my mouth and not a word came out. Even if I lied and claimed

Galan had burnt the scrap of skin and I'd had nothing to do with it, Sire Rodela would find a way to blame me. It pleased him to blame me.

He smiled to see me so afraid. "I warned you what would happen if you prattled to Sire Galan. Did you forget what I said I'd do? Let no man—nor woman, either—say I don't keep my word."

He stepped back to his pallet, and when he stooped to pick up his dagger, I ran. Instead of trying for the door, I pushed aside the curtain and dashed through Consort Vulpeja's chamber to the slit I'd cut in the tent wall the night of the dwale smoke. I'd never stitched it up again, leaving it open most days for light and air; today it was tied shut with laces against the cold wind. I cut the knot with my little knife. The hole was big enough for me and not for Sire Rodela. I clambered through headfirst, but he caught up to me before I was halfway out and dragged me back into the tent by my ankles. As I lay on the ground, he kicked me in the belly and I couldn't breathe. He pulled me to my feet with his arm around my neck, squeezing my throat in the crook of his elbow, and he put the point of his dagger under my ribs. He was behind me and I couldn't see his face. "Don't fret," he said in my ear, "I shan't kill you." I didn't believe him. He hauled me across the chamber, and I saw Sunup sitting on the cot and I wanted to call to her to run for help, but neither sound nor breath could get past the grip around my windpipe. Consort Vulpeja stared.

He took me to his pallet. The knife pricked through my dress. I went where he dragged me and didn't have the strength to hinder him. He pushed me down facefirst and I lay there gasping, thinking if I could only fill my bellows, I could move, I could beg. I would have begged. But I had no chance, for he kicked me again in the side, under my ribs, and I choked out a scream and curled up, and as I did I saw his face. Only a skull could wear a wider grin.

He was calling me a tattling bitch and a skinsheath and a mudhole and other things, but what he said didn't matter. His rage was huge and famished. And what was I to this rage? Not even its cause. It needed no cause. But it had an appetite for my terror.

Sire Rodela turned me over with his boot and lay on top of me—not as a man who wants to couple would lie, but backward, with his bent knee under my chin, jammed against my throat, and his heavy thigh across my rib cage. His green leggings were coarse and wrinkled and patched over one buttock. His boots were clotted with dried mud. My world had shrunk to this, to Sire Rodela, and I saw every minute particular with clarity.

He pulled my skirt up to my waist and grasped some of the short coppery hairs at my crotch to pull the skin taut, and he laid the edge of his blade against me and began to saw. He meant to skin me, as he'd said he would. He meant to take my woman's beard for a trophy. I heaved, I kicked, but he outweighed me and I couldn't shift him off. He said, "Be still! You wouldn't want the dagger to slip, would you?" And he pressed his knee harder against my windpipe.

There was this mercy, that pain and fear became distant, along with my body. What was left of me calculated how I might stay alive one moment to the next. If he didn't stab me, he'd choke me to death soon. I had no wind left and blood roared in my ears and there were black swarms like flies crawling over my eyes. I discovered my left arm was pinned under him but my right was free, and I found my knife in that hand; I'd used it to cut my way out of the tent. Now I stabbed where I could reach him, leg and haunch and flank.

His body might have been ironwood, for all I could carve it. He was cursing and telling me if I'd only lie still, it would be sooner done.

Then I did lie still. I relinquished possession of my limbs. I had but one thought, a coward's thought, the hope that he would leave me alive when he was done.

And I could do nothing else, because he choked the breath out of me and blackness brimmed over.

When I came to myself, I was on Galan's pallet. Sunup had a cloth pressed to my wound. It hurt to breathe; the air scraped down my windpipe with a sound like an armorer's file across steel.

Sunup had run for help and fetched the Crux's cook. He had come with the great bone cleaver, because he was cutting up a sheep's carcass when she found him, but he never had cause to use it. She said that when they came in Sire Rodela was still lying backward across me. Cook called his name from the doorway and he got up with a deliberate carelessness and straightened his jerkin and put his dagger in his sheath and something else into his pouch, and with his foot pushed the skirt down over my thighs. It was soon wet with blood. He was bleeding too, from many little holes—five, the priests counted when they tended to him—but both Sunup and Cook marked that his leather prickguard was still laced tight.

Now Cook was sitting cross-legged beside me with the cleaver resting across his thighs. It lay there as if he'd forgotten it, but I felt safer in the company of both cleaver and Cook anyway. Cook had the same grizzle to his beard as his master, the Crux, and the same lines graved beside his mouth, the same set to his jaw; they were as like as brothers born on opposite sides of the bedsheet. He ruled his kitchenboys with scorn and a hammer fist and a pinch of praise for the sauce, and in that he also resembled his master.

I tried to ask him if Sire Rodela was there, and discovered it hurt even more to talk than to breathe. The sound I made was not much like speech.

He understood enough to answer, "Gone. I doubt he'll be back."

I sat up and my arms trembled under my weight and my eyes swam with dark motes and tears. After a moment I pushed away Sunup's hand to see what Sire Rodela had done. A rabbit's skin is loose and comes off clean, and underneath the body is whole and neat, the muscles bound with tendon. I was not skinned so tidily. There was a raw stripe in the thicket of wiry hair at my groin, a red and white furrow about the length of my thumb. The flesh wasn't thick there and he'd gouged down to the girdle bone. There was a puncture in my thigh; perhaps the knife had slipped after all. I didn't even feel the holes he'd pricked in my back, not till later. I took the rag from Sunup and pressed on the wound. The bleeding was already stanched, except for a trickle. I must have been insensible for a long while. I wished I still was, for the pain of the cut clamored at me now.

Dread came again and I was shaking. I thought how Sire Rodela would have crushed my windpipe if he'd leaned just a little harder.

I would make him rue that he'd left me alive.

Sire Galan came home after dark and went straight to his tent without greeting anyone on the way. When I showed him what his armiger had done, fury turned him white-faced. The first thing he asked was whether Sire Rodela had taken me, whether he'd pricked me. I said, "Only with his knife," in a voice so rough he flinched at the sound. He demanded to know why I hadn't sent for him at once. I began to weep, saying I had no idea where he was—did he think we could find one ant in a wheat field? Then he chastised Noggin for leaving the women alone in the tent, even though I was the one who'd sent him on an errand. He struck him with a gauntlet and shouted while Noggin begged for mercy with his arms over his head and Spiller and Rowney and horsemaster Flykiller stood by without a word.

At that moment Consort Vulpeja began to laugh. It chilled us all, I think, to hear her laughing alone in her dark chamber. Sunup ran in to see to her and after a while she subsided.

Galan looked stunned; the fury had ebbed and left him aground. He dropped his gauntlets and tugged off his helmet and cap and wiped his face with his hands.

He squatted next to me and asked, "Do you know where he went?"

I shook my head. My throat was closed tight, between the swelling and the crying.

"Why did he do this? Because you refused to lie with him?"

I shook my head again.

"Why then? Tell me why."

The words had to be forced out, one by one, against the pain of speaking. "He came back. Opened his strongbox, his pouch. Gone." I looked to Spiller for help but he shied away from my eyes.

"He thought you'd robbed him?"

"Not coin," I said. I stopped to wheeze, helpless for a time to do more.

It was Rowney who stepped forward to finish the tale. But before he could finish it, he had to start at the beginning, when Sire Rodela had killed Sire Bizco. Galan did not show so much as a flicker of surprise at this. He'd given us all a beating for hiding Sire Rodela's wound without once asking how his armiger had come by it; no doubt he'd guessed the next day, when the body was found.

Rowney seemed to find the words slow in coming and, once they were said, very bald, a poor disguise for shirking our duty toward our master. Galan fixed him with a stare and bid him spur on his laggard tongue. He listened in pitiless silence as Rowney told how Sire Rodela had threatened us with harm if we told Sire Galan, or anyone else, and how he'd waved a piece of Sire Bizco's scalp like a banner. "Though I wasn't there when he came home," Rowney added, "I couldn't help but see he was wounded. So he threatened me too." Here the skin tightened around Galan's eyes at the reminder: he'd not seen it, after all, though it was plain to see.

Galan said to me, "Were you so afraid of him?"

I looked down. He hadn't asked before why I had failed him, but the question had lain between us. Fear was only part of the answer. I couldn't explain the rest to him, for shame of it. I couldn't say that in this I had been more his drudge than his woman. When Galan and I had quarreled, the night Sire Rodela was wounded, then I was his woman. By morning I was his drudge and nothing more, the distance to him impassable for days and days—had he forgotten so soon?

Drudges keep many secrets from their masters.

Now he was angry with me, with my silence. "You should have brought this trouble to me. Did you think I couldn't guard you from my own armiger?"

I gestured, refusing the question, for the answer was right before him. I saw him wince, as if he'd heard his own words too late. "But if you'd told me," he said, "if I'd had forewarning . . ."

Spiller spoke up then, and under Galan's eye he stuttered and stammered, saying it was not only that Sire Rodela had frightened us—after all, it was his way, we were used to it: one day he'd offer to fry us, the next roast us on a spit—but we'd all thought the wound was just a scratch, it would heal quickly, and there'd be no need to tell about such a little thing. No need to worry Sire Galan about it. But Sire Rodela had caught the fever and still he'd refused the carnifex and we'd thought the dead man was at fault for his worsening. "And so we burned it—the scalp—and we were just about to tell you about it, Sire, when you came in that day and gave us a whipping."

I watched Galan's face closely as he listened. His countenance changed little, but what I saw now I didn't expect: a slackening, an easing that bespoke relief. He turned to me and said, "So you were the first to hand when he came home and found his prize was gone."

I shrugged and looked away. This was what he cared to think.

"Or was there more? Something else you've kept from me?" He put a finger against my cheek and turned my face toward him.

Galan was so glad Sire Rodela's prick had not trespassed where he was tenant. That was all that concerned him. Of course there was more, yet nothing to tell. Should I have run to Galan over a few insulting words and caused discord between them? Should I have complained of Sire Rodela's eyes, of how often I'd chanced upon him watching me? And yet it was never lust I thought I saw, but something more like greed. Never lust until I lay under him and felt his prick stiffen against my side before I fainted. I too was glad that Cook had come in before he could do more. But surely Sire Rodela had done enough.

"Must there be more?" I asked.

Galan's face was close. One coil of hair hung over his brow, lank with sweat, and he pushed it away. His eyelids came half down and his gaze went elsewhere, nowhere, before coming back to me. "No," he said.

CHAPTER 12

Ordeal

alan went to find Sire Rodela. He left behind his helmet with the serene metal face on the visor. When we parted he wore no more expression on his face than that mask, and his calm was chilling. Except for his eyes. His eyes were restless, they burned what they touched. I was glad to see him go. I had a bellyful of that same fire and would not be content until Sire Rodela was dead. I never doubted Galan would see to it.

But the Crux had other ideas.

He and the other cataphracts had returned to camp from the tourney field that evening before Galan. Since Galan had been forbidden to ride, he trained apart from the others and stayed at his exercises longer; no one knew what he did exactly, save for his men.

When the Crux had found supper wasn't ready, he'd bellowed at Cook, and Cook had told him why. They'd found Sire Rodela without any trouble, for he'd gone to his pallet in the priests' tent for a nap.

So before Galan was three strides from his doorway, he was invited to the Crux's tent. Spiller, who'd crept out after him though Galan had forbidden it, came back to give us this morsel of news and left just as quickly to scavenge more. He returned to say that armigers guarded the Crux's tent and he couldn't get close. The cataphracts were all inside.

Galan's men jawed this over, but it was all gristle and no meat. Spiller would not stop talking; he was filled with glee to think of Sire Rodela dragged before the Crux, though he'd have been happier to see Galan skewer him outright. I lay on the pallet with my back to them and my face to the wall. I watched the shadows waver and knew I'd been robbed. The Crux had found out. He would blunt the edge of Galan's rage. If it did not happen now, it would not happen.

In a little while they came for me. The Crux sent his armiger, Sire Rassis, and Divine Xyster. The priest told me to show him the wound. I did as he asked so they wouldn't lay hands on me. It was one more humiliation I owed to Sire Rodela. I hitched up my skirt and untied the bandage soaked in woundwort I'd put on not long before, while my rising blood clothed me in a flush of shame. I kept my gaze averted from Divine Xyster. He brought the lamp closer to scrutinize the wound. Rowney turned away, but Noggin and Spiller gawked openly.

My breath ran quick, scratching so loudly the priest could hear it. He lifted my chin and looked at the marks on my throat. Whatever he saw, it was bad enough for him to give a small grunt.

He said, "So, can you speak?"

I said, "If I must," and was reminded what it would cost me. It felt like a fishbone was trapped in my gullet.

When they brought me to the Crux's tent, it seemed they didn't care to hear me speak after all. They asked me no questions. I stepped inside the doorway and with a darting glance found Galan across the tent. He sat unmoving and impassive. But when he met my eyes, I saw something more: I saw how he compelled himself to stillness. Constraint showed in the line of his jaw, in the set of his shoulders, in the way one hand prisoned the other on his lap. The Crux had snared him and now he had to sit still before his fellows while all the privy matters of his household, even his sheath, were displayed to them and held up for judgment; sit still before me while Sire Rodela knelt just a few paces in front of him, within his reach. I saw the shame of it and looked away before he could.

The pavilion could have been taken for a manor hall, it was so large and richly furnished, except that the north wind leaned on the walls, making them shudder and complain, and set the oil lamps swinging on their chains and the hangings to swaying. I couldn't begin to reckon the cost of the carpets that covered the floor, or the tapestry behind the Crux, depicting the Sun and the Moon worked in gold and silver thread on a field of blue Heavens—had there been enough oxcarts to carry all this?—and then I wondered how I could think of such a thing when the sinews of my legs unraveled like poorly spun thread and it took all my strength to stand upright.

For there were too many men. The cataphracts were seated all around the tent, wearing surcoats touched with shades of green, each so embellished with gold thread and beads and fine embroidery that pattern vied against pattern and none stood out. The plumes and bird wings fixed upon their hats were teased by the wind. In this crowd three men were marked by the plainness of their garb: the Crux in a surcoat of somber green velvet, unadorned except for the godsign picked out in diamonds on his right breast, and a collar and hat of glossy black fur; Galan bareheaded beside him, the only man in armor, half shining and half drab in his polished neck-plate and his canvas-covered brigandine studded with rivets. His sword arm was clad in glinting scales and his shield arm in red linen underarmor. And there was Sire Rodela, clothed in his short leather jerkin over a tunic and threadbare hose. Though he was kneeling, he didn't look sufficiently cowed. He leaned back on his heels, looking over his shoulder at me.

All their eyes were on me.

I saw this much before a word was said. When I backed up I found Sire Rassis stood between the doorway and me. I hung my head and stared at the carpet underfoot.

Divine Xyster crossed the tent to take his place with the other priests, who sat to the left of the Crux while Galan sat on his right. The carnifex described my wound and Sire Rodela didn't trouble to deny he'd made it. There was blood on my skirt for everyone to see and though some was Sire Rodela's, most was mine. Plainly the damage was inconvenient to Galan, and that was of some account and cause for some sly amusement among the assembled cataphracts.

I kept my head down and peered from under my brow, careful not to look any man in the eye; it would be taken for insolence. I didn't know why I was there. If Sire Rodela had treated a horse as he'd treated me, would they have brought it to the tent for show? Perhaps they meant to parade me up and down so they could calculate my worth against the damage done and set the fine Sire Rodela must pay. I guessed they'd rate me far below a warhorse and maybe somewhat above a palfrey. Soon I wouldn't have to guess, I'd know my price to a nicety. Their smiles made me angry, and that was good. It stiffened my legs against the trembling.

There was no amusement in the Crux's voice. He leaned on the arm of his high-backed chair and said, "She will mend, Galan. It's not reasonable to ask full quittance when she will mend. Or have you no further use for her now that Rodela has scarred her?"

I hadn't thought of that.

Galan said—and I marked he did not answer the question—"I'll tell you what quittance will satisfy me. Give me leave to fight him and I'll gladly put an end to the quarrel by putting an end to him."

The Crux said, "I won't give you leave. Are you such a fool as to think any quarrel ends with one death? You've already started one feud, and now you would cause strife within the clan."

Galan said, "I'm not the cause of this strife. *He* caused it. I don't deserve this of him. I gave him a place as my armiger as a favor to a cousin, because we shared a grandfather—and because you asked it of me. There were others I would rather have had on my shield side, yet I always treated him with courtesy."

"Was it courteous to burn off his hair?" asked the Crux.

Galan was silent.

"Was that perchance over the woman too?"

There was a further silence that admitted it and I didn't dare look up. My face was hot.

In a grudging voice Galan said, "He's ever envied what was mine, but I never thought he'd be forsworn. I took him for better."

Sire Rodela said, "I'm not forsworn, *Cousin*. The armiger's oath says I must serve and defend you; it says nothing about your sheath. Though I did serve her, and gladly. I served her as she deserved." His back was to me, but I could tell by his voice that he wore a smirk.

One of the cataphracts—I think it was Sire Pregon—called out, "I heard she gave you what *you* deserved. She poked you full of holes."

"Those were just thorn pricks. Divine Xyster lets more blood with his little quill. It was as good as a tonic to me."

A snort of laughter escaped someone and the Crux scowled. "Do I understand you right?" he asked Sire Rodela. "Do you boast of winning a fight with a *woman*?"

"No, Sire," the armiger said in a chastened tone. "It was no fight. It was . . . a mishap. I merely wanted a keepsake, a lock of her hair, and can I help it if she lost her temper and perforce a bit of skin came with the hair? I didn't mean to harm her."

I jerked up my head and looked to Galan. Everyone knows what it betokens for a man to have a keepsake of a woman's hair. Hair from the head is a sign of her favor. Hair from the woman's beard that hides her quim means he's pricked her. Sire Rodela hunted me; he wasn't done with me yet. Every part of me shook now, not just my legs. I crossed my arms and dug my fingers into the flesh above my elbows until it hurt.

If Galan should believe him . . .

But Galan was half out of his chair and shouting, "Uncle, he lies. Do you expect me to abide this?"

The Crux answered, "Sit down! You'll abide what I tell you to abide. And do not call me uncle again today, for today I answer to all the houses, Falco, Musca, and all, as well as to Crux. We must all answer if we let this little squabble—over a sheath, mind you—grow into a rift that divides the clan."

He turned on Sire Rodela. "What is the meaning of this so-called keepsake? Did you force the sheath to lie with you?"

"I never forced her," Sire Rodela said, "yet I did lie with her now and then. She was willing enough before she grew fickle. All I asked of her today was a little token of the fondness she once showed me."

Gods defend me. He had insinuated as much before. But the boldness of the lie took my breath away as surely as a belly blow. They'd never take the word of a sheath against a man of the Blood.

I spat on the Crux's fine carpet. Sire Rassis shoved me hard and my legs gave way and I fell onto my hands and knees. I braced my palms on the ground and fought for breath. My throat burned. Over the thump of blood in my ears, I heard the Crux ask, "What does the sheath say? Is this true?"

I looked up at him, but for fear of meeting his eyes I ventured no farther than his grizzled beard and the grim line of his mouth. My guts twisted. Such a hard knot in my belly, such a tangle of words, and I couldn't find any of use. "No, Sire."

Sire Rodela shrugged. "Of course she'll not admit it. But I know how she wallows under a man as well as Galan."

The Crux looked at me. "I misjudged," he said. "I should never have let Galan bring this sheath. I was sure she'd be gone inside a tennight—for Galan is a man whose fancy wanes faster than the Moon. Yet here she is and here is trouble."

Oh, the armiger had been clever. No one ever blamed a man for being willing if a woman was—even, perhaps, his master's woman. He had made his malice look like a lover's spat; he'd dressed his master in a cuckold's horns (and many cataphracts were glad to see it, for envy's sake) and vaunted himself. That wasn't the worst he'd done. The worst was that Galan sat so stiffly, so far from me across the tent. Surely he knew Sire Rodela had lied; he'd thrown the lie back in his teeth. Yet I feared Sire Rodela had bred in him a maggot of doubt.

I got to my feet again, though my legs misgave me. I was tired of cringing like a scolded dog and refused to hang my head lower than Sire

Rodela's. I looked up and my gaze caught on a lamp hanging from a tent pole, swaying gently; the spout was a woman's head, and flame flickered from her open mouth. I thought of the Dame and begged her, if she could hear me, to lend me her aid. And I felt her come near carrying Wend's shears, a little pair of snippers such as used to hang from her girdle. She cut the knot that bound my words.

I spoke in the High and heard her inflections. "There's your trouble, Sire," I said to the Crux, pointing at Sire Rodela. "He does lie, he lies on the face of it, don't you see? For if you put his face by Sire Galan's face, is there any woman blind enough to choose him? *I* am not so blind." Some cataphracts laughed, and I felt I could gather them up, carry them with me. "But if he were half as ugly or twice as fair, I'd not risk my place for him or any man, for I'm content with it."

Now I looked at Galan and there was misery in the way he looked back. "I am content," I said again, to him. "And besides, when does Sire Rodela claim he coupled with me? Sire Galan knows I've been by his side nearly every night since he took me into his household, and those few nights, he knows right well, Sire Rodela accompanied him. And in the day, I was always with one or another of my master's drudges and Sire Rodela was always under Sire Galan's eye. He must take you for fools if he expects you to believe him!"

I knew at once I'd overstepped—I should never have called them fools. They did not laugh now. Their silence hardened against me.

Sire Rodela was quick to answer. His tone was mocking, even in the face of the Crux's bleak regard. "You may remember, Sire, that there were four nights when Galan was otherwise occupied in the matter of a certain wager. I suppose the sheath was galled because he spent himself elsewhere. Anyway, she let me know there was room on the blanket, and it mattered not a whit to me whether she opened her legs to satisfy her jealousy or her appetite. I didn't care to question, as long as I could have her."

"You were with him those nights, guarding him," I said, and my voice cracked. He made it sound so likely. It was the careless way he spoke, as if he couldn't be bothered to lie about it. He gambled away the Crux to please the cataphracts, and it seemed to me he'd won them.

Sire Rodela shrugged and turned toward me. "But you know better, don't you? I left the jack to stand guard and slipped back to the tent."

"I'd sooner take a viper to my bed."

Sire Rodela smiled. "So you say now. You sang sweeter before."

Galan was gripping the arms of his chair as if he held himself in it by force. He turned to his uncle and said, "He lies and lies and lies and you let him. What kind of man is this, with so much malice in him? He has a taste for flaying. He skinned that armiger—do you remember him?—he was found in the sea with a piece of his scalp missing; he skinned my sheath because she wouldn't do his bidding, because she burned that scalp to placate the dead; and now he'd use his sharp tongue to part her from me. Don't you see he means to flay me too?"

But the cataphracts did not see. The lie was simpler than the truth and easier to believe. And Galan had said too much; though his words were balm to me, they discomfited his fellows. I could see it on their faces as they glanced at each other.

Galan went on regardless. "Every word he says adds to his offense and all you can say to me is *sit down*—as if I were a child. Will you give me no remedy, Sire? Must I bear this insult? Any man of you would answer him as he should be answered, with a sword—must I bear it just because he's in my household?" Now he rose to his feet and his words ran headlong. "Surely it makes the offense greater that he's my cousin and that he's sworn to me, though he takes his oath to be as thin as the vellum it was writ on. Will you leave me no remedy but murder? I'd rather kill him fair, but any way, I mean to kill him."

Galan took a stride toward Sire Rodela as if he'd do it there and then, but quick as he was, the Crux was quicker, and Galan found him standing in his way with a naked sword. He pushed Galan hard with the fist that held the hilt, so hard he stumbled backward and sat in his chair again. The Crux laid the sword flat on the floor between Galan and Sire Rodela. In the voice he used in the field to command his men, the voice that could cut through the sounds of battle, he bellowed, "The first man to step over this blade will feel it bite his neck. Now sit down and be silent!"

He turned on Galan. "I shall put you in a baby's gown and tie a napkin around your neck if you don't master yourself. Are you still unweaned? Do you still play at spindles at your nurse's knee? You are of a man's estate but you've the temper of a child and a child's tantrums. You'd think he'd laid hands on your wife, not your sheath! You have two women in your bed now and Rodela has none, and did you think even so to have a quiet household?"

The words hailed down on Galan but he didn't seek shelter. He met the Crux's glare with one of his own. This was unjust. They both knew Galan had sent for Consort Vulpeja to end the feud he'd begun, not for a bedmate.

The Crux came forward until his boots brushed the sword on the ground. He loomed over Sire Rodela and spat out his words. "I never before blamed my father for siring so many bastards on his concubine, but today I'm ashamed of him for making me kin to you. Did you think I'd judge you lightly for sticking your little dagger in your master's sheath? If your story is true, you betrayed your master not once but many times—and you left him with only a worthless jack to guard his back. Now you have the bad grace to boast of it. Perhaps you think your quittance will be less if the sheath proves faithless and therefore worthless. You forget it's *your* faithfulness in question. Hers is of no importance here. And if your claim is false, if you've lied to make mischief, I'll give you special cause to regret uttering it." Sire Rodela's shoulders hunched about his ears and his eyes looked no higher than the tops of the Crux's boots—and still he carried his head too stiffly; there was defiance in it.

The Crux turned his back on Sire Rodela and resumed his seat. He straightened the folds of his surcoat over his thighs. He waited until the silence became wearisome, and then he said, "As Sire Rodela says one thing and the sheath another, there's but one way to find out, and that's by ordeal." Now he looked at me and for the first time I met his eyes directly. "When we're done here tonight, we will give her to the dogs. If she's lying they'll sniff it out. If she's telling the truth—and keeps a stout heart—they'll leave her unharmed."

I was thickheaded and slow to understand. And yet part of me was quicker: a wail began deep in the belly and crawled upward. I ground my teeth to prevent its escape.

The Crux watched me with a cold eye and deigned to address me. "I've given you leave to speak freely tonight and you've been bold enough to call a man of the Blood a liar. If you wish to recant your words, you may do so now, and stand for a liar yourself—and escape the dogs."

Galan began to rise and the Crux said to him, "Be still!" He said to me, "Well? What's your answer?"

I bowed my head. My throat was dry. I swallowed and swallowed and each time came a jabbing pain.

Trial by ordeal. For themselves, the Blood reserve trial by combat. For us, there is the ordeal. When I lived under the Dame's rule, such things were only rumors, but under Sire Pava I had seen it once when a village woman accused his horsemaster, Harien, of taking her against her will. The steward had given her the black drink, which is supposed to poison those who lie and spare those who tell the truth. She didn't survive it, but still I believe she didn't lie, for other women had whispered of Harien too; afterward they didn't dare.

I'd never heard of an ordeal by dogs. It was more fearful to me than poison. I'd run from the gazehounds in the Kingswood and seen them tearing at the stag. These war dogs were fiercer still, bred and trained to hunt foot soldiers and bring down galloping horses, the better to get at the horsemen's throats. Fleetfoot and Ev still slept with the pack, for they'd made themselves useful to Dogmaster and gained a place among the dogboys; but the dogs didn't know me. I avoided their pen. Was it true they could smell falsehood? For sure they could smell fear. Even I could smell it now in the stink of my own sweat. They would savage me for it. I had no faith the truth would shield me.

The Crux said, "Do you admit you lied?" Now it was my turn to feel the brunt of his contempt. Mud is easily scraped from a boot, he'd said of me once. And he'd said, "Keep her out of my way or I'll feed her to the dogs." He'd rid Galan of me one way or the other.

I looked up. Galan too waited for my answer. His brows were drawn together in a frown and his eyes were in shadow. He was a jealous man and Sire Rodela knew it; he'd counted on it. I said to Galan and Galan alone, in all the room, "Whether the dogs prove to be wise judges or as foolish as men, I told the truth. I swear to it." I spoke in anger that he should need this from me, but even as the words were out I saw that I had misunderstood his look. He lifted his hand as if he would reach across the room and cover my mouth.

"No," he said, his words overtaking mine. "Sire, I beg you, don't make her suffer this ordeal. This is a matter within my household, and no one else's concern. And I believe her."

"You may believe what you please. To be sure, it's none of my concern if you are fond to foolishness. But what's between you and Rodela *is* my concern," the Crux said. "It's why we are met here tonight. I would know whether he lies."

Galan said, "Then give Rodela to the dogs instead. It will save you bother, for they'll tear him to pieces." Now he made Sire Rodela out to be no better than a mudman; the insult did not go unnoticed, to judge by the muttering of the cataphracts.

The Crux said coldly, "If you're so sure of your sheath, why object to the ordeal? The manhounds will leave her unscathed if she's faithful. And if not, good riddance."

"Sire, I know my armiger and my woman, I know them by heart, and I don't need dogs to tell me which of them is faithless. But if it's proof you're after, give me leave to fight Rodela and I'll prove on his body that he is false."

"It is the third time, by my count, that you've asked this of me tonight," said the Crux, "and I'm weary of it. The answer is no, the answer will always be no. You started a feud with Ardor over a woman and set the whole Marchfield into an uproar, and now you'd do the same for our clan. I've been patient with you, because I know you tried to mend the feud you began. When you took Consort Vulpeja to your household, you took a man's part and tried to sow accord where you had earlier sown discord. But discord is a weed that often overgrows the crop. The gods are more vengeful than we are and were not appeased. So when will you learn not to beget feuds in the first place? Will you learn this after you've turned the Moon against the Sun, setting the house of Musca against Falco until we've let blood all over the floors of our keeps? Or will you learn now, beforehand, and stay your hand and be ruled by the clan's good?"

Galan made no answer. What the Crux said was wisdom, no doubt. I had hoped Galan would choose another time to grow wise.

"Now, Galan," the Crux went on, "will you keep your temper or must I walk you up and down like an overheated horse?"

The cataphracts had been quiet; I'd almost forgotten they were there. Now one smiled and the next stretched out his legs and another whispered to his neighbor. The Crux had allowed a little levity to ease his men's disquiet, like a swallow of ale for a thirst. A swallow was all.

Galan turned his face away from the Crux and I saw how the cords of his neck stood out and his jaw clenched. He looked down at the hands that lay useless in his lap. How easily his uncle had made him look a fool, a hothead; how well he had hobbled his rage. Galan said no more of dogs.

"Well then. Good then," said the Crux. He looked around the tent, he gathered up the men in his sight, but his glance passed through me as if I were unseen. He said, "This isn't such a grave matter, after all. We've no need to consult the Council of the Dead or study omens to read the will of Crux. Yet it will be a grave matter if we are not agreed, today, to make an end to it. Otherwise there will be rumors and whispers and disputes, men taking this side or that, and I will not have it."

He paused and leaned forward in his chair. "Does any man here doubt Sire Galan was wronged? An armiger should be as a shield arm to his cataphract, his master. His *master*. Should a man be on guard against his own arm lest it strike him? A cataphract has the right expectation that his armiger will shield not only his body but also what lies within the bounds of his protection: his lands, his chattels, his women. Rodela, instead, struck at what lies closest to Galan, he attacked him in his very bed. Whatever Rodela did to the sheath, whether he lied about it or not—and I will speak of that later—he did disgrace his oath."

The Crux raised his voice and made his pronouncement. "For this offense I settle on Sire Galan the Musca village that lies at the eastern end of Crookneck Pass, on Hunchback Mountain, and its pastures, fields, coppices, herds, and peoples, and the tolls, taxes, and rights pertaining to it."

There was a pause. Galan twisted in his chair, never looking at his uncle. I wondered if the Crux was done, if that was all. It was less than it seemed, and more. A Musca village would be nothing but a huddle of tumbledown crofts on a stony mountain flank. Even so, the house of Musca could not afford to lose one. It was well known how poor they were, and how proud. They'd hazarded all the coin they could rub together to equip Sire Rodela as an armiger, in hopes that he'd win enough plunder to become a cataphract himself in the next campaign. It was the best they could do, though every other house in the clan had at least one cataphract in the troop. Now he'd bring home nothing but sorrow. If he lived.

Into the silence crept Sire Alcoba's voice, lightly. "A village is a high price to pay for trifling with a sheath's virtue—even a Musca village. Even a virtuous sheath, if such a prodigy exists."

It raised a laugh. But the Crux frowned, and Sire Rodela bristled, saying, "Now you mock my house. I'll not have my house brought into this."

The Crux answered the armiger sharp: "Then you should not be standing before me, for no man stands without his house." Next he turned his attention to Sire Alcoba and said, just as sharply, "Make no mistake, I'm more lenient here than Rodela deserves. Do you count an oath worth so little? I know you bear a grudge toward Galan for costing you your armiger and your horse. Perhaps you're glad to see him spited. But you'd do well to remember it took two to make that wager."

Neither man was unwise enough to speak.

He looked to Galan then, and waited until his nephew raised his head and met his eyes. It seemed a long time. "You are proud, as you should be," the Crux said. There was no contempt in his voice now. "But sometimes pride must march with policy. Enmity between houses would be a far greater wrong than you suffered today; it would be a wound in the body of the clan. I ask that you accept this quittance and take no further vengeance. I know it doesn't satisfy your blood, but I ask that if it satisfies your reason, you will agree to be ruled by it." He waited again, until Galan gave a curt nod and looked down. Galan never glanced my way.

Then the Crux said, "There is something further. Rodela, having made a mockery of his oath to Sire Galan, can serve him no longer. If Sire Alcoba agrees, Rodela will become his armiger, to take the place of the far better man Alcoba lost to Galan's foolish feud. That should quit Galan of any debt Alcoba could claim." He looked to Sire Rodela kneeling before him, and there was enough scorn in his voice to singe the armiger's hair all over again. "I'm sure you'll agree to this," he said, "because if you don't, you'll be sent home in a cart with the dames. And if Alcoba finds you unsatisfactory or catches you up to mischief, I'll give him leave to deal with you as he pleases. Will you swear faithfully to him?"

Rodela mumbled something so small I couldn't hear it.

"What's that?" the Crux said.

"I will," said Sire Rodela, somewhat louder.

"And now you'll thank me. For the sake of your house and for your father's sake, I've left you the wherewithal to redeem your name."

Under the weight of the Crux's gaze, Sire Rodela bowed down and down until his forehead touched the ground. He stretched his hands out before him, palms up, and half of what he said was lost between his lips and the ground, but he did abase himself and swear he was grateful for the Crux's mercy; he didn't deserve it, he was unworthy. The Crux watched with a grim satisfaction while Sire Rodela offered up every humble word he owned, his mouth so crammed he choked on them. If there was more resentment than gratitude in his tone, no matter.

Still the Crux wasn't done. He looked at his cataphracts and said, "Perhaps it escaped your notice that tonight Sire Galan accused Rodela of killing an armiger of Ardor and stealing part of his scalp. It did not escape mine. I won't weigh that matter here. If it's true—and I daresay it is, I mark Rodela doesn't deny it—it is better left to the gods, the ancestors, and a certain angry shade to punish him for desecrating the body of a foe. I think the shade has begun already." There was an uneasy laugh at this. "But listen well: there are trophy collectors in every war, men who come home with a sackful of ears so they can say 'I slew this many.' Such men bring misfortune home to their kinfolk, and I'll have none of that in my company.

"Now we'll put the sheath to the ordeal, and soon we'll know whether she lies or Rodela lies. I shall leave it up to each of you, if Rodela proves false and a profaner, to decide whether you wish the company of such a man."

A shunning. The Crux laid the burden on his men to make the final judgment, to choose the cruelest punishment. Sire Rodela's back stiffened. His open hands became fists. He made no pretense of gratitude now.

It gave me another reason to face the dogs: to know he would be shunned. Almost reason enough.

The Crux stood and picked up his sword from the ground. Before he sheathed it he prodded Sire Rodela in the ribs. "Get up," he said, and waited for the armiger to get to his feet. With a glance across the tent, he summoned his own man, Sire Rassis, who took Rodela by the elbow and marched him to the doorway. All the while the Crux took care to stand between Sire Galan and his former armiger.

I stepped aside. Sire Rodela's eye sockets were dark as bruises and his cheeks, above the beard, were pasty. The Crux had dealt him many blows. He'd been humiliated before his fellows, and he faced shunning. Yet when he passed me, he smiled.

No remedy but murder. Galan had said it, and now his blood was cooler and he would accept what requital the Crux allowed and take nothing more. Sire Rodela had been brought low, but not low enough to suit me. It was not safe to let him live. If I survived the ordeal, I'd see to it myself. And then I'd tread his ashes in the mud.

Sire Rassis jerked his arm and they were out. The Crux was just behind, with Galan and the priests at his heels. The other cataphracts were rising, and the gabble of their voices rose also. The Crux spoke to me and his voice cut through the clamor. "Are you ready?"

Galan came close and said, "Don't do this."

Then we were out the door and the cataphracts spilled from the tent after us, around us. The thinnest new Moon hung in the sky. At home in the mountains, it would mark the month of Ingathering. The herders would be bringing the sheep and goats down from the high pastures before the snows, and driving the pigs into the Kingswood to forage for the fallen acorns granted them yearly by the king. Did the months have different names here, by the sea?

There were no clouds. The wind had swept them away.

Galan's hand gripped my wrist as tightly as if he held the hilt of his sword, and he pulled me against the tide of the crowd until I stopped. "Why are you doing this?" he asked. "Tell the Crux you lied."

"I didn't lie."

"I know that. I don't require proof."

"You say that now. Later you'll wonder."

The Crux was on his way back to us, the cataphracts moving aside for him.

Galan looked as if I'd struck him. "Have I earned this much of your distrust? Please . . . I'm begging. Say you lied."

He had no armor from me. And he was right, I distrusted him. Oh, surely he believed me. But could he live with me, if I said I'd coupled with Sire Rodela when his back was turned? He forgot the other cataphracts, how they'd scorn him for it.

I too was wounded. He'd asked me to do something he'd never do: claim a vile lie for truth and bear the shame that would come with it. He asked because a drudge has no honor to lose, no word to break—never tells the truth when a lie is safer. I had lied before, many times, to my betters. And yet I couldn't do it now. I was just discovering this myself. Still, I was angry Galan had not known it.

The Crux was upon us. "Has she changed her mind after all?"

I put my free hand over Galan's hand and leaned close. "I do trust you—as I trust my own heart." I couldn't leave him with bitter words, if they were the last he was to hear from me.

There was no time. I pried his fingers loose from my wrist and walked toward the dog pen while the new Moon looked down: Crux showing his thinnest sickle smile.

The manhounds' pen backed onto the horse corral. Most of them slept, but they kept sentries. When we came close one began to bark and another took it up and soon there were four or five yammering at us. They woke Dogmaster. He came to the high wooden gate, walking between his charges as they roiled about his legs. I saw Fleetfoot and Ev and two other dogboys sit up across the pen, roused from their sleep amongst a dozen or so dogs lying head to flank, sharing heat.

Dogmaster hushed the dogs but their silence was no better. One growled low, the teeth showing white against the black muzzle.

When the Crux spoke his voice was just as low. "She's going in for trial by ordeal. Open the gate." He pointed his thumb at me, not condescending to use a finger.

Dogmaster looked dismayed but said nothing. He felt for the latch in the dark and swung the gate half open. Behind me, the noisy crowd pressed forward: cataphracts and armigers and drudges who'd come running as soon as word had flown between the tents. They'd brought torches. Somewhere Rodela was watching too.

I knew exactly where Galan was. I could feel him, a silence just behind my right shoulder. I had silenced him. No matter how close he stood, I was alone in this.

Not quite alone. A god came unwelcome. Rift again, in the avatar of Dread.

I faltered, I balked. I had thought I was afraid before, and counted myself brave because I made my legs walk to the dog pen when they were unsteady. That was nothing compared to this. Dread seized me, inside and out, and I held on to the gate so I would not fall. My palms were wet. Dread drove my heart too fast, my mind too slow. I never knew that fear could hurt so much, that its pains were so various, both sharp and dull.

I couldn't understand courage. I couldn't find it in myself. How does a man go to battle? Not the cataphract in all his armor, but the drudge, the foot soldier. How does he face it with no honor of his own to spur him, knowing that whether he lives or dies, he'll win less praise than his master's horse? Rift must give the gift of recklessness as well as fear, or the god of war would have no soldiers. They'd all run away.

I would run if I could move.

While I hung on the gate, the crowd grew quiet.

I tasted salt and didn't know if it was sweat or tears. I prayed to Rift to take Dread from me, and send instead the Warrior to make me brave. But it was dangerous to pray to Rift. I should never have sought Rift's help to find the dwale; Dread was the price the god exacted for it.

Rift did not relent. It was a far humbler divinity who came to my aid: Dogmaster, who was a god to his hounds, at least. I saw some promise of mercy in Dogmaster's eyes, some pity. I believed he wouldn't let the dogs kill me. He stood with his hand on the gate and held it steady as I leaned against it. A dog whined, legs braced, hackles raised. The man growled and the dog quieted.

Fleetfoot and Ev were behind him. They'd come halfway across the pen to see what was happening and the rest of the dogs had come with them.

They looked so small. The backs of the great manhounds came above the boys' waists. The dogs wore their winter coats of short, thick fur; most were fawn colored, but a few were of dun brindled with black. They all had black masks and ears. The boys wore their leggings and nothing else, and their skin shone pale in the dark. They looked sleepy, puzzled, cold. Fleetfoot folded his arms over his bare chest and shivered. Ev grasped a dog's ruff.

Why was I so afraid? The boys had no fear.

I remembered the war dogs let loose on Summons Day to please the crowd, how they'd torn the fallow deer to pieces on the tourney field.

I tugged on the gate and Dogmaster let it swing open. I took one step and another, still holding the gate for support, and he stood aside. The wind dried the sweat on my brow and chilled me. I heard Galan move, the rattle of metal against metal.

I was inside, but Galan was inside too, one step behind me, and Dogmaster closed the gate after us both. There was a sigh and a mutter from the crowd. Galan moved up on my right. He'd left his sword behind, outside the gate. He held out his shield arm and I clung to it to keep from falling to the ground. I felt the stiff, quilted linen under my hand. He kept his sword arm down in front of his body. The leather sleeve covered with metal scales was something better for the manhounds to chew on than our flesh. He gave me one glance, that was all—and, I swear, a fleeting smile—before turning his face toward the dogs.

Reckless heart. No wonder Chance loved him. He never cared what odds.

Then I thought: perhaps this was not of his choosing. Maybe by binding him, I'd bound him to die alongside me. Yet I wouldn't have unbound him at that moment if I could have, not for the world.

"Easy now, steady," he said. He was talking to the dogs, I think.

The lead dog, a great tawny bulk with hoarfrost on his shoulders and muzzle, was the first to try us. He lunged to within a few paces and barked and snarled and barked again, while we stood still. Other manhounds came up in turn, and then a mob of them, legs and tails and ears stiff with fury, spittle flying as if they aimed to outdo their leader, or at least impress him. The barking riled the horses in the corral next to the dog pen; some dashed here and there and some neighed, ready to do battle.

So much bluster. It would have been laughable, if I hadn't seen what the dogs could do when they were minded to. They did not advance or fall back. They did not tire of howling. The din battered me. My joints loosened and Galan bore me up, his arm as solid as stone. He turned his right shoulder toward the leader and let his hand hang loose. All the while, he talked. He called the dogs lads and bade them be quiet in a stern voice, like a tutor admonishing a pack of rowdy boys.

The grizzled leader stopped barking and began to growl. The rumble sent tremors through me. The manhound was quivering too, but not with fear. He came a pace closer.

Galan said, "Watch him. Watch him. He can't quite make up his mind." I didn't realize at first he was talking to me, for his voice didn't change.

There was foam on the dog's blunt muzzle, on his jowls. He had a huge head, a deep and wide chest. The folds of fur around his neck and the hair standing on his hackles made him seem even more massive. He surely weighed as much as Galan. I'd heard the war dogs ate as well as any man of the Blood. They were costly to keep, which is why the pack numbered less than four hands. Which was more than enough.

The manhound looked me in the eye and my own hair stood on end. I looked away quickly. His eyes caught the torchlight and shone pale and gold; a dog should not have such pale eyes.

Galan said, "I saw this ordeal once, at my father's keep. The man broke and ran. Don't run. If you run, he'll know what you are. He'll know you for prey."

That shamed me. I was more cowardly than that man, for I lacked the strength to run. My legs would not do my bidding. Even a beast would have more courage. It's said the stag has a special bone next to his heart to keep him from dying of fear when he's pursued. My own heart was not so fortified.

And there were dogs behind us now, between the gate and us.

"The manhounds are like soldiers," Galan said. "They'll kill a fleeing enemy sooner than one who stands to fight. Don't mistake me—they're brave enough to take on a bear at bay—but it's the chase that heats their blood. They're not much use in a melee, for they can't tell friend from foe, but they serve right well in a rout. And our own foot soldiers know that if they break in the face of the enemy, they'll have the dogs loosed upon them."

Would Galan tutor me now? I was not a horse or a dog or a child, to be soothed by a steady voice, no matter what was said. And yet I was steadied regardless, as if his voice made some small refuge. As if he spoke of matters that didn't pertain to us, not now, not urgently.

The leader commenced to bark again, a deep bronze clangor, peal after peal. Now I thought I heard confusion under his threat. Dogmaster had let us in, Dogmaster stood quietly by. The manhound didn't know what his god required of him.

The other dogs were strident. With every bark their warm breath smoked in the cold. They jostled flank to flank. I looked past them and saw Fleetfoot and Ev standing alone, huddled together for warmth; the dogs had left them, every one roused against us. Fleetfoot's mouth was open, a dark circle.

Galan said, "We mustn't try his patience. Can you stand alone?"

I didn't quite understand, but I shook my head: no to whatever he meant.

"You must," he said. "You must stand now, else you'll forfeit what you came for, whether you leave here whole or not."

I shook my head again. No.

"If he decides to attack, crouch down and cover your throat and the back of your neck. Keep your head down. I'll be your shield. I doubt very much my uncle will let the dogs kill me."

I looked sideways at him. His voice was calm, but I marked the sweat glinting on his forehead and cheeks. He smiled at me.

"I'll take a step back now," he said. And when I didn't let go of his arm, he said, "Come now. Sooner begun, sooner done. You're a brave one, my beauty. I know you have the heart for it." He used to say such things to Semental, I had heard him.

My eyes stung. "Go then," I said, but I couldn't loosen my grip. He nodded and took his arm away.

When Galan stepped back the chief manhound took another step forward. Now he spoke to me alone and his barking sounded hoarse, full of rumble and whine, and I knew he tired of this. One more stride and he would reach me. The other dogs surged around him, yelping, but none dared go in front. It was past enduring that Galan had left me to face them and I thought—knowing it was unjust—that I could have borne it better if he'd never come inside the gate at all.

Death was a mere pace from me, but the dead were far away; I took no solace from the finger bones in my pouch. If I called on the Dame or Na, how could they help? Once my own journey began, I'd be alone. There's no overtaking one who left beforehand.

I had no prayers left. I felt how small I was, and how vast the gods. Vast and indifferent. Even Dread had abandoned me. It had filled me like a roaring wind and like a wind had passed through, and I was hollowed out.

I had crossed my arms over my breast. I lowered them slowly. I took care not to meet the manhound's eye, knowing that he, like the Crux himself, would take offense at such presumption.

There was to be no such mercy as dying of fear. I had stopped shaking. A gust of wind wrapped my skirts about my legs and brought to me, over the animal reek of the dogs and my own body, the wintry scent of the north: stones, heather, moss. I tasted dust.

Let it be quick.

The manhound came that last stride, not in a rush but with deliberation, and nosed my hand. His tail came upright and wagged once. He stepped back and gave a short bark to warn me not to be too familiar. And so, in that manner, he did pass judgment: he adjudged me neither prey nor enemy nor master, whatever else I might be. Whatever else was of little concern to him. Other dogs crowded close to get my scent, and by the order of their coming, I knew their rank in the pack. They too must pass judgment, for each approached warily and left appeased. Last of all, Fleetfoot and Ev came up, and one touched my arm and the other clasped my shoulder. Fleetfoot's breath came short, as if he'd just run a long race. Ev's eyes and nose had been leaking. His hand was cold.

I heard Galan behind me. "I think we might go now," he said, and his voice was thick. "Slowly. Don't turn around." I felt his hand on my back and I leaned against him. I was trembling again.

We backed two steps, three, four, and the lead manhound sat on his haunches and yawned, showing every tooth. But his eye was watchful.

Dogmaster whistled, the gate opened behind us, and we were out.

The Crux was standing just outside the pen with a torchbearer beside him. The ruddy light picked out the pale scar that ran across his brow and next to his left eye, close enough to pucker the eyelid. The lines beside his mouth were graved deep. He spared me a glance, a look that considered and perhaps reconsidered, and made me rue he ever had cause to notice me.

He fixed his eyes on Galan next, and did not let go. "Well, Galan," he said.

"Well, Sire Adhara dam Pictor by Falco of Crux," said Galan. "Or may I call you uncle again?"

"That will be up to your father, when I tell him what he sired. A dirtlover."

Galan's smile never changed. "You don't need my father's leave to disown me, First of Crux."

"Don't you think you've tempted me enough for one night? You've always been willful and spoilt, though not for lack of chastisement—but this was, of all your follies, the most foolhardy—to make this ordeal your own, and thereby make it false."

"Why, Uncle, it was to keep it true that I entered the pen—lest you be overly tempted to pluck out a certain troublesome thorn. And can you dispute she faced the dogs alone and they let her live?"

"I would you hadn't said that, boy," the Crux said balefully. "For the fondness I once bore you, I'll let you outlive the insult. But you'd best stay out of my sight until you recollect that I don't need some green sprig to teach me not to cheat. *I* taught *you*. Next time you try me, you might well be lopped off."

Galan knelt and put his forehead to the ground, but it was too late. The Crux turned his back and stalked away. I knelt beside Galan and put my hand on his back, on the stiff brigandine, and felt him shake. He was a long time with his face to the ground. Some stayed to stare, then wandered off to their gossip or their pallets.

When Galan straightened up his cheeks were wet. "My tongue is cursed," he said.

CHAPTER 13

Auguries

hat night I trembled and Galan soothed me, and when I turned, restless on the cot, he turned with me and would not let go. The heat of his skin drove some of the chill from me. I was beholden to him; he'd given me a gift beyond recompense, beyond acknowledgment. I had nothing to give in return, not even my purest gratitude. For Sire Rodela had tainted even that, when he cut me with his blade and his lies, and marred me so I hardly recognized myself.

I wanted what was stolen from me. After Galan slept I thought of nothing else. Pains kept me awake, a burning at my cleft where I'd been skinned, the scraping of every breath. I don't know when I first thought of poison. It was in my mind as if it had always been there, how I'd kept the rest of the dwale; how the Dame had said the black berries tasted sweet and wholesome.

In the morning my voice was gone. My throat was barred with a dark bruise.

The Crux sent his three Auspices over at first light. They wore their regalia of green robes and peaked hats, and by that we guessed their purpose. There had been too many wounded in our tent, too much sickness; there had been hatred let loose and blood spilled—worse, a woman's blood, and worse yet, a mudwoman's. The priests came to cleanse us of this defilement and to make sure that ill will and ill fortune did not escape our tent to endanger others.

We were all awake, having risen before dawn as usual. Galan was in his underarmor, breakfasting on dry bread and mincemeat while his jacks fastened up his laces. He'd not been forewarned of the Auspices' visit and he was offended, or so I thought when I saw the lines gather between his brows. He took it as a rebuke from the Crux, and well he might, after the way they'd parted; yet there was no denying the Crux was within his powers to protect the clan—and his errant nephew—from further harm.

So he welcomed the priests courteously, each by their full name, and set us all to do their bidding. They had scant courtesy for him. Divine Hamus had us bustling until the tent was arranged to his liking, telling us there was no time to dither. Noggin ran to fetch Flykiller and the horseboy Uly, for they said all of Galan's men save his foot soldiers should be present; his women too. The curtains about Consort Vulpeja's chamber were tied back. She lay with the blanket pulled up to her chin, her head turned on the pillow, her eyes following the priests.

First they sought to know the cause of the trouble in Galan's tent, what shades or gods had been offended. They'd brought four birds in cages: two white doves, two black crows. Inside the tent, on the space we cleared for him, Divine Hamus unrolled a length of white cloth. He was the smallest priest, the roundest, the mildest in seeming, but he was the Sun's Auspex and led the way in all sacrifices. He took a dove and a crow from the cages and wrung their necks without spilling blood, and the priests watched gravely as the birds staggered and jerked and flapped until their deaths caught up with them.

He skinned the birds and laid the empty, feathered husks to one side, wings and heads and feet still attached. The rest was divided into parts, even down to the bones, each part belonging to a god and having three signs to be read, one for each avatar. These little clots of flesh were laid out on the white cloth and the priests bent over them, poking and pointing, and as they consulted, their tall hats nodded and bumped together.

A hush had settled on all of us, all the watchers. Galan sat upon a stool and looked on with a pinched face; Spiller's jaw hung slack and Noggin sniffled and Rowney crouched in a corner as far from the priests as he could get; Flykiller sat motionless, but if he'd been a horse, I'm sure we'd have seen his tail switch and his hide twitch, for his unease showed in his staring eyes.

I felt that prickling on my neck that comes when the gods have been invoked. Just then I feared the Auspices more than the gods, for I thought they'd come to lay blame and I'd get more than my due.

Before yesterday I was Galan's sheath and nothing uncommon. Today I was Galan's folly. Unlike his other folly, the wager, he'd get no glory of it. The Crux had called his nephew a dirtlover because of me. He had said it and others would repeat it, and the next time it was thrown in Galan's face, he'd not be able to let it pass, and there'd be more bloodshed.

If the priests pointed to me, if the signs pointed to me, I wouldn't be able to make an answer, for the swelling in my throat had stoppered up my voice. I couldn't even whisper.

When the priests had done conferring, Divine Hamus beckoned Galan over and showed him a thin gray worm he'd found in the entrails of the crow. The Auspices had no difficulty interpreting this sign. As the crow was the male body of the household, the tripes pertained to Rift, and gut worms belonged in the domain of the Queen of the Dead, this could only mean that the malice of a male shade was at work, and who could this shade be but Sire Bizco? Since last night the whole troop knew how Sire Rodela had courted affliction by defiling a corpse, stealing a scrap of scalp and leaving the rest to rot instead of burn; he'd not been satisfied by taking a life, he must rob the man of his peace as well. It wasn't the least of his offenses, though the requital for it had been left to the gods and the dead and not undertaken by the Crux.

It could easily be seen—said Divine Hamus—that the shade had not only made Sire Rodela's wound fester, he'd made his mind fester too. Clearly the shade had moved him to skin me and make a false accusation against me; in his right mind he'd never have done it. Now Sire Rodela was shunned. Sire Alcoba, his new master, had refused him shelter last night. He bade him sleep across the threshold, outside the tent, that he might be stepped on more conveniently as Sire Alcoba went in and out. Sire Bizco was avenged: the armiger's downfall was neatly accomplished.

There should be no trace of the dead man left in the tent to haunt us. His scalp had been burned days ago and Sire Rodela's belongings tossed outside into a mud puddle last night, and with them any stray hairs; and his living malice by rights should have followed Sire Rodela, his tormentor, and not clung to us.

But the worm said otherwise.

To drive Sire Bizco's shade from the tent and to cleanse us of the blood and enmity with which he'd befouled us, Divine Hamus and Divine Tambac each took a wing of the crow and swept everywhere, from floor to ceiling, over chests and pallets and sacks, over Consort Vulpeja's cot and blanket, over the rest of us too, from head to toe. I shivered when the feathers brushed my face. They sang all the while, an eerie song with words in some secret tongue. Divine Xyster droned low while Divine Hamus keened, and Divine Tambac's voice, a quavering thin thread, stitched between them.

When they had finished sweeping, there was a pile of dust and scraps and crumbs and mouse droppings and a few bones—for Noggin didn't sweep as often as he ought—on the earthen floor. They burned this on the brazier along with the wings of the crow, and candlebark and bitter herbs that made a sweet and pungent smoke, and when all was ash, the priests ended their song and seemed satisfied.

Now they turned to the dove, and the omen they'd found in her corpse, which stood for the female body of the household. Her heart was enlarged and too pale a red, which could clearly be seen when it was laid next to the crow's. When they cut it open, the chambers were seen to be malformed. Trouble with Ardor in all its avatars, Smith and Hearthkeeper and Wildfire, they said, and didn't look far for cause, for there was Consort Vulpeja, Ardor's child, on her sickbed watching.

I felt then as though a great black wing had swept over me and gone. I was so glad to be overlooked. I had wronged the Auspices, thinking they would dare offend the gods by pretending to read what wasn't written. Yet their interpretation was faulty, for they didn't see that I had also been marked by Ardor. Since the Smith had saved me in the Kingswood, there had been many days—such as yesterday, in the dog pen—when I felt abandoned by the god, by all the gods, and other days when I'd mistaken my own fancies for Ardor's bidding; now I couldn't have said whether I'd served the god well or no, but I felt unknown purposes still at work in me. Here was another sign, in that pale engorged heart, of Ardor's swollen will.

The more I thought on this sign, the more I feared it showed an ill will. My relief gave way to misgivings.

The priests went to stand about Consort Vulpeja's bed. In silence she beckoned to Sunup, and the girl helped her to sit and took a place on the cot behind her so she could lean against her, back to back. Her hair being unbound for sleeping, Consort Vulpeja covered it with the blanket, and with this gesture wrapped herself in modesty, in dignity. She kept her eyes downcast.

Divine Xyster said, "Consort, it's a marvel to see you so much better." The last time the carnifex had seen her was the morning after the dwale smoke, less than a tennight ago, before she had forced herself to eat and so smoothed the hollows of her cheeks and changed the pallor of her skin from whey to cream.

Galan was standing behind the priests with his arms crossed. He muttered, "Indeed, she grows better and her temper grows worse."

"Ill temper?" asked Divine Hamus.

Galan shrugged. "She curses at my sheath like a foot soldier."

When Consort Vulpeja spoke at last, her voice was small and bewildered. "Your pardon, Sire, but what am I to do if the drudge needs correction? She's disobedient and clumsy besides." She appealed to the priests. "Surely such faults must be plucked up at once by the root, or they will spread."

"You misuse her," Galan said.

"I fear you're too lax with her, Sire. It's made her impudent. 'Smite a drudge and he will favor you, favor a drudge and he will spite you.' As you see, I can't smite her, for I'm too weak. If I speak to her roundly, it's less than she's owed." Her words were hard, but her voice was soft.

Galan took a step closer. "She healed you. You owe her your life, not your curses." I wished he hadn't said it, for Divine Xyster peered at me where I stood behind Spiller. I didn't want him curious.

Her cheeks flushed red. She forgot to be gentle; she raised her eyes and her voice and cried, "Do I, Sire? I'll not be indebted to her. I'd as soon she took my life back—I no longer want it."

I thought how she must have had more guile before, when she was a maid and played coy day and night. Now she was so overstrung she couldn't sound one note long before it began to sour. She played upon my faults and sounded her own: ire and obstinacy.

Or it may be that her temper had indeed been sweet and demure and guileless before Galan had won his wager. Not that she was blameless, even so. Even the most demure maid knows what treasure she must guard. She'd brought dishonor on herself and her house and clan, dishonor and all that followed after—poison, her father's shameful death, and feud. So many blows. The sign of her house was the anvil, and it was certain the Smith was still at work on her; she altered daily under his hammer. Some metals strengthen in the forging, others prove brittle and are cast aside. I feared she was near breaking.

Galan didn't know that she meant what she said, that she'd set her mind on dying. Since the eve before yesterday, she'd taken no food from my hand or Sunup's.

Divine Xyster rubbed the bridge of his long nose. Divine Hamus said to her, "You don't wish to live?"

She covered her face with the blanket.

The priests, all three of them, turned to Galan. He shrugged.

"Have you quarreled?" Divine Hamus asked him.

"No. To me she's as meek as a mouse to a cat, but I've heard how she shrews behind my back. On my part, I've never said a cruel word or raised a hand against her."

Consort Vulpeja drew her knees up and bent over them. From under the blanket came her voice, choking. "Cruel. You are cruel. Why did you ever send for me if you didn't want me? You'd have been kinder to leave me to die in my father's tent."

Galan said, "I found I couldn't let you die. Not because of me."

Her back shook, but no sound escaped save for a few dragging breaths. Even through the blanket I could see how thinly her flesh covered her bones, and how slight she was, narrow in the shoulders, narrow as a boy at the hips. Sunup laid a hand on her back. I wondered which was worse for her, Galan's indifference or his pity.

Galan said, "I swear to you now, I'll take no other concubine of the Blood while you live. You shall be the only one. You'll have a respected place in my household. Soon you'll go home, and I'll send word to my wife to give you your own apartments in the keep, your own drudges. She'll treat you with all due courtesy, I assure you." He said to the priests, "I can do no more. Isn't it enough?"

"It's generous," Divine Tambac said. "It's handsome."

But Divine Hamus put his hand on Galan's arm and looked up at him, his round face solemn. He said, "No, it's not enough. You must give her children too. No woman should be without children. If you're not fortunate enough to plant one before you part, then give her hope of it when you return."

Consort Vulpeja kept her face hidden under the blanket. She was so still, listening for his answer, it seemed she'd stopped breathing. She couldn't see, as I could, the answer already there on his face.

"No," Galan said. "She'll get no bastards from me to trouble my household. I gave her honor back. That will have to content her."

No bastards to trouble my household. I flinched to hear him refuse her so bluntly, and then to see her fall across the cot wailing. It didn't ease me that he denied her bed and bastards, for thinking that if the childbane should fail and I should come by one of his bastards myself, it would come unwelcome. As for Divine Hamus, he was displeased, but forbore to argue. As they say, a man can be commanded to his duty, but his prick answers to no one.

I turned away just as Galan said again, this time with more entreaty than anger, "I gave her honor back."

By the time the Auspices took the last augury outside the tent, the Sun had already quartered the sky. We came to watch, all except Consort Vulpeja, who wept in her bed, and Sunup, who stayed to tend her. Crux Sun was warm on our faces though the air was cold. We'd not seen her so unveiled for many a day and our shadows were black at our feet. The sight of her lifted my spirits; surely Crux's smile was a good omen to put against all these warnings.

Divine Tambac opened the cages and let the two remaining birds fly free, that they might seek out any threats to Galan from outside his household. The birds flew off south-of-west across the Heavens, brimful with blue. The wind had changed since the night before; now it blew from the mountains instead of the Hardscrabble and pushed the birds seaward with a strong hand. Far out over the water, the dove could be seen trying to beat her way back, slipping sideways.

On a clear night any fool can point to the sky, to any one of the twelve directions, and read which god rules it at a given hour, for the godsigns are there writ large in the stars, moving in their slow circle dance. But Divine Tambac, Auspex of the Heavens, knew the stars in his bones. No clouds could hide them from him, nor could the bright Sun of day. He knew where they were at every moment, in every season.

Galan said to him, with a wry smile, "I daresay you'll tell me to expect more trouble from Ardor. I don't need birds to warn me of that."

Divine Tambac kept his hand over his brow, shadowing his eyes. His eyesight must be sharp, for he watched long after the two birds had vanished from my sight. Then he turned his gaze on Galan. His eyes were bright and the skin around them was scored with crow's-feet from years of squinting at the Heavens. He said, "A man is a fool who guards only one gate of his keep. Trouble can come by any road."

Galan nodded, his smile gone.

The priest said, "Sacrifice a cock to Rift tonight, for Rift follows close on Ardor's heels. You may find favor there."

Then Divine Hamus put his hand on Galan's shoulder and said, "I didn't wish to speak of this in her presence, but I fear your concubine is in grave danger."

"But she's getting well," Galan said. "She's gained flesh and strength since she came to me. It's only her temper that worries me, how she cries and laughs and rails without restraint."

Divine Hamus shook his head and told Galan that the omen of the dove's heart had been plain, and plainer still Consort Vulpeja's despair. "It would be best if you yourself would give her some hope—but since you refuse, we must try another cure for her melancholy. If you can afford it, I'll send for the Initiates of Carnal. I've heard there are some here at the Marchfield. They'll know what to do." He had lowered his voice. We overheard him nevertheless, Spiller and Noggin and I. We were sitting on our heels near the corner of the tent, catching the warmth of the Sun hitting the canvas wall.

Galan asked what it would cost, and when he heard the answer exclaimed that by the time Consort Vulpeja was settled at home, he'd be stripped to his hose and have to run about half naked.

Divine Hamus said, "Find the money, or all you've spent on her till now will be ashes on the wind—she'll come to her pyre before ever she reaches your keep. If I go to the Initiates today with payment, they should be able to start the rites tomorrow."

Galan stared bleakly at the priest and I thought he'd refuse, but he went into the tent and brought out his jewelry: his great jade pendant of a gyrfalcon stooping for prey, a cap sewn with pearls, his armbands and bracelets, the small gold knives he wore on his sleeves when he went to dine—all these he gave to the Auspices. They said it might do.

Spiller watched with his mouth hanging open, and when the priests had gone and Galan stood before the doorway frowning at their backs, he elbowed me in the ribs and hissed in my ear, "The Initiates of Carnal! They'll teach her such tricks as will have his prick in harness and her with the whip and reins. You'd better look sharp!" Noggin whinnied so loudly at this that Galan turned our way.

I'd heard much of the Initiates from Mai and the whores. Enough to cause me disquiet. Their jests about the cult were bawdy and tinged with an envy that came near to awe. Whores worshiped Carnal, after all, in the avatar of Desire; they paid taxes to the temple and kept her shrine in their tents for protection; they did her work. The cheapest two-copper drab kept an idol of naked, fat Desire, even if it was just an amulet of unglazed clay to string around her neck. And Mai served Carnal too, in her fashion; she once told me she'd dedicated herself to furthering the aims of Desire after the god gave her Sire Torosus.

The Initiates kept the god closer still. Desire was rumored to possess them during their rites and leave them with certain gifts. They were called upon to heal the various afflictions to which dames and maidens are prone, such as barrenness, nagging, grief, sulking, disobedience, jealousy, pining for love, cuckolding or refusing their husbands—no need to go on, the list is endless. Each woman they cured became an Initiate in turn.

Mai claimed that the Initiates were more apt to work their cures on discontented men than the wives and concubines those men sent to them. The men never guessed, being well satisfied when their women came home sweet and docile; before long they were docile too, led about by their dangle. So the jest went, anyway.

In truth, the mysteries of the cult were a well-kept secret, privy only to a few women of the Blood. Mai and the whores knew no more of them than any other outsiders. But, as often happens, the less known, the more said.

So I wondered: would the Initiates undertake to cure Consort Vulpeja—or Galan?

Though the morning was half gone when the priests left, there was still unwonted bustle about our camp. The Crux and his men had gone off to the tourney field, but he'd left orders that Sire Alcoba and Sire Fanfarron should move their tents, each taking the other's place on the opposite side of the compound. He didn't think it wise for Sire Alcoba to dwell next to Galan any longer.

Sire Fanfarron's drudges set up his pavilion next to ours. It was painted on the front with dancing cranes, the crane being the emblem of his house, but the sides and back were a dingy green. Such was the man too I'd heard: all front and bluster and nothing much behind.

Galan watched in silence, then turned and went into his tent again. When he'd finished arming he tucked his helmet under his arm and went to see Consort Vulpeja. She was still weeping behind her curtain. One couldn't help but hear.

He murmured something and she grew quiet, but when he came from her chamber, she began to sob again. He looked at me and grimaced. "Have I been so cruel to her, do you think?"

I opened my mouth and a croak hopped out.

He caught me up in an embrace that pressed me hard between rivets and scales and an arm like iron. "Never mind, never mind." He lifted my chin. "The swelling will go down by tomorrow and no doubt then you shall fill up my ears as usual. Today, lie abed for once and let Sunup tend to you." He smiled and gave me a kiss. The smile was worried and the kiss as hard as the embrace.

For a moment I didn't fear the Initiates or the Crux or anyone. I was proud to be Galan's folly. He'd faced the dogs for me, and no one, not even his uncle, could have been more amazed at it than I was.

If I was his folly, he was mine. *He was mine.* I took his lower lip between my teeth, and when he drew back his smile had changed. Desire came at my summons, avid and fierce, and she seized both of us.

But Galan only laughed. He called for his men and set off for the training fields, and left Desire to fatten on anticipation.

Then the camp was quiet, save for the drudges about their chores. Noggin sat cross-legged on his pallet, mending Sire Galan's second set of underarmor and breathing loudly through his mouth; he snored even when he was awake. I did lie abed but soon rose again. I was restless and couldn't bear hearing Consort Vulpeja cry. I fixed broth and put soothe-me in it to make her sleep, but she dashed the bowl from my hands and shrieked at me. I drank the rest of the soothe-me myself, for I was in need of it, and at last I slept in the drowsy afternoon.

CHAPTER 14

Wildfire

Rumormongers pay snitches for tidbits of gossip. Most snitches are drudges—and why shouldn't they snatch a few coins where they find them, since their masters are so closefisted?—and drudges are everywhere and often go unseen. So it's likely someone in our camp earned a few copperheads by telling a rumormonger that it was Sire Galan's armiger, Sire Rodela, who killed Sire Bizco and defiled his body. As for why the tittle-tattle didn't tell the rest—that Rodela was Galan's armiger no more and had gone to stay with Sire Alcoba—that is anyone's guess.

When Ardor's men came they went straight for Galan's tent. It was easy to find, for his banners flew beside it. They carried oil and pitch and torches and went without stealth, for the fighting men were gone to the tourney field and the training grounds. A bagboy belonging to the clan of Growan allowed he'd seen them coming. They came on horseback without haste or concealment, and they never dismounted.

By the time the bagboy gathered his wits and began to shout, others had seen them. Too late, for the deed was already done, it was quickly done, and the men rode off in more haste than they'd come, leaving Consort Vulpeja, their own kinswoman, behind in the burning tent.

I woke to Sunup's screams.

Dulled by sleep and soothe-me, I sat up on my pallet. That was a mistake. The tent was flooded with stinking black smoke, turbulent, hot, full of grit, a substance more like water than air. I feared I'd drown in it. It entered my nose and mouth and I coughed and gagged. My eyes burned and ran with tears. I could see no farther than my own hand, except for bright puddles of flame above me and rivulets of flame on all sides. This was no natural fire. It spread from everywhere at once.

My mind was as thick as the smoke, moiled with terror. I couldn't tell east from west, north from south, or whether the doorway was behind or before me. But Sunup was screaming—I'd never heard such a scream from anyone before, man or beast, yet I knew it was Sunup—and the sound goaded me. It was the one thing I understood. I rolled on my belly and pulled my sheepskin cloak over my head and began to crawl toward her with my nose near the ground, where the air was less foul. Before long her screaming stopped, for the more she cried out, the more smoke she took in. She coughed and she whimpered, and then she was silent. By then I knew where I was. Sunup hadn't left Consort Vulpeja's side. I was crawling away from the door.

No breath to spare for prayers or curses, though I was full of both, all muddled together. Only breath enough to hitch along, elbows and knees, belly scraping the ground. I was afraid to uncover my head. I hid from the fire in the stifling dark under my cloak. As if the flames wouldn't find me if I couldn't see them.

It seemed a long while before I encountered an ankle with my outstretched hand and then an upturned heel. The bones of the ankle were fine as bird bones, which told me nothing, but the heel was rough and hard, and by that I recognized Sunup. By working my way up, I came to her head and found her limp and insensible. I put my hand over her mouth and felt a faint breath.

I uncovered my head and saw that while I had crawled, the fire had outpaced me. Now the tent was lit by a glowering light, revealing a landscape of fire and smoke: torrents of fire flowing above my head and streaming along the walls; roiling smoke pressing downward instead of rising. Everything upside down. A rain of sparks going up. Rags flying around us. A fierce, hot wind stealing the breath from my mouth. The air heavy with ash.

I dreaded to burn. The dogs would have been more merciful.

I moved as quickly as I could but I was hindered by coughing and blinded by smoke and tears. Sunup was under my hand. She'd fallen by the foot of Consort Vulpeja's cot. The concubine was on the bed, but I couldn't see her. Nothing but a smudge of shadow.

I'd have to come back for her.

I took off my cloak. It was splotched with small fires I hadn't felt through the heavy sheepskin, and I smothered them. I crouched and wrapped the cloak around Sunup. Fire was writing its way across the thin white linen of the curtain around Consort Vulpeja's chamber, leaving a black scrawl. I dragged Sunup under the burning tatters, bending low. I held my breath as long as I could, and when I gasped again I was scorched all down my windpipe.

We were in the very maw of Wildfire now, and it roared with tongues of flame. I hadn't truly heard till now that it roared at me. I felt its greed. I'd once presumed to think Ardor had some use for me—this was the use, then: to feed on.

Well, we must be cooked first. This was no time to crawl. I hoisted Sunup in my arms. She was a light but unwieldy burden, her arms and legs and head dangling slackly. When I straightened up I felt heat enough to sear the meat off my bones with me still standing. Even the ground was blazing, for the dry heather in the pallets had kindled.

The tent was ten strides square, no more than ten strides. I could go that far. I blundered toward the door, through the brightness, through the darkness. I found my way by what was underfoot, the brazier, Galan's strongbox, meal sacks, casks. Fire caught at my skirts.

I could have sworn I'd left the door flap tied open. Now it was hanging down in our way and all ablaze.

I went through nevertheless, half-carrying, half-dragging Sunup. The heavy canvas raked over me and set my headcloth, my hair, and the back of my dress afire. Someone took Sunup from my arms and then seized hold of me and rolled me over the ground to put out the fire.

The man squatted by me. He wore Hazard's red feather in his cap. I sat up and coughed and couldn't stop coughing. I was helpless with it; I thought the bellows of my lungs would turn inside out. The drudge looked worried, but when he saw I'd live, he clapped me on the back and ran off, and I never saw him again to thank him.

I stopped coughing and began to wheeze. Over the roar of the fire, I heard shouts and the frenzied bleating of our milk goat, tethered to a tent stake. My eyes still smarted and watered ceaselessly. There were drudges, a crowd of men and boys, rushing about to fetch water, but I couldn't see well enough to tell those I knew from strangers. I could make out the tent, what was left of it, and the smear of smoke rising high above it. The canvas was waxed to keep out rain; men threw water on it and the water ran off and fire danced back. There were holes eaten in the roof and walls and nothing but flames visible within.

I had no voice to call for help for Consort Vulpeja. I knew I must get up. But I was as unsteady as an infant who can't find her own feet, and can only get about by crawling. Sunup lay where she'd been dropped, still insensible. I went to her on hands and knees. There were burns on her feet and her cheek. Despite the heat of the fire, despite my cloak, she was shivering. Even so, I needed the cloak and I took it from her, after dragging her farther from the fire.

I found a shallow, muddy puddle and soaked the sheepskin in it, thinking that if it were wet it would shield me better from the flames. Even this little exertion made me gasp, and every gasp seared deep. I could think clearly again and my mind moved apace. I began to reckon what I should have done when I was inside the tent—what I must still do. Yet for all the haste of my thoughts, my limbs were laggard.

I pulled the wet cloak over me and the weight bore me down. I got one foot under me and then another, but couldn't balance without the prop of one hand on the ground. I rubbed my eyes to clear them, and what I saw stole my strength and I fell to my knees again.

The fire was swift and I had been slow, too slow. Our tent ropes had been smeared with pitch. They'd burned like wicks, and now the strands were parting.

The tent lurched like a drunkard. It leaned, it leaned farther and farther, and then it collapsed with a great whomp and an exhalation of hot air and sparks and soot. A shout went up and the men stopped scurrying and stood gawping. A surprised laugh from one, a cheer from a few others: the fire was beaten, stifled when the tent came down.

Then little flames got up and began to dash over the hills and valleys the canvas made over what lay underneath.

I heard Sunup sob and call for Consort Vulpeja.

A voice I recognized shouted nearby, berating the onlookers. It was the Crux's cook. He roared that not a man among them had a feather's weight of sense, and bade them go to the cliff path and form a line to pass buckets upward.

I waved to him, having no voice to call out. His face and tunic were spattered with blood and I thought he had been injured. He came over and helped me stand. When I pulled urgently at his sleeve, he shook his head. He knew already; he'd not forgotten Consort Vulpeja.

Cook followed me around the tent. I pointed to the large hummock over the concubine's cot and he pulled out his long knife and began to cut. He shouted for water and more water, he cursed the men who brought it for being too slow. They emptied their buckets over the fire and steam rose up with the smoke. Cook was hardened to heat after all his years at the hearth fire. He cut through the burning canvas quickly and lifted it away with his bare hands.

She was not on the cot. She must have crawled under it for shelter. She lay faceup on the ground with her hands folded, as she had been taught was proper, and I thought at first she was alive because she wasn't burnt, not even her shift. Except for soot around her nostrils and on her eyelids and cheeks, she was unmarked. But she was dead.

I had saved Sunup instead. Sunup, mudborn.

Men and boys crowded close behind us. Most of them were cooks and kitchenboys and bagboys; any drudge or foot soldier with time to waste was down at the tourney field watching the Blood fight. They had come running from all over the Marchfield when they saw the smoke, for Wildfire was everyone's concern. Wildfire gets hungrier the more it feeds; it would have leapt from tent to tent with the wind and devoured the king's hall if they'd not kept it penned inside Sire Galan's tent. I suppose they'd done well to do that much. For us it was too little.

When they saw Consort Vulpeja, a hush came over them. Soon they'd begin to talk, and the tale would be carried all over the Marchfield. It would find its way home to the king's court, to Galan's keep, to his wife.

I put my sodden cloak over the concubine, leaving her face uncovered. It wasn't fitting they should see her in her shift. When I'd done that, I didn't know what else to do. The ground where I knelt was hot, so I crawled away. I sat by Sire Fanfarron's tent, which was pocked with small holes where sparks had caught before they were doused.

I meant to go back for her. It was Hazard who chose for me, Hazard in every aspect, blind Chance and ruthless Peril and unyielding Fate. If I had touched Consort Vulpeja's foot first, surely I would have saved her. But then Sunup would have died, and I could not regret that she lived.

I regretted everything else. I should have saved them both. I hadn't thought, that was the trouble. I hadn't thought of the hole in the canvas wall beside Consort Vulpeja's cot. I could have widened the opening, gotten us all out. But the wall was a wall of flames—and I had no knife, for I'd taken off my belt with the sheath when I lay down to rest. Why, then, hadn't I picked it up? For now the belt was lost and the knife and my herbs with it. And Consort Vulpeja.

Maybe if I'd gotten out first, I could have found help in time for both of them. If I hadn't crawled . . . I never thought the fire could move so fast.

I should have cut my way out from inside when I had the chance—but already the wall was blazing, I couldn't get near it. And I had forgotten my knife.

And so on, round and round.

The priests say the dead see more clearly the farther they travel from us in the afterlife, until at last they see more like gods than men. The burden the dead carry on their journey is remorse. Duties left undone, even omissions that went unnoticed in life, often prove the most burdensome, and some deeds that seemed great to the living, for good or ill, turn out to be but a small matter.

Passions do not long survive the body. Only regret. Powerless regret, for shades can't set the balance right or turn aside any harm their past deeds will yet bring to the living. For the first time, I understood what a torment that will be: the heavier the remorse, the longer the journey.

Crux Sun smiled down. I no longer saw anything benign in her smile. Rain and rain and rain, a month of rain, and today, when water from the sky would have been a blessing, she showed us her face.

Ardor had spared me and taken Consort Vulpeja and I was baffled by it. All that I'd done to save her life, all that Galan had done: useless. I'd been so sure, for a time, that I fulfilled Ardor's purpose. Now I wondered if I'd thwarted Ardor's will when I healed her, and she was always meant for dying. But if I'd displeased Ardor, surely Wildfire would have eaten me?

Or was it Hazard all along? Consort Vulpeja and Galan merely followed the path Fate ordained, and I, perforce, followed them.

And so on, round and round.

Sunup found me, and we huddled together. She bore the pain of her burns without complaint, but when she saw Consort Vulpeja she cried and called for her mother, and I was reminded she was a child. I comforted her and I was comforted, because she was alive. But my thoughts trudged in circles, mule yoked to a millstone, grinding small.

The Crux rode up at a gallop by way of the east-of-north road with his men behind him. Others followed, among them the king himself, come to see the cause of the smoke. They crowded so close around our camp that horses stumbled over the tent ropes and the tents began to wobble. Sunup and I pressed close to Sire Fanfarron's pavilion so we wouldn't be trampled, and we found ourselves facing a horse's hindquarters covered in a fine barding stamped with red diamonds. We could see little else.

King Thyrse had a voice like a brass horn when he needed it, and when he roared, he was heard. He sent the idle onlookers away, drudges and Blood alike, and we could see again. There were heads of other clans present. The king bade them come to his hall that evening, and they left, though it was clear that the First of Rift, at least, begrudged the dismissal. Three or four cataphracts of Prey remained with their men, for a king is always attended. But they didn't stay so close to the king's elbow as to imply distrust of the clan of Crux.

For the Blood of Crux were there, armed, as they had come from the tourney field. All save one—Galan. The Crux stood beside the king.

Though our tents were near his hall, I'd only seen King Thyrse so close once, when we came to the Marchfield, and his clothes had been plain and worn. Today he was attired more like a king. His surcoat was of mail so fine it was nearly as soft as cloth, patterned all over with godsigns worked in countless gold and silver links. An armorer could go blind making such a hauberk. It was for show: gold and silver will not stand up to blows. He wore a cowl of rare white fox fur and his undersleeves were pinned back to show a lining of red fox. His face, in this splendor, was merely a man's face—an angry face—with nothing about it to say: *here is a king*.

The king didn't speak and no one else would speak before him. He gazed at the ruined tent. The flames were gone but smoke and stink rose from it. Galan's banners had been hacked down and stolen.

Cook came up dragging a corpse by the heels. He let it fall at his master's feet and he knelt beside it. Now I understood the bloodstains on Cook's tunic. The man's throat had been cut. It gaped wider than his open mouth. Blue and rose ribbons were sewn to the shoulders of his grubby leather jerkin: the ribbons, the jerkin, his face and hair were spattered with blood.

King Thyrse said, without surprise, "Ardor."

The Crux spat on the carcass and wiped his mouth. His face was tight with disgust. "You did well," he said to Cook.

Cook bowed low, his face nearly touching his knees, and crawled away backward, to put himself out of sight of the king and his master. There was no pride in the curve of his broad back; instead I saw shame and, perhaps, reproach. I suppose he'd done well to catch the man and butcher him like a pig—but better he'd stayed at the fire, where we needed him. Yet it should never have fallen to Cook and his kitchenboys to safeguard our camp.

No one, not even the priests—whose omens were clear now it was too late—had expected Ardor to come during the day when the fighting men were gone. It was as clever as it was craven. But why should this surprise the Crux, or any of us, after Sire Voltizo and his false weapon? The honor of Ardor was counterfeit.

Yet the feud had been over till they found Sire Bizco's mutilated corpse. That was Sire Rodela's doing. There were, in feuds as in tournaments, or even war itself, certain proprieties. Once those bounds were overstepped, one base act was answered by another, and where would it end?

All this blame to share, and my burden was not lessened one whit.

"They sent their jacks," said the king.

"Their hands are still sullied, Sire," the Crux said.

"Indeed," the king said in a dry voice.

But Sire Rassis, the Crux's armiger, spoke up, saying, "He's no jack. I know him, King Thyrse. He's my wife's cousin's husband's brother—armiger to Sire Pisar." He was careful not to say his name.

Cook rubbed the dead man's face with his sleeve, and sure enough, there was Ardor's godsign on his cheek.

"And who is she?" asked the king, inclining his head toward Consort Vulpeja, her face very white amidst the heap of blackened canvas.

"She's late of Ardor herself," the Crux said.

"Is she the one?"

"Indeed," said the Crux, in a voice as dry as the king's.

The king stepped over the dead man and approached Consort Vulpeja. He was not three paces from us; Sunup and I never moved, for fear we'd be noticed and sent away. He lifted the cloak from the concubine and covered her up again, and I heard him sigh. When he straightened up he said, in a voice meant to carry, "Have you ever seen such a wonder? Wildfire took her gently—she isn't marred. Surely this is a sign the god Ardor has taken her back and counted her offense paid and her honor cleansed. But the clan Ardor, which killed her, what of their honor? May the god curse their hearths for loosing fire in the Marchfield."

It might just as well be said that Ardor, the god, had not wanted her, for she was left untouched. But if the king said her death was the coin to redeem the reputation she'd pawned, that was the way the rumormongers would sing it. They'd sing of the curse too. Even the gods must heed a king's curse.

The king looked from the concubine to the crowd around him. "And which of these men of yours is the hotspur who made the wager? It's his tent, surely."

The Crux answered, "He's not here, Sire. He goes on foot these days, and goes alone. But I've sent for him."

"I would see the man behind so much mischief."

"He has much to answer for," said the Crux. "But not all of it."

"Oh, Ardor will answer too, you both shall answer. This feud will not come with us to war. I'll have an end on it."

A lesser man might have knelt before the look on the king's face, but the Crux merely bowed his head.

King Thyrse said, "Send your man to me when he comes. And, if you please, attend me tonight in council and we'll settle this matter."

When the king was gone, the Crux said, "Not empty-handed. It will never be settled without steel."

Not long after, Galan came running. He ran all the way from the hills where the Crux's jack, Tel, had found him. He ran while his men rode, and when he arrived he was at his last extremity of wind. He bent double, his hands on his knees, and fought for air with great tearing gasps. When he mastered himself he straightened up. He was helmetless. His cheeks were flushed but his brow was pale. He wiped the sweat from his face with his quilted sleeve and looked about him.

By then the Sun was westering over the sea, a flock of small clouds scattered about her. Her golden light dazzled and spared nothing. All that had been laid waste was made clear. When the shadow of a cloud passed over us, the dimming was a relief.

Galan's eyes sought me out where I stood by Sire Fanfarron's tent, and when he found me I know he found some ease, though his face was still grim. Then he looked down at Consort Vulpeja and his mouth twisted.

I didn't go to him. His fellows came, cataphracts and armigers alike; they offered him their voluble anger, which suited better than sympathy. Ardor had outraged them all. Someone brought Galan a horn cup and he tilted his head and drank quickly, and when he lowered the cup there was a trickle of red wine on his chin. He handed back the cup and nodded, courteous by rote. The cloud passed, the Sun came forth again, and his eyes were dark under the shadow of his brow, staring at Ardor's handiwork. Though the crowd pressed him close, he stood as if he were alone.

One man stayed away and that was Sire Rodela. He couldn't keep from grinning. He looked my way sometimes and I took care not to look back, but I saw just the same.

The Crux took Galan's arm and spoke in his ear. Galan inclined his head, for he was the taller by a palm's breadth, and they turned and went together to the Crux's tent, and all the while Galan's tongue was locked behind his teeth, and not one word, not one sound escaped.

Spiller was loud where Galan was silent; he cursed enough for three men, as if the clan of Ardor cared what he thought of them. It was Rowney who put us all to work—Galan's men, even his foot soldiers, and me—taking up the burned canvas to see what, if anything, might be salvaged under it. Soon we were all smeared crown to heel with soot and ash.

Spiller said, "No wonder Noggin isn't here, for he's always missing when there's work to be done," and Rowney sent a boy to fetch him. By the time the boy came back, Noggin had been found.

He looked like a charred branch. The wall of the tent had fallen over him in tattered folds, and he lay under it with his knees drawn up to his chin. His skin was blackened and most of his hair had burned away. His lips were drawn back, showing a mouthful of teeth unsullied by the fire. They looked as big and yellow as horses' teeth in the ruins of his face. It had to be Noggin, it could be no other.

I hoped he'd slept through his death, that the smoke drowned him before the fire got to him. For certain, I'd not heard a sound from him, nor known he was there. But where else would he be but on his flea-ridden pallet behind the meal sacks? And what else would he be doing but sleeping?

Spiller said he was too lazy to live. Sunup began to sob. Hers were the only tears shed for Noggin, unless his mother wept when she heard the news. Daft Noggin, my shadow. There was little malice in him. He loved to laugh when others laughed, even when the wit buzzed high above his head, even when it stung him.

Rowney and I wrapped him in a piece of canvas and laid him beside Consort Vulpeja. Fuel was scarce, so they'd share a pyre. It would burn hot enough to consume everything but a few handfuls of bone and grit and ash, and the priests would grind those in a mortar until there was no remnant a shade could recognize of the body left behind.

Consort Vulpeja wouldn't have chosen Noggin as an attendant, but no matter. She wouldn't be troubled with him long. There are no drudges to serve the dead, no companions on that road.

* * *

Mai came to bring Sunup home, came near as quick as rumor ran through the Marchfield. She gathered up her daughter in her ample arms and Sunup cried again, this time for her own pains, as if only her mother could console her.

We'd borrowed Sunup and I had no claim on her now that Consort Vulpeja was gone. Better she should go home, I knew, but I'd grown fond of her and her ways. It was in her nature to watch and wonder much and ask little, to see where she was needed and serve without stinting. Yet she could also be giddy as any child when she felt at ease. She'd never been so merry with us, in Galan's uneasy household.

Mai made soothing sounds, but her eyes, meeting mine above Sunup's head, were small and stony in the folds of her thick eyelids. I pointed to the bruises across my throat, to let her know I was mute. But she did not need me to tell her of the fire and who had set it; rumor was beforehand.

"They killed her after all," she said. "May canker blister them and dry up their sacs, and may their wives go barren." She made a gesture as if she were scattering seeds or ashes.

A curse from Mai might well be as potent as a king's. I made an avert sign to ward it off, for fear it would fall on us as well as the clan of Ardor.

Sunup hung around her mother's neck until Mai set her down, saying the girl had grown too heavy, we'd fed her too well. But when Sunup's feet touched the ground, she began to cry again. She sat down, saying it hurt to stand.

I knew how she suffered. I hadn't felt my burns as much when they first happened. Then came heat and pain, and now a cold fire that leached warmth from every part of me and left me shivering.

I knelt beside her. The soles of her feet were black with a crust of charred skin and ash. Under the blackness was an angry red. Her feet must have dragged through the fires on the floor when I carried her out of the tent. She had other lesser burns as well, on her cheek, her back, and her limbs. I knew better than to apply soothing ointments or heavy bandages—though I had none, they'd all burned—or even to wash her wounds with water, cold or hot. Such measures would only keep the fire trapped in her body. The Wildfire was still burning inside her, inside both of us, and must be put out.

In our village there'd been a woman who could draw fire from burns. When she was done small burns healed without scars, and even large ones healed smooth, almost like new skin, but shiny. People said she made no sort of fuss at all when she healed; it came easily to her, they said, because her father died before she was born. Fatherless people have that gift, whether or not they ever learn to use it.

I'd learned to douse another sort of fire, since I'd cured Catnep's firepiss. I'd been called to the bedsides of many women ridden with fever. If the fever was mild, I let it be, to serve as a cleansing fire to burn away the dross of other ailments. But when a woman's skin was hot as embers, when she was so parched her blood turned thick and dark and she wandered in fever dreams, I'd sing a prayer and warm my hands on her and then let the heat go. It was a simple matter, when the gods permitted it. If not, I could do nothing.

I squatted back on my heels and looked to Mai. She nodded, and with a groan she settled herself on the ground beside Sunup and took her hand. I touched Sunup's heels lightly with my fingers. She winced, though she made no outcry. I held my palms before her soles without touching her, as if she were a brazier. I felt no warmth, but I knew the fire was there, burning inward toward the thin bones of her feet.

It was strange to ask Ardor for help now, when Ardor Wildfire had of late seemed so hungry for my death. There had been something gleeful in the flames reaching for me, and no notion of mercy.

But if Wildfire had meant to kill me, I would have died.

I had no voice to sing so I whistled to the wayward flame that burned in Sunup, as one might whistle to a dog: a scrap of a tune, a few notes of the firethorn song that had served me well as a healing prayer. But the Wildfire in her was more wolf than dog, and wouldn't heed me.

I leaned closer and blew on the soles of Sunup's feet to put out the flame, but my breath only made it leap higher. Sunup whimpered at the pain of it. I could sense the fire now, though it gave off neither heat nor light. When I looked sideways it was almost there, a dark flickering in the corner of my eye. It was all through Sunup: it had entered her bellows when she'd breathed the smoke and it had burrowed under her skin and now it was licking the length of her bones. As I breathed in I felt the fire advance toward me, as if it were curious. Every time I inhaled it came closer, and so I coaxed it breath by breath until I took a deep breath and it followed that wind right into me. The fire flared up as it left Sunup and she screamed. And suddenly I was in the burning tent again, breathing sparks.

I must have pulled too much heat from Sunup. I was seared inside. I didn't know what to do with the fire, how to let it out of me. I lay on my side, gasping, and Sunup quivered and cried so hard she ran out of breath. Her face was blanched, where it wasn't streaked with soot and tears.

But the soles of her feet were no longer such an angry red under the blackened skin. I knew that she'd heal and never have a scar.

In a while I mastered myself. Mai heaved herself to her feet and helped me stand. She took my face between her hands and gave me a hearty kiss on the lips. "For Sunup," she said, "I'll give you anything."

I shook my head, still unable to speak.

"Let me give you my shawl. You can't refuse me—even a harlot hides her wares better." And it was true: my dress was so burned about the back and shoulders that nothing but rags and thread held the sleeves to the bodice.

Even a slight weight against my burns was painful, but I bore it to let her know I was grateful. Pinch took Sunup on his back, and she lifted her face on her slender stalk of a neck to kiss me when we parted.

I didn't know how to heal myself. To this day I wear the mark of Ardor Wildfire, a constellation of shiny scars on my back where the burns were slow to heal, and there's fire in my joints at every change in the weather. I'm sure that when I go to my pyre, they'll find my bones are charred already.

After Mai left I folded the shawl and set it aside to keep it from the grime, and rejoined Galan's men, searching amidst the ruins of the tent for anything Wildfire might have scorned. It was better to stoop and grub than to think of my pains.

Spiller had been jealous of this duty and disinclined to share it. He chased away Galan's foot soldiers, claiming they'd steal what little was left and he had only two eyes to watch them and none in the back of his head. He showed unaccustomed diligence, digging in the corner where Noggin used to sleep until the ground was all pocked with holes (for even the poorest drudge has something precious and a place to hide it). Rowney chided him for wasting time and Spiller showed him his back and went on digging. I hope he was disappointed; Noggin's hoard was more likely to be shells and shiny pebbles than coins.

Rowney and Flykiller and Uly and I gleaned from the ashes braziers and buckles, pots and lamps, spoons and knives, and a few pearls and beads of garnet, jet, and jade from Galan's clothes. There was little left of cloth and leather and wood, though the fire had been capricious, sparing such things as should by reason have burned: an oak cask full of wine, sacks of meal, Semental's harness and barding, which had been packed away in cloth and straw. Consort Vulpeja's linen chest was merely scorched, the garments inside smoked and stained. They would burn nevertheless, with her. I kept one piece of cloth from the pyre, for she'd barely touched it: the length of embroidered white lawn Dame Hartura had given her just two days before. Sunup should have it. I didn't think the concubine would grudge her this consideration, though she would have grudged me.

The fire had mutilated Galan's splendid plate armor, which had lain unused in the tent since he'd been forbidden to ride. The silver inlay had melted, the blued iron had blackened, and the velvet lining had burned away, along with the leather laces and straps. It might be mended, but how to afford the armorer?

We found the metal fittings of Galan's strongbox as well as the money he'd locked away in it, still in a leather purse; of the strongbox itself, nothing remained but charcoal. The purse had been light already, most of the coins paid to Ardor for Consort Vulpeja. We counted what was left, Spiller and Rowney and I, keeping an eye on each other. We had cause to want to know whether our master was penniless. He was, near enough—seven gold coins and a few lesser ones might see a village through a bad harvest, but he'd started with a hundred times as many (so Spiller claimed).

The fire had taken less from me, for I had less to take. I crouched and raked through a heap of burned twigs and bits of sacking, all that remained of Galan's pallet, and found a few precious things: my knife, the copper fire flask, my awl, a needle, and the finger bones of the Dame and Na. There was just enough color left to tell one bone from the other.

I'd buried my valuables elsewhere, underfoot in Consort Vulpeja's chamber where the other drudges, save Sunup, seldom entered. I dug up the purse of coins I'd earned from my dealings among the women of the Marchfield. Under it I'd buried plants too dangerous to be left where anyone could find them: what was left of the dwale, the berries in a gourd gnawed by the damp, the roots in a sack. And under that, in a packet of oiled vellum wrapped with red cord, the firethorn berries I'd carried all the way from the Kingswood. They had nearly killed me once—or saved my life, it was hard to say. I opened the packet and found the berries shriveled and dark under a bloom of mold. I wondered if they kept their potency. No matter, I wouldn't cast them away. Amidst the black ashes and the stench I was suddenly reminded of the Kingswood, of orange berries among smooth gray thorns and of the blue flowers of tread-me-down pushing up through fallen leaves; the smell of a spring thaw.

I kept the berries, both the dwale and the firethorn, twisting them into my headcloth and tucking it well in. The purse was heavy—it weighed more than Galan's—but I was gladder to see the dwale than my money; the money would not stretch far in the Marchfield, but the poison would suffice. I did not need much.

I rolled my belongings in a scrap of unburned canvas and tied the bundle to a belt made of rope, which I hung under my skirts, out of reach of pickpockets. Now I was wearing all I had left—except my cloak, which I'd lent to Consort Vulpeja until she would no longer need it. I was richer than I'd been in the Kingswood, by a knife and a purseful of coins, the dwale and two finger bones. But I felt poorer, being robbed; even the slippers Galan had given me, which had pinched my feet, were dear now that they were gone. The loss that cut deepest was my belt with herbs. Wildfire had chewed it and spat out the buckle and a scrap of twisted leather. When I had my voice again, I'd ask Mai for some childbane. I prayed she'd saved some for the higher price she could fetch later; I prayed I'd need it, that my tides would come soon. If not the childbane, there were other plants I'd heard could put an end to the unborn, if taken before the quickening.

Galan went to see King Thyrse in the king's hall, as he was bid to do. He was gone so long the other cataphracts had time to doff their armor and don their clothes and eat their supper too. By the time he came back, the Sun was low over the sea, hidden behind the cliffs. The light had gone from gold to ruddy and now it was turning blue; the wind that skirled between the tents, east from where the darkness rose, brought a chill.

He found me sitting where his tent used to be, with his horse soldiers. We sat beside two heaps, one much larger than the other. The small one was all we'd salvaged of his goods; the large one was a muck and welter of ash and soot and charcoal, slag, charred leather, remnants of cloth, potsherds—the useless. A little warmth still came from it. This had been Galan's place and we had no other, so we stayed there, despite the stench of smoke, eating food Cook had brought us after the Blood had supped: bread and oil, colewort stewed with a bit of ham. Such a hunger beset me when I saw the food that I couldn't eat fast enough to quell it. Every swallow scraped its way down my raw throat and, for my pains, called for a swallow of ale after it. The ale might have been water; the more I drank, the more sober I felt.

I stood and Galan embraced me hard. Rowney hunched his shoulders and attended to sopping his bread in the colewort juice. Spiller opened his mouth and shut it again upon a wiser thought.

Galan stayed silent, his cheek against my temple, his arms tight around my ribs. I held him just as tightly and felt as much as heard how his breathing was choked and shallow, how in a while it came easier. He smelled of sweat, without the taint of smoke. We had no shelter from other eyes now, no shelter except the dusk that had followed on the heels of the Sun. But his fellows granted him the grace of a little time with his household—what was left of it. They looked elsewhere. I doubt it was from courtesy. More likely they feared contagion; King Thyrse had sent Galan back to us unharmed, but he was shrouded in the king's displeasure.

I'd covered myself again with Mai's shawl. It slid from one shoulder and Galan said, "You've been burned, your back is raw! Why haven't you tended to this?"

I shrugged. The burns, inside and out, would heal as Ardor willed it, or not at all. I had other pains as well, which Sire Rodela had given me, and all insistent.

Galan sighed. "You've taken more wounds in my service than any of my men."

I found my voice for the first time that day, but it was no louder than a rustle. I said, "Not so. Weren't you told? Your bagboy is dead, burned in the fire."

"I hadn't heard," he said.

Speaking made me cough and Galan loosened his grip until the fit passed. Though he was gentle with me, I felt him stiffen with anger. Noggin was another loss for which he would hold Ardor accountable.

I hid my face against Galan's brigandine. There was little comfort in it, for the green canvas was studded all over with rivets that held the metal scales inside the vest. It was a fine time to weep but my eyes were dry. I whispered, "You said once I brought you luck, but if I did it was bad luck. You've lost everything."

"No," he said, with such certainty I looked up to see what was in his face, and found a smile tucked in the corners of his lips. "Not everything." He kissed me on the eyebrow and the bridge of my nose, but it was the smile I wanted, and I found it tasted as sweet as I expected. I touched his cheek and throat and the back of his neck, for I wanted the comfort of his flesh and everywhere else he was armored.

Then Galan raised his head and began to laugh. This laugh stung me. It was too sudden and too mocking. He said, "How can you call me unlucky? Hazard favored me today, surely, for I gave all my jewels to the priests, before the fire, to cure the concubine, and now there's no need. I'm richer than when I left you this morning."

I said it was nothing to jest about, and he said it was the kind of jape the gods play on mortals—and shouldn't we learn to laugh with them?—else we'd spend all our days weeping.

This strange mood of his, this bitter mirth—it galled me. Na used to say: "The more you laugh, the more you'll end by crying." She always had an apt saying at the ready, and when had I ever listened? She'd also told me: "If you make your bed of brambles, you'll get pricked."

I took my arms from around his neck and stepped back, but he kept a hand on the small of my back and I did not get far.

Galan said, "Why so silent? Your looks scold, but you say nothing."

"Surely the king has scolded you enough for one day."

"Oh, you're a wise shrew," he said. "You know when to bite your tongue."

"Not so wise," I said, very low so the others wouldn't overhear. "Didn't I advise you to bring that concubine to your tent, and she died anyway? And all your coins wasted."

"Are you in mourning for my money?" He still smiled, but he dropped his arm. We stood eye to eye, but not touching. "Perhaps you liked me better . . . richer."

"It's not your money I mourn, but her suffering. I wish I'd held my tongue, that she'd died in her clan's tent without waking."

"Without honor," Galan said.

"Then I wish I'd never wakened her when she came to your tent, for her life was misery then. Needless misery." I'd seen her day after day, fighting to live, wishing to die, all on a smile or a word from him, and her fortitude and suffering were of no account as honor was accounted. And what was her honor worth, if money could buy it?

Did I say Consort Vulpeja's suffering was needless? It was her dying that was needless. I'd preached to Galan of his faults often enough, but now I said nothing—nothing of my own culpability, of how I'd failed in wit and courage both. How I'd been close enough to Consort Vulpeja to save her life, and had let her die instead.

"Come," Galan said. "Come here," and he took my arm and drew me away from the others. Some paces away, on the other side of the midden that had been his tent, he stopped. Over his shoulders I saw Spiller watching us. He leaned toward Rowney to say something and laughed; Spiller was ever too fond of his own wit.

Galan put his hand on the nape of my neck and pulled me toward him. His thumb rested against the pulse under my jaw. "All these foolish wishes," he said. "Are you an Auspex, that you could have foretold her death and saved us all the trouble?"

I looked sidelong at his face, afraid of what I might see. I was caught by his eyes. The pupils were wide and black in the dark, intent on me.

"I found you by Chance, and I took you for a trinket that would bring me luck, only to find Hazard's gift was greater than I knew. None of us can be certain of what lies ahead, we can only set one foot before the other. But Hazard has given me a lodestar, for you have a wise heart, and when I followed your heart, you led me true. Even though," he said, and that smile came again, "even though you had to goad me like a mule with every step."

I shook my head, remembering the glimpse I'd had of Fate's kingdom in the palm of the Dame's hand, how I'd known at last what Ardor required of me. How I was mistaken. "When you followed me you were misled."

"You sought to save me from grief, and Vulpeja as well, and now grief has come to us anyway and you say it was all for naught. But the one thing you led me to do was the one thing I did well. No matter that I must now go begging to my uncle for shelter, I don't regret it."

I turned my head away from the touch of his hand, his eyes. A harsh wordless sound came from my throat. He pulled me again into his arms.

"Would you take so much on yourself?" he asked. "You're blameless in this. The maid had her reckoning to make, as I do. I won't quarrel with Hazard, complain that Fate's road is too hard when—after all—we chose it, that maid and I, with our first misstep. I own the blame for it, for I persuaded her—but I won't claim what isn't mine. It was Rodela who broke the peace, and the clan of Ardor who set fire to the tent. Their contemptible deeds are none of my doing, and they must make their own reckoning. The gods will not let them go unscathed; nor will I."

I saw the anger in his face before he hid it again, as neatly as if he'd pulled down the visor of a helmet. But his arms were too tight around me. "I suppose you think you could have saved her, is that so? Don't you see the gods have had their sport with us? They gave us the concubine's life only to take it later. It was in their hands all along, not ours. Let them carry the weight of it."

I saw the truth of what he said, and I did let the gods take that burden. I let it go. The gods send us tribulations, but they also give us this solace: though we may never know their reasons, there is purpose in what befalls us, and we must bend to their will, lean on their strength. Even a king cannot command his own destiny, but must rather face the destiny he's given. Why then should I feel shame that the gods had overmastered me?

I felt as if I'd been stooping under a great weight, and when it was lifted from me, I could weep at last. I paid Consort Vulpeja her due of tears. She was never dear to me, but I owed her that much for her bravery. It was a woman's courage, of a sort men disregard. It had shone in her despite her frailty; it cast a light that death couldn't put out, for courage is never wasted.

I wept because I was alive and she wasn't, because I had what she would never have, and pity and gratitude were so alloyed they made a piercing blade.

The Crux made room for Galan and his household in a corner of his capacious tent, near the doorway. Before we set foot inside, his body servant, Boot, stood over us drudges to make sure we scrubbed the soot from our skins and beat the ashes from our clothes.

There was little rest for anyone that night. The king had called the heads of the clans together to his hall after supper, and sent them away again in a trice, for what he had to say was quickly delivered. The feud would end by noon on the morrow. The Blood of Ardor and Crux would settle it between them in a mortal tourney. "I'll lose men I could well use," the king had said, "but no matter, if I'm rid of this pestilential feud."

The Crux came back smiling. He called for his Auspices and bade them take the omens. They consulted the starry vault of the Heavens, the shapes of the clouds passing over the newly risen Moon, the dartings of the nighthawks, and proclaimed that the signs—on balance, notwithstanding certain obscurities—suggested the day would be favorable to Crux.

He called for his men, and said to them, "Some of you have learned how to strike a man on his visor with a lance and knock him off his horse. It's a fine feat and you may well be proud of it. But you've played too long at tourneys and now you must forget such niceties. The king has granted us our fondest wish, and tomorrow we will have our chance at Ardor. There will be no quarter. Do you understand? I swear this before you all: I will not yield and lose the tourney and honor with it. If any man of you quits the field while you can still fight, or cries for mercy, I'll kill you myself when I have leisure. Don't look to the king to interfere, for he tells me he's content to let the troublemakers in his army execute each other. When noon comes we'll count those left standing—so keep your legs under you if you can, eh?"

Then his men's voices rang out and their laughter was loud and hard. I listened, hiding behind the skirts of the Crux's tent, and marked how they clapped Galan on his back, when not an hour before they'd avoided him. If the Crux hadn't been there, I daresay they would have congratulated him for starting the feud and providing the occasion for their joy.

But there was still a pyre waiting at the charnel grounds on the sea cliff north of the Marchfield, and Consort Vulpeja to send on her way with the ceremony due her. We went by torch and lamplight, and the path was a chalky smudge under our feet. There was another path stretching toward us across the sea, a silver shimmer cast by the Moon, and it followed as we went, as if inviting the unwary to turn and tread upon it—one of the trickster's many false promises.

Consort Vulpeja was laid atop the pyre on a bed of heather, with her meager possessions set around her. Noggin, wrapped in canvas, was placed crosswise at her feet. The priests and armigers emptied their oil lamps on the pyre so it would burn hot and fast. Galan put a torch to it.

So Wildfire took his concubine after all. When the shroud had burned away and she was sheathed in flames, she was seen to move. Her limbs twitched, she bent at the waist and her head turned. This happens sometimes; they say it means the shade will be restless. But she turned her head away from us and toward the sea as if she were eager to be going. It gave me a fright, it was so lifelike. My eyes watered freely, for the pity of it. And from the smoke.

The Auspices called on Crux to strengthen the warriors on the field tomorrow. They made much of the concubine now that she was dead. The cataphracts warmed their anger by her pyre. There were few among them, I should think, who did not need fuel to stoke their battle fever, for cold doubt will dampen those fires in a long night. After the burning Galan smeared one streak of soot across his forehead. He'd wear the mark until she was avenged or he was dead.

It was late when we returned to camp. Now the Blood shut out the night and the wind and crowded into the Crux's tent, so many of them they must perforce rub elbows and sit knee to knee. Only the night before, the cataphracts had gathered for a different occasion, and ended by putting me to the ordeal. Now there were twice as many men, for the armigers were there as well; and all of them would face their own trial tomorrow. No one noticed me. I stayed on Galan's pallet in the corner, out of sight behind a stack of wine casks, and I watched.

The Crux's drudges lit five or six braziers and a lavish quantity of lamps and candles, and the light flowed heavy and gold, like honey, among the men. The air was thick with the fug of smoke, ale, spilled wine, and such cloying attars as the Blood wear to cover up their honest sweat, and I was glad our pallets were near the door, where the drafts slipped in, bringing cold and the smell of turf and saltwater, swelling the canvas walls of the tent.

How they buzzed, clamoring of what they'd do on the morrow. I heard Sire Pava wager he would win three swords, and Sire Fanfarron answered he proposed to do better; he'd follow Sire Rodela's fashion and take pelts to hang upon his horse's caparison. And I saw Sire Rodela lean forward into the light from where he sat behind Sire Alcoba's shoulder, and say he wanted but one trophy tomorrow, and that was a fine suit of armor; he'd be sure to take the cataphract's measure before he took the trouble to kill him—and when he smiled, I saw teeth glinting under the coarse fringe of his mustache, and how his lower lip jutted above his beard. Sire Alcoba leaned away from him with a sour look, but Sire Fanfarron guffawed. Others laughed too. I thought: *So this is how they shun him.* It was all forgotten how he'd lied; or what did it matter, since I was a sheath and no harm done after all? And I knotted my hands in my skirts and swallowed bile.

Men show something of their natures the night before a battle. The loud ones drank too much and spoke too freely. Others sat quietly over their cups, perhaps afraid, or aloof from such foolishness. Some slipped away to say their prayers before the shrine in the priests' tent, and came back pensive. The Crux moved among them and wherever he went his laughter rumbled and tumbled like boulders rolling down a mountainside. He mocked his men's boasts or roused them from their silences, and even those he twitted basked in his regard.

Galan did not boast. He sat on a low stool, leaning against a tent pole, and others came to him. In that warm light I couldn't see the weariness and strain that had of late been graved upon his face. There was, instead, a smile that came now and then as he talked, and even at times when he sat alone, a smile disclosed in the corners of his eyes and mouth, the slight droop of his lids, the lift of an eyebrow.

Oh, he was glad the king had put steel in his hands and given him leave to use it. He was glad to the marrow of his longbones. All his joy was forged of rage; watching Consort Vulpeja burn had only made him keener. He didn't seem to reckon the chances of a man on foot in a cavalry charge.

I had reckoned them. From the moment I heard that the king had called for a mortal tourney, I counted him a dead man.

Sometime in the middle of the night, the Crux sent his men away, bidding them to pray and to make their bequests before the priests, for some had beggared themselves and some had bettered themselves since we'd come to the Marchfield, and every man should take thought to what he'd leave behind. He told them to rest if they could, but how could anyone sleep on such a night? Soon they'd begin the slow and meticulous task of donning armor, each cataphract in his own tent with his armiger to attend him. The king had wasted no time; they must be ready by sunrise to finish by noon.

There had been more bluster in the Crux's tent than you might find in a summer thunderstorm, and now came a quiet like that which follows the rain. The Crux called for one of his varlets to rub him down, and he stripped and sat on a stool while Boot kneaded the knots from his sinews. The Crux's chest was broad, the muscles in his limbs long and ropy; one leg had a thick white scar from groin to kneecap.

He hadn't spoken to Galan all evening, and now that they were alone—save for their men and me—his silence was more marked.

Galan sat with his head turned away, the lamplight unsteady on his face. He had no need to prepare for the morning, for he still wore his armor. It was all the clothing he had left after the fire. His jacks had already brushed the mud from his metal fitments and polished his buckler and helm; he'd honed his weapons himself to make certain of the edge. All was accomplished but the waiting. Behind his head shone the quarter Moon, woven of silver thread in the tapestry that hung across the tent. There was bread and wine before him on a small table, for he'd had no supper. He reached for the bread, one of Cook's best white loaves, and pulled off a piece with his deft fingers. But instead of eating the bread, he set it back down and stood abruptly.

He knelt before the Crux as Rodela had knelt the evening before, but there was submission in his back, humility in his neck. His uncle stared at him with no warmth at all, not even that of anger. And waited, for Galan was slow to speak.

At last he said, "Sire, my offenses are many, but there is one in particular I wish did not lie between us—that I misspoke when I doubted your justice last night."

"Wishing won't unsay it," said the Crux.

"I spoke in heat."

"Men say what they mean when they forget to guard their tongues."

"Maybe. But don't we sometimes grow wiser on reflection? I know you for a just man. I own I shouldn't have doubted you. Will you permit me to ask your forgiveness?"

"You thought me corrupt, but you're the one who corrupted the ordeal. There will always be questions, now, about the truth of it."

Galan said nothing. He kept his head bowed low and I couldn't see his face.

His uncle gave a sour laugh. "Have you learned at last not to quarrel with me?"

Galan looked up at him. "Sire, I am your penitent. Absolve me, I beg you, so I don't have to go into battle tomorrow carrying this regret."

The Crux beckoned to his jack, Tel, to bring him his underarmor. Tel knelt to pull on the red leggings, thick with many layers of linen and stitching, and to lace them up. The Crux looked over his head at Galan. He said, "I have had it in mind to forbid you the tourney."

Then sly hope whispered to me that Galan might outlive the next day. The heart is a fool and will listen to any sweet insinuation.

The Crux lifted his arms so his shirt of linen underarmor could be pulled over his head. Boot and Tel tugged at it on either side. When the Crux's head emerged, he said, "Did your tongue swim away, Nephew? Have you nothing to say?"

"I'm in your hands, Sire. I'll do as you command."

"Will you, now? I'm not accustomed to finding you so biddable." The Crux's voice was cutting and his stare just as sharp.

Galan looked away from his uncle's gaze and down and waited in stillness. I thought perhaps he submitted himself to Fate as much as to the Crux.

And yet, how could I trust such meekness from him? I saw the same distrust in the look the Crux gave him.

He frowned at Galan. "You'd lack your own armiger."

Galan's head came up. "That's just as well, isn't it, Sire? Seeing that my armiger was faithless."

"I can't let you ride. My word will not bend so far."

"I'd never ask it."

"A man afoot will not last long."

Galan shrugged. His eyes were steady on his uncle.

Now the Crux's mail leggings were girded on. They fit snugly, with many points to fasten them to the underarmor. When the Crux spoke again, his voice was rough. "I dread to tell my brother his son died before ever we got to war. But this is your battle, I can't keep you from it." He put his hand on Galan's shoulder.

Galan got to his feet and smiled, his face so bright I looked away. "Don't grieve for me, Uncle. I'm not dead yet."

I turned my back to them and my face to the wall. I lay on my side; anything else was intolerable. I had kept pain at a distance and now I made it welcome. It had its own pulse and everything yielded to it. Galan and the Crux talked on, but I no longer listened.

Hope was a viper.

It was near dawn before Galan came to lie down beside me in all his armor. I kept my back to him and looked over my shoulder and there he was with his head propped up on one hand.

Rowney and Spiller had been lying on their pallets nearest the door, whispering. When Galan came they fell silent. Tourneys were for the Blood only, though jacks had been killed trying to get their wounded masters off the field. Maybe they fretted about the dangers to come tomorrow; more likely they'd been wagering on the outcome.

"You went to sleep in your clothes," Galan said behind me. He began to untie my headcloth. He unwound the headcloth twice, three times, and I lifted my head so he could do it. He let down my hair and I hissed when I felt it against my burns.

"Your pardon," he said, and combed it to one side with his fingers. Then he laid his head down with my hair for a pillow. He took care not to touch my shoulders. "Is there much pain?" he asked.

"Sufficient," I said.

"Where Rodela cut you?"

"Not so bad. The burns have nearly driven it out of my mind."

A small laugh, a puff of air against my neck. "That's a blessing."

Galan's hand was on my shin, under my skirts. He wore a metal prickguard, which was cold even through the wool of my dress. "Tomorrow," he said, in a voice so quiet I had to turn my head to catch it, "no—today—I'll kill my bastard cousin."

I rolled toward him and groaned, but he said to keep still.

I said, "You can't."

He said, "Many men will die today. Why shouldn't he be one of them?"

"You swore, you gave your word you'd abide by the Crux's judgment."

"Hush," he murmured. "I never did swear. He said—if my reason was satisfied—do you remember? And reason tells me it wouldn't be safe to let Rodela outlive me. Do you pretend you don't want him dead?" And he pushed my skirts up and bared my legs. I felt the kneecop and the scales affixed to his leather kilt against my skin.

"No."

"Well then," he said, and his hand was busy undoing the laces of his prickguard.

"You must not," I said. But I didn't move away.

"Why not?"

"I can't lie on my back or my belly, it hurts either way."

"I have considered it," Galan said in my ear. "Get on your hands and knees."

I thought if he mounted me like a dog, he'd be quick as a dog, and that was just as well. I feared the pain, and feared the Crux too, that he might see us there in the dark corner. Yet I wouldn't deny Galan. I wanted him. It wasn't desire I felt, but longing. I longed for him as if I'd already lost him.

Galan was not quick, he was one to linger if it pleased him. I braced against his weight but he did not shove into me so much as sink, and the pain was overtaken slowly at first and then faster. And Desire brought me her gifts after all: the craving of any bitch in season, forgetfulness. We were long past tenderness and he was relentless and I didn't want him to relent, I wanted the slickness and his hands on my hips and his gasps and the moans jolted out of me. I wished I could see his face but I'd take this. I could take it. I raised my head and my hair clung to my face, and though my eyes were open, I was blind. Metal from his armor galled as he dug into me, and when he was in so deep that it hurt when he moved, he shuddered and bent over me, his hands on the ground beside mine, and bowed his head, breathing hard.

I said *no* when he withdrew. I was not ready for it to end and this day to begin, I would never be ready. I lowered myself onto my side and he lay in front of me this time, face-to-face, knee to knee.

For a while we were silent.

"Did I hurt you?" he asked. "You're crying."

I shook my head.

He put his arm over my waist and his forehead against mine. "Dear heart," he whispered, "if I die today . . . I have thought on it . . . there are some here who would treat you well. Pava, you know—but you might also go to Sire Lebrel; he's often admired you."

He might as well have struck me. I doubled over and put my arms over my head and wailed, but the sound was stifled, I couldn't get it out. I couldn't breathe. I'd thought only of his death, not what might happen after. And he'd pass me to another as a man might leave a favorite horse to a favored friend. Not even a friend, he had no friends now.

"Listen, listen!" He pulled my arms away from my face. "Do you think I'm not jealous? Even as a shade I'll know when another man touches you. But if Rodela should outlive me—though I mean to see he doesn't—you'd best find yourself a new cataphract. Rodela will kill you if he can. You need a protector."

A thin keening escaped me at last and I began to weep. Galan said *hush, hush* soothing me like a child. But even as I tried to hold back the sobs lest they be heard, even as I was overtaken and harrowed by them, my thoughts went on ahead with a terrible clarity.

When the weeping had passed, Galan kissed me and rolled on his back to fasten his prickguard. In that moment his face looked pure, his utter self, washed clean of the smiles that had played about his mouth and the frowns that had troubled his brow. Only the ash on his forehead marked him.

If he would not hear me now, he'd never hear me. I said, "Galan, there will be sacrifices before the tourney, I suppose."

He turned his head toward me and nodded.

"Then you must give my mare to Hazard. The mare you let me ride."

"Must I?" His eyes were wide and dark.

"And you must pray to Hazard—to Fate—to relieve you of Sire Rodela. You must not meddle with him."

"Mustn't I?"

"You have enough enemies on the field, you don't need another. Leave Rodela to the gods—even if he should survive the tourney, I think he'll not live long. Promise me to leave him be."

"I'll do what's needful. I won't promise otherwise." His eyes had narrowed.

I saw he was displeased, yet I went on. "Didn't you tell me this very evening that I had a wise heart, that I led you true? Why will you not listen to me now?"

"Because in this matter, my head is wiser than your heart. I know Rodela too well. Let a dog live and he'll bite."

"It's your hot blood that speaks, not your wise head."

"Is your blood so cold, then?" He was glaring now.

For a while I was silent, turning over in my mind words that might persuade and also mollify him, for the more I insisted, the angrier he became. But no words came to me save the truth, and that I couldn't say. That resolve that I'd taken in heat to kill Sire Rodela had indeed grown cold, cold as winter. And though I couldn't kill him in hot rage, I'd kill him nevertheless.

It was only yesterday that Sire Rodela had stolen part of me. A long, empty night and a long, eventful day since. In the night I had lingered over the idea of steel; it was voluptuous to imagine driving a blade into him. But I kept coming back to poison. I had the dwale to hand, yet how to give it to him? He was not such a fool as to take food from me. In the day, still I fretted over this puzzle—never asking whether I should kill him, only how it might be done. Even the fire hadn't driven such thoughts away for long, for he'd rekindled the feud that killed Consort Vulpeja—he might as well have carried a torch himself. Had I wished to forget Rodela, the pains he'd given me would not permit it; they kept faithful company.

The unrequited desire for someone's death is like unsatisfied lust, in this way: it will not leave you be. I had suffered it before, hating Sire Pava, but he'd been beyond my reach.

Rodela's death was mine. I found I was jealous of it. And furthermore I saw as plain as could be that Galan had missed his chance to kill him clean, and if he did it now, it would all begin again. Even if—as he claimed—he would not be forsworn, the gods did not take a man at his word, but at what he meant by it. Among all the dangers of the day, this one he could avoid. He shouldn't carry this to battle with him and tempt the gods again.

I was angry with Galan for his obstinacy, yet why should he be otherwise? He didn't know I claimed Sire Rodela's death for myself, and I couldn't tell him. I saw the danger in speaking; but silence was dangerous too.

"No—I see you're not cold-blooded, but rather too warmhearted," he said, after a long pause. I didn't like the way he said this, or the upright lines that gathered between his brows, or the tightening of his lips so that a crease appeared at either corner. "For you claim your heart tells you I should spare Rodela."

I nodded.

"Then I ask myself," Galan said, "why is your heart so solicitous of him? Perhaps he didn't lie after all. Maybe you won't be sorry if he outlives me. Maybe you already have your next man."

In my outrage I hit him with my fist, a glancing blow under the eye. He blinked but did not flinch. Now the emptiness of his face was frightening, barren instead of pure, a wasteland.

So wrong. It would never go well with him—I was too forward in my speech and he too ready to take offense. Always when I thought I saw the way most clearly, then I was snared by the unforeseen.

"I can promise you this," he said, rising to his knees and setting his scaled kilt to rights. "If he's in reach of my sword, I'll strike him down—because if Chance puts him in my way, can I refuse her gift?"

I cursed that jealousy of his that had turned him from me. His doubt lay just under the skin. I had only to scratch and he bled distrust. He stood and I grabbed his ankle. My voice had been ill-used and I could hardly make myself heard. "Sire, how can you doubt me now? You know he lied. Please . . . it can't be borne."

He moved away from me and nudged Spiller with his foot. "Rouse up, lads. We mustn't be late."

Not long after, I heard the Crux say to Galan, "This is why I can't abide women on a campaign. They're always wailing."

CHAPTER 15

Mortal Tourney

he saying is that hearts break, but that's not what happened to me. Instead my heart was squeezed and squeezed, my body a fist around it. After a while there was nothing left but a hard pit, like the stone of a fruit, small and heavy. And my breath clouded the cold air and I found I was not dead, after all.

I stood on a hill above the tourney field, and all the other inhabitants of the Marchfield were there too, spreading around the horizon, and every one of them jostling for a better view—and the Sun was a handspan high, spilling gold over the land, and the sky was a sheer deep cobalt above the sea—and I saw what a fool I was; I saw the more clearly because my heart was stony. I saw how a man astride a courser becomes one with it, they become a great singular beast, much more fearsome than a man who stands on his own legs. Put ten, twenty, thirty of these beasts together, put a man among them, and see how small he is. That's how small Galan was, standing below me on the tourney field.

And I knew my concern over Sire Rodela, whether Galan should or should not kill him, was a trifling distraction. Galan must have known, as I knew now, that he'd be the first to die today, ridden down in the charge. I'd shied from it; perhaps he had too, with his jealousy, his threats and promises. He was a man, after all, he would boast.

I saw Galan looking up at the sky and I followed his gaze to see white gulls and black ravens and, high above them, two falcons tilting as they wheeled.

The crowd was restless. A great altar had been set up between the lines, and the procession of sacrifices was long. While the clans of Crux and Ardor fought on the field that day, so too their gods would contend, and each clan vied to make the most lavish offerings. And each warrior prayed to his forebears or to Rift or Hazard or any god whose favor he sought, and sent his prayers winging on their way with blood: *Make my armor strong and my arm stronger.* I saw my mare Thole among the horses dedicated to Hazard, and wondered if Galan offered her on my advice or to make me rue it. She died and I felt nothing.

So many animals slaughtered, one by one: oxen and horses, goats and sheep, roe deer and fighting cocks. Among so many opposing prayers, not all could be answered. If any god might listen to me, it would be Ardor—but today Ardor was Galan's enemy, and therefore mine. Today my prayers were leaden, and couldn't rise.

It had been four tennights and a hand of days since we came to the Marchfield, and I'd never seen such a crowd, not even on Summons Day. When the word went out that the king had called for a mortal tourney, his whole army came to watch, along with the queenmother's Wolves. The merchants left their stalls guarded by boys who followed as soon as their masters' backs were turned—and the armorers came, and the goodwives, butchers, shepherds, laundresses, shipwrights, and the bare-legged children who dug shellfish in the tide pools. Then came those who preyed on the rest of us, the pickpockets and strongarms, peddlers of pisspot ale, two-copper whores. And every man sporting a sprig or a ribbon, green for Crux or rose for Ardor, and tempers dry as kindling. Every one in motion, shoving downhill to get closer to the field, pushed back by the Blood of Prey and Rift, who guarded the boundary, herded this way and that by varlets clearing space so that their masters could see the tourney from seats under their bright canopies. Every one gossiping, bickering, quarreling because one stepped on another's toes. Every one wagering. The oddsmen gave the two clans an even chance, though Ardor outnumbered Crux by four cataphracts. The odds were eleven to one against Galan.

We drudges of Crux watched from a hillside south of the tourney field, nearest to our clan's line. Flykiller had chased some kitchenboys from a boulder and now we stood upon it, a head above the crowd, with Fleetfoot and Galan's horseboy, Uly. Flykiller's long reach and his glower kept others away from our perch.

The Sun rose and shadows retreated across the field. It was a clear cold day: no fog, no clouds, nothing but smoke from the smudge pots and braziers, mist from our mouths. I'd draped Mai's shawl over my headcloth to cover my shoulders, but the Sun found my burns and set them afire again. Elsewhere I was chilled.

Priests examined the entrails for omens and the carcasses were dragged away. There'd be such a feast after this tourney that the meanest beggars would eat.

A rumormonger nearby amused the restless crowd in the lulls between sacrifices. He rode upon the shoulders of a massive fellow who bore him with the sullen patience of an ox. His long, bony legs dangled around the man's neck. His standard, a hollow tongue of cloth, waggled on the pole when the wind caught it. For a copperhead he'd make up a riddling rhyme about one of the warriors on the field, and many a drudge asked for one about his master. They were not all flattering. I had a few coins knotted into my shawl, and I gave two copperheads to Fleetfoot to bid the man come closer.

The rumormonger looked down at me and I up at him. He wasn't one I'd seen before. I said, "That man afoot down there, who is he?"

He said,

Who started the trouble that troubles the king?
He crowed like a rooster, though he's just a chick.
The Crux hopes to tuck him safe under his wing.
But he'll die all the same if he doesn't fly quick.

"I don't want one of your riddles. I want his name."

"Sire Galan dam Capella by Falco of Crux. And you're his sheath, so why do you ask?"

I was not surprised he knew Galan. A rumormonger should know every man of Blood in the Marchfield by his insignia, his armor and horses, his manner of fighting. But if he knew of me, surely he was good at his trade. I said, "Will you stay by me and keep him in sight and tell me how he fares?" I showed him two silverheads in my palm. His mount gave me a wink, which was startling; the man seemed so like a beast, I'd almost taken him for one.

The rumormonger looked at the coins and said, "Keep your silver. This is as fine a spot as any to stand."

Down on the field they were also restless. There were more than seventy horsemen, all told, and each man kept his stallion on a short rein to make him prance and stamp and toss his head, to show off the fine arch of his neck.

I saw Galan among them, leaning on the shaft of his scorpion, trusting his fellows to keep their mounts from trampling him. On his baldric he bore his two swords, the greater and the lesser, and his mercy dagger. His buckler hung by a hook behind his hip; it served better as a weapon than a shield, with its sharpened rim, spike in the center, and a pair of sword-catcher horns jutting from the sides. There was no hiding behind it, for it didn't even cover his forearm.

His scorpion looked like a twig next to the war lances carried by the other cataphracts for use in the charge. These lances had ironwood shafts, twice a man's height and thick as a man's arm at the base, and leaf-shaped heads of the best steel to punch through shield, plate, mail, and underarmor to find blood and bone. No other weapon could do so much against a man in a metal carapace.

And Galan was not well armored. From where I stood the green canvas of his brigandine looked dull, save for the rows of rivets glittering in the Sun. The fire had taken his shining cuirass of plate, and he must gamble on speed. Soon we'd see if it served him. He had his back to me. When he turned his head, I saw his visor was down, the silver face in the beak of the iron gyrfalcon.

They carried away the altar, and two boys ran along the lines of mounted men with painted kites trailing behind them. Wind took the kites and lifted them as high as the birds overhead: the sign of Crux to the south, the sign of Ardor to the north.

The Blood began to roar and beat weapons against shields. The spectators raised their own clamor of whistles, hoots, shrieks, ululations, bellows, chants of praise and mockery. I covered my ears against this uproar and before I knew it—before I was ready, how could I be ready?—the warriors set spurs to their horses and the horses surged forward. I felt the pounding of hooves through the ground, as if the hills were hollow as a drum.

Galan moved when the horses moved, but soon he was left behind and all alone. Some spectators taunted him, calling him a coward, but those of us nearest to him saw clearly that he did not hold back, nor did he hurry. He strolled. The ribbons on the shaft of his scorpion fluttered and the banner of his house snapped in the wind, and he looked, in the arrogance of his grace, as though he set out to cross the king's hall rather than a battleground.

He had walked perhaps a quarter of the way across the field when the two lines of horsemen met in the middle, and I learned what was meant by a mortal tourney.

This time the cataphracts didn't aim to score points—so many for a hit to the helmet, so many to break a lance, so many more for unhorsing a man. This time the hills resounded with the clang of metal against metal instead of the crack of splintering wood. Many men were toppled from their saddles. Horses skidded, fell, thrashed on the ground. The lucky ones—men and horses both—staggered to their feet again. The dead were left lying underfoot, along with those too sorely wounded to help themselves, and at this distance no one could say which was which, not even the farsighted rumormonger. Though we all could see that Sire Choteo of Crux was dead, impaled on a lance through his chest. The melee boiled around them. Horsemasters rode into the field to lead remounts to their masters. They carried mercy daggers to kill the horses too injured to mend. I saw a jack cut down as he tried to drag his master to safety.

The rumormonger sang out the names of the fallen and cried victory for Crux in the charge. We'd lost five men to Ardor's seven, and many in the crowd around me shouted huzzah and waved their green-sprigged caps in the air. But how could the fallen be counted while men were still dying? For the battle hurried on heedless of such victories, swifter by far than a tourney of courtesy.

All this while Galan walked across the field.

There were four cataphracts of Ardor who passed through the charge unscathed and found, on the other side, Galan strolling toward them. Likely they'd come looking for him. I imagine they felt joy, seeing how harmless he looked, this troublesome man.

They converged, three coming from the left flank and one from the right, and each man put spurs to his warhorse, racing to be the one to ride Galan down. The three on the left galloped side by side and nearly neck and neck, and two of their armigers followed some lengths behind. The cataphract on the right looked to reach Galan first.

Galan went right. As if he were eager to meet his own death, he ran toward the cataphract bearing down on him. The rider ("Sire Tropel, house of Lamna," the rumormonger called out) lowered his lance to take Galan in the chest. At the last instant Galan darted across the horse's path and past the lance head, and drove the lance downward with the shaft of his scorpion. The lance plowed into the ground, jolting the horse and shaking

Sire Tropel half out of his saddle. Galan hooked him under the arm with the claw of his scorpion and pried him the rest of the way out. The lance fell one way and Sire Tropel another, and in that moment of falling, he left his element and became hapless and awkward. His foot caught in the stirrup and he was dragged along the ground, shouting and flailing. The horse cocked his head to see what was behind him and bolted.

Then Chance peeked under her blindfold and gave Galan a wink, we all saw it. As the stallion swerved, going crabwise to escape his own rider, he crossed the path of the three cataphracts who were still coming for Galan at full tilt. The one on the swiftest horse was ahead by two strides with his lance lowered, and he couldn't pull up in time. He struck Sire Tropel's mount below the withers with such force the lance pierced the stiff leather barding and buried itself in meat and bone, and the two horses collided, and then the other two slammed into them. There was such a thunderclap when they came together, I felt my teeth jar in my head.

A horse heaved himself up and stood with his reins trailing. That left three stallions on the ground in a moil. Sire Tropel's courser had been killed and the other two were hurt. The riders were thrown, winded, maybe wounded, and trapped in their mounts' caparisons as the horses rolled and churned. Galan ran toward them. The wagers were flying, the odds shifting: it looked to be a fairer fight.

Sire Tropel lay under his dead horse. All I could see of him was his helmet and shoulders and an arm so askew it must have been wrenched from its socket. We could tell he was alive because he rolled his head from side to side. When Galan reached him he steadied Sire Tropel's head under one foot and leaned down. Maybe they spoke.

The crowd howled, demanding a kill, and I knew he should do it, for a dead man could bring him no harm. But he spared Sire Tropel, and as he did the rumormonger cried, "Sire Virote's armiger, Sire Nidal, House of Accendo!" and Galan turned away from Sire Tropel to find a man charging him on a rawboned chestnut.

The armiger slashed downward with his sword and Galan swept the blow aside and clouted the chestnut on the rump with the scorpion to send him on his way. Then Galan jumped up on the flank of Sire Tropel's dead horse and everybody laughed to see him waiting so patiently for the armiger to wrench his courser around and come at him again.

The rumormonger said to me, "No fear—the man's a fool—he has Sire Galan on his left now, and the scorpion has the longer reach." And Flykiller said, "True, and his horse has an iron mouth and won't answer to the bit. But Sire Galan should have a care."

Before the armiger was close enough to swing his sword, Galan struck at his mount, raking the horse across the eyes with the scorpion's claw. And there was Sire Tropel lying helpless in the horse's path, and the chestnut stumbled over him and planted one hoof squarely on his helmet and fled, blinded, across the field. He carried away Sire Nidal, who never did land a blow, and raucous hoots followed him as he went. Galan jumped down to firmer ground and a sound came out of me that was almost a laugh, but hurt like crying. I took a breath.

The rumormonger shouted to the crowd. "Sire Tropel's a dead man, and Sire Nidal's a deserter! Six men rode against Sire Galan, and two he's accounted for. 'Ware of the rest!"

The Crux had once chided his men for failing to see past the points of their swords, and hadn't I done the same? For as I'd watched Galan toy with Sire Nidal, I'd failed to see that two of the men who'd charged him had disentangled themselves from their fallen mounts with the help of a third, an armiger, and now that armiger was scrambling toward Galan's back holding a sowpricker, with the two cataphracts close on his heels.

The rumormonger bellowed the men's names, their houses. He might have started on their ancestry next, but one of the hotspurs was so eager to reach Galan first that he grabbed the armiger's ankle and tripped him. So Chance granted Galan another boon, and he was ready for it. As the armiger fell forward, Galan turned and dropped to one knee—leaning sideways to avoid the sowpricker—and caught him on the scorpion's sting the way a hunter would catch a charging boar. The rumormonger sang, "That makes three!" Galan flipped the man onto his back and there he lay with the scorpion quivering in him. Galan hauled on the haft, but it wouldn't come free.

Watchers on the hill shouted warnings and I couldn't draw breath enough to make a sound. Men had broken from the melee in the middle of the field to ride to Galan. The Crux himself was coming at a gallop with some of his men strung out behind him, fending off pursuers. And yet there were men of Ardor before the Crux in this race. I found I was gripping Fleetfoot's shoulder and I let him go, and my right hand found my left and clasped hard. I dug my nails into my skin, in need of some sensation, for I was unfeeling. My heart was too shrunken and hard, too paltry a thing to compass this day. But if my heart had not been deadened, how could I have borne it?

I wondered if Galan saw them coming. No matter. He could only fight those within reach.

The two cataphracts afoot closed with Galan and he dodged them long enough to draw his sword and unhook his buckler. One of the men hewed at Galan with mighty swings, while the other thrust at him from behind a long kite-shaped horseman's shield. Galan sidestepped, he reeled, now hidden from me, now in sight. I thought I saw some blows get past his guard.

I was too far away. Some stroke would take him from me and I wouldn't know it, as if there were nothing between us. But why should I want to know the moment and manner of his death? If not now, then surely by noon. If not this battle, the next.

A cataphract pitched onto his face with Galan's sword between the breastplate and backplate of his cuirass. "Well done, well done!" the rumormonger bellowed. "Sire Lenador has fallen—it looks to be mortal—and he's the fourth!" and there were cheers from the crowd on our hillside. But the other cataphract was shoving Galan with his wooden shield, jabbing at him over the top of it. Galan kicked the shield and turned it sideways and struck into the opening. The man staggered and recovered and bashed Galan with the shield's edge. Now it was Galan's turn to stumble. He backed up and the man came after him, and by then the foremost of the riders had reached Galan.

He came at a gallop and caught Galan with the shoulder of his horse and flung him sideways through the air, over the backs of the three downed stallions. Galan's sword wheeled overhead, catching the light. He hit one horse's neck and the high cantle of another's saddle and slid over the side of a rump. He sprawled, unmoving. The two injured horses whinnied and struggled to get up, to get away. Their legs folded under them. One rolled and let out a high scream and hid Galan from me.

Then there were many horses in the way, with riders.

He'd been thrown with such force—he'd landed so hard. I told myself he could be dead, but couldn't believe it.

I asked the rumormonger, "Do you see him?"

He looked down at me and shook his head.

I stood on a boulder on a hill, my bare feet gripping the stone, my hand shielding my eyes from the searing light, and from this distance the tourney looked to me like a rough sea, iron and silver. Horses rose and plunged and the Sun beat on every wave. I sought Galan. I searched so intently I forgot to breathe, and all the world was caught, for a moment, in my pent breath.

I looked away, and my eyes blurred and I saw a green afterimage of the Sun burning in the center of my vision. In the corners of my eyes, I saw shadows. Even now, as the Sun rose toward noon and the shadows dwindled, they grew blacker and more substantial. They mocked the warriors, mimicking their shapes, imitating their deeds, and they leapt like fire and flowed like water.

I pulled the end of my headcloth free. There were two knots in the cloth: here where I'd hidden the dwale, and there the firethorn. I unwrapped the firethorn berries and they were hard and shriveled. I crammed them into my mouth.

I chewed and swallowed and the taste was sour and tainted with mold. I thought of Ardor's generosity, how this time it might kill me. Maybe I misused the gift. I didn't care, because I'd begun to hope and hope made me rash.

In the Kingswood once, I'd become my own shadow. I'd left my wooden body and flown. If it was a dream, I trusted it was a true dream.

My mouth flooded with spit and I swallowed and swallowed again. I'd been cold all day and now I felt fever coming. I called it to me and it came fast and made me burn, sweat, and sway. My legs shook. Flykiller looked at me strangely and took hold of my arm. He looked odd too, with all that darkness tangled in the hairs of his beard, his face a patchwork of shadows under his brow, his nose, his lips, in the grooves beside his mouth. Around his head was a haze of a color I couldn't name, one of the infinite shades of black.

I remembered in the Kingswood my shadow had been tethered somehow. I hadn't strayed far or stayed long away. How far could the tether stretch before it broke? If it did, surely I'd go from shadow to shade.

If there was any difference between one and the other.

In another woods at dark-of-the-Moon I'd bound Galan to me. I hadn't understood the rites and afterward had cause to doubt they'd done anything at all. Yet there were times I was sure of a bond between us, and when it pulled taut I knew I was caught fast by a line coiled around my heart.

Today my heart was useless. I felt the pull right in the belly, a barb in the womb, sharp as fear.

In my dream I'd gathered up my shadow until it was dense, and made some sort of shape I could inhabit. But it's the way of dreams to give us knowledge we haven't earned. Now I found, too late, that I no longer knew how it was done.

Already I was going where I was tugged. Some small part of me stayed behind, a steward who kept the body standing upright, heard the shouts of the crowd, and beheld a dazzlement of light. The rest of me seeped into shadow. When water flows, a single drop can't keep apart from the rest, it's all one. So it is with shadows. I had no shape but what was borrowed, and that was changeable. And suddenly my senses were boundless, overwhelmed. Where did that flash of orange come from, that sound of a man groaning, the taste of ale, the touch of silk, the weight of mail and plate, the stench of blood? From everywhere and nowhere I could place.

I was dispersing. I don't know what would have become of me if not for the cord that tethered me to my body and to Galan. It hummed a tone so low it could only be felt, not heard, and something reverberated in a higher note, and that sound was me. I was not shadow after all, but I could move through it.

I pooled underfoot in the pitted surface of the boulder and I ran downhill, and it was easy to go under the crowd, flowing from shadow to shadow. When I reached the edge of the tourney field, I was daunted by the light. It seemed to me that only shadows had depth and shape and hue, and what was in the light was flat and colorless, too brilliant. But I saw darkness ahead among the rocks and turf on the broken ground, and I hid from the Sun in the shadow of one blade of grass or another, and I made myself so small I was little more than a longing.

I found my way toward that tumult of men, and darkness was beneath their feet and the bellies of their horses.

I found Galan under a horse, or rather a horse's crumpled leather barding. He dragged in a breath and coughed it out again. There was sweat in his eyes, sweat slick in the armpits. He lay on his buckler and one of the shield's sword-catcher horns dug into his thigh. The iron scales of the brigandine chafed through the sodden padding of his underarmor. Something jabbed him in the shoulder—the sharp toe of a mailed boot. The foot twitched when Galan shifted away. An injured stallion wheezed, his flanks shuddering. The smell of horse, the smell of piss. The clangor of battle outside, the drone of a fly inside. Nearby, a mindless whining whimper. Unbearable heat. Dim light leaking through the eye slits of his helmet.

I knew this because I cloaked myself in Galan's shadow.

It was a strange intimacy. When he moved I perforce moved under him like any shadow. But where it was dark under his helm, his armor, I was free to embrace him like a second skin. I nestled in the whorls of his ear and heard what he heard. I felt the working of his sinews, the hinging of his bones. I slid between his fingers and his grip.

I knew what he felt; the body cannot lie. I knew by his dry throat and constricted wind, by the taste of his sweat, by the knotted muscles of his shoulders and the twitching of his lips that he was afraid.

I knew when he reached for his smallsword how it came welcome into his hand. He crept from his little shelter under the stiff leather barding and the light smote him. He crawled over the two helpless horses and found the vulnerable spot at the throatlatch that the neck barding leaves bare, and slit their throats. The blood spattered and the horses tried to rise under him as they died.

He rolled because of a sound he understood and I did not, and a sword struck where he'd just been, stabbing deep through the barding into the flank of a dead horse. Galan scrambled to his feet and found his attacker circling to try again, but empty-handed now. He was an armiger on a roan horse, and he meant to ride Galan down.

Galan raised his buckler and smallsword. His arms were too stiff, his grip too tight. He made his sinews loosen, and by this I felt his will and how it strove with his fear, muscle by muscle. He couldn't swallow. His tongue cleaved to the roof of his mouth.

The armiger was too bright for me. I saw only his shadow, how he and his mount were one creature dancing toward us over the rough ground, swelling and shrinking. Then Galan blinked, and I saw the man again. He wore a mail hood under a basin-shaped helmet. The links jingled as he came on.

I felt Galan tense and I knew he'd move, yet still he took me by surprise. He sprang onto the backs of the dead horses and from there vaulted right over the roan, taking the rider with him. I clung to the hollows behind Galan's knees and anklebones when he leapt, and I felt the play of his hamstrings and the swell of the muscles in his calves and thighs. I was also in that shadow left behind when his feet left the ground, and I fled into the shadow of the horseman and out the other side.

He twisted in the air and took the armiger under the chin with the round rim of the buckler, driving the iron links of his hood into his throat and crushing his windpipe.

They hit the ground and the armiger broke Galan's fall, jerking under him. The horse shied at the men underfoot. Galan rose and caught the stallion's reins and cut his throat. The horse tottered and collapsed and soon stopped moving, but the armiger went on writhing and choking in a dreadful silence.

Galan turned away, we hastened away, and left the man to live or die by the mercy of the gods.

Up on the hill, the rumormonger shouted that Sire Galan was building a fortress of dead horses, and for a moment I was standing on the hillside looking down, and then I heard Galan again, gasping in the confines of his helmet while he jumped from one horse's rump to another's withers, over treacherous ground. The hard leather of saddles and barding, knobbed and ridged, turned underfoot. Girths and reins and buckles caught at his feet. Nothing caught me. I skimmed over all this, under his heel and toe. The horses had subsided awkwardly, heads twisted. One eye looked up through an iron mask. Their legs were so many broken branches. The bare flank of the roan was slippery with a foam of sweat and blood.

Galan sheathed his smallsword, for he'd found his scorpion again. The man he'd speared with it was still alive. He'd driven it into his belly through the mail hauberk and it had stuck fast in his girdlebone. The man lay between two horses, curled up around the weapon, his hands gripping the shaft. I slid across his body when Galan stood between him and the Sun. The armiger was taking a long time to die. He whimpered with every exhalation. His helm had a plain visor with one long slit for the eyes and many holes pierced to let in air. I slipped into the shadow under the helm. His features were stretched and twisted in his agony.

And I was in the shadow over Galan's face, under the silver mask of his visor, and I felt his grimace and tasted the sour tang in his mouth. He stepped on the man's chest and pulled hard until he freed the scorpion and a quantity of blood. It made an end to that terrible whimpering.

Galan stood still for no more than ten or twenty heartbeats, out of reach of his enemies, and he pushed up his visor and looked around and caught his breath. I took refuge in the hollows under his cheekbones and brow, between his parted lips.

And I looked too, from the shadow under his eyelid. He was not alone. His uncle was there. And Sires Guasca, Meollo, Erial, Lebrel, Pava, Alcoba, and most of their armigers. They were all around: his kin, his friends. They'd cast a circle around him.

In an eyeblink I saw more men of both clans riding his way, or maybe I saw that from the hill. But almost all of me was in shadow now. I no longer heard the rumormonger, only the roar of the crowd and the din of battle: the clang of metal on metal, thuds, grunts, shouts, screams, neighs, hoofbeats, the creak of leather.

The battle had come to Galan; Crux contested with Ardor as if he were the prize. I was glad, thinking his clansmen had come to save his life. So when the Crux shouted, "'Ware, Galan!" and lifted his sword to let a cataphract of Ardor ride past him, I didn't understand why.

Galan's pulse never jumped and his breathing was steady. He, at least, was not surprised.

The cataphract was on a huge stallion. I saw what Galan saw, how the painted leather barding flapped against legs of a dirty dun color, with white fetlocks. The courser lumbered toward us like a drafthorse. But I also saw the shadow around the man, how the darkness had the color of fear.

Galan snapped down his visor and smiled under it. "My thanks, Uncle," he said under his breath.

Then I knew. They did him honor to leave the killing to him.

As his enemy rode toward him, before Galan moved, I felt the hair rise on his neck and scalp. The skin tightened across his forehead. He trembled. There was a humming in his ear. I knew this feeling: it was the presence of a god. He said a word: "*Hazard.*" Not Chance or Peril or Fate, not any one aspect, but the whole. I didn't taste fear now. Something else. Exaltation.

He started to run over the backs of the fallen horses. Though he was surefooted, he stumbled when barding gave under his weight, slid when a saddle turned around a girth. He didn't hesitate. Every slip became a leap, every mischance the next chance. This was Hazard's gift to one who hazarded all: the ability to balance on the sharp edge of the blade that divides life and death.

Hazard had him, he was possessed. Yet never was he more in his own possession, in command of all that he knew and all that he was. As if the god did not ride him—the god was of him.

A grin was fixed on his face. How right the scorpion felt in his grip. How long it made his reach, our reach. I was the shadow of the weapon and the arm that held it. The ribbons danced as he swung and I streamed over the ground. I felt the haft shudder in Galan's hands as the sickle-shaped claw bit into bone. The horse careened and fell, hamstrung. The man without the horse was nothing.

There was recklessness in him, to take some harm if it would get him what he wanted. Or maybe he was reckoning all the while, with the ruthless judgment of a man who has set aside fear and hope, that if he tarried to ward a blow, he'd miss his chance to strike faster, to strike first. I couldn't know for certain, his thoughts were then beyond my ken, and yet I knew every blow that he received, for I was between their weapons and his flesh: how the skin split and the bruises spread on his back, his thigh, his inner arm, his shin. I didn't feel pain, because he felt none. He was heedless of his wounds.

Galan shouted, "Send me another!" and Sire Alcoba sent him two, a cataphract and his armiger. The armiger rode his courser straight at the heap of dead horses and men as if he'd overleap it, but the horse balked and the man was half over the pommel already and his neck was bare, for he had no neckguard. As Galan struck, the muscles of his belly clenched and his breath pushed out in a hoarse bark: *Ha!*

The cataphract hit Galan from behind and knocked him facedown over a fallen horse. There was blood in his mouth and he swallowed it. Before his eyes, tufts of mane braided with bright ribbon. I was under Galan and I wrapped myself around him as he rolled and jabbed at the underbelly of his assailant's mount. The stallion reared, his hooves above our heads. The cataphract leaned over with his mace, looking for Galan in the darkness under the horse, and Galan brought him down.

He moved faster than I could think, and yet I moved with him, for a shadow must keep pace. And I battened on his swiftness and force. I tasted his want and it was my own: to overthrow his enemies, to grind them down. It was not their deaths we craved so much as their devouring.

Time lurched, now racing, now lagging; I began to lose moments.

Galan broke a rider's leg with the shaft of his scorpion and pulled him from his horse and stood upon his arm and punched holes in his helmet and skull with the venom, the scorpion's spike. And we were screaming.

I crawled into the open mouth of a dead man, across a glazed and sightless eye, and felt satisfaction. Yet we were not sated.

A horse was disemboweled and ran away tripping on his own guts. Galan must have done that. I don't remember. He had his fortress of dead horses. They had to clamber to us now. They couldn't reach us on horseback.

Two teeth were loose and wobbling in his jaw. His cheeks were stiff. His grin had become a snarl. There was a longsword that had belonged to someone else in his hand. The scorpion and buckler were long gone. We struck and the metal sang; struck again and found the true spot on the edge where the sword cut without jarring. Some fool left himself open for a thrust and we shoved hard, all those layers to reach the flesh, grunting as the blade went home, ripping it out sideways to finish him fast. Every man was the same man, faceless in his helm or with a face of fear or pain or anger. The same enemy over and over, and we were growing weary of it. One leg shook. Exaltation had soured to impatience, the taste of wrath.

The blood spilling from the enemy had been warm, but it was cool against Galan's skin. He burned so hot he scorched even me, his shadow, and in feeling this I knew myself apart from him again, for a moment. Time enough to feel fear.

If any god rode him now, it was Rift, who sows fear and reaps destruction, who gathers the dead like so many sheaves. It was a thought too great for me to hold, for I was diminished, a scrap of self.

There was a gorgeous shadow streaming around Galan, as if his shade had grown too large for his body to contain. His heat consumed me, and I was the smoke of his flame and our shades commingled.

A cataphract climbed up the mound of fallen men and horses. He carried the insignia of the Ardor's own house on his banner, the smith's forge with a fire burning in its heart, so it was fitting that he wore the finest plate armor I'd ever seen, with overlapping bands at every joint so that he could move with ease. His visor was smooth and inlaid with a pattern of flames in gold and copper.

The armor was useless as a prize; the man was tall and thin as a sapling and it could never be remade to fit. That was Galan's thought and mine. By then there was no difference.

All that was left of me was a flaw in his eyes, a throbbing in his bloodstream.

I saw everything doubled, shadowed. There was a black nimbus around the enemy, and by its tinge I knew he was too calm. I hoped the heavy plate would make him clumsy, but his attack was audacious and fast. A flare of darkness warned me it was coming. I huffed and scrambled out of the way.

A breath or two, while I eyed him. Where had he been hiding, that his armor was so clean, not yet besmirched with mud and gore? His freshness was a jape. He mocked me with it. I'd sully that perfect armor and trample him like the others.

He came in high and I swept his blow aside with an armored hand while I thrust low. When my sword hit his thighguard, it jarred my arm. His blade darted back to slice through the padding of my left sleeve and into the flesh above the elbow. That stung me; it was the first pain I'd felt since the battle began.

Then fear nattered at me, fear wavered on the point and edge of his blade. I blinked away the sweat and drew my mercy dagger. My left arm had been weakened by the cut, but I could still grip. Another blink, and I lunged.

We might have been laboring alone on the field, for I heard no sound but our panting and groans, our blows. He was well schooled, his elegance only a little marred by the uneven footing of dead men and horses. He pierced my thigh; he tried to bleed me to death with little pricks, aiming where I had least protection. Blood ran down my leg and arm, making the linen underarmor bind like swaddling clothes. I waded through air thick as water.

But I knew his moves, every one. By the way he combined one form with another, by his very precision, I knew his swordmaster, I knew his name. The Ardor's son. They'd kept him safe that he might find me when I was weary. A ferocious glee was rising in me. He hadn't killed today and that would be his downfall, for I was bent on his death and he—though he didn't know it—hesitated at mine.

And his shadow reached for me first and I knew where he meant to go. I knew I could kill him. He was beginning to understand. His shadow flickered and changed hue.

Now he was forgetting half of what he'd been taught, and all I had to do was follow my sword's lead, slide from counter to counterattack along the length of the blade. And I struck and struck again, but my sword rang against his armor. They'd used the best steel and I could hardly dent it. There were so few chinks. I studied them all. My fury burned cold now, and measuring.

A blow against his shins weakened his leg. I tried to get under his neckguard and my sword nicked on his cuirass. Two more blows and the blade shivered. I dropped it and he lunged and I caught the blade of his sword in my gauntleted hand and pulled him close and drove my dagger into the small gap where his steel prickguard was laced to his mail leggings, and left it there. I wrested his sword from him and bashed him so hard with the pommel that I stove in his helmet and rocked him back on his heels. He raised his arms to fend off the blows, and I turned the sword and jabbed him in the armpit. He fell to his knees and I hammered him across the visor, cursing every time I struck. The visor flew off, and I drove the hilt into his nose and he toppled over.

And that should have ended it, but the man trapped my legs between his and brought me down. I fell on him, and we wrestled for the sword in a close embrace. His nose was broken and his breath bubbled and blood ran down his cheeks. We rolled and I was wedged between two horses. He loomed over me. But I found my mercy dagger lodged in his groin and I pulled it free with my left hand. I saw fear widen his pupils before I drove the blade under his chin, to the hilt. A spray of blood got through the eye slits of my visor.

I pushed him off me and saw his shadow seethe and roil away like smoke, and so his shade departed.

What was left had been more boy than man, with a downy beard.

I climbed to my feet and looked for the next enemy. The palms of my gauntlets were sticky with clotted blood. I picked up the man's sword. There was pain from the old belly wound; maybe I'd torn it again. I was gasping, hot as a hearthstone and thirsty. I licked my lips and tasted blood and salt.

To stand still was to know these things. To collect myself, to slip into shadow again, to hide underfoot. The Sun was high overhead. It gave too much light and we shrank from it.

And we looked for the next man we must kill, and the next, but there was no one at hand. The locus of battle had shifted and left us stranded on our fortress of corpses. We began to search among them, among the dead.

And I, on the hill, began to fall. Sometimes I've dreamed of falling only to start awake, heart racing. This was worse: I plummeted from a great height or a great distance and woke to find myself still falling. For a perilous moment I didn't know who I was, where I was. The eyes were filled with sun splotches and shadows. And all those pains—at the groin, across the back, around the neck and down the throat, into the bellows—and the pricking in the limbs, the burning skin—surely those pains and those limbs were none of mine. The sap of strength was gone and there was nothing inside but weak and brittle pith that couldn't bear me up. The legs were giving way.

I was truly falling. It was no dream. I'd been pushed from my perch on the boulder. A strong hand grabbed my arm as I went down. Flykiller pulled me up and saved my life.

The spectators had begun to move toward the tourney field, and we were in the midst of them. As those nearby pressed against us, so were they pressed. There was no contending against that force. A grain of sand might as well defy the tide.

Later I found out a brawl had started on our hill. Who knows how it started and what does it matter? When the knives and cudgels came out, a good many drudges ran to see the scuffle or to join in, but more tried to flee, pushing others as they went. At the churning edge of the crowd, the brawl became a riot. We were trapped inside. I heard grunts and shouts, shrieks and curses. Someone shoved against the burns on my back. Flykiller stiff-armed the man away and got behind me to shield my back, but he too shoved. He had no choice. His thick arm was wedged between us, under my shoulder blades. I lost Mai's shawl. There were hands on me I couldn't fend off. Fleetfoot was ahead and there were people between us. I called his name but he never heard.

I came close to slipping into shadow again, slipping away. I had but to give myself to the vertigo, for I'd never stopped falling; I was still neither here nor there, not entirely, as if I'd left motes of self scattered over the field in the shadows under stones and blades of grass. I was plagued by wayward perceptions. Fever burned. My feet stumbled along at a distance, as if they made their way without me. I saw the crowd one moment and the next a throng of shadows. I blinked to banish the swarming darkness, and saw the rumormonger had lost his mount but kept his banner; it moved away overhead, the pole swaying, as he was carried off in some eddy. Uly was at my side. He had the wild, startled stare of a walleyed horse. He drove his elbow into my ribs to give himself another handsbreadth of room. The skin was stretched tight over my own grimace and I knew I looked no different.

Rift Dread had us all, we were the god made manifest in a swarm, we were a mob.

We moved downhill toward the field like an avalanche. The embrace of the crowd was such I feared my ribs would crack; I feared if I let out one breath I might not have room for the next. As we moved some were carried along and others submerged, clutching at their neighbors for help, finding none, until they disappeared under our feet. And I trampled them too.

The Blood of Rift and Prey, who guarded the field, met the crowd and tried to turn us back. Their horses sidled, presenting well-armored flanks, and the riders thrust with the wooden butt ends of their scorpions or used their swords like cudgels, sparing us the edge. Some drudges at the front of the mob were caught between the wall of horses and the surge of men coming downhill and died standing up, crushed to death. I couldn't see what was happening down there, surrounded as I was by taller men, but the screams were terrible to hear. And when the horsemen checked us, we felt that force come uphill like a wave. The man in front of me lurched backward and Flykiller bore me up.

There was no room to fall now. A boy swooned, eyes rolling and head lolling, and the crowd carried him.

I wondered if Galan still lived, and then the thought was gone.

Down by the crowd's forefront, a few drudges were so desperate they ducked under the horses' bellies or around their hindquarters and dodged the weapons of the Blood and ran onto the tourney field, looking for safety. Men of Prey and Rift turned to ride them down, hunting those who profaned the consecrated ground, and now they showed no forbearance, they used their sharp blades. But fewer Blood were left to hold back the multitudes.

We were going faster, stumbling over the rocky ground. I could breathe again. Flykiller grabbed my sleeve, which was nothing more than a rag hanging from my bodice; a pull, a tear, a few threads broken, and he was gone and my sleeve with him. I was running with the rest, a headlong stampede.

As I ran I found myself praying—not to the gods, not even to Ardor—but to the Dame and Na, whose bones I still carried. As if they could intercede for me now.

I came to an upended smudge pot with coals smoking around it, and after it a shambles that marked the southern boundary of the field, the dead and wounded under our feet.

Now we were among the riders and the riders were among us. Most of the horsemen bore the banners of Rift and Prey, but I saw some of the Blood of Ardor, and even a few of Crux, turn from killing each other to strike us down, outraged by the vermin scuttling about the legs of their horses. Rift Warrior must have put a battle frenzy on those men of Crux, and blindness, for most in the mob wore a sprig of their green. The metal skins of the warriors shone against our dingy garments, our dull flesh. They rode into the throng wearing their frightful masks, and they scythed us and threshed us under hooves, and we ran to and fro, colliding, tripping over the fallen, dodging the boulders that littered the field, sliding and sticking in the bloody muck.

I ran with the other drudges, as if I could hide in the swarm, as if any of us could hide. And maybe the others prayed for the same thing I did: let them take the one next to me, and the next, just so I am spared. There is a selfishness Dread teaches, to hold our own death dear and that of others cheap.

We sounded like pigs at slaughtering time, squealing and screaming. There was that stink too, of bodies opened up. I couldn't believe we held so much stink. The Blood were careless, and left many to die a slow death. No butcher would do that.

I felt a spatter of rain from the cloudless sky and wiped my face and my hand came away red. I turned, and there was a whore behind me in a striped skirt. She took two steps before she fell. I might have known her, but her head was gone. Gods, the blood is so pent up inside us, it bursts forth like a fountain.

I saw, but I couldn't make a world out of what I was seeing: scintillas of light, specks of darkness, everything shimmering. I swayed, blinded. As if vision were a trick and I'd forgotten the mastery of it.

Someone ran into me and knocked me down. I scrambled to my feet and I could see again and there was a horseman bearing down on me and people scattering from his path. I knew by his light armor that he was a priest of Rift. He went bareheaded, with a shaven pate. A grotesque face had been painted on the top of his skull and he bent his head to show me this face and I mistook it for his own. I thought he was my death. I stood still, caught in Dread's paralysis, and he came so close the stirrup brushed my arm, and the wind of his passing brought the smell of horseflesh and sweat and leather; I heard the chuffing of the courser's breath.

The priest struck as he passed. His sword licked out and parted my headcloth with a sure touch. The cloth fell and my hair came unbound; it was dark with sweat and clung in coils to my face and neck, my burned back. I saw by his face, his real face, not the one painted on his skull, that this was sport to him. He clucked to his mount and they leaned as one, man and horse, and circled me in the tightest possible compass. He culled me neatly from the flock. I stooped to pick up my headcloth—my mind was empty as a poor man's purse—and the sword hissed over my head and lopped off a hank of hair. He made his courser rear over me, and at last I ran, ducking low, clutching the scraps he'd made of my headcloth.

He spared me. Maybe he disdained to kill any of us. His sword was not bloody.

I fled toward the edge of the tourney field and met the mob still rushing downhill. I was no longer part of it, having gathered up some of my scattered wits again. I tucked up my skirts as I ran, and I made my way against the current, dodging the runners and the riders, leaping over the slain, making my way west along the boundary of the field, toward safer ground, where the crowd thinned and the bodies lay less thickly strewn about.

It was nearly noon. The Heavens were empty of clouds but full of birds: gulls and ravens, kites and fish hawks and falcons, starlings and swallows. Up where the Sun climbed, the sky blazed white; elsewhere it was a lucid blue. I was alive for this moment and maybe the next, and I ran as if the Queen of the Dead followed at my right shoulder and Dread at the left. I meant to outrun them both, then go to ground like the prey I was. I wanted no more of crowds.

I headed for a ravine between the hills, for a stand of twisted scrub oak and a marshy place hidden behind it where the water came up from the ground and collected from the rains, where I'd gathered stanchmoss and cresses. I knew this ground and what could be found there, from many days spent wandering over these hills with Noggin at my heels when I was supposed to be watching tourneys.

A thud and a crack and I was facedown on the turf and I heard a horse galloping away that I had never heard coming. I'd been struck on my back, near a kidney, and the pain was so sharp I thought I'd been stabbed. I strove to breathe, and couldn't. Couldn't. Couldn't. Until the pain tore open and let in some air. And then I breathed until I could crawl. I crawled under a rock outcropping that cast a small shadow, blessedly cool and dark, and I felt safer out of the Sun's eye. I trembled with fever. Pain beat on me in waves.

At last the tide of pain went out. I felt my back and I wasn't bleeding, and I knew I'd live. And I felt, for the first time since I'd fallen so far and so suddenly back into my body, that I was in one place, every last and least remnant of self called home. For the body knew what the shade had forgotten: I was mortal and not ready to die.

Yet I wasn't wholly restored. Once I'd been all of a piece, now I was a fist around a handful of shards. Or less than that. If I opened my hand, I might find only a hum, a song.

It seemed a long time I was there. I raised my head. The tourney went on, and also the hunt. I heard them both and the sounds were different. And there was Sire Rodela's bay horse, in mask and barding painted green and ivory, nosing about for faded tufts of grass among the stones. The bay tore at the grass and chewed, his bit jangling. I saw the horse plain, without a halo of shadow. It hurt to look, the Sun was so fierce.

Beyond him two cataphracts of Prey rode the boundaries of the field with their armigers trailing behind. They rested the butts of their scorpions on their thighs. The blades winked in the sunlight. The horsemen watched the crowd that covered the heights to make sure that no one strayed—and the spectators on the western hill were wise enough to keep to their place, though there was movement among them, swirls that troubled the backwater. They were noisy with whoops and catcalls. Someone threw a stone and an armiger's mount shied. The silks and awnings and pennants of the Blood dotted the hill, bright as the first spring flowers in a wintry meadow.

No more than fifty paces to that haven in the ravine. Behind me there was havoc, ahead a seeming peace. Yet my way was barred. I feared to pass those men who guarded the field; they might be eager to join the sport of their fellows.

I backed away from them, around the rock outcropping. And on the other side I found Sire Rodela. He sat propped against the stone with his hands dangling laxly over his knees. His head was bowed and he looked nearly dead. The man lying beside him was dead beyond a doubt. His helmet was gone and he had cuts across his neck deep enough to lay bare his backbone. A cataphract, to judge by his fine armor; one of Ardor's, by his banner. So Rodela had won that armor he had boasted of last night.

I stopped in front of Sire Rodela and he looked up at me. His helmet was of leather with an iron noseguard and iron ribs. One of his cheekguards was missing and the other dangled by a strap. The whites of his eyes were startling against the blood on his face. He blinked and lifted his hand, a vague gesture. I stood with my back to the Sun and he was in my shadow.

"Water," he said.

It must be he didn't know me.

I thought of Galan seeking Sire Rodela, and then of what Galan had said: *If Chance puts him in my way, can I refuse her gift*? There was no doubting my luck, but as to Chance—I couldn't be sure.

I remembered the taste of Galan's wrath, how I'd fed on it when I was a shadow. How it felt to be as absolute as a sword, forged for one purpose. Hard, sharp, swift, bright. I was alloyed of baser metals. I couldn't summon Galan's wrath. Neither could I summon my own, for I was still estranged from myself.

I must do without it.

All this I thought between two heartbeats. I said, "Give me your helmet and I'll fetch some water."

When he fumbled for the strap that held his helmet under his chin, I went to him and unfastened the buckle. I pulled off his helmet and the padded cap came with it. It was soaked with blood. His scalp had split where he'd been struck above his right temple—perhaps a blow from a mace—something heavy rather than sharp. I could see the injury plainly because of his bald crown. The hair was matted flat below it. The blood was darker than I expected, blackish, and it welled up from the wound and ran from his nose too, and clotted in his mustache and beard. I pressed the spot with my fingers and found it pulpy to the touch under the skin. Maybe my woman's touch would sicken him, taint his blood, and I wouldn't have to poison him. Maybe he'd die of the wound without my help.

Sire Rodela raised his arm and pushed me away. "Get off," he said. He swayed and put a hand on the ground to support himself. One knee flopped sideways. He was panting.

I dumped the sodden cap on the ground and looked at the helmet. Two of its iron ribs had been driven inward. He'd been struck more than once.

I looked up and saw that the two cataphracts and armigers who guarded the boundary were trotting away, still with their eyes on the crowd. I was afraid to run, but staying was no better. I sprinted toward the ravine between the hills with Sire Rodela's helmet in my hand and when I reached the stand of scrub oak, I ducked and pushed my way in. The oaks were not much higher than my head. Rusty leaves clung to the black twigs, clattering as I passed. Acorns rolled underfoot and briars caught my skirts.

When I looked back I saw they had not done with killing. Riders on the slope herded the crowd uphill. On the tourney field, they chased drudges down one by one. I should stay in the thicket and hide. I was safe there.

One moment I determined to kill him, and the next I dithered. A straw was stiffer than my resolve. Why should it be hard to kill a man? I knew how it felt. I'd given myself to Galan, and Galan had killed. Hadn't I felt the elation, the lunge, the thrust? Now the horror of it came unbidden and I was weak.

I'd seen the Blood make meat of us, meat and offal. It didn't trouble them at all.

If he was dying anyway, there was no need.

Suppose he lived. There'd be no better chance.

I pushed through tall swamp rush. The ground was soft. I stepped from one tussock to the next and the mud squelched between my toes. The seep had no open water, not even a puddle, but water oozed up everywhere. I knelt in a clearing where stanchmoss and goosecress and slue cabbage grew, and my skirts were soaked to the knees.

I set the helmet down next to me and scooped up muddy water in my hands to drink. When I'd drunk my fill, I pressed the helmet into the mire to let water lap over the rim.

Then I saw what token Sire Rodela had carried to the tourney inside his helmet: short wiry copper hair on a scrap of flesh—my own flesh—stitched to the leather with a waxed thread. He hadn't dared to wear it on his crest, as he'd worn the trophy he took from Sire Bizco. But he had worn it nevertheless, and it was worse to me that he kept it inside, close to his own skin.

Rage came unsummoned then, and I shook with it.

I tore the flesh free of the helmet, and picked out the bits of hair and skin left under the threads. I found it hard to touch what he'd stolen from me, but I tucked the remnant under my bodice. I'd burn it when there was time.

The water was brown, flecked with bits of chaff, and it grew ruddy when it mingled with Sire Rodela's blood. A water strider slipped into the helmet and I flicked it away.

I set the helmet down against a tuft of sedge. There were stones everywhere and it wasn't hard to find what I sought: a smooth stone, nearly flat but for a dip in the center like the hollow of a palm, and a round rough stone that fit my hand. Mortar and pestle. I had carried the scraps of my headcloth with me. Now I spread them on the ground. The priest of Rift had sliced the headcloth into three pieces with one cut. One scrap still had a twist knotted into it, and through the linen I felt the shriveled berries of the dwale. I emptied the dwale into the hollow of the stone: eight berries. I wasn't sure it would be enough.

I spat on the berries and ground them, I spat again and ground hard, and Sire Rodela's face was under the pestle. The black flesh of the berries smeared between the stones. And I prayed, for I was sure Ardor would hear me now. Didn't we share this enemy? Sire Rodela had defiled Ardor's offspring as he'd defiled me. *Ardor Smith, make me a weapon in your hand.*

And what god would I offend by this act? Gods and men, and many of them, no doubt. *Ardor Wildfire, hide me from their sight.* I would I had a poisoned kiss, he'd die and no one the wiser. I picked out the seeds and scraped the paste into the helmet with a twig and rinsed the mortar and pestle with water, careful to save every drop.

I crept back to the edge of the thicket. I saw men in the distance, riding, running, fighting, but there was such quiet at our end of the field that kites and ravens were already settling on the dead. One of the armigers on patrol rode at the birds and sent them flapping. I waited for the warriors to pass me, and when I judged them far enough away, I hastened to Sire Rodela, hitching up my wet kirtle to keep it from clinging to my legs.

Sire Rodela heard me coming and turned his head. The movement made him wince and groan. I put the helmet in his hands but he couldn't grasp it, so I held it for him. My hands were steady. He emptied it in four gulps, and water ran down his chin and made a runnel in the blood. There were flecks of black berry in his beard. I wiped them off with my hand and cleaned my hand on a tuft of grass. I thought he might complain that the water was foul, but he only looked at me as I squatted before him. His face was in full sun and he squinted, dazed. One pupil was small as a pinprick, the other huge. His skin was mottled white and purple, where it wasn't covered in blood. His jaw hung slack and breath came quick and shallow.

I picked up the bloody padded cap and set it on Rodela's head, and tied the laces under his chin. I put his helmet on over the cap, which took some effort, for it fit snugly. He never raised a hand to stop me, though he leaned sideways and I had to prop him up.

So I was startled when he lifted his hand to take a lock of my hair between his fingers. "So bright," he said. "Brighter than what I had of you."

I jerked away and stood up. He knew who I was, after all.

He looked up at me; he couldn't hold his head steady and it tilted on his neck. "I knew you were fond," he said, and one side of his mouth smiled.

I took a step backward and tripped over the dead cataphract, and sat down abruptly. Rodela's head flopped forward and he moaned.

Though it was foolish of me, I bowed my head and stayed there, sitting on the ground. It was strangely silent, but for the roaring in my ears.

Die now! I thought. But I knew he wouldn't die quickly: neither the wound nor the dwale would kill quickly.

There was a mace by my hand, the dead cataphract's mace, and I thought how I should take it up and finish Rodela. I'd taken a coward's way, a woman's way.

But I couldn't pick up the weapon. I shuddered to think of swinging at his head. I knew the sound it would make as it struck.

I'd called *him* a viper. Who had the stronger venom?

I'd killed him and I was glad. I should be glad.

If only he would die soon.

I heard the footsteps, but kept my head bowed, my eyes closed. Just then it was too much trouble to save myself. I felt the coolness of a shadow between the Sun and me. I knew him before I looked up, before he spoke.

"Well met. I've been seeking everywhere for one and the other of you, and here you are together."

Galan had taken off his helmet and hung it from a hook on his baldric. The crown of his head was sunlit but his face was dark. I thought of how he'd left me that morning, how his jealousy had spoiled our parting. Now he'd found me with his former armiger, and I feared he might suspect me of anything—except what I had done.

"By chance," I said. "I was running and nearly stumbled on him. And I could go no farther . . ."

He leaned toward me. "It cuts me to see you afraid of me, for I know I deserve it."

"I never . . ."

"I know." He touched my cheek. "Are you hurt? What is this blood?"

I heard weariness in his voice, no suspicion. It was like a fever, his jealousy. It waxed hot and then it broke. But it would come back.

"Not mine," I said. I struggled to my feet, hampered by my wet skirts, and he reached out a hand to me and didn't let go.

I'd doubted my welcome; I'd doubted that he lived, after I'd been riven from him so suddenly. Now there was certainty of both, and I could do nothing but weep. My stony heart held a seed after all, and joy put forth a slender root and a green shoot that cracked the stone. I hid my face against his shoulder and pressed myself against the whole length of him, clad in all that cloth and leather and metal, and wished that, like his shadow, I could lie against his skin.

Oh, but it was better to be in the body and alive, both of us alive and shaking. I said his name. It was the only word that came to me.

He made me look at him. Sweat and blood had dried on his face, and he wore the smudge of Consort Vulpeja's ash on his brow. He looked sallow as wax, and when we kissed I felt the bones of his skull, his teeth, and thought how thin was the veil of flesh that covers us.

He said, "The way you sat there so still—I feared . . ."

"I'm unharmed and you're alive, praise the gods for it—I can't think how else we lived so long this morning!" I kissed him again, laughing and crying at once. "But we're not safe yet. We should get to shelter."

Galan said, "Didn't you hear the king's horn? The tourney is over. The king put an end to it when the mudfolk overran the field. And it was noon anyway, near enough; no one can say he favored us. Gods—when I saw the green in their caps and knew our men were among those who ran—and you might be with them . . . But it's finished now, the killing is over. They're all dead or run off. All dead."

Galan let me go and fell to his knees. He was trembling violently.

I knelt beside him and didn't flinch when he put his hand on my shoulder and his fingers dug into my burns. He stared at Rodela, who had slumped over on his side. It was plain he was alive, by his rattling wheezing breath. "What of him?" he asked.

"Dying," I said. "His skull is broken."

"The carnifex might cure him."

"No, it's mortal, I'm sure of it."

He eased his grip on my shoulder and looked at me. His straight brows were knotted; his eyes could not quite hold steady on mine. "I meant to kill him."

"No need. Better that you didn't." I looked down. I wished he had, then I wouldn't have done it.

"I meant to." He put his hands upon his thighs and leaned forward and made a sound as if he were in pain, and I thought he must be feeling his wounds at last. But he said, "What was one more among so many?" and he clasped his arms over his belly and bent until his forehead almost touched his kneecops.

That is what I'd told myself.

I heard him gasp as if he stifled sobs, but when he straightened up, his eyes were dry. "Truly, I don't know how many," he said. "Shouldn't I know? I can't remember them all. I must wait for the tallies." He began to rock back and forth, still shivering. "They think this will be an end, but it will never end. I killed the Ardor's son. That's one I know for certain. He was good but I bested him." He laughed. "A thing to crow about—killing a beardless boy."

I put my hand on his arm to stop his rocking. "Who won, Galan? Did anyone win?"

He looked at me in disbelief. "Why, can't you see?" he asked. "The honor is ours."

CHAPTER 16

Tallies

here was not much wood left in those hills, but what little there was went under the ax: the scrub oak in the hollows, too scrawny to suit the shipwrights, the old thorn hedgerows between pastures, the twisted trees that here and there clung to the cliffs. All of it—and even timber herded down-river from the mountains and bought for silver in the marketplace—burned that night to feed the pyres of the Blood.

The feast was over; the living had poured a little wine from every cup for the fallen, friend and enemy alike, with praises for their valor. Those who hadn't earned praise were flattered instead, for the dead must be sent on their journey garlanded about with fine words. They wouldn't be spoken of by name again, not for a long year.

The cliffs were crowded with those who came to honor the dead and those who came for the spectacle. Last night we'd gone there to burn Consort Vulpeja. Galan had avenged her; he'd washed his face of the mark of her ash. I wondered if her shade was content with so many deaths laid against hers, if it made amends for all he'd denied her in life.

Galan stood before the pyres clothed in a borrowed surcoat and firelight, sparks darting about his head. Not long ago his fellows had kept a certain distance lest his bad fortune tarnish them. Now they crowded close, they touched him as if he were a talisman.

I'd been as close to him as his own shadow, closer maybe. Hadn't I? Already I mistrusted my memory. It was as if I'd awakened from a dream, sweating and crying in its grip, and the dream had faded in the light of day. It was made of fragile stuff that could not withstand remembering, and tore to pieces as I tried to gather it up.

One thing was certain: I'd nearly lost myself in shadow, nearly given myself up to Galan. It had been as mortal a danger as the trampling mob and the riders who struck us down. I was still paying the cost, for I'd come back to myself somehow smaller than I was before, ill fitting. I rattled inside my skin like a dried bean in a pod.

And there was grief at the distance between us, the ordinary distance that now seemed so vast, each of us alone in our separate bodies. The binding I'd tied between us was a paltry thread, badly spun.

The taste of the firethorn berries was still sour on my tongue, but it might have been someone else who'd stood on that hill, swallowed them down. I could no longer recall what I'd been thinking, why I'd hazarded so much. I should not have done it.

I turned my back on the crowd and the fires and sat on a rock with my legs over the cliff edge. The wind came from the land and pushed like a palm against my back. I gripped the stone to keep from falling into the vastness of sky and water; I was worn thin and the wind had more substance than I did. Whether I closed my eyes or kept them open, I saw the same sights.

That afternoon, when the tourney was done, the Sun had glared as she climbed down toward the sea, and under her glare the bodies littering the field had looked like sea wrack, like drab empty garments tumbled by the wind. I heard the discordant moans and cries of the wounded calling for their mothers or cursing the gods or praying, and under those sounds the smothering silence of the dead. I'd gone back to look for Fleetfoot where the mob had met the horsemen, where the dead lay in heaps. I hoped I wouldn't find him there. I was one of many searchers: some looked for kin or friends, others scavenged for coins the dead hid in their purses, about their clothing, in their mouths.

How could I have kept Fleetfoot safe? Impossible—and yet I hadn't even thought to try, and the promise I'd made to Az was the more burdensome because I'd borne it too lightly. So I ran and ran in haste, calling his name. Every lanky boy I saw, I thought was him—and there were many boys. I turned them over, wiped blood from their faces. All of them had a blind stare, the living and the dead.

And I too was blind, blind and deaf to any other need; I held to my small purpose, as if it could serve to hold back the vastness of that desolation. But then I came upon the sheath Suripanta, entrails spilling from her belly, and stayed by her until she died. I gripped her hand as she traveled slowly inward to meet her death, and I wept, not for grief, but for weariness and despair. She never knew I was there.

I could not weep all day. After a time I got up again and wandered over the field, and it was then, after I stopped searching, that I began to find. I found Uly, Galan's horseboy, and he was dead; I found others of my acquaintance, foot soldiers and whores and peddlers from the market, and yet it was hard to say for sure I knew them, for death steals resemblance.

I found a woman—a laundress, by the look of her chapped hands—lying with her skirts about her hips and one leg broken below the knee, twisted and torn. Her face was clammy and her rough sunburnt skin had gone gray, and she cried out when I touched her and screamed at me to stop. Nevertheless, I straightened her broken leg and bandaged it, and bound it to her sound one, having no better splint, and she went from screaming to cursing to sobbing. I tied her skirt about her ankles so she wouldn't be molested and gave her water from a dead man's flask. She'd lost her little boy, who was of an age to crawl, and I found him wailing nearby and tied him to her wrist. She asked me to look for her husband, and I said I would. But how could I?

I left her lying there and set off to find some stanchmoss, and on the way I found a man calling for water and a woman bleeding, and that was how it went. I'd start a task only to find, sometime later, that I'd forgotten what I came for and even what I'd done. I'd never seen so much of what was inside us; those rents in the flesh bared what should have been hidden. And I'd never known how much a person could endure and live.

There were other healers on the field. I saw the stancher, the boneset, and even the midwife tending to the women. Two women I helped took heart from it, and aided me. The men had their carnifices, a few horse-gelders and such. One had a blazing hot brazier on a barrow and a handful of irons that he applied to the stumps of the maimed men. I could tell where he was by the screaming.

The injured women were cold, and I was fevered. I bound their wounds with rags stolen from the dead, I took them water, and I laid my hands on them and gave them warmth to stop their shivering. I no longer tarried to see the dying on their way, not when there were those who might yet live.

No matter how much heat I gave away, I burned, the fires fed with wrath. There is prayer in healing, so I suppose I prayed, after a fashion. But I didn't plead for any god's favor.

Whatever whim of the gods had spared me that day, had spared Galan, I knew them for what they were: carrion eaters. I saw Rift Dread descending on the dead mudfolk, manifest in the swarms of gulls and ravens and kites, dogs and thieves. And other gods came to feed as well, stooping to suckle on the last breath of the dying. Even under the bright stare of the Sun, the killing ground seemed overshadowed by great wings.

They feasted on what was left of the mob while their descendants, the slain cataphracts and armigers of the Blood, were gathered up and laid before the king in decorous rows, and every last and least of their belongings accounted for.

The Blood came down from their perches on the hills to gaze upon those killed in the tourney and reckon, with some awe, by how many the dead of Ardor outnumbered those of Crux. I didn't see or hear the tallies read, for by then—though the Sun was still high—I toiled in a darkness lit by one face at a time; by then the wide tourney field had grown as small as one wounded person and the next. But I heard about it afterward: how a priestess of Rift read from a long list, giving each dead man's name and the name of his killer, as attested by witnesses; how she paused so that anyone who wished to dispute the disposition of the prizes could do so; how eight times Sire Galan's name was called and there was only one objection, and that from Galan himself, who refused to claim the kill, saying it was Hazard's doing and therefore Hazard's prize. How King Thyrse had spoken, saying the feud was honorably ended, and those lost in the battle had died as men should, and their shades would be content; saying further that we'd disembark within the next hand of days, for the wind and tides and omens were all favorable, and commending us to the gods, who had drunk deep of our libation that day.

So the dead of the Blood were tallied with rites and speeches. No one counted the dead mudfolk. They were heaved into carts and taken to the charnel ground on the cliffs, stacked for burning.

It was not until the Sun went down behind the sea and I walked back to camp behind a cartload of wounded men that I found Fleetfoot. He was in the dog pen. Though he was a good runner, he hadn't outrun danger. He'd lost half of his left hand, severed through the palm, and part of two fingers from his right. It was plain he'd held up both hands to ward off a blade. I'd seen many such injuries that day. As if flesh could be a shield. The manhounds had licked his wounds and Ev had bandaged him.

I was glad to find him alive; I dared hope that the little clay man with an acorn heart Az had given him would see him home safe, that he'd live long enough to father children and tell them the tale of how he was maimed. But he said he'd not go back to the village, to Az, even if Sire Pava released him.

He'd not go home poorer than he set out and useless besides. He sat with his arm resting on a dog as we spoke over the thorn and stone wall of the pen, and soon he hung his head and said no more.

I turned toward the pyres and the flickering light slid over my eyes. I couldn't banish the visions I saw, but neither could they fill me, for I was a dull husk emptied of the long day; it had brimmed over, spilled away.

CHAPTER 17

Leave-taking

That night I lay long awake, waiting for Galan on the pallet in the corner of the Crux's tent. He sat on a footstool and leaned back against his uncle's chair, and his uncle's forearm rested on the arm of the chair close to Galan's head, and though they didn't touch, there was such ease in their proximity, such affection, as I'd not seen since the Crux had learned of Galan's wager. Galan was forgiven and all was well with him, not a care in the wide world. No matter that his uncle still forbade him to ride: the Crux was a man of his word, and no one, least of all Galan, expected him to bend or break it.

Galan turned his head and smiled at something Sire Alcoba said, and the Crux spoke to both of them and Galan laughed. Then he stood and drained the last wine from his cup and wended his way through the press of his kin, his companions. He took up a clay lamp on the way, and came to me carrying that little glow. He crouched and set the lamp on the ground. The lamplight tickled Galan's chin, sent shadows up the hollows of his face. Some of those shadows were bruises he'd taken in the tourney. His cheek was cut where a rivet had scraped him and his lower lip was swollen and split. He smiled.

I was wrong about the bond between us. It was neither as thin nor as weak as a thread. It was a wick. Somehow it burned and was not consumed.

Deep in the night Sire Rodela stole my hard-won sleep. He startled us all awake with a great roar, followed by ceaseless shouts. He wouldn't be quieted. I could hear him too well, because he was in the priests' tent under the care of the carnifex, and there were only two canvas walls between us. I wanted to stop up my ears or run away, but I feared what he might say and so must listen. He cried out *stinking vixen* and *uppish insolent honeypot* and *slippery stinking mudhole*. He swore I had a serpent's eye and I'd put that eye on him and Galan to ruin their peace. He ranted that he'd whittle me down, he'd skin me and make my hide into a prickguard, a sheath for his sword. Yet he never said my name, never said I'd given him aught to drink.

I lay beside Galan with my head on his arm and felt his limbs stiffen and his pulse begin to race. Between his silence and Rodela's din, I was between anvil and hammer.

Sire Rodela shrieked that the priests were trying to poison him and he'd feed them their own tongues if they didn't leave him be; in the next breath he entreated them to untie his ankles and let him go. He cursed Sire Galan and the Crux, begging the gods to drag them under the sea and choke them with mud for the wrong they'd done to him. But before long he was wailing that the gods despised him, and then his lamentations turned to rage and he vowed to spite the gods for abandoning him. With the names of so many others on his tongue, I hoped no one took note of what he said against me.

The shouts drove Galan out of bed. Before the glimmer of first light, he rousted Spiller and Rowney, for there was much to be done. I huddled under the blanket while his warmth leached away.

At dawn I was driven outside by my own stink. The smoke and ash of the fire clung to my dress, and there was the reek of my own fear sweat and the foul discharges of the wounded I had tended. I'd scrubbed off the worst of it the night before and hung the dress to dry while I slept, but the stench remained and now my skirts were damp and cold. I sat by the wall of the Crux's tent in the Sun, for the warmth she gave, shielding my eyes against her. The pains I'd forgotten the day before, in the press of greater miseries, came back importunate and would not be denied.

I had my needle and a bit of thread Boot had given me, and I sewed the torn sleeve of my dress onto the bodice. The sleeve had come off in Flykiller's hand when we ran down the hill, and he'd saved it for me. It's bad luck to mend a garment while you're wearing it, but I had no other clothes. I stitched the pieces of my headcloth back together too, with crooked stitches I was ashamed to make. Such a simple task, and it was almost more than I could do. Before long Spiller came by and dropped Galan's red linen underarmor into my lap and told me to fix it. It was a jack's duty, but I didn't refuse. He and Rowney had many repairs to make to Galan's harness and weapons, straps and laces and buckles and rivets to replace and metal scales to sew on tight, and cleaning besides.

The padded shirt and leggings were stiff and brown with dried blood, and full of holes that must be mended before washing to keep the stuffing from oozing out. Each hole matched one in Galan's skin. I took up his shirt and bent my head to the work and was glad no one marked how my fingers trembled, without strength or sureness—while Sire Rodela screamed.

A hand of days, more or less, before we embarked for war, and the fire had left Sire Galan ill prepared. Before the tourney the Crux and his fellows had given him garments and supplies to replace what he'd lost, generous gifts, but still he summoned clothier and tentmaker, jeweler and armorer to commission what was lacking.

When the clothier came, Galan called for me to help him choose the best of his stuffs, for I knew a good weave and a fast dye. Sire Rodela bellowed, and Galan would not show that he heard, would not raise his voice, and the clothier leaned closer, flinching and nodding. Galan ordered a quantity of garments for himself, tunics and hose for his varlets, and three overdresses and four underdresses for me.

I asked, "Why so many dresses? Why these bright colors?" for he refused to buy the dark wool I urged on him, a green so drab it was nearly brown, like turf in winter. He said if he left it to me, I'd go about in rags, and he wouldn't have it said he was a skinflint.

Galan gave the man twice what the garments were worth, and never minded that he was cheated; the extra coins would buy lamp oil for stitching all night, for he wanted them delivered in two days.

He was a rich man again, with gold enough to waste, purses and purses of gold: ransom for the arms and armor of the seven men he'd killed.

All morning the Auspices of Ardor and Crux met at the king's hall to dicker over these ransoms. It was a solemn business, and delicate, to satisfy the dead and the living and their kin too. By inches they arrived at a price, redeeming each equipage for about half what it cost when it was new—at which price both sides had aimed from the beginning. This swelled the pride and purses of the living; as for the dead, a shade cares nothing for money, but will tarry and be troublesome if the armor he lived in, sweated in, bled in, died in, hangs for show in his enemy's hall, or worse, is worn by his killer.

The weapons and armor were collected by grim drudges, overseen by the Auspices to ensure that not one buckle went astray. They required a cart to take away all that Galan had won. But there was one man who wouldn't accept a ransom, and that was Sire Rodela. The Auspices offered him gold and he roared that the armor was his and he meant to use the helmet for a pisspot and no one could gainsay him—and he laughed and taunted the man he'd killed by name as if his shade stood before him.

Divine Xyster made excuses to Ardor's priests, saying a broken skull had made Sire Rodela unreasonable. I knew better. The way he veered from fury to terror, the way he laughed and lamented, put me in mind of Consort Vulpeja after she breathed the smoke. He howled about the same torments that had troubled her, which I'd thought were mere dreams: shades and black dogs and crawling insects. Why should they both rave of such visitors, unless the dwale had sent them?

The jacks had wagers on if and when Sire Rodela would die and whether Sire Mordaz, armiger to Sire Lebrel, would perish first (he had been stabbed through the bellows); Spiller said Rodela would go soon, he'd heard he was vomiting black blood, but Rowney put five copperheads on him, saying the carnifex must have favorable signs, and besides, the sowpricker was too mean to die. Galan had given his jacks heavy purses and they were in a hurry to lighten them.

Rodela did not seem to lose strength, though he spent it freely. I saw a ragged god-bothered revelator crouching behind the priest's tent, listening to him. Sire Rodela's words tumbled out in a mob, a hundred of nonsense for every one of sense, but they say the words of a dying man are potent; the more obscure they are, the more profit can be made of them. I feared what the revelator might divine, and chased him away.

Sometimes, for a blessed while, Rodela was silent. Never for long.

Sire Galan went to watch Flykiller try his new warhorses up and down the hills outside the Marchfield (with half the men in our camp looking on), to judge which to keep and which to sell. He'd won nine horses. There would have been more if he'd not killed so many from under their masters; most of these mounts had been kept in reserve and never entered the battle. There was jesting among his fellows, some good-natured, some envious, about how it was that a man forbidden to ride had won a stableful of stallions.

So Galan was not there when Divine Xyster called the other priests into their tent, and all their servants and the Crux's varlets as well, and Sire Rodela commenced to scream worse than ever. He screamed and screamed and sobbed, and Divine Xyster shouted, "Hold him steady!" and I couldn't guess what they were doing except they made Rodela suffer. I thought of the peephole I'd cut in the wall of their tent to spy on Galan and wondered if they'd discovered it. But I couldn't bring myself to look.

Later Boot told Spiller and Spiller told me that the carnifex had drilled two holes in Sire Rodela's skull and he'd bled some watery substance that was only a little pink, and then Divine Xyster had plugged the holes with wads of precious amber resin. I asked Spiller why it was done, and he said to drive Sire Rodela's tormentors out. For certain (Spiller said) he was possessed by the shade of Sire Bizco, returned to take revenge, and a crowd of wights who'd crept in behind him through the crack in Rodela's head—and that was why the armiger had so many voices. But I doubted that any spirit dwelling in the wind would give up such an airy palace to be prisoned in the stinking confines of Rodela's skull. It was the dwale that spoke in him: Rift's medicine, Rift's poison. Divine Xyster, with all his omens, had failed to guess that his torments had another cause than his wound.

By the time the priests finished with him, Sire Rodela was hoarse and his shouts tore the air itself. When Galan came back he found me sitting on the ground by the doorway with my hands over my ears. It was a clear day up above in the blue vault, but down below, a glittering haze hung in the air, turning golden as the afternoon waned.

Galan squatted next to me, looked me in the eye. "I thought you said he was dying."

I looked at him and made no answer.

"Are you weeping for him? How can you weep?"

"If he was a horse, they'd have given him mercy by now."

"I'm content that he should suffer," Galan said. But I saw how pinched his face was, how the muscles shifted in his jaw.

I covered my face with my arms. "I just want it done, I want him shut up. Is there no one who'll put an end to his misery? Give me your mercy dagger and I swear I'll do it myself."

Galan unsheathed his dagger and offered it to me. My fingers itched for the hilt, but I pushed it away. Even if the Auspices and the Crux himself had stood aside and given me leave, I couldn't find the strength in me to use it. So quickly I was forsworn.

"As I thought," Galan said. "You're too soft to go to war. You can neither endure your enemy's suffering nor steel yourself to end it."

I wanted to tell him I was not so soft. I wanted to tell him how I'd given Rodela poison, made him drink and wiped his chin clean, but I bowed my head and cried instead.

* * *

The Sun descended and pulled the cloak of twilight after her. King Thyrse invited the clan of Crux to his hall for a victor's feast and still Sire Rodela bawled.

The night before, the king's army of cooks had roasted the sacrificial meats and fed the whole Marchfield, but this night all their labors and arts were for Crux. Even our jacks and horsemasters were invited, for they'd played their small part in the tourney; they ate at trestles set up outside the round hall on the bare muddy ground where all the roads of the Marchfield met.

The wind had quieted. I could smell the food and also the pyres of the drudges burning on the cliffs. Cook gave me barley bread and horsemeat stewed with pease and onions; the bread was black and dense and coarse, but at least when it was swallowed you knew for a long time you'd eaten something, unlike the pale bread of our betters.

The weather had turned a few nights ago and the north wind had driven away the clouds and sea mists, and after it came the east wind bringing the smell of the mountains and a cold fiercer than the damp chills of autumn. There had been a time in the Kingswood when I'd learned to endure winter's bite, going barefoot in the snow, going without fire, without comfort, like any animal. I'd lost the knack of it.

Now the wind harried me back into the Crux's tent. My fever had broken at last and I couldn't stop shaking. I lit a meager fire in the brazier by our pallets and huddled beside it. The Crux's servants went about their many chores.

Rodela screamed that maggots were eating him. He began to weep, and over his sobs I heard music coming from the king's hall, but couldn't make out the words. No doubt there were songs about the tourney; the king never traveled without his rhapsodists, for how else are great deeds to be remembered?

The men returned late, flushed with too much drink and self-importance, and crowded into the Crux's tent. Even over their hubbub, Sire Rodela could be heard.

Since the victory, whores and rumors had overrun our tents, more plentiful than rats. I couldn't walk for stumbling over whores, and as for the rumors, truth did not deter them. On the contrary, it needed but a dollop of truth for lies to spawn and flourish.

So when I heard from Spiller after the feast that there was a secret plan afoot (but drudges are everywhere, and nothing is secret) to begin the war by stealth—and to begin it on the day after the morrow—I doubted him. Rowney said it was true and still I doubted. We sat around the brazier in our dim corner of the Crux's tent, eking out the fuel by feeding one leathery strand of sea hay at a time to the fire. The air bladders popped and sizzled and the salt made the flames run blue.

Spiller said King Thyrse had used the occasion of the feast to offer the clan of Crux one last prize for winning the tourney: an honor, a dangerous honor. He had asked them to help take the city of Lanx, south-of-west across the Inward Sea, which commanded a fine harbor. It was the key to unlock a kingdom. If they could capture and hold the port, the army would stay well supplied for the long march inland to the capital of Incus.

The king said they would go hidden in the bellies of fishing boats, and so steal past the walls and water gates of Lanx to gain by treachery what would otherwise cost him a long, cold siege. The port was well defended everywhere except from within, being divided by an old feud between clans so evenly matched that neither side could win a victory. It needed but a little weight added to one side to tip the scale.

In a few days, so the king said, he'd follow with the rest of the army, but an army is ponderous and slow, and for this purpose he had need of a dagger rather than a bludgeon. And would they be that dagger? And they had all cheered.

"I don't believe you," I said. "There are only thirteen cataphracts left, and Sire Rodela and Sire Mordaz are likely to die of their wounds, and if they do there will be just ten armigers. What use are so few?"

Spiller said, "Ask the clansmen of Ardor what use! They can tell you right enough. They lost half their strength against us. The king needs men who can fight as well on foot as on horseback—and one of you, he said, has the mastery of it, and if the rest do half as well as Sire Galan, you'll be worth three times your number." He was as pleased by this remark as if he'd thought of it himself.

Sire Rodela was barking, howling—with a sort of laughter, I supposed, for it didn't sound like crying. He was as tormented by gaiety as, moments before, he'd been afflicted by terror. The men ignored him so well that I wondered if I was the only one who listened, the only one who heard. I was glad there were no words in his laughter.

I looked at Rowney and he shrugged, saying, "No fear, we go with a good company of kingsmen and the queenmother's best Wolves—and some priests of Rift, I heard. And besides, the queenmother has followers in the city, clans loyal to her and not Prince Corvus."

Prince Corvus, the queenmother's son. Rumormongers belittled him in songs, calling him Prince Cuckold, and the quip had gone round the Marchfield that he was half the man his mother was (which wasn't meant to flatter her either, to be sure). The betting favored a quick victory, with odds that we'd be home before Longest Night. But songs can be purchased and rumors can be sown, and maybe it suited the queenmother that we should think her son a weak, beardless boy, soon to bow to her chastisement. Now I wondered: in his own country, did they call Corvus king?

I said, "I still don't see—"

Spiller said, "We'll steal in at night and catch them in their beds," and he scraped his thumb across his throat.

"I daresay they won't all be sleeping," Rowney said, and he lay back on his pallet and stared at the ceiling.

"Then we'll catch them coupling, and skewer two at once, eh?" Spiller said. "Anyway, I don't wish for more help. The fewer we are, the better the loot. Didn't you hear the king say they were rich over there?"

"Huh," said Rowney.

Spiller couldn't keep still. One of his legs jigged up and down and he fidgeted with the fire on the brazier, poking and prodding it to death. All bravado and no bravery, was Spiller; I knew he'd spent the tourney hiding in the jacks' enclosure and hadn't ventured out once. But if he was afraid now, he hid it under a smirk. "Harien said their women go about in dresses so thin you can see right through. All the goods showing and no need to peek under skirts to find out who's plump and who's scrawny. And no need to share, either. There will be two or three apiece, he says."

"Your tongue is loose on both ends, Spiller," I said. "Better watch it doesn't flap away."

Spiller grew cross with me and would say nothing further, useful or otherwise. He left and came back shortly with a whore. I sat with my back to them while he went at her noisily, bidding her turn this way and that. Rowney was next, and he was quieter but not so quick. When he was done she went off with a rustle of skirts and clink of coins. Soon after, Spiller began to wheeze in his sleep.

The day after tomorrow. After all these tennights dallying in the Marchfield, time for trouble to breed more trouble, now we found out what the king had been awaiting: messages sent and received, good omens, fair winds—and a fleet of fishing boats. I'd known the war would come and yet when the time came I was taken by surprise.

I hugged my knees and rocked. When I'd decided to go with Galan, I'd been ignorant of war. It had been no more to me than tales told about the king's doings, songs about battles so ancient that those who survived them had long since died of old age, tapestries with woven blood spurting from woven wounds. But my ignorance proved to be willful, for surely it was all there in the tales, the songs, the tapestries, if I'd chosen to look: the cruelty under all that splendor. But the songs and stories lied when they gave war shape and purpose. Would I have believed the wanton waste of battle, the squandering of life and suffering, if I'd not seen it myself? And the waste of meaning, for Hazard stalked the field, choosing one to be killed and another maimed and another to go unscathed, and not for anything a man had done or failed to do. Fate gives us what we've earned, but it was Chance who held sway, careless and sightless Chance.

I'd seen and still I couldn't take it in. When I thought of the bodies we'd stacked on carts to be taken to the cliffs for burning, I was benumbed. I had to call the dead before me one by one—Uly and Suripanta, Snare the foot soldier and Cowslip the whore, Sire Choteo and his armiger, so many others—to make of grief a blade so I could feel it cut.

I'd seen battle and riot and it was but a shadow of the war to come. We'd bring down Rift's wrath on strangers and they'd visit it in turn on us. And what would become of me in a strange country in wartime, if—when—Galan died? He'd sent the Queen of the Dead many new subjects yesterday and cheated her of his own death. She'd claim it yet.

If not for the mortal tourney, I wouldn't have known Galan as I knew him now. All the Blood were bred to war and raised to it. But not all were granted the ruthless, reckless, headlong bent for destruction that Galan had discovered in himself yesterday, that I'd tasted in him when I was his shadow.

I'd taken him for a pleasure lover, I'd thought the Crux was not far wrong when he called him an idle dillydallier; I'd gone with him for the pleasure he gave me and because there was a certain want in his eyes when he looked at me, something I took to be more than lust. As if there were some lack in him only I could remedy, some craving for my particulars. And I didn't wonder at the time whether he desired what I truly was or what he fancied me to be.

Then I found out that look was one of his talents, and how he used it. Still I flattered myself it was for me alone—and somehow I was not wrong.

Now I knew his power and speed, the havoc under his skin. He was a living blade, and how could I, his sheath, contain him? When I bound him to me, I bound myself to all that he was and all he might become. And if mortal tourney had wrought such a change, what would war make of him?

I'd stared at the brazier without seeing it, and the fire was nearly out. I leaned over and blew on it gently, fed it some more sea hay. Sparks scurried away. *Ardor Hearthkeeper, grant me your blessing,* I prayed, as I always pray. It is well to remember that the gods are not all wrathful. But even in the Hearthkeeper's domestic flame, I saw Wildfire and war.

And Sire Rodela shrieked that Sire Bizco was coming for him out of the sea, his flesh in rags, torn by crabs.

I heard the Crux raise his voice and say, "This is more of your foolishness."

I turned and saw he was speaking to Galan. The other cataphracts had gone back to their tents while I sat musing. Sire Rassis, the Crux's armiger, leaned away from the lamplight, drinking and watching. He was a dour man always, but since yesterday he'd been morose; his boy Ob had died, trampled on the hill.

Galan said, "Uncle, have you never clapped eyes on a woman and said, 'That one is mine'?"

"Perhaps I did. But I found a night or two would cure me. You're the same way; I recall you were infatuated above once a week with one skirt or another. Why then should you squander any jot of your patrimony on a clod picked up in a field on Carnal Night?"

"I'm within my rights," Galan said.

"Within your rights and out of your right mind. That's a good holding, and should go to a good man. Your horsemaster, your falconer—a steward would not be ashamed to have it."

"She shall have it, Uncle," Galan said. "Call the priests to list it in the Landsbook."

I stood up, and the motion caught the Crux's eye. He glanced my way and I crouched back behind the wall of wine barrels, which had been breached by one feast after another. Galan's back was to me, I could see only the edge of his cheek and the stubborn set of his shoulders.

When the Crux spoke next, his voice was heavy. "Just when I think you are a man, you play the boy again. What will your father say, your wife? Your honor is bright now, and I don't wish to carry it back to your father, when this war is over, spattered with mud." I heard his weariness, his disappointment—a heavy burden; I wouldn't have wanted to bear it. There was a long pause, and Galan didn't speak.

The Crux said, "I wish I'd sent you walking home, but I've condemned you instead. It is for love of you that I counsel you not to do what you'll regret, maybe in days, maybe in tennights—when your shade has time for reflection and she is long left behind."

Galan turned his head and I saw his profile, lit by a many-branched standard hung with oil lamps. "Have the Auspices told you I'm bound to die?"

"All of us are bound to die. But it doesn't take a priest to foretell *your* future. Common sense will do it."

Galan turned back and I lost sight of his face. "Well, Uncle, a dying man must make his bequests, and this is mine."

When the Crux spoke next, patience was stretched thin over his ire. "If you must make provision for her, give her a room in your keep for as long as you live, and if you don't come home, your kin will not be obliged to waste good land on her."

Galan said to Sire Rassis, "If it please you, would you ask Divine Hamus to come and bring the Landsbook?"

Sire Rassis scowled and didn't move until the Crux gave him leave with a jerk of his head. The Crux leaned toward Galan and lowered his voice. "She's befuddled you, boy. From the first she tied a leash to your dangle and made you parade after her like a dog. It isn't natural—she's a canny, and you'd see it for yourself if she hadn't thrown mud in your eyes."

"No doubt I earned the reputation of always following my prick's lead," Galan said. "But no more. And you're wrong—she's a greenwoman, indeed, but no cannywoman. She wouldn't stoop to charms or curses—she's too tenderhearted for her own good. Just today I caught her weeping over Sire Rodela, though he's done her nothing but harm. And don't you remember how she cured my concubine? She was nearly a skeleton and Firethorn put flesh on her again. She advised me to offer for her—is that a canny at work?—so that I might end the feud. And so I would have, if not for Rodela."

"What of Rodela? Have you heard how he raves, accusing her?"

"I mark how he accuses us all, Sire, even you."

Silence fell between them, but not all around, for just then Sire Rodela could be heard lewdly moaning, and he began to grunt "*Bitch, bitch, bitch, bitch,*" as if he thrust himself into a woman, as if that were the only sweet talk he knew.

"She hexed him. And she probably hexed the maiden too, out of jealousy, and made her sick in the first place."

"Why then would she cure her?"

"To gain your trust. Or so she'd be well enough to send home to trouble your wife. And why do you suppose she came so unscathed from the same fire that killed your concubine? There's not a woman alive but will play you false; the more forthright she seems, the more wary you should be, for she's sure to be hiding something."

The truth cut, for I was indeed hiding something; I'd stooped to charms and worse—to poison. For the binding I could be cast out, for the poisoning burned alive or strung up or drowned in the sea in a bag full of stones. And if Galan knew of this, he'd know too much of me. But I was more pricked by the lies, by the Crux's implacable, inventive distrust.

I wanted to spit those lies back in the Crux's face, to deny everything, even what was true. But I stayed silent and hidden. To be so forward as to defend myself would condemn me further in his eyes.

The Crux said, "She's a canny, and she's snared you somehow. I have but to look at you, boy, to know it. And if proof were needed, proof was given when you followed her into the dog pen, for that was a foolhardy act, even for you. I thought the Initiates had cured you, but I see their work isn't done."

"The Initiates," said Galan. "So that's why the priests kept my falcon pendant when they gave my jewelry back to me—you've set the Initiates of Carnal upon us. You meddlesome—" He checked himself and sat still, as if he feared he might say something the Crux could not forgive.

The Crux stared back at him.

Galan's lips twitched. He began to laugh. "Oh, Uncle! All the Initiates of Carnal, all their secret rites and sacred powers, all defeated by one little sheath! For I'm not altered, except in this: I had been selfish, thinking to keep her by me, but now I want her safe at home. She's better fitted for peace than war. She won't endure it long."

Their talk had led roundabout to this end, and I'd followed blind and stumbling—for I'd never, not for a moment, guessed he meant to send me away. The Initiates must indeed have cured him, if he could suffer the thought of parting. I could not.

Then I did what I knew to be folly. I braved the daunting stare of the Crux to cross that long, figured carpet; I stood before Galan with my fists clenched at my sides and said, "I won't go."

Galan reached out and wrapped his hand around my fist. "I'm sending Flykiller back with the horses, since I may not ride, and I've charged him to see you home safe."

Every bone in me turned stubborn. "I have no home." *Unless you are my home.*

"You do. In my household, in my keeping."

"No doubt your wife will be pleased to look after me. You promised as much to your concubine when you wanted to be rid of her."

The Crux said, "She's not so tender as you paint her, is she?"

I flinched and kept my back to the Crux. Galan looked at me with his straight brows pinched. He said, "Uncle, enough. More than enough."

Divine Hamus came in with Sire Rassis. It was the priest's task to keep the Landsbook, in which he recorded the wills of each cataphract and armiger in the troop as to the disposition of their lands, chattels, and goods; such bequests change as often as fortunes change in wartime, for one day a man may be poor, the next rich, and the day after, dead. Divine Hamus unfolded the book, a long, pleated sheet of linen he carried always in a pliant leather case wrapped around him like a baldric.

Galan gripped my fist hard. He said, "Bear witness that I give my sheath Firethorn tenancy, for her lifetime, of my holding that lies on Mount Sair and is bounded by the Needle Cliffs to the north, Wend River to the east and south, and to the west the Athlewood; the stone house and byres, the lands, the rights to coppice and pasture, the spring." To me alone he said, "We used it for a hunting lodge when I was a boy, to go falconing on the cliffs. It's high land with a long view. You shall have a fine garden on the terraces. I think you'd like a garden."

The Crux was silent, his face bleak as granite. Divine Hamus wrote it all down fair in his book, and began another copy on a small sheet of sized linen.

I looked down at Galan's fist around mine. His knuckles were swollen and bruised. He let go of my hand; my skin had gone white under his fingers. He said, "I shall think of you there. I want you there when I come home."

"And if you don't come home?"

"I will."

"You're always so careful of your word—would you now make a promise you can't keep? And if you do come home, when would I see you? Once a twelvemonth, I suppose."

That made Galan glower at me. "I think you'll find me at your door quite often. If you don't want me there, you can shut it."

"She's ungrateful," the Crux said. "But she supposes right. You have your duties in Ramus, in your father's keep. I shall have need of you too. Better give her a room above your stables, if you must have her. Without a bolt on the door. So you can visit whenever you please."

I turned to look at the Crux. He looked back at me with a glint in his eye like a spark struck from steel, and a little smile on his lips. He delighted to see us at odds. But the quarrel was Galan's and mine. I wouldn't quarrel with him too.

I said to Galan, "What about your precious luck? Didn't you say that Hazard gave me to you?"

"Well, that may be," he said. "But you are too much at hazard. Shall I count the ways you nearly died in the last hand of days?"

"You must take me for a coward. There were twenty times you could have been killed yesterday, and you won't turn back." I crossed my arms over my ribs and squeezed hard to quell the shaking.

"I know your courage—I trusted my life to it in the ordeal, and you stood fast. But where will you be if I'm killed in Incus and you're alone in a foreign kingdom? In Pava's hands or Lebrel's. Or anyone's."

"So you told me yesterday morning," I said bitterly. "You'd pass me on."

"Yesterday Sire Rodela could still do you harm, and you were in need of a cataphract's protection. Today I can't abide the thought of another. Spare me. Go home."

I almost told him why I could not go, almost let it slip past my teeth how on one dark-of-the-Moon I'd dug up a womandrake root. She had two legs already and I gave her a face, arms, and a quim with my knife. She was as heavy as an infant and as wrinkled as an old woman. I'd wound the cord around her, I'd wrapped her about the head, the heart, the crotch, and I'd tied her hand and foot and buried her again in the mud.

I felt that cord dig into me everywhere I'd tied it round the womandrake. It was choking me; there was darkness in my eyes. How could I still be bound if he was free?

I hunched my shoulders. "I won't go." I blinked to clear my eyes and tears brimmed over.

I heard the Crux say, "Quarrelsome, rebellious, obstinate—insolent—I see why she caught your fancy. She shares your faults."

Galan sat back in his chair. "She may quarrel all she likes. There is no argument. She's going home."

The Crux said, "You're well rid of her. Better if you'd discarded her, but at least she'll be out of sight. You'll find, I think, she's soon out of mind as well." I heard satisfaction in his voice. Galan had given him what he wanted after all.

Divine Hamus handed Galan the small folded sheet of linen on which he'd made a copy of the bequest. The priest would not look at me. He'd kept silent as he did his duty, but the hard look of disdain—no, disgust—on his soft round face spoke for him. Galan gave the sheet to me and I unfolded it and read; I let them see I knew my godsigns. It was all there, nothing stinted, nothing omitted.

Sire Rodela was shouting, his voice rough, straining, breaking. "*Spiller, bring me my sword! Where's my sword? Whoreson coward, give it to me or I'll run you through!*"

The Crux told Divine Hamus, "See to it that Divine Xyster keeps him quiet tonight, or none of us will rest."

The carnifex tried a sleeping draught, but Rodela spat it out. So they gagged him. They hobbled him and staked him to the ground inside the tent so he couldn't wander, and it took five men to do it, or so I heard.

When he was silent at last, I drew a deep breath and it was as if I'd forgotten to breathe all day. But the next breath stuck in my throat.

When did it cross my mind to do what Galan asked of me, to go to the house provided and wait, tending a garden?

Not at first, when we were back behind the wine barrels, when the Crux and his men had retired and all was quiet except for Spiller snoring. Galan doffed his velvet hat and unbuckled his baldric and unclasped the armband that held his little golden knives. He winced as he pulled off his surcoat and dropped it on the ground. He treated the garment carelessly, though it was embroidered with a winter hunting scene of owls and hares, and trimmed with lace threaded with gray pearls. It was a gift from Sire Guasca, and too tight across the shoulders. His eyes were skittish. He was ashamed—maybe because we'd quarreled before the Crux and I'd proved ungovernable—or because he'd given me too much and he regretted it.

I didn't care why, for I was in a fine rage that gripped the back of my head and buzzed in my ear. I pushed him. "You think you can dismiss me now? Maybe you want another sheath, more to your fit—someone tough and leathery, perhaps, or else tarted up with jewels and gaudy paint."

Galan took my wrist and pulled me down to sit on his pallet. Our knees were touching and mine were shaking. I'd been shivering all evening and now I thought I might clatter apart. He met my eyes and wouldn't let me look away, and his anger answered mine. "This is unworthy," he said. "I thought you had more sense."

"I'm not—I'm not your *horse,* to be sent home to the stables when you please. I chose to come with you, and I'll choose when to go. I'm not yours to dispose of."

"You are mine." He reached out and pulled off my headcloth.

"I'll go if you don't want me. Swear you don't want me," I said, and pushed him down on his pallet. He took a handful of hair and pulled me after him.

"I won't be forsworn," he said.

I thought I'd won our quarrel when my hands were on his shoulders holding him down and I slid over him and his eyelids came half down and he turned his head aside and I leaned to take kisses from the corner of his mouth. But I was greedy and took my pleasure too soon and when I tired he turned me under him. The pains came back to me, the sting of the wound Rodela had given me, the burns on my back scraped raw. But scratch an itch until it bleeds and still it feels good and you scratch some more. I wrapped my legs around him and he bucked against my grip. He braced himself on stiff arms and he watched me with that appraising air I'd marked at times before, as if he reckoned how best to grind me small. He drove the breath out of me and all constraint and I let him do as he pleased—I would have let him do anything—but even so I thought of other women, how he must have watched and toyed with them. He was too complacent and I'd devour him for it. I did try.

I suppose it was a draw: for every argument, an answer. One couldn't best the other, not for long.

Afterward his prick was smeared with blood and so were my thighs, as if I'd had a maidenhead after all. He was appalled and asked if I was hurt. I said, "It's my tides. I am sorry for it, truly. I didn't know or I'd have warned you. They came early and unexpected."

I wanted to drift or sink toward sleep—already I was heavy and half submerged—but Galan wore a dark look on his face as he lay down facing me. I took it for disgust, because the Blood think a woman's tides will defile them, causing sickness and worse. But I was glad they'd come.

"I thought you had quickened by now," he said. "Are you barren? Surely not."

One doesn't speak of childbane to a man. I shrugged one shoulder and said, "It's for the best. Since you don't want bastards—to trouble your household, you said once. Well, you'll get none from me." Then I remembered I had no childbane left. It had burned in the fire, and unless I could get some from Mai, unless it grew in that other kingdom across the sea, my boast would be hollow.

"Yours, I want," he said.

A shock of heat went through me, and I couldn't have said why: anger that he meant to breed me or pleasure in it. Or even that I'd so far vanquished his dead concubine.

Nor did I dream of going to that high stone house, his hunting lodge, when at last we slept.

I dreamed I was stifling. I was small and stifling and hot under heavy linens. I was in a box, a chest. I heard screaming that went on and on. I'd been told to be quiet but I couldn't stop whimpering. The box was opened and a hand reached in and grabbed my leg. I woke covered in sweat, and Galan was saying, "What's wrong? What's wrong?"

"Nothing. Just a dream." I lied, for it was not merely a dream, it was a true dream. I knew it by its reek of smoke and flesh burning.

Galan was right, I wasn't fit for war. That he was—was frightening.

Nor did I consider leaving Galan and taking the peace he offered when one of the priests' varlets came running to the Crux's tent in the morning to give him the news: Sire Rodela had died sometime in the night, choking on his own spew.

Divine Xyster had gagged Rodela and the Crux had told him to, and they didn't disown the blame but neither did they linger over it. The blame that was mine I kept to myself. I had expected to be glad when he died, but I wasn't glad, only a little less afraid.

No one forbade me to follow when they took Sire Rodela to his pyre on the charnel grounds at the edge of the sea cliff. The wood had been bought at great price and drenched with oil so it would go up quickly, as Rodela was likely to have a restless shade.

The Crux poured a libation for him, but all he'd say in his praise was that he was a brave man. Galan wouldn't give one word to his shade, and for a libation he spat on the ground. He stalked away, and left me there by Rodela's pyre.

Nearby the dead drudges were burning. The bodies had been laid two deep in a long row, and piled with sea hay and gorse and thistles gathered from leagues around. There was no wood to squander on mudfolk. They'd been burning since yesterday. With such poor fuel the pyres would not burn hot, so they needs must burn long. When rigor had overtaken the dead, some had been caught in awkward gestures, an arm upraised, legs akimbo, head twisted. Now they shifted under a blanket of ash.

I held the end of my headcloth over my nose against the stench. Cook, who stayed to tend Rodela's pyre after the others had gone, said he'd seen and smelt worse in his years of going to war, and he told me, for kindness, that I should hie off home before I learned what he meant. I shook my head.

When no one was watching, I threw the scrap of flesh and hair Rodela had stolen from me—which I'd stolen back—on his pyre, so the smoke would carry my words to his shade: while fire gnawed his flesh and cracked his bones to get at the marrow, I told him under my breath how I'd killed him. I didn't regret his murder. Perhaps remorse would come to me when I died, and my shade would have to bear it.

But I swore to myself that if ever I had cause to kill again, it would not be by a slow and chancy poison.

It was when I turned my back on the pyres and the sea, and came down into the clamor and commotion of the Marchfield, all stirred up by news of the war's imminence—walking alone, as I hadn't walked for many tennights, and any man who dared to hoot at me or reach for me got a look that reminded him sharp to mend his manners—and how and when had I come by that look?—it was then I knew that no matter how I denied it, I was tempted by thoughts of an aerie for myself alone, a garden, the Athlewood, which carried such a welcome-sounding name.

I went to the tents of the clan of Delve, seeking Mai, and I found her sitting on a boulder with her back to the Sun. The day was cold but the Sun was warm. Tobe pulled on the piebald dog's tail, the dog whined and bared his teeth, and Sunup picked Tobe up and sat him down not far away, and he began to whine too.

I didn't like the look of Mai's face: her wattles hung too slack, as if she'd lost substance, her skin was a shade too gray. Her feet were so swollen she'd given up wearing shoes.

"Are you well?" I asked her.

She shrugged. "I'm just tired, always tired. Too much to do."

Horses' bardings and caparisons, sacks and casks and bundles were heaped and strewn about the yard, and more provisions coming in carts and on backs, and varlets bustled everywhere, most at cross-purposes and cross besides.

"And you?" Mai said.

"Oh, what shall I do? Sire Galan means to send me home—he's given me a house, some land—he gave it before the Crux and all and they put it in the Landsbook."

"Do? Why go, I suppose." She spoke offhand, but the look in her black eyes was not altogether amiable.

"I can't go—you know why—even if I wanted to."

"What do you mean?"

"The binding, of course."

"Oh, child, sit down, sit down!" she said.

I sat down beside her, both of us with our backs to the Sun. Her bulk cast a great shadow and mine a little one, and when I leaned toward her, the shadows merged.

"You said there was no way to undo it, Mai, and no way to bind one without the other, but the Crux found a way to free Galan, and I'm still bound, and how can I bear it?"

"Oh, indeed? How did the Crux do such a thing?"

I whispered, "The Initiates of Carnal."

Mai laughed. "Balderdash!" It was a hard, mocking laugh and I took it hard.

Sire Torosus came out of his tent, squinting in the sun, the crow tracks gathering at the corners of his eyes. He smiled at Mai and nodded at me, and strode off, shouting at one of his men, "No, not that one! Use this one!" He came to Tobe sitting in the yard and stooped over him. "Well, little man, what's the fuss?" he asked, and Tobe squealed and crawled away as fast as he could, and they had a chase. Sire Torosus pounced and snatched him up and swung him this way and that until Tobe screamed with delight. When he put him down, Tobe waddled after him. If Tobe lived to be a lad, would his father keep him close, have him serve at table, clap him on his shoulder and say with pride his son would make a fine man? Or would Sire

Torosus grow distant, set his mudboy to herding sheep on a mountain suitably far away?

Tobe trusted his father's affection—he was too young to know better. But Mai trusted too, and she was no innocent. When I set out to be a sheath, I thought it was all between a man and his woman, for a campaign or two; I never expected to see a family.

Mai laughed at me, so sure of herself that she teased me for doubting. I envied her certainty.

She turned to me and said, "Listen, I told you about the binding that day because you needed something to ease your mind. I told you it couldn't be undone so you'd believe in its potency, and belief would give you strength. I didn't know you then. I didn't know what you could do."

"So it can be undone?"

"If it can be done at all, surely it can be undone."

"Why do you speak in riddles? Answer me plain—how can I undo it?"

"Dig her up and cut the cord and burn her," Mai said. "That might work."

"*Might*?"

She shrugged. "Well, you're a cannywoman, after all. I don't know quite what you did when you made the binding. If you managed to twine your lives together in her, there may be no way to tease those strands apart gently; and if they are severed that might harm the both of you. Or you might cut them, only to find that something more holds you two together."

"Maybe, might, maybe. I'm no canny and you know it."

"Aren't you? What do you suppose a canny is, then?"

"You are, for one." But it had been easier to deny when the Crux had said it. Uncanny—*that* I could own. Ardor had given me strange gifts: I could see by shadows, travel by shade, I could draw fire and give warmth. But shouldn't a canny be knowing, be shrewd? I blundered my way forward; what use to see in the dark if I didn't know where to go?

Mai only grinned. But soon the grin turned sour. "So he means to send you home."

"Yes—with his horses. He's putting us all out to pasture until he comes back."

She gestured around her, as if to compass the whole Marchfield. "How many of us will come back? Not above half, I'd say. Take his gift and thank him for saving your life—that's what I'd do."

"Would you truly leave Sire Torosus?"

"I would. This time I would." She shifted on her buttocks and sighed. "Every day I feel my travails coming closer, and I'm worn out dreading it. You'd think having birthed nine living children, praise the gods, it would come easier. But this boy has a lot of Mischief in him."

Now the envy was on her part, and pity on mine. I'd seen fear in her eyes before, but never so bare.

She said, "I'll miss you when the time comes."

"I mean to make Sire Galan change his mind," I said.

"By Hazard, you have all the luck! Why do you kick against it?"

I shook my head. I couldn't say why. Now I saw myself going to a place I'd never seen but that already sounded like home. And on the way we'd stop by the river to camp, and I'd leave the fire to go threading through the bogs in the dark to find that place where I'd buried the womandrake root—if it could be found, I'd find it, for I always knew where I was, even when the Sun was down. I'd build a pyre for her and light it with a coal from my fire pouch. I'd burn it all up, that tangled, knotted snarl that trammeled us both. And when—if—Sire Galan rode up to the house on the mountain, he'd be surprised to find me cooler than was my wont.

I felt then as if I were burning, blood ablaze in my veins like oil in a lamp, shining through my skin. I clasped my knees and bent my head and rocked, and when tears fell the drops seared my cheeks and arms.

"It's hard," Mai said. "I know it's hard, my dear. If you must leave, godspeed. And if you come with the army—whether Sire Galan forbids you or no—you can always stay with us. We'll make you welcome."

Sunup, who'd been listening as she always did, without appearing to, came over and leaned on me, saying, "Yes, stay with us! Please!"

And at that I cried some more.

I'd let a day pass, and if it was the last day, I'd wasted it. There was not such a bustle among our tents as in the tents of Delve, but rather stealthy preparations. Tomorrow they'd leave the tents standing, the baggage half packed, the horses in the corral, and go unheralded. They were taking only arms, armor, and scant provisions. Jacks wrapped the armor tightly against the sea spray and salt air. They'd be three or four days crossing if the wind held. They'd all fight afoot in the coming battle, cataphracts, armigers, and jacks, even the Crux himself, for they'd fight within walls.

If it was the last day . . . I stood on a narrow knife edge and never before had I seen the world divided so starkly between one side of a blade and another. For when I'd left with Galan to be his sheath, I'd known less than I knew now.

Az had read the bones for me then, and the Dame and Na had been cryptic, or so I'd thought. But the Dame had warned of aimless wandering, that I might be swept away in flood—which was war, surely—and yet told me I might discover in that flood a wellspring, if I had the resolution for it; and Na, hadn't she warned me of a prison, which might be that stone house on the mountain, and of the shackles with which I'd bound myself and Galan?—unless I made of that prison a shelter, unless the binding rooted us, one in the other, gave us the strength to withstand flood and all.

The pouch Az had given me had burned with the tent, but I still had the bones, which I'd stitched into a seam in my kirtle. I rubbed them through the cloth. I could prick out those stitches, cast the bones on the ground, ask again. But what more would they say than what they'd already said? They'd been freer with their advice when they were alive, those two. And I was smitten with grief for a moment, missing them as they were when their bones had been girded about with flesh, missing their dear faces, their hands always busying about, and how they spoke their minds, their minds full of twists and turns and hidden places, so that even knowing them both so well, they surprised me daily. Our shades are but a revenant of all that; even if they are the better part of us, they are only part, and it doesn't suffice the living to know they go on when the rest is ash.

And what did Ardor have to say to me, that god who'd singled me out? Ardor, like all gods, was triple, and spoke contradictions. But I had only two hands, there were two sides to the blade: on the one was a stone hearth holding the Hearthkeeper's fire, and me burning beside it, consumed with unquenchable longing. On the other, war: war as a furnace in which Sire Galan, an army, a kingdom, would be melted down and reforged, and I might be alloyed in that crucible, and between the Smith's hammer and anvil made part of something new, or I might be dross, burned away as ash or spilled as dull slag on the furnace floor; or war as Wildfire born in lightning or careless spark, free of any man's control, devouring keeps and cities, man, woman, child, and Galan and me, insatiable, until there was nothing left to gnaw but coals. Ardor said all these things, and as to what the god would have me do, said nothing.

The priests tell us—when we are beset by calamities—that everything happens by the will of the gods. They mean to comfort us, but it was no comfort to me. Why then do the gods keep us ignorant of their purposes?

Why must we stumble, err, go astray? That too is their purpose, the priests say. But they don't say why.

They'd go tomorrow with the changing tide. Every day the tides rose and fell and yet I'd failed to mark the time of their passage. I'd learned the land: the dun folds of the hills, the sloughs and hummocks, the crumbling cliffs, the running and standing waters, even the tide pools and the pebbled shore; I knew where jillybells flourished and a lonesome beech had rooted in a cranny. But I couldn't say when the tide went out. I'd turned my back on the sea, not wanting to think of what lay on the other side.

He should have shunned me for my tides that night but the blood was slick between us. Even as I strove against Galan and toward him, when I closed my eyes I saw the sea and a ship skimming over it, a fleet of ships. They had oars as well as sails and their holds were full of men. Silver scales of armor glimmered in the dark.

I blinked and Galan's eyes were on me and his face was shining with sweat. I closed my eyes again and saw the ship, the sea, and balked at following farther. I'd never seen a city, didn't know what it might look like or the nature of water gates, didn't want to see Galan running up stone stairs two at a time with his short sword in one hand and his dagger in the other. Nor who met him coming down. When I opened my eyes, his were closed. His head was tilted back and the cords stood out on his neck. I lifted my head and tasted him.

Such was our hurry he was quickly done. He lay on me with his mouth against my ear. I could feel his breath stir my hair.

"Galan, when does the tide go out? When do you sail?"

"Dawn."

I put my hand over my mouth, but Galan pulled it away. I was sorry he saw my weakness, the tremor on my lips. I clasped him tight and hid my face against his shoulder, and we were silent awhile. I thought if we could stay this close, peace between us for once, peace from all the world, if we were granted the small span left of the night, if we could go drowsing into some dream together, I'd thank the gods for it; I'd not complain anymore of their cruelty.

But Galan stirred and sat up with his shirt twisted around him, his hose gaping. He tightened the laces and got up, and fetched the oil lamp and his baldric. When he sat down cross-legged, flame wobbled on the clay spout of the lamp and a little smoke drifted by his head. He drew his mercy dagger from its gilded sheath.

"I would have something more of you before I go," he said. "Something for luck."

"I never brought you luck. You must see that by now."

"Still, I want it," he said. The knife lay quiet on his lap, one hand on the hilt, the other resting on the blade. His eyes were intent.

"Do you mean to skin me like Rodela did?"

He smiled at that. "Nothing so painful. A lock of your hair is all."

"Take it," I said. It was not after all such a small thing he wanted; I knew what could be done with hair or fingernail parings.

He cut a hank from my forelock about the thickness of a finger. Then he unwrapped the leather braid that formed the grip around his dagger hilt. Spiller had replaced it only that day, for the old one had been clotted with blood. He started to unbraid the fine thongs. "Help me," he said, for his hands were stiff. I saw what he meant to do. I twisted each thong with a lock of hair and braided the three back together, holding the end in my teeth. The leather was stronger and less slippery than the hair and kept it from unraveling. One end of the braid went through a hole in the tang that slid into the hilt. The cord was wound crisscross around the hilt again—this he did, for he knew the trick of it—and the other end cunningly tucked under. When he was done the hilt glinted with fine coppery thread, copper that would never turn to verdigris.

Galan turned the dagger in his hand and felt the edge with his thumb. He took out the whetstone he carried in a wallet on his baldric and began to draw the blade over it. The sound scraped at me.

"Will you not come to sleep now? Come and sleep."

He shook his head.

"Spiller and Rowney spent all day on your blades and armor. There's no need."

"Some things a man does for himself." He went about his task with patience, coaxing the blade to yield its finest edge. He spat on the stone and pulled the dagger toward himself with smooth strokes, again and again, bent to his work, his hair falling over his brow and hiding his eyes.

I think he said, "The king says there will be knife work," or maybe I dreamed it, for when next I looked he was sharpening his lesser sword. One edge caught the light and winked at me. This sword was made to pierce armor, with a narrow, triangular blade to stiffen it for the thrust. It tapered to a point that could fit in any chink. His great sword had a nick in it. He'd ordered a new one; his scorpion was with the armorer to be fitted for a new shaft. All his forethought and still he was behindhand. Nothing would be ready in time.

Through the linen shirt I could see spots of blood on his arm, soaked through the bandages. Not a man left alive of the clan who wasn't sore hurt, and some worse than Galan, and yet the king chose them to fight his battle. He must mean to be rid of them all; they'd go to their deaths thanking him for the privilege.

And if Galan lived through this, there'd be another battle and another, and if he lived through this war, another and another. How could I wish to be a sheath and watch him sharpen his blades as a man sharpens his sickle daily during harvest before going to the fields?

There is no man or woman who is not beset by dangers. A plowman might step on a viper one morning, or a woman die giving birth; a child might fall into a well. There is sickness in every season. The Queen of the Dead rules all of us, sooner or later—but to go courting her was another matter: to worship Rift, to feed the god's appetite.

Metal slid over stone. The wind had risen again, it swelled the canvas and tugged the ropes, and I felt we were in motion, sailing over the hills. There were others still awake in the tent. I saw their shadows on the walls and ceiling. Someone threw candlebark on a fire. I think it was Divine Hamus, for soon I heard the low drone of a chant. It was deepest night, and dawn was as far ahead as dusk was behind, and I thought how strange it was that I was there and not lying on my pallet of sweetfern in the manor, by the Dame's bed closet, dreaming.

I lay on my side with my head resting on my bent arm. There was no way to turn that didn't hurt. We hadn't been careful, not at all.

Galan ran an oily rag down the blade of his sword. He pulled a strand of dried sea hay from our little store of kindling and threw it in the air and his sword flicked out and cut it in two. The pieces fell on me. I brushed them off. He knew I was watching.

He should have been afraid, but he seemed content, as if the rasp of the whetstone had soothed him as much as it had riled me. He looked at me and lay down his sword. There was the quirk of a smile.

I'd followed him for that look and that smile. And surely more than one god had meddled to put me in Galan's path and him in mine. The gods have a hand in anything that makes us foolish. They give and snatch their gifts away and leave us knowing we are bereft, when before we were ignorant. But not yet, not now.

Galan said farewell without words, in every last kiss, farewell to eyelids, earlobes, brow and nape, the hollow of the throat, the tender skin in the crook of the arms, hard knuckles and rough palms. He suckled me like a child and called the milk to rise until my breasts felt heavy with it and milk flowed between my thighs. Farewell to the hard rib ridges, the haunches, the hollows, farewell the long legs and their runs of sinew, rises of bone; farewell the furze and the enfolded quim, the anus rose, the buttocks' cleft, the small of the back, the knobbed spine, even the raw underflesh laid bare by fire and Sire Rodela's knife, farewell even to the quick of me. I felt as if my shadow had slipped its bounds again to mingle with his, and I was seeing myself through his eyes; that was my taste on his tongue, and his desire was mine, until I had to say *no more* and *come here*. Then farewell in the way he sheathed himself in me all at once, farewell again, again, and were we born to fit so tight or had I taken his impress, had I whetted him smooth? He laid claim to my every last reserve only to say *farewell*. And I wouldn't say it, I refused.

A while, a little while of lying close and still before Galan looked up and the Crux said above my head, "Time to be moving," and Galan sighed and took himself away.

Everyone was now awake and bustling, but all in a strange hush. The horses and dogs were restless and made more noise than the men. Galan and I stood outside, between the tents. The black sky had a blue hem and the east wind smelled of snow. He let me under his cloak and told me not to cry. He said he'd come back to me. It was not a thing he could know, that he'd come back. I still had a quarrel with him; I kept it hidden.

I also quarreled with myself, being so divided in two that one would go where he bade me, and the other meant to follow against his will and rely on his welcome, and dare the Crux to stop me. The two would not be reconciled.

Silence fell between us and the tight grip of his arms slackened. There was nothing more to do but say, "May the gods keep you," and let go. I stepped back into the cold outside his cloak. Now I wished he'd leave if leave he must, so he wouldn't stand there looking at me so straight. I feared I might give way under that look. He said farewell and turned away, and as soon as he did, I regretted my wishing. I hid between the tents and bent around the pain in my belly, which was like a sickness.

The troop set off on the north road and I roused myself to follow. They were so few: the cataphracts and armigers, and after them the jacks and some five hands of foot soldiers who were deemed worth the trouble of their passage. Even fewer cataphracts than I'd supposed, for Sires Ocio and Fanfarron were too badly hurt to go, though their wounds weren't mortal. They were left in the care of their men and to Cook's rough medicine; the carnifex was going where he'd be needed most.

There was no pomp in this creeping out of the Marchfield. Dogs started barking and the drudges up early about their chores stood and stared, and so much for secrecy. A pack of the queenmother's men, her gray Wolves, joined our clan on the way. When they reached the open ground past the tents, King Thyrse was waiting on his horse with his men about him. Now there were more, but still not many. Not enough, surely, for what they were asked to do.

Flints in the road jabbed my bare feet; the men moved ahead like a mist, dim in the dim light, Galan among them. I couldn't find him in his cloak and hood. No one turned to see if I followed. When the Sun's light breached the horizon, the men began to talk, to laugh, and to hasten.

The king saw them off and so did I, standing on the cliff above the cove. The ships were as I'd dreamed them, with rows of oars and square sails, long and nimble in the water. Their prows were sea serpents. The sails were dyed gray-blue, a color between the sea and the sky, and they vanished long before the darker hulls disappeared.

Soon the Marchfield too would vanish, the city would be folded up and stowed away, and we'd leave behind desolation. But they say flowers come up plentifully after a battle, and surely the tourney ground and the cliffs and the hills thereabouts were churned and harrowed as if under a plow, and surely the seeds were pressed down deep and nourished by a rich rain. Maybe next spring the wasteland would bloom and the pink and white dog roses clambering over the hills would be tinged with red. None of us would be there to see it.

What need, after all, to decide? I'd decided when I chose not to run on Carnal Night, when I stayed with Galan after the fickle UpsideDown Days were over. I'd decided on the road, in the Marchfield, even when he was careless, even when he was cruel—by the river, where I'd buried the womandrake, beside the tent as he lay wounded, in his shadow. He'd chosen me and I'd chosen him, from the first. And he'd been the first to see our fate, to chafe against it, to admit it, always the quicker one and the braver. But this time he was mistaken.

Mai had played a trick on me, meaning well by it. Doubt was my affliction and she'd given me solace, a counterfeit assurance of what—all along—was mine to know. Strange that certainty and doubt can live side by side, the heart's conviction, the mind's disbelief.

But Mai had taught me better than she realized when she taught me the binding. I'd fed the womandrake my faith, and she'd taken from it an animal strength and heat to match her rooted endurance, her will to grow. She'd go on whether we lived or died this winter.

In spring she'd rouse and burgeon. I'd planted her upright, and she'd send forth rootlets, she'd fatten, she'd grow welts of woody flesh around the cord that wrapped her, that plait of hair and lamb's wool. And from her head would sprout the tender shoots of bryony, from those shoots tendrils would grow with an astonishing green speed, clambering over bracken and osier, up willow and ash, her long tresses twining everywhere, setting white flowers to bloom in the leaf shadow and berries to follow.

For I'd never dig her up. I'd not be forbidden what was mine unless the Queen of the Dead herself forbade me: mine to sleep so close beside him that when one turns the other must turn, mine to wake with him, to rise and cover our shining limbs with clothes and eat porridge, mine to hear him banter with his men or curse when Spiller straps the armor too tight, to stir up the hearth fire at night to watch light dance over his face—for even in wartime, surely, there must be the commonplace deeds of which lives are made, and lives together made; mine to see what he'd see, a new kingdom with trees and herbs unknown to me, cities with towers and golden domes, inhabitants strange in their customs and speech, all such sights never seen before. Mine to trudge beside him, for both must walk now, though the way is stony and muddy and winter howls down on us; mine to know his bruises, his wounds, the hour of his death, if death should come to him first—the travails too are mine, if the rest is mine.

A few flakes of snow drifted down. The water had turned gray under the clouds advancing swiftly from the eastern mountains. Where the Sun shone through, terns swooped and plunged into a dazzle on the water.

The Auspices had promised the king a favorable wind and the wind had come, cold and steady and laden with snow, to blow his chosen men west. They were gone and the rest of the army would not wait on their messages before we followed, for if the city wouldn't fall by treachery, it must fall by siege. The queenmother would have her war, a gift from her brother the king.

But for all that kings and queens can command the flood of war and bid it ebb and flow, the gods will have their way with us. I would cast myself on that flood and maybe I would founder. Like so many foolish mortals, I fancied myself to have a sail, an oar, I dared ask mercy of the wind, I thought that by striving I might turn this way or that, when all the while I went where I was bound to go, carried willy-nilly on the great swell, scratching a little vanishing wake over the surface.

Acknowledgments

Some creative writing teachers are gatekeepers who believe their job is to keep out the riffraff. Abigail Thomas throws open the gates and says, “Come on in.” Without Abby and her class, the Tuesday Night Babes, I would not have started writing this book again after abandoning it for years, or seen it through. Thanks to Kathleen O’Donnell, comrade-in-arms, for brainstorming and commiserating.

Thanks to Merrilee Heifetz and Nan Graham for their welcome. Thanks to my editor Alexis Gargagliano for helping me delve deeper.

I was a reader first and always. My thanks to the writers of science fiction and fantasy who took me on journeys to imaginary worlds. To create Firethorn’s society, I drew on works by historians, anthropologists, sociologists, and journalists; I read army survival manuals, oral histories, herbals, and travelers’ tales; I am indebted to the authors, above all, for showing me our own beautiful, strange, and terrible world.

My father Roland has always been my guide in the woods: for teaching me the names of trees and feeding me pigweed, roadkill, and grasshoppers, my thanks. Thanks to my mother Carolyn for being a beacon, not just for me, but for many. And thanks to Cornelius for having faith in me all these years.

About the Author

SARAH MICKLEM had jobs in a restaurant, printing plant, sign shop, and refugee resettlement agency before discovering that graphic design was an enjoyable way to make a living. She wrote *Firethorn* while working as an art director for children's magazines in New York City. She lives with her husband, poet and playwright Cornelius Eady, in Washington, D.C., where she is writing the second book of the Firethorn trilogy.